CHRISTMAS IN MODERN STORY

An Anthology for Adults

Edited by

MAUD VAN BUREN
and
KATHARINE ISABEL BEMIS

NATAL PUBLISHING LLC
ARS LONGA, VITA BREVIS

Copyright© 2024 Natal Publishing

All rights reserved

PREFATORY NOTE

This volume is the outgrowth of a librarian's search each holiday time for stories to meet the ever growing demand from clubs, schools, societies, and home circles for something "Christmassy" to read aloud. Several great stories that are read over and over, Christmas after Christmas, have purposely been omitted. These can be found in other collections. If our readers gain from this anthology even a little of the gracious spirit manifested by the authors in the writing of the stories and again in granting permission to reprint, the compilers can but feel that their work has been well worth while.

Owatonna, Minnesota,
May 16, 1927.

NOTE OF APPRECIATION

The editors of this volume desire to express their deep appreciation to the authors and publishers whose permissions for use of copyright stories have been so courteously and generously granted. Without this splendid spirit of coöperation this collection of Christmas stories would have been impossible.

Contents

The Candle in the Forest
Temple Bailey

Christmas on the Singing River
Jefferson Lee Harbour

The Shepherd who Watched by Night
Thomas Nelson Page

Christmas at the Trimbles'
Ruth McEnery Stuart

The Gift of the Manger
Edith Barnard Delano

God Rest You, Merry Christians
George Madden Martin

To Springvale for Christmas
Zona Gale

Emmy Jane's Christmas
Julia B. Tenney

David's Star of Bethlehem
Christine Whiting Parmenter

A God in Israel
Norman Duncan

Van Valkenberg's Christmas Gift
Elizabeth G. Jordan

A Beggar's Christmas
Edith Wyatt

A Christmas Mystery
The Story of Three Wise Men
William J. Locke

A Christmas Confession
Agnes McClelland Daulton

The Day of Days
Elsie Singmaster

Holly at the Door
Agnes Sligh Turnbull

Teacher Jensen
Karin Michaelis

Honorable Tommy
Mary E. Wilkins Freeman

The Sad Shepherd
Henry van Dyke

Christmas Bread
Kathleen Norris

THE CANDLE IN THE FOREST[1]
Temple Bailey

The Small Girl's mother was saying, "The onions will be silver, and the carrots will be gold——"

"And the potatoes will be ivory," said the Small Girl, and they laughed together.

The Small Girl's mother had a big white bowl in her lap, and she was cutting up vegetables. The onions were the hardest, because one cried a little over them.

"But our tears will be pearls," said the Small Girl's mother, and they laughed at that and dried their eyes, and found the carrots much easier, and the potatoes the easiest of all.

Then the Next-Door-Neighbor came in and said, "What are you doing?"

"We are making a beefsteak pie for our Christmas dinner," said the Small Girl's mother.

"And the onions are silver, and the carrots gold, and the potatoes ivory," said the Small Girl.

"I am sure I don't know what you are talking about," said the Next-Door-Neighbor. "We are going to have turkey for Christmas, and oysters, and cranberries and celery."

The Small Girl laughed and clapped her hands. "But we are going to have a Christmas pie—and the onions are silver and the carrots gold——"

"You said that once," said the Next-Door-Neighbor, "and I should think you'd know they weren't anything of the kind."

"But they *are*," said the Small Girl, all shining eyes and rosy cheeks.

"Run along, darling," said the Small Girl's mother, "and find poor Pussy-Purr-up. He's out in the cold. And you can put on your red sweater and red cap."

So the Small Girl hopped away like a happy robin, and the Next-Door-Neighbor said,

"She is old enough to know that onions aren't silver."

---

[1] By permission of the author and "Good Housekeeping."

"But they are," said the Small Girl's mother, "and the carrots are gold and the potatoes are——"

The Next-Door-Neighbor's face was flaming. "If you say that again, I'll scream. It sounds silly to me."

"But it isn't in the least silly," said the Small Girl's mother, and her eyes were as blue as sapphires, and as clear as the sea; "it is sensible. When people are poor, they have to make the most of little things. And we'll have only a pound of steak in our pie, but the onions will be silver——"

The lips of the Next-Door-Neighbor were folded in a thin line. "If you had acted like a sensible creature, I shouldn't have asked you for the rent."

The Small Girl's mother was silent for a moment, then she said: "I am sorry—it ought to be sensible to make the best of things."

"Well," said the Next-Door-Neighbor, sitting down in a chair with a very stiff back, "a beefsteak pie is a beefsteak pie. And I wouldn't teach a child to call it anything else."

"I haven't taught her to call it anything else. I was only trying to make her feel that it was something fine and splendid for Christmas day, so I said that the onions were silver——"

"Don't say that again," snapped the Next-Door-Neighbor, "and I want the rent as soon as possible."

With that, she flung up her head and marched out of the front door, and it slammed behind her and made wild echoes in the little house.

And the Small Girl's mother stood there alone in the middle of the floor, and her eyes were like the sea in a storm.

But presently the door opened, and the Small Girl, looking like a red-breast robin, hopped in, and after her came a great black cat with his tail in the air, and he said "Purr-up," which gave him his name.

And the Small Girl said out of the things she had been thinking, "Mother, why don't we have turkey?"

The clear look came back into the eyes of the Small Girl's mother, and she said, "Because we are content."

And the Small Girl said, "What is 'content'?"

And her mother said: "It is making the best of what God gives us. And our best for Christmas day, my darling, is a beefsteak pie."

So she kissed the Small Girl, and they finished peeling the vegetables, and then they put them with the pound of steak to simmer on the back of the stove.

After that, the Small Girl had her supper of bread and milk, and Pussy-Purr-up had milk in a saucer on the hearth, and the Small Girl climbed up in her mother's lap and said,

"Tell me a story."

But the Small Girl's mother said, "Won't it be nicer to talk about Christmas presents?"

And the Small Girl sat up and said, "Let's."

And the mother said, "Let's tell each other what we'd rather have in the whole wide world——"

"Oh, let's," said the Small Girl. "And I'll tell you first that I want a doll—and I want it to have a pink dress—and I want it to have eyes that open and shut—and I want it to have shoes and stockings—and I want it to have curly hair——"

She had to stop, because she didn't have any breath left in her body, and when she got her breath back, she said, "Now, what do you want, Mother—more than anything else in the whole wide world?"

"Well," said her mother, "I want a chocolate mouse."

"Oh," said the Small Girl scornfully, "I shouldn't think you'd want that."

"Why not?"

"Because a chocolate mouse—why, a chocolate mouse isn't anything."

"Oh, yes, it is," said the Small Girl's mother. "A chocolate mouse is Dickory Dock, and Pussy-Cat-Pussy-Cat-Where-Have-You-Been—and it's Three-Blind-Mice—and it's A-Frog-He-Would-a-Wooing-Go—and it's——"

The Small Girl's eyes were dancing. "Oh, tell me about it——"

And her mother said: "Well, the mouse is Dickory-Dock ran *up* the clock, and the mouse in Pussy-Cat-Pussy-Cat was frightened *under* a chair, and the mice in Three-Blind-Mice ran *after* the farmer's wife, and the mouse in A-Frog-He-Would-a-Wooing-Go went *down* the throat of the crow——"

And the Small Girl said, "Could a chocolate mouse do all that?"

"Well," said the Small Girl's mother, "we could put him *on* the clock, and *under* a chair, and cut his tail *off* with a carving knife, and at the very last we could eat him *up* like a crow."

The Small Girl shivered deliciously. "And he wouldn't be a real mouse?"

"No, just a chocolate one, with cream inside."

"Do you think I'll get one for Christmas?"

"I'm not sure."

"Would he be nicer than a doll?"

The Small Girl's mother hesitated, then told the truth. "My darling—Mother saved up the money for a doll, but the Next-Door-Neighbor wants the rent."

"Hasn't Daddy any more money?"

"Poor Daddy has been sick so long."

"But he's well now."

"I know. But he has to pay money for doctors, and money for medicine, and money for your red sweater, and money for milk for Pussy-Purr-up, and money for our beefsteak pie."

"The Boy-Next-Door says we're poor, Mother."

"We are rich, my darling. We have love, and each other, and Pussy-Purr-up——"

"His mother won't let him have a cat," said the Small Girl, with her mind still on the Boy-Next-Door. "But he's going to have a radio."

"Would you rather have a radio than Pussy-Purr-up?"

The Small Girl gave a crow of derision. "I'd rather have Pussy-Purr-up than anything else in the whole wide world."

At that, the great cat, who had been sitting on the hearth with his paws tucked under him and his eyes like moons, stretched out his satin-shining length, and jumped up on the arm of the chair beside the Small Girl and her mother, and began to sing a song that was like a mill-wheel away off. He purred so long and so loud that at last the Small Girl grew drowsy.

"Tell me some more about the chocolate mouse," she said, and nodded, and slept.

The Small Girl's mother carried her into another room, put her to bed, and came back to the kitchen—and it was full of shadows.

But she did not let herself sit among them. She wrapped herself in a great cape and went out into the cold dusk, with a sweep of wind; heavy clouds overhead: and a band of dull orange showing back of the trees, where the sun had burned down.

She went straight from her little house to the big house of the Next-Door-Neighbor and rang the bell at the back entrance. A maid let her into the kitchen, and there was the Next-Door-Neighbor, and the two women who worked for her, and a daughter-in-law who had come to spend Christmas. The great range was glowing, and things were simmering, and things were stewing, and things were steaming, and things were baking, and things were boiling, and things were broiling, and there was the fragrance of a thousand delicious dishes in the air.

And the Next-Door-Neighbor said: "We are trying to get as much done as possible to-night. We are having twelve people for Christmas dinner to-morrow."

And the Daughter-in-Law, who was all dressed up and had an apron tied about her, said in a sharp voice, "I can't see why you don't let your maids work for you."

And the Next-Door-Neighbor said: "I have always worked. There is no excuse for laziness."

And the Daughter-in-Law said: "I'm not lazy, if that's what you mean. And we'll never have any dinner if I have to cook it," and away she went out of the kitchen with tears of rage in her eyes.

And the Next-Door-Neighbor said, "If she hadn't gone when she did, I should have told her to go," and there was rage in her eyes but no tears.

She took her hands out of the pan of breadcrumbs and sage, which she was mixing for the stuffing, and said to the Small Girl's mother,

"Did you come to pay the rent?"

The Small Girl's mother handed her the money, and the Next-Door-Neighbor went upstairs to write a receipt. Nobody asked the Small Girl's mother to sit down, so she stood in the middle of the floor and sniffed the entrancing fragrances, and looked at the mountain of food which would have served her small family for a month.

While she waited, the Boy-Next-Door came in and he said, "Are you the Small Girl's mother?"

"Yes."

"Are you going to have a tree?"

"Yes."

"Do you want to see mine?"

"It would be wonderful."

So he led her down a long passage to a great room, and there was a tree which touched the ceiling, and on the very top branches and on all the other branches were myriads of little lights which shone like stars, and there were gold balls and silver ones, and gold bells and silver ones, and red and blue and green balls, and red and blue and green bells—and under the tree and on it were toys for boys and toys for girls, and one of the toys was a doll in a pink dress!

At that the heart of the Small Girl's mother tightened, and she was glad she wasn't a thief, or she would have snatched at the pink doll when the boy wasn't looking, and hidden it under her cape, and run away with it!

The Boy-Next-Door was saying: "It's the finest tree anybody has around here. But Dad and Mother don't know that I've seen it."

"Oh, don't they?" said the Small Girl's mother.

"No," said the Boy-Next-Door, with a wide grin, "and it's fun to fool 'em."

"Is it?" said the Small Girl's mother. "Now, do you know, I should think the very nicest thing in the whole wide world would be *not* to have seen the tree."

The Boy-Next-Door stared and said, "Why?"

"Because," said the Small Girl's mother, "the nicest thing in the world would be to have somebody tie a handkerchief around your eyes, as tight, as tight, and then to have somebody take your hand and lead you in and out and in and out and in and out, until you didn't know *where* you were, and then to have them untie the handkerchief—and there would be the tree—all shining and splendid——"

She stopped, but her singing voice seemed to echo and re-echo in the great room.

The boy's staring eyes had a new look in them. "Did anybody ever tie a handkerchief over your eyes?"

"Oh, yes——"

"And lead you in and out, and in and out?"

"Yes."

"Well, nobody does things like that in our house. They think it's silly."

The Small Girl's mother laughed, and her laugh tinkled like a bell. "Do you think it is silly?"

He was eager. "No, I don't."

She held out her hand to him. "Will you come and see our tree?"

"To-night?"

"No, to-morrow morning—early."

"Before breakfast?"

She nodded.

"Gee, I'd like it."

So that was a bargain, with a quick squeeze of their hands on it. And the Small Girl's mother went back to the kitchen, and the Next-Door-Neighbor came down with the receipt, and the Small Girl's mother went out of the back door and found that the orange band which had burned on the horizon was gone, and that there was just the wind and the sighing of the trees.

Two men passed her on the brick walk which led to the house, and one of the men was saying:

"If you'd only be fair to me, Father."

And the other man said, "All you want of me is money."

"You taught me that, Father."

"Blame it on me——"

"You are to blame. You and Mother—did you ever show me the finer things?"

Their angry voices seemed to beat against the noise of the wind and the sighing trees, so that the Small Girl's mother shivered, and drew her cape around her, and ran on as fast as she could to her little house.

There were all the shadows to meet her, but she did not sit among them. She made coffee and a dish of milk toast, and set the toast in the oven to keep hot, and then she stood at the window watching. At last she saw through the darkness what looked like a star low down, and she knew that the star was a lantern, and she ran and opened the door wide.

And her young husband set the lantern down on the threshold, and took her in his arms, and said, "The sight of you is more than food and drink."

When he said that, she knew he had had a hard day, but her heart leaped because she knew that what he had said of her was true.

Then they went into the house together, and she set the food before him. And that he might forget his hard day, she told him of her own. And when she came to the part about the Next-Door-Neighbor and the rent, she said,

"I am telling you this because it has a happy ending."

And he put his hands over hers and said, "Everything with you has a happy ending."

"Well, *this* is a happy ending," said the Small Girl's mother, with all the sapphires in her eyes emphasizing it. "Because when I went over to pay the rent I was feeling how poor we were, and wishing that I had a pink doll for baby, and books for you, and—and—and a magic carpet to carry us away from work and worry. And then I went into the kitchen of the big house, and there was everything delicious and delectable, and then I went into the parlor and saw the tree—with everything hanging on it that was glittering and gorgeous—and then I came home," her breath was quick and her lips smiling, "I came home—and I was glad I lived in my little house."

"What made you glad, dearest?"

"Oh, love is here; and hate is there, and a boy's deceit, and a man's injustice. They were saying sharp things to each other—and—and—their dinner will be a—stalled ox—And in my little house is the faith of a child in the goodness of God, and the bravery of a man who fought for his country——"

She was in his arms now.

"And the blessing of a woman who has never known defeat." His voice broke on the words.

In that moment it seemed as if the wind stopped blowing, and as if the trees stopped sighing, and as if there was the sound of a heavenly host singing——

The Small Girl's mother and the Small Girl's father sat up very late that night. They popped a great bowlful of crisp snowy corn and made it into balls. They boiled sugar and molasses, and cracked nuts, and made candy of them. They cut funny little Christmas fairies out of paper and painted their jackets bright red, with round silver buttons of the tinfoil that came on a cream cheese. And then they put the balls and the candy and the painted fairies and a long red candle in a big basket, and set it away. And the Small Girl's mother brought out the chocolate mouse.

"We will put this on the clock," she said, "where her eyes will rest on it the first thing in the morning."

So they put it there, and it seemed as natural as life, so that Pussy-Purr-up positively licked his chops and sat in front of the clock as if to keep his eye on the chocolate mouse.

And the Small Girl's mother said, "She was lovely about giving up the doll, and she will love the tree."

"We'll have to get up very early," said the Small Girl's father.

"And you'll have to run ahead and light the candle."

Well, they got up before dawn the next morning, and so did the Boy-Next-Door. He was there on the step, waiting, blowing his hands and beating them quite like the poor little boys in a Christmas story, who haven't any mittens.

But he wasn't a poor little boy, and he had so many pairs of fur-trimmed gloves that he didn't know what to do with them, but he had left the house in such a hurry that he had forgotten to put them on.

So there he stood on the front step of the little house, blowing on his hands and beating them. And it was dark, with a sort of pale shine in the heavens, which didn't seem to come from the stars or to herald the dawn; it was just a mystical silver glow that set the boy's heart to beating.

He had never been out alone like this. He had always stayed in his warm bed until somebody called him, and then he had waited until they called again, and then he had dressed and gone down to breakfast, where his father scolded because he was late, and his mother scolded because he ate too fast. But this day had begun with adventure, and for the first time, under that silver sky, he felt the thrill of it.

Then suddenly some one came around the corner—some one tall and thin, with a cap on his head and an empty basket in his hands.

"Hello," he said. "A Merry Christmas."

It was the Small Girl's father, and he put the key in the lock, and went in, and turned on a light, and there was the table set for four.

And the Small Girl's father said: "You see we have set a place for you. We must eat something before we go out."

And the Boy said: "Are we going out? I came to see the tree."

"We are going out to see the tree."

Before the Boy-Next-Door could ask any questions, the Small Girl's mother appeared with her finger on her lips and said: "Sh-sh," and then she began to recite in a hushed voice,

"Hickory-Dickory-Dock——"

Then there was a little cry and the sound of dancing feet, and the Small Girl in a red dressing-gown came flying in.

"Oh, Mother, Mother, the mouse is *on* the clock. The mouse is *on* the clock."

Well, it seemed to the Boy-Next-Door that he had never seen anything so exciting as the things that followed. The chocolate mouse went *up* the clock and *under* the chair—and would have had its tail cut *off* except that the Small Girl begged to save it.

"I want to keep it as it is, Mother."

And playing this game as if it were the most important thing in the whole wide world were the Small Girl's mother and the Small Girl's father, all laughing and flushed, and chanting the quaint old words to the quaint old music.

The Boy-Next-Door held his breath for fear he would wake up from this entrancing dream and find himself in his own big house, alone in his puffy bed, or eating breakfast with his stodgy parents who had never played with him in his life. He found himself laughing too, and flushed and happy, and trying to sing in his funny boy's voice,

"Heigh-o, says Anthony Rowley!"

The Small Girl absolutely refused to eat the mouse. "He's my darling Christmas mouse, Mother."

So her mother said, "Well, I'll put him on the clock again, where Pussy-Purr-up can't get him while we are out."

"Oh, are we going out?" said the Small Girl, round-eyed.

"Yes."

"Where are we going?"

"To find Christmas."

That was all the Small Girl's mother would tell. So they had breakfast, and everything tasted perfectly delicious to the Boy-Next-Door. But first they bowed their heads, and the Small Girl's father said,

"Dear Christ-Child, on this Christmas morning, bless these children, and help us all to keep our hearts young and full of love for Thee."

The Boy-Next-Door, when he lifted his head, had a funny feeling as if he wanted to cry, and yet it was a lovely feeling, all warm and comfortable.

For breakfast they each had a great baked apple, and great slices of sweet bread and butter, and great glasses of milk, and as soon as they had finished, away they went, out of the door and down into the wood back of the house, and when they were deep in the wood, the Small Girl's father took out of his pocket a little flute and began to play, and he played thin piping tunes that went flitting around among the trees, and the Small Girl hummed the tunes, and her mother hummed the tunes until it sounded like singing bees, and their feet fairly danced, and the boy found himself humming and dancing with them.

Then suddenly the piping ceased, and a hush fell over the wood. It was so still that they could almost hear each other breathe—so still that when a light flamed suddenly in that open space it burned without a flicker.

The light came from a red candle that was set in the top of a small living tree. It was the only light on the tree, but it showed the snowy balls, and the small red fairies whose coats had silver buttons.

"It's our tree, my darling," he heard the Small Girl's mother saying.

Suddenly it seemed to the boy that his heart would burst in his breast.

He wanted some one to speak to him like that. The Small Girl sat high on her father's shoulder, and her father held her mother's hand. It was like a chain of gold, their holding hands like that and loving each other——

The boy reached out and touched the woman's hand. She looked down at him and drew him close. He felt warmed and comforted. The red candle burning there in the darkness was like some sacred fire of friendship. He wished that it would never go out, that he might stand there watching it, with his small cold hand in the clasp of the Small Girl's mother.

It was late when the Boy-Next-Door got back to his own big house. But he had not been missed. Everybody was up, and everybody was angry. The Daughter-in-Law had declared the night before that she would not stay another day beneath that roof, and off she had gone with her young husband, and her little girl, who was to have had the pink doll on the tree.

"And good riddance," said the Next-Door-Neighbor.

But she ate no breakfast, and she went out to the kitchen and worked with her maids to get the dinner ready, and there were covers laid for nine instead of twelve.

And the Next-Door-Neighbor kept saying, "Good riddance—good riddance," and not once did she say, "A Merry Christmas."

But the Boy-Next-Door held something in his heart that was warm and glowing like the candle in the forest, and so he came to his mother and said,

"May I have the pink doll?"

She spoke frowningly. "What does a boy want of a doll?"

"I'd like to give it to the little girl next door."

"Do you think I buy dolls to give away in charity?"

"Well, they gave me a Christmas present."

"What did they give you?"

He opened his hand and showed a little flute tied with gay red ribbon. He lifted it to his lips and blew on it, a thin piping tune——

"Oh, that," said his mother scornfully. "Why, that's nothing but a reed from the pond!"

But the boy knew it was more than that. It was a magic pipe that made you dance, and made your heart warm and happy.

So he said again, "I'd like to give her the doll," and he reached out his little hand and touched his mother's—and his eyes were wistful.

His mother's own eyes softened—she had lost one son that day—and she said, "Oh, well, do as you please," and went back to the kitchen.

The Boy-Next-Door ran into the great room and took the doll from the tree, and wrapped her in paper, and flew out of the door and down the brick walk and straight into the little house.

When the door was opened, he saw that his friends were just sitting down to dinner—and there was the beefsteak pie all brown and piping hot, with a wreath of holly, and the Small Girl was saying,

"And the onions were silver, and the carrots were gold——"

The Boy-Next-Door went up to the Small Girl and said, "I've brought you a present."

With his eyes all lighted up, he took off the paper in which it was wrapped, and there was the doll, in rosy frills, with eyes that opened and shut, and shoes and stockings, and curly hair that was bobbed and beautiful.

And the Small Girl, in a whirlwind of happiness, said, "Is it really *my* doll?"

And the Boy-Next-Door felt very shy and happy, and he said, "Yes."

And the Small Girl's mother said, "It was a beautiful thing to do," and she bent and kissed him.

Again that bursting feeling came into the boy's heart and he lifted his face to hers and said, "May I come sometimes and be your boy?"

And she said, "Yes."

And when at last he went away, she stood in the door and watched him, such a little lad, who knew so little of loving. And because she knew so much of love, her eyes filled to overflowing.

But presently she wiped the tears away and went back to the table. And she smiled at the Small Girl and at the Small Girl's father.

"And the potatoes were ivory," she said. "Oh, who would ask for turkey, when they can have a pie like this?"

CHRISTMAS ON THE SINGING RIVER[2]
Jefferson Lee Harbour

There was always a crowd in waiting when the stage-coach arrived in the shabby little mining-camp of Singing River. As a rule, the crowd assembled on the long, wide platform in front of the post-office, which was also the stage-office, the hotel, the general store, and the center from which radiated the social life of the camp. Above the post-office was a small and dingy hall lighted with dripping tallow candles; and such public amusements or entertainments as there were in Singing River were given in this hall. The platform in front of the building was the favorite "loafing-place" of the miners. The arrival of the stage-coach was the connecting-link between Singing River and the great outside world from which the little mining-camp was so far removed. The nearest railroad station was one hundred miles distant, and there was no town within fifteen miles any larger than Singing River, which was but a little hamlet of log-cabins, tents, and slab shanties far up the mountainside above the little Singing River in the rocky gulch below. The Singing River was a narrow and shallow stream; but its crystal-clear waters surged in foamy wavelets around moss-covered boulders and went singing on so merrily that there was perpetual music in even the darkest and gloomiest parts of the gulch. But there was ice over the river for seven months of the year, and then nothing was to be heard but the dreary sound of the wind as it went moaning or shrieking up and down the long, dark cañon.

The winters were long and bitter in Singing River. Snow began to fly as early as the last of September, and it still lay deep in the gulches and in the narrow, rocky streets of the camp while the wild flowers were blooming in the far-distant valleys.

But on the December day when this story opens, the stage arrived a full hour in advance of the usual time, and only a few of the men of the camp were at the post-office

---

[2] Reprinted from "St. Nicholas Magazine" with permission.

when Dave Hixon, the stage-driver, drew rein before it, amid the gently falling snow. There were no passengers on the outside seats, and no inside occupants were to be seen. Apparently the big stage was empty.

"Light load this trip, Dave," said big Jim Hart, the postmaster, as he came out to get the limp and unpromising-looking mail-bag.

"I should say so," replied Dave, as he took off his wide-brimmed felt hat and slapped it against the side of the coach to rid it of the snow that had fallen upon it.

"I reckon travel is about done for this season over the Shoshone trail, an' they'll soon stop sendin' the coach up here even once a week, an' then we'll be clean shut off from everywhere. No passengers this trip—eh?"

"Only two, an' there's so little of them that I reckon they've rattled round like peas in a pod inside there."

Then Dave leaned far downward and, twisting himself around, called out to some one within the stage:

"Hello, there, youngsters! You all right?"

A shrill, childish voice replied: "Yes, sir."

"Well, you'd better crawl out o' that an' git in where it's warmer, an' git some o' Ma'am Hickey's hot supper. Hey, Ma'am Hickey, I've fetched you a kind of a queer cargo!"

This last remark was addressed to a large, round-faced, motherly-looking woman who had come to the door of the hotel part of the building with her apron over her head.

"What's that you say, Dave?" she called out loudly and heartily.

"I say I've fetched you a kind of a queer cargo. You just come out an' see if I hain't."

He jumped down from his high driver's seat and flung open the stage door as Ma'am Hickey came over to the edge of the roadway. Reaching into the coach, Dave picked up what appeared to be a round bundle on the back seat, and set it out in the snow with a buffalo robe around it. The robe fell to the ground, and there was revealed to the amazed bystanders a girl of about nine years with big dark eyes that looked calmly and yet appealingly at the staring group. The next moment Dave had set a yellow-haired boy of about five years down beside the girl.

"There you air!" said Dave, the stage-driver. "Got 'commodations for this lady an' gent, Ma'am Hickey?"

"Well, I'll make 'commodations for 'em, if I have to turn you out o' your bed to do it," said Ma'am Hickey, as she dropped to her knees before the little boy and took him into her arms, saying as she did so:

"Why, bless your heart an' soul, little feller! I declare if it don't feel sweet to git a child into my arms once more! An' whose boy air you, anyhow?"

"Papa's," replied the boy, shyly, with a slight quivering of his lips and an attempt to release himself from Ma'am Hickey's embrace.

"An' where is papa, honey?"

"Here."

Ma'am Hickey looked around toward the men as if expecting some of them to come forward and claim the child; but they too were looking around inquiringly as the crowd grew in numbers, attracted by the news of the arrival of the stage. Noting the boy's quivering lips and half-frightened look in the presence of all those strangers, his sister stepped toward him and patted his head gently with her mittened hand, saying as she did so:

"There, there; don't you cry, Freddy. Sister will take care of you; yes, she will."

"Where did you little folks come from?" asked Ma'am Hickey, rising to her feet with the little boy in her arms.

"From Iowa, ma'am."

"Ioway!" exclaimed Ma'am Hickey. "You don't ever mean to tell me that you have come all the way from Ioway to this place all by your lone selves?"

The girl nodded her head and said:

"Yes, we did. We had a letter to the conductors on the trains telling them where we were going, and we got along all right; didn't we, Freddy?"

The little boy nodded his head solemnly, too much awed by his strange surroundings to speak.

"Well, if that don't beat anything I ever heard of!" exclaimed Ma'am Hickey. "If I'd been your ma you wouldn't've done it!"

The little girl kept looking into the faces of the men who

crowded about them, and said:

"I don't see my papa anywhere. He said that he would be here when the stage got here with us; but I don't see him at all."

"What is your papa's name, deary?"

"Richard Miller."

The men looked at each other blankly. Some of them opened and closed their mouths without uttering a sound. Big "Missouri Dan" uttered an exclamation under his breath. Ma'am Hickey held up one finger warningly. Then she stooped and kissed the little girl on the brow, and said gently:

"You come right into the house with me, little folks. I'll get you a real nice hot supper, an' then I think you'd best go right to bed after your long ride."

When the cabin door had closed behind them, Big Dan said to the miners around him:

"Well, if this ain't what I call a state of affairs! To think of them poor little tots trailin' 'way out here from back in Ioway only to find their daddy a day in his grave! Cur'us how things turns out!"

"What's to be done?" asked a long, lank, red-whiskered man called "Cap."

"Shore enough," drawled out an elderly man who had been chewing the end of his long gray mustache reflectively.

"I move that we go over to my shack an' talk the matter over," said Big Dan; and, without waiting for his motion to be voted upon, he started toward his cabin, a small log affair a short distance around the rocky road. The men around the post-office followed Big Dan, and, when they were in his cabin, seated on benches and nail-kegs or sprawling on buffalo robes in front of the fire in the big open fire-place, one of the men said:

"What does all this mean, anyhow? You know that I've just come down from Mount Baldy, an' all this is Greek to me."

"Well, it's just this-a-way," replied Dan. "Three days ago a man come into camp on foot from over towards Roarin' Fork. He was so sick when he got here he could hardly speak, an' 'bout all we got outo' him was that his name was Miller. Pneumonia had set in mighty hard, an' in less than two hours after he got here he couldn't speak at all, an' he didn't live twelve hours. We laid him under that little clump o' pines down near the bend in the Singin' River not ten hours ago; an' now here in comes the stage with that boy an' gal, ev'dently the prop'ty o' this same Miller, who ain't here to meet 'em, an' who won't ever meet 'em in this world. It goes without sayin' that they ain't got no ma. If they had, she'd never let 'em come trailin' off out here all by theirselves. It's mighty tough on 'em."

"That's right," agreed the man called Cap. "I'm old an' tough as ever they make 'em, but I ain't fergot my own childhood so fur as not to 'preciate just how them pore little young uns will feel when they reelize the sitooation. I feel fer 'em."

"So do I," said a stalwart fellow of about thirty-five years. "I've got a couple o' little folks o' my own back East, an' that boy reminds me a sight o' my own little chap."

The men were still discussing the strange and sad occurrence, and the question of the future of the children was still unsettled, when the door of the cabin opened and Ma'am Hickey appeared. Her eyes were red and her voice was unsteady as she said:

"I just run over to say one thing, boys, an' that's this: Don't one of you dast to breathe a word to them pore little darlin's about where their pa is until after Christmas. They're not to know that they are orphans until after that time. Their ma died last spring, an' their pa sent for 'em to come out here to him. It's a mighty rough place to fetch 'em to, but the little girl says that an aunt of hers was to come on from California an' be with 'em this winter, an' their pa wrote that he would likely go on to California in the spring—pore man! He's gone on now to a country that's furder away than that!"

She wiped her eyes on the back of her hand before adding:

"It jest about broke my heart to hear them two pore little things talkin' about Christmas, an' wonderin' what their pa would have for 'em, while I was undressin' 'em for bed. An' I made up my mind that they shouldn't know a thing about what has happened until after Christmas; an', what's more, some o' you men kin jest stretch your long legs hoofin' it over to Crystal City to git 'em some toys an' things to make good my promise to 'em that if they hung up their stockin's Christmas eve they'd find 'em full next mornin'. Now you boys remember that mum is the word in regard to their pa. Leave it to me to pacify 'em in regard to his not comin' for 'em. They're the cunnin'est little things I ever saw, an' it's jest too terrible that this trouble has had to befall 'em!"

When good Ma'am Hickey had gone back to the hotel, Big Dan slapped his great rough palms together and said:

"I tell you what, boys! Let's give them two little unfortinists a jolly good Christmas! I'm fairly sp'ilin' for somethin' to do, an' I'll hoof it over to Crystal City an' git a lot o' Christmas gimcracks for 'em."

"I'll keep you company," said Joe Burke, the man who had two little ones of his own back East. "Travelin' on snow-shoes over the mountain passes at this time o' the year is ruther dangerous, an' it's not best to start out on a trip alone. Then I guess I know more about what would please the youngsters than you would, Dan."

"I ain't ever took occasion to mention it before, but I happen to know a little about what children like, my own self, seein' as I have had two o' my own," replied Big Dan. "They both died the same week. It happened nearly forty years ago, but these two little wayfarers stragglin' into camp this way brings it all back to me."

No one in the camp had ever heard Big Dan speak so solemnly, and there was silence in the room when he added:

"I reckon I know enough about children to know that a big doll with these here open-and-shet kind o' eyes allus takes the fancy of a little gal, an' that a boy allus likes somethin' that'll make a racket. But I'll be glad o' your comp'ny, Joe."

Ma'am Hickey appeared again before the conference came to an end.

"They're cuddled up in bed in each other's arms, cheek to cheek, the pore little dears," she said. "I pacified 'em in regard to their pa without tellin' any actual fib, an' they went to sleep content. The little boy's tongue went like a trip-hammer when he finally got it unloosened, and he jabbered away fast enough. But most he talked about was Christmas. He's set his heart on a steam-engine that will go 'choo, choo,

choo,' an' if you boys can find such a thing in Crystal City, you buy it an' fetch it along with you, an' I'll foot the bill. The little girl is doll-crazy, like most little girls, so you must get her one, or more than one. An' of course you'll lay in plenty o' candy; an' if you can lug home a turkey or two on your backs I'll get up a Christmas supper for 'em to eat after we've had the tree."

"The tree?" said one of the men, inquiringly.

"Yes, *sir*; the tree! Of course them little folks must have a tree. They say they want one, an' why shouldn't they have it, with the finest Christmas trees in the world right at hand here in the mountains?"

"Where you goin' to have the tree, I'd like to know?" said a burly miner.

"In the hall over the post-office."

"Well, if you ain't plannin' a reg'lar jamboree!"

"Course I am!" replied Ma'am Hickey. "Got any objections?"

"Better keep 'em to yourself if you have," said Big Dan. "For what Ma'am Hickey an' them two little youngsters says—goes."

"That settles it," said Ma'am Hickey, with a laugh.

Crystal City was a long distance from Singing River, and the mountain trails were hard and dangerous to travel at that time of the year. The stage would not make another trip until after Christmas, and it might be a month before it returned after it left the camp.

Big Dan and Joe Burke set off at daybreak the morning after the arrival of the two little wayfarers. The men had "chipped in" for the purchase of "gimcracks" for the tree, and they had been so generous that Big Dan said just before he started for Crystal City:

"We'll have to have the biggest pine we kin git for the tree. You chaps have it all set up in the hall by the time we git back."

"You sure you got that list o' things I wrote down for you?" asked Ma'am Hickey. "Men ain't got any kind of a mem'ry when it comes to shoppin'."

"I got the list right here in this pocket," replied Dan, patting his broad chest. "If we have good luck we'll be back by noon day after to-morrow, an' that night is Christmas eve, so you'll want the tree all ready. Did the little folks sleep good?"

"They never stirred; but once the little boy laughed out in his sleep an' said somethin' about a steam-engine. Both of the children are sleepin' yet."

An hour later the children were up and were eating their breakfast in Ma'am Hickey's cozy kitchen, which was also the dining-room of the hotel.

"Will my papa come to-day?" asked Freddy, as he helped himself to a hot doughnut.

"Don't worry none about your papa, deary," Ma'am Hickey said. "We'll see to you all right. Let's talk about Christmas."

"I never talked so much about Christmas in all the born days of my life as I talked about it in them two days," said Ma'am Hickey, afterward. "It was the only way I could git their minds off their pa."

Ma'am Hickey's account of the Christmas tree at Singing River is so much more interesting than any account I could give of it, that I think it best to let her tell about it in her own way:

"You see, Big Dan an' Joe Burke got back all right the middle of the afternoon the day before Christmas. They looked like a pair o' pack peddlers, an' they were about fagged out, for they had had a hard time of it pullin' up over the mountain trails in a snow-storm. Joe said he didn't think he could have dragged himself another mile for love nor money. He had two big turkeys on his back besides a great lot of other things.

"Well, the men in the camp had been busy, too. They had cut a big pine an' set it up in the hall over the post-office, an' the way they had dec'rated the hall with evergreen was beautiful. You couldn't see an inch of the ugly bare logs nor of the bare rafters. They set to an' scrubbed the floor an' washed the winders, an' strung up a lot o' red, white and blue buntin' I happened to have in the house, an' I tell you the little old hall did look scrumptious. I kep' the children in the kitchen with me, where I was makin' pies an' cake an' doughnuts most o' the time. I give 'em dough to muss with, an' let 'em scrape the cake-dishes, an' tried to keep 'em interested all the time, so they wouldn't ask about their pa.

"When Big Dan an' Joe got back the other men had a great time riggin' up the tree. We was afeerd they wouldn't be able to buy Christmas-tree candles in Crystal City; but, my land! they got about ten dozen of 'em, an' no end o' tinsel an' shiny balls an' things to hang on the tree, an' a lot o' little flags to stick in among the evergreen dec'rations. We had no end o' common taller candles on hand, an' the men were perfectly reckless with 'em. I reckon they put as many as two hundred of 'em up around the room. An' what did they do but go an' rig Big Dan up as Santy Claus! They wrapped him up in a big bearskin one o' the boys had, an' put about a quart o' flour on his long, bushy whiskers to whiten 'em, an' they put a big fur cap on his head, and he did look for all the world like Santy his own self. Yes; an' he had a string o' sleigh-bells they got at the stage-office stable; an' them boys ackshully cut a hole in the roof so Santy Claus could come down through it! La, if you want things carried through regardless, you let a lot o' Rocky Mountain boys take it in hand. They won't stop at nothin'. I reckon they'd h'isted off the hull roof if it had been necessary to make the appearance of Santy true to life. Such fun as the boys had over it all! An' of all the capers they cut up! Seemed like they was all boys once more! Me an' Ann Dickey an' Mary Ann Morris were the only women in the camp, an' we had our hands full gittin' up the Christmas supper we intended havin' after the tree. Mind you, there wasn't a child in camp but just them two pore little orphans, an' all that fuss was on their account. If you think rough miner boys can't have the kindest o' hearts, you just remember that. Every man seemed to be tryin' to outdo the others in doin' somethin' for them little folks.

"Well, I jest wisht you could have seen them children when the time come for 'em to go up to the hall an' see their tree! Little Freddy he give a yell o' joy that most split our ears, an' he just stood an' clapped his hands, while his sister kep' sayin', 'How lovely it is! Oh, isn't it beautiful?' Then Freddy he screeches out: 'Oh, there's my choo-choo engine! Goody!' An' how little Elsie's eyes did shine when she saw no less than *three* dolls on the tree for herself! There was enough stuff on that tree for a hull Sunday-school, for the men had been that reckless in sendin' to Crystal City for things.

"Then I wisht you could have seen those children when Big Dan come in all rigged up as Santy Claus! That was the cap-sheaf o' the hull proceedin's! First we heard his bells outside, an' him callin' out, 'Whoa, there!' like as if he was talkin' to his reindeers. Then he clim up the ladder the boys had set outside, an' presently down he come through the hole in the roof. I jest thought little Fred's eyes would pop clean out o' his head when that part o' the show come off! An' what fun there was when old Santy went around givin' the boys all sorts of ridiculous presents! He give old Tim Thorpe a tiny chiny doll, an' big Jack Ross a jumpin'-jack, an' Ben Anderson a set o' little pewter dishes; an' he fetched me a great big old pipe, when they knowed I hated the very sight o' one. I tell you, it was real fun!

"Well, the things had all been distributed, an' the children were loaded down with presents, an' me an' the two other women were about to go downstairs to take up the supper, when the door of the hall opened, and a strange man stepped in. When he saw the children he give a kind of a little outcry, an' the next minute he was down on his knees before 'em, with an arm around each child, an' he was kissin' first one an' then the other. We all jest stared at each other when little Elsie clapped her hands together and said:

"'Why, papa!'

"An' that's jest who it was! The man named Miller who had died a few days before was a cousin o' the children's pa. It seemed that his cousin o' the name of Miller had been sent to meet the children, because their pa had been sick an' wasn't hardly strong enough to come away over to Singin' River for them. He lived in a little camp only about twenty miles away, but it was a hard road to travel for a well man, even. So this cousin he come, an', from all we could make out, he had lost his way in a storm, an' had laid out a night an' got so chilled it had brought on pneumonia. When he didn't come back with the children after two or three days, their pa got oneasy, an' he set out himself to see what was the matter. He wasn't hardly fit to travel, but he come anyhow, an' he was all tuckered out when he got to Singin' River. Then he was so nervous an' kind o' wrought up that no one thought it to his shame that he jest broke clean down an' laughed an' cried by turns, kind o' hystericky like, over the children.

"We did have the best time at the supper! A storm had come up, an' the wind was roarin' an' howlin' in the cañon an' up an' down the Singin' River, an' the sleet was dashin' ag'in' the winder-lights; but that jest made it seem more cheery an' comfortable in the cabin, with a roarin' fire o' pine-knots in the big fireplace at one end o' the cabin, an' the teakettle singin' on my big shinin' stove at the other end. Mr. Miller he set between the two children, an' he'd hug an' kiss 'em between times. We made him stay two whole weeks in Singin' River to rest up an' git real well, an' then a hull passel o' the boys went with him to git the children home. The boys rigged up a sled, an' tuk turns drawin' Elsie an' Freddy over the trails an' away up over Red Bird Mountain. I reckon it was a ride they won't ever forgit; an' none of us that were there will ever in this world forgit that Christmas on the Singin' River."

THE SHEPHERD WHO WATCHED BY NIGHT[3]
Thomas Nelson Page

The place had nothing distinguished or even perhaps distinctive about it except its trees and the tapering spire of a church lifting above them. It was not unlike a hundred other places that one sees as one travels through the country. It called itself a town; but it was hardly more than a village. One long street, now paved on both sides, climbed the hill, where the old post-road used to run in from the country on one side and out again on the other, passing a dingy, large house with whitewashed pillars, formerly known as the tavern, but now calling itself "The Inn." This, with two or three cross-streets and a short street or two on either side of the main street, constituted "the town." A number of good houses, and a few very good, indeed, sat back in yards dignified by fine trees. Three or four churches stood on corners, as far apart apparently as possible. Several of them were much newer and fresher painted than the one with the spire and cross; but this was the only old one and was generally spoken of as "The Church," as the rector was meant when the people spoke of "the preacher." It sat back from the street, in a sort of sordid seclusion, and near it, yet more retired, was an old mansion, also dilapidated, with a wide porch, much decayed, and to the side and a little behind it, an out-building or two, one of which was also occupied as a dwelling. The former was the rectory, and the smaller dwelling was where the old woman lived who took care of the rectory, cleaned up the two or three rooms which the rector used since his wife's death, and furnished him his meals. It had begun only as a temporary arrangement, but it seemed to work well enough and had gone on now for years and no one thought of changing it. If an idea of change ever entered the mind of any one, it was only when the old woman's grumbling floated out into the town as to the tramps who would come and whom the preacher would try to take care of. Then, indeed, discussion

---

[3] From "The Land of the Spirit"; copyright, 1913, by Charles Scribner's Sons. By permission of the publishers.

would take place as to the utter impracticability of the old preacher and the possibility of getting a younger and liver man in his place. For the rest of the time the people were hopeless. The old preacher was not only past his prime but his usefulness. Yet what could they do? No one else wanted him, and they could not turn him out. He was saddled on them for life. They ran simply by the old propulsion; but the church was going down, they said, and they were helpless. This had been the case for years and now as the year neared its close it was the same.

Such was the talk as they finished dressing the church for Christmas and made their way homeward—the few who still took interest enough to help in this way. They felt sorry for the old man, who had been much in their way during the dressing, but sorrier for themselves.

This had been a few days before Christmas and now it was Christmas eve.

The old rector sat at his table trying to write his Christmas sermon. He was hopelessly behindhand with it. The table was drawn up close to the worn stove, but the little bare room was cold, and now and then the old man blew on his fingers to warm them, and pushed his feet closer to the black hearth. Again and again he took up his pen as if to write, and as often laid it down again. The weather was bitter and the coal would not burn. There was little to burn. He wore his old overcoat, to save fuel. Before him on the table, amid a litter of other books and papers, lay a worn Bible and a prayer-book open, and beside them a folded letter on which his eye often rested. Outside, the wind roared, shaking the doors, rattling the windows, and whistling at the key-holes. Now and then the sound of a passing vehicle was borne in on the wind, and at intervals came the voices of boys shouting to each other as they ran by. The old man did not hear the former, but when the boys shouted he listened till they had ceased, his thoughts turned to the past and to the two boys whom God had given him and had then taken back to Himself. His gray face wore a look of deep concern, and, indeed, of dejection, and his eye wandered once more to the folded letter on the table. It was signed "A Friend," and it was this which was responsible for the unwritten Christmas sermon. It was what the world calls an anonymous letter and, though couched in kindly terms, it had struck a dagger into the old man's heart. Yet he could not but say that in tone and manner it was a kind act. Certainly it had told the truth, and if in tearing a veil from his eyes it had stunned him, why should he not face the truth!

He took the letter up again and reread it, not that he needed to read it, for he knew it by heart. Every sentence was seared into his memory.

He reread it hoping to find some answer to its plain, blunt, undeniable statements, but he found none. It was all true, every word, from the ominous beginning which stated that the writer felt that he had "a clear duty to perform," down to the close when with a protestation of good-will he signed himself the old man's friend.

"You must see, unless you are blind," ran the letter, "that your church is running down, and unless you get out and let the congregation secure a new and younger man, there will soon be no congregation at all left. No men come to church any longer and many women who used to come now stay away. You are a good man, but you are a failure. Your usefulness is past." Yes, it was true, he was a failure. His usefulness was past. This was the reason doubtless that no Christmas things had come this year—they wanted to let him know. It pained him to think it, and he sighed.

"You spend your time fooling about a lot of useless things," continued the anonymous friend, "visiting people who do not come to church, and you have turned the rectory into a harbor for tramps.

"You cannot preach any longer. You are hopelessly behind the times. People nowadays want no more doctrinal points discussed; they want to hear live, up-to-date, practical discourses on the vital problems of the day. Such as the Rev. Dr. —— delivers. His church is full." This also was true. He was no longer able to preach. He had felt something of this himself. Now it came home to him like a blow on the head, and a deeper pain was the conviction which, long hovering about his heart, now settled and took definite shape, that he ought to get out. But where could he go? He would have gone long since if he had known where to go. He could not go out and graze like an old horse on the roadside. There was no provision made for such as he. No pensions were provided by his church for old and disabled clergymen, and the suggestion made in the letter had no foundation in his case: "You must or, at least, you should have saved something in all this time."

This sounded almost humorous and a wintry little smile flickered for a moment about the wrinkled mouth. His salary had never been over six hundred dollars and there were so many to give to. Of late, it had been less than this amount and not all of this had been paid. The smile died out and the old man's face grew grave again as he tried to figure out what he could do. He thought of one or two old friends to whom he could write. Possibly, they might know some country parish that would be willing to take him, though it was a forlorn hope. If he could but hold on till they invited him, it would be easier, for he knew how difficult it was for a clergyman out of a place to get a call. People were so suspicious. Once out, he was lost.

At the thought, a picture of a little plot amid the trees in the small cemetery on the hill near the town slipped into his mind. Three little slabs stood there above three mounds, one longer than the others. They covered all that was mortal of what he had loved best on earth. The old man sighed and his face in the dim light took on an expression very far away. He drifted off into a reverie. Ah, if they had only been left to him, the two boys that God had sent him and had then taken back to Himself, and the good wife who had borne up so bravely till she had sunk by the wayside! If he were only with them! He used to be rebellious at the neglect that left the drains so deadly, but that was gone now. He leant forward on his elbows and gradually slipped slowly to his knees. He was on them a long time, and when he tried to rise he was quite stiff; but his face had grown tranquil. He had been in high converse with the blessed of God and his mind had cleared. He had placed everything in God's hands, and He had given him light. He would wait until after Christmas and then he would resign. But he would announce it next day. The flock there should have a new and younger and abler shepherd. This would be glad tidings to them.

He folded up the letter and put it away. He no longer felt

wounded by it. It was of God's ordaining and was to be received as a kindness, a ray of light to show him the path of duty. He drew his paper toward him and, taking up his pen, began to write rapidly and firmly. The doubt was gone, the way was clear. His text had come to his mind.

"And there were in the same country, shepherds abiding in the field, keeping watch over their flock by night, and lo, the Angel of the Lord came upon them, and the glory of the Lord shone round about them. And they were sore afraid. And the Angel said unto them: Fear not, for behold, I bring unto you good tidings of great joy, which shall be to all people. For unto you is born this day in the City of David a Saviour which is Christ the Lord. And this shall be a sign unto you. You shall find the Babe wrapped in swaddling clothes lying in a manger."

Unfolding the story, he told of the darkness that had settled over Israel under the Roman sway and the formalism of the Jewish hierarchy at the time of Christ's coming, drawing from it the lesson that God still had shepherds watching over His flocks in the night to whom He vouchsafed to send His heavenly messengers. On and on he wrote, picturing the divine mission of the Redeemer and His power to save souls, and dwelling on Christmas as the ever recurrent reminder of "the tender mercy of our God whereby the Day Spring from on High hath visited us."

Suddenly he came to a pause. Something troubled him. It came to him that he had heard that a woman in the town was very sick and he had intended going to see her. She had had a bad reputation; but he had heard that she had reformed. At any rate she was ill. He paused and deliberated. At the moment the wind rattled the shutters. She did not belong to his flock or, so far as he knew, to any flock, and once when he had stopped her on the street and spoken to her of her evil life, she had insulted him. She had told him that he had better look after his own people instead of lecturing her. He turned back to his paper, pen in hand; but it was borne in on him that he was writing of watching over the flock by night and here he was neglecting one of his Father's sheep. He laid aside his pen, and rising, took down his old hat and stick, lit his lantern, turned down his lamp, and, shuffling through the bare, narrow passage, let himself out at the door. As he came out on to the little porch to step down to the walk, the wind struck him fiercely and he had some difficulty in fastening the door with its loose lock; but this done he pushed forward. The black trees swayed and creaked above him in the wind, and fine particles of snow stung his withered cheeks. He wondered if the shepherds in the fields ever had such a night as this for their watch. He remembered to have read that snow fell on the mountains of Judea. It was a blustering walk. The wind felt as if it would blow through him. Yet he stumbled onward.

At length he reached the little house on a back street in the worst part of the village, where he had heard the sick woman lived. A light glimmered dimly in an upper window and his knocking finally brought to the door a woman who looked after her. She was not in a good humor at being disturbed at that hour, for her rest had been much broken of late; but she was civil and invited him in.

In answer to his question of how her patient was, she replied shortly: "No better; the doctor says she can't last much longer. Do you want to see her?" she added presently.

The old rector said he did and she waved toward the stair. "You can walk up."

As they climbed the stair she added: "She said you'd come if you knew." The words made the old man warmer. And when she opened the door of the sick-room and said, "Here's the preacher, as you said," the faint voice of the invalid murmuring, "I hoped you'd come," made him feel yet warmer.

He was still of some use even in this parish.

Whatever her face had been in the past, illness and suffering had refined it. He stayed there long, for he found that she needed him. She unburdened herself to him. She was sorry she had been rude to him that time. She had been a sinful woman. She said she had tried of late to live a good life, since that day he had spoken to her, but she now found that she had not. She had wanted to be a believer and she had gone to hear him preach one day after that, but now she did not seem to believe anything. They told her that she must repent. She wanted to repent, but she could not feel. She was

Christmas in Modern Story

in the dark and she feared she was lost. The old man had taken his seat by her side, and he now held her hand and soothed her tenderly.

"Once, perhaps," he said doubtfully, "though God only knows that, but certainly no longer. Christ died for you. You say you wanted to change, that you tried to ask God's pardon and to live a better life even before you fell ill. Do you think you could want this as much as God wanted it? He put the wish into your heart. Do you think He would now let you remain lost? Why, He sent His Son into the world to seek and to save the lost. He has sent me to you to-night to tell you that He has come to save you. It is not you that can save yourself, but He, and if you feel that it is dark about you, never mind— the path is still there. One of the old Fathers has said that God sometimes puts His children to sleep in the dark."

"But I have been—You don't know what I have been," she murmured. The old man laid his hand softly on her head.

"He not only forgave the Magdalen, for her love of Him, but He vouchsafed to her the first sight of His face after His resurrection."

"I see," she said simply.

A little later she dozed off, but presently roused up again. A bell was ringing somewhere in the distance. It was the ushering in of the Christmas morn.

"What is that?" she asked feebly.

He told her.

"I think if I were well, if I could ever be good enough, I should like to join the church," she said. "I remember being baptized—long ago."

"You have joined it," he replied.

Just then the nurse brought her a glass.

"What is that?" she asked feebly.

"A little wine." She held up a bottle in which a small quantity remained.

It seemed to the old preacher a sort of answer to his thought. "Have you bread here?" he asked the young woman. She went out and a moment later brought him a piece of bread.

He had often administered the early communion on Christmas morning, but never remembered a celebration that had seemed to him so real and satisfying. As he thought of the saints departed this life in the faith and fear of God, they appeared to throng about him as never before, and among them were the faces he had known and loved best on earth.

It was toward morning when he left; as he bade her good-by he knew he should see her no more this side of Heaven.

As he came out into the night the snow was falling, but the wind had died down and he no longer felt cold. The street was empty, but he no longer felt lonely. He seemed to have got nearer to God's throne.

Suddenly, as he neared his house, a sound fell on his ears. He stopped short and listened. Could he have been mistaken? Could that have been a baby's cry? There was no dwelling near but his own, and on that side only the old and unoccupied stable in the yard whence the sound had seemed to come. A glance at it showed that it was dark and he was moving on again to the house when the sound was repeated. This time there was no doubt of it. A baby's wail came clear on the silence of the night from the unused stable. A thought that it might be some poor foundling flashed into his mind. The old man turned and, stumbling across the yard, went to the door.

"Who is here?" he asked of the dark. There was no answer, but the child wailed again and he entered the dark building, asking again, "Who is here?" as he groped his way forward. This time a voice almost inarticulate answered. Holding his dim little lantern above his head, he made his way inside, peering into the darkness, and presently, in a stall, on a lot of old litter, he descried a dark and shapeless mass from which the sound came. Moving forward, he bent down, with the lantern held low, and the dark mass gradually took shape as a woman's form seated on the straw. A patch of white, from which a pair of eyes gazed up at him, became a face and, below, a small bundle clasped to her breast took on the lines of a babe.

"What are you doing here?" he asked, breathless with astonishment. She shook her head wearily and her lips moved as if to say, "I didn't mean any harm." But no sound came. She only tried to fold the babe more warmly in her shawl. He took off his overcoat and wrapped it around her. "Come," he said firmly. "You must come with me," he added kindly; then, as she did not rise, he put out his hand to lift her, but, instead, suddenly set down the lantern and took the babe gently into his arms. She let him take the child, and rose slowly, her eyes still on him. He motioned for her to take the lantern and she did so. And they came to the door. He turned up the walk, the babe in his arms, and she going before him with the lantern. The ground was softly carpeted with snow, the wind had died down, but the clouds had disappeared and the trees were all white, softly gleaming, like dream-trees in a dream-land. The old man shivered slightly, but not now with cold. He felt as if he had gone back and held once more in his arms one of those babes he had given back to God. He thought of the shepherds who watched by night on the Judean hills. "It must have been such a night as this," he thought.

As they reached his door he saw that some one had been there in his absence. A large box stood on the little porch and beside it a basket filled with things. So he had not been forgotten after all. The milkman also had called and for his customary small bottle of milk had left one of double the usual size. When he let himself in at the door, he took the milk with him. So the shepherds might have done, he thought.

It was long before he could get the fire to burn; but in time this was accomplished; the room grew warm and the milk was warmed also. The baby was quieted and was soon asleep in its mother's lap. And as the firelight fell from the open stove on the child, in its mother's arms before the stove, the old man thought of a little picture he had once seen in a shop window. He had wanted to buy it, but he had never felt that he could gratify such a taste. There were too many calls on him. Then, as she appeared overcome with fatigue, the old man put her with the child in the only bed in the house that was ready for an occupant and, returning to the little living-room, ensconced himself in his arm-chair by the stove. He had meant to finish his sermon, but he was conscious for the first time that he was very tired. But he was also very happy. When he awoke he found that it was quite late. He had overslept and though his breakfast had been set out for him, he had time only to make his toilet and to go to church. The mother and child were still asleep in his room, the babe folded in her arm, and he stopped only to gaze on them a moment and to set the rest of the milk and his breakfast where the young mother could find it on awaking. Then he went to church, taking his half-finished sermon in his worn case. He thought with some dismay that it was unfinished, but the memory of the poor woman and the midnight communion, and of the young mother and her babe, comforted him; so he plodded on bravely. When he reached the church it was nearly full. He had not had such a congregation in a long time. And they were all cheerful and happy. The pang he had had as he remembered that he was to announce his resignation that day was renewed, but only for a second. The thought of the babe and its mother, warmed and fed in his little home, drove it away. And soon he began the service. He had never had such a service. It all appeared to him to have a new meaning. He felt nearer to the people in the pews than he ever remembered to have felt. They were more than ever his flock and he more than ever their shepherd. More, he felt nearer to mankind, and yet more near to those who had gone before—the innumerable company of the redeemed. They were all about him, clad all in white, glistering like the sun. The heavens seemed full of them. When he turned his eyes to the window, the whole earth seemed white with them. The singing sounded in his ears like the choiring of angels. He was now in a maze. He forgot the notice he had meant to give and went straight into his sermon, stumbling a little as he climbed the steps to the pulpit. He repeated the text and kept straight on. He told the story of the shepherds in the fields watching their flocks when the Angel of the Lord came upon them, and told of the Babe in the manger who was Christ the Lord. He spoke for the shepherds. He pictured the shepherds watching through the night and made a plea for their loneliness and the hardship of their lives. They were very poor and ignorant. But they had to watch the flock and God had chosen them to be His messengers. The wise men would come later, but now it was the shepherds who first knew of the birth of Christ the Lord. He was not reading as was his wont. It was all out of his heart and the eyes of all seemed to be on him—of all in pews and of all that innumerable host about him.

He was not altogether coherent, for he at times appeared

to confuse himself with the shepherds. He spoke as if the message had come to him, and after a while he talked of some experiences he had had in finding a child in a stable. He spoke as though he had really seen it. "And now," he said, "this old shepherd must leave his flock; the message has come for him."

He paused and looked down at his sermon and turned the leaves slowly, at first carefully and then almost aimlessly. A breath of wind blew in and a few leaves slid off the desk and fluttered down to the floor. "I have been in some fear lately," he said, "but God has appeared to make the way plain. A friend has helped me, and I thank him." He looked around and lost himself. "I seem to have to come to the end," he said, smiling simply with a soft, childish expression stealing over and lighting up his wan face. "I had something more I wanted to say, but I can't find it and—I can't remember. I seem too tired to remember it. I am a very old man and you must bear with me, please, while I try." He quietly turned and walked down the steps, holding on to the railing. As he stooped to pick up a loose sheet from the floor he sank to his knees, but he picked it up. "Here it is," he said with a tone of relief. "I remember now. It is that there were shepherds abiding in the fields, keeping watch over their flocks by night, and the light came upon them and the glory of the Lord shone round them and they were sore afraid, and the Angel said unto them:

"*'Fear not, for behold, I bring unto you good tidings of great joy which shall be unto all people; for unto you is born this day in the City of David a Saviour which is Christ the Lord.'*"

They reached him as he sank down and, lifting him, placed him on a cushion taken from a pew. He was babbling softly of a babe in a stable and of the glory of the Lord that shone round about them. "Don't you hear them singing?" he said. "You must sing too; we must all join them." At the suggestion of some one, a woman's clear voice struck up,

"*While shepherds watched their flocks by night*," and they sang it through as well as they could for sobbing. But before the hymn was ended the old shepherd had joined the heavenly choir and gone away up into Heaven.

As they laid him in the chamber on the hill opening to

the sunrise, the look in his face showed that the name of that chamber was Peace.

They talk of him still in his old parish, of the good he did, and of his peaceful death on the day that of all the year signified birth and life. Nothing was even known of the mother and babe. Only there was a rumor that one had been seen leaving the house during the morning and passing out into the white-clad country. And at the little inn in the town there was vague wonder what had become of the woman and her baby who applied for shelter there that night before and was told that there was no place for her there, and that she had better go to the old preacher, as he took in all the tramps.

CHRISTMAS AT THE TRIMBLES'[4]
Ruth McEnery Stuart

PART I

Time: Daylight, the day before Christmas.
Place: Rowton's store, Simpkinsville.

First Monologue, by Mr. Trimble:
"Who-a-a, there, ck, ck, ck! Back, now, Jinny! Hello, Rowton! Here we come, Jinny an' me—six miles in the slush up to the hub, an' Jinny with a unweaned colt at home. Whoa-a-a, there!

"It's good Christmas don't come but once't a year—ain't it, Jinny?

"Well, Rowton, you're what I call a pro-gressive business man, that's what you are. Blest ef he ain't hired a whole row o' little niggers to stand out in front of 'is sto'e an' hold horses—while he takes his customers inside to fleece 'em.

"Come here, Pop-Eyes, you third feller, an' ketch aholt o' Jinny's bridle. I always did like pop-eyed niggers. They look so God-forsaken an' ugly. A feller thet's afflicted with yo' style o' beauty ought to have favors showed him, an' that's why I intend for you to make the first extry to-day. The boy thet holds my horse of a Christmas Eve always earns a dollar. Don't try to open yo' eyes no wider—I mean what I say. How did Rowton manage to git you fellers up so early, I wonder. Give out thet he'd hire the first ten that come, did he? An' gives each feller his dinner an' a hat.

"I was half afeered you wouldn't be open yet, Rowton—but I was determined to git ahead o' the Christmas crowd, an' I started by starlight. I ca'culate to meet 'em all a-goin' back.

"Well, I vow, ef yo' sto'e don't look purty. Wish she could see it. She'd have some idee of New York. But, of co'se, I couldn't fetch her to-day, an' me a-comin' specially

---

[4] From "Moriah's Mourning" by Ruth McEnery Stuart. By permission of Harper & Brothers.

to pick out her Christmus gif'. She's jest like a child. Ef she s'picions befo' hand what she's a-goin' to git, why, she don't want it.

"I notice when I set on these soap-boxes, my pockets is jest about even with yo' cash-drawer, Rowton. Well, that's what we're here for. Fetch out all yo' purties, now, an' lay 'em along on the counter. You know *her*, an' she ain't to be fooled in quality. Reckon I *will* walk around a little an' see what you've got. I ain't got a idee on earth what to buy, from a broach to a barouche. Let's look over some o' yo' silver things, Rowton. Josh Porter showed me a butter-dish you sold him with a silver cow on the led of it, an' I was a-wonderin' ef, maybe, you didn't have another.

"That's it. That's a mighty fine idee, a statue like that is. It sort o' designates a thing. D'rec'ly a person saw the cow, now, he'd s'picion the butter inside the dish. Of co'se, he'd know they wouldn't hardly be hay in it—no, ez you say, 'nor a calf.' No doubt wife'll be a-wantin' one o' these cow-topped ones quick ez she sees Josh's wife's. She'll see the p'int in a minute—of the cow, I mean. But, of co'se, I wouldn't think o' gittin' her the same thing Josh's got for Helen, noways. We're too near neighbors for that. Th' ain't no fun in borryin' duplicates over a stile when company drops in sudden, without a minute's warnin'.

"No, you needn't call my attention to that tiltin' ice-pitcher. I seen it soon ez I approached the case. Didn't you take notice to me a-liftin' my hat? That was what I was a-bowin' to, that pitcher was. No, that's the thing wife hankers after, an' I know it, an' it's the one thing I'll never buy her. Not thet I'd begrudge it to her—but to tell the truth it'd pleg me to have to live with the thing. I wouldn't mind it on Sundays or when they was company in the house, but I like to take off my coat, hot days, an' set around in my shirt-sleeves, an' I doubt ef I'd have the cheek to do it in the face of sech a thing as that.

"Fact is, when I come into a room where one of 'em is, I sort o' look for it to tilt over of its own accord an' bow to me an' ask me to 'be seated.'

"You needn't to laugh. Of co'se, they's a reason for it—but it's so. I'm jest that big of a ninny. Ricollec' Jedge

Robinson, he used to have one of 'em—jest about the size o' this one—two goblets an' a bowl—an' when I'd go up to the house on a errand for pa, time pa was distric' coroner, the jedge's mother-in-law, ol' Mis' Meredy, she'd be settin' in the back room a-sewin'; an' when the black gal would let me in the front door she'd sort o' whisper: 'Invite him to walk into the parlor and be seated.' I'd overhear her say it, an' I'd turn into the parlor, an' first thing I'd see'd be that ice-pitcher. I don't think anybody can *set down* good, noways, when they're ast to 'be seated,' an' when, in addition to that, I'd meet the swingin' ice-pitcher half way to the patent rocker, I didn't have no mo' consciousness where I was a-settin' than nothin'. An' like ez not the rocker'd squawk first strain I put on it. She wasn't no mo'n a sort o' swingin' ice-pitcher herself, ol' Mis' Meredy wasn't—walkin' round the house weekdays dressed in black silk, with a lace cap on her head, an' half insultin' his company thet he'd knowed all his life. I did threaten once-t to tell her, 'No, thank you, ma'am, I don't keer to be seated—but I'll *set down* ef it's agreeable,' but when the time would come I'd turn round an' there'd be the ice-pitcher. An' after that I couldn't be expected to do nothin' but back into the parlor over the Brussels carpet an' chaw my hat-brim. But, of co'se, I was young then.

"Reckon you've heerd the tale they tell on Aleck Turnbull the day he went there in the old lady's time. She had him ast into the cushioned sanctuary—an' Aleck hadn't seen much them days—an' what did he do but gawk around an' plump hisself down into that gilt-backed rocker with a tune-playin' seat in it, an', of co'se, quick ez his weight struck it, it started up a jig tune, an' they say Aleck shot out o' that door like ez ef he'd been fired out of a cannon. An' he never did go back to say what he come after. I doubt ef he ever knew.

"How much did you say for the ice-pitcher, Rowton? Thirty dollars—an' you'll let me have it for—hush, now, don't say that. I don't see how you could stand so close to it an' offer to split dollars. Of co'se I ain't a-buyin' it, but ef I was I wouldn't want no reduction on it, I'd feel like ez ef it would always know it an' have a sort of contemp' for me. They's suitableness in all things. Besides, I never want no reduction on anything I buy for *her*, someways. You can charge me reg'lar prices an' make it up on the Christmas gif' she buys for me—that is, ef she buys it from you. Of co'se it'll be charged. That's a mighty purty coral broach, that grape-bunch one, but she's so pink-complected, I don't know ez she'd become it. I like this fish-scale set, myself, but she might be prejerdyced ag'in' the idee of it. You say she admired that hand-merror, an' this pair o' side-combs—an' she 'lowed she'd git 'em fur my Christmas gif' ef she dared? But, of co'se, she was jokin' about that. Poor little thing, she ain't never got over the way folks run her about that side-saddle she give me last Christmas, though I never did see anything out o' the way in it. She knew thet the greatest pleasure o' my life was in makin' her happy, and she was jest simple-hearted enough to do it—that's all—an' I can truly say thet I ain't never had mo' pleasure out of a Christmas gif' in my life than I've had out o' that side-saddle. She's been so consistent about it—never used it in her life without a-borryin' it of me, an' she does it so cunnin'. Of co'se I don't never loand it to her without a kiss. They ain't a cunnin'er play-actor on earth 'n she is, though she ain't never been to a theatre—an' wouldn't go, bein' too well raised.

"You say this pitcher wasn't there when she was here—no, for ef it had 'a' been, I know she'd 'a' took on over it. Th' ain't never been one for sale in Simpkinsville before. They've been several of 'em brought here by families besides the one old Mis' Meredy presided over—though that was one o' the first. But wife is forever a-pickin' out purty patterns of 'em in catalogues. Ef that one hadn't 'a' give me such a setback in my early youth I'd git her this, jest to please her. Ef I was to buy this one, it an' the plush album would set each other off lovely. She's a-buyin' *it* on instalments from the same man thet enlarged her photograph to a' ile-painted po'trait, an' it's a dandy! She's got me a-settin' up on the front page, took with my first wife, which it looks to me thet if she'd do that much to please me, why, I might buy almost anything to please her, don't it? Of co'se I don't take no partic'lar pleasure in that photograph—but she seems to think I might, an' no doubt she's put it there to show thet she ain't small-minded. You ricollec' Mary Jane was plain-featured, but Kitty don't seem to mind that ez much ez I do, now thet she's gone an' her good deeds ain't in sight. I never did see no use in throwin' a plain-featured woman's looks up to her *post mortem*.

"This is a mighty purty pitcher, in my judgment, but to tell the truth I've made so much fun o' the few swingin' pitchers thet's been in this town that I'd be ashamed to buy it, even ef I could git over my own obnoxion to it. But of co'se, ez you say, everybody'd know thet I done it jest to please her—an' I don't know thet they's a more worthy object in a married man's life than that.

"I s'pose I'll haf to git it for her. An' I want a bold, outspoke dedication on it, Rowton. I ain't a-goin' about it shamefaced. Here, gimme that pencil. Now, I want this inscription on it, word for word. I've got to stop over at Paul's to git him to regulate my watch, an' I'll tell him to hurry an' mark it for me, soon ez you send it over.

"Well, so long. Happy Christmas to you an' yo' folks.

"Say, Rowton, wrap up that little merror an' them side-combs an' send 'em along, too, please. So long!"

Part II

Time: Same morning.
Place: Store in Washington.

Second Monologue, by Mrs. Trimble:

"Why, howdy, Mis' Blakes—howdy, Mis' Phemie—howdy, all. Good-mornin', Mr. Lawson. I see yo' sto'e is fillin' up early. Great minds run in the same channel, partic'larly on Christmas Eve.

"My old man started off this mornin' befo' day, an' soon ez he got out o'sight down the Simpkinsville road, I struck out for Washin'ton, an' here I am. He thinks I'm home seedin' raisins. He was out by starlight this mornin' with the big wagon, an', of co'se, I know what that means. He's gone for my Christmas gif', an' I'm put to it to know what tremenjus thing he's a-layin' out to fetch me—thet takes a cotton-wagon to haul it. Of co'se I imagine everything, from a guyaskutus down. I always did like to git things too big to go in my stockin'. What you say, Mis' Blakes? Do I hang up my stockin'? Well, I reckon. I hadn't quit when I got married, an' I think that's a poor time to stop, don't you? Partic'larly when you marry a man twice-t yo' age, an' can't convince him thet you're grown, noways. Yes, indeedy, that stockin' goes up to-night—not mine, neither, but one I borry from Aunt Jane Peters. I don't wonder y'all laugh. Aunt Jane's foot is a yard long ef it's a' inch, but I'll find it stuffed to-morrer mornin', even ef the guyaskutus has to be chained to the mantel. An' it'll take me a good hour to empty it, for he always puts a lot o' devilment in it, an' I give him a beatin' over the head every nonsensical thing I find in it. We have a heap o' fun over it, though.

"He don't seem to know I'm grown, an' I know I don't know he's old.

"Listen to me runnin' on, an' you all nearly done yo' shoppin'. Which do you think would be the nicest to give him, Mr. Lawson—this silver card-basket, or that Cupid vase, or——?

"Y'all needn't to wink. I seen you, Mis' Blakes. Ef I was to pick out a half dozen socks for him like them you're a-buyin' for Mr. Blakes, how much fun do you suppose we'd have out of it? Not much. I'd jest ez lief 'twasn't Christmus—an' so would he—though they do say his first wife give him a bolt o' domestic once-t for Christmus, an' made it up into nightshirts an' things for him du'in the year. Think of it. No, I'm a-goin' to git him somethin' thet's got some git-up to it, an'—an' it'll be either—that Cupid vase—or—lordy, Mr. Lawson, don't fetch out that swingin' ice-pitcher. I glimpsed it quick ez I come in the door, an', says I, 'Get thee behind me, Satan,' an' turned my back on it immejiate.

"But of co'se I ca-culated to git you to fetch it out jest for me to look at, after I'd selected his present. Ain't it a beauty? Seems to me they couldn't be a more suitable present for a man—ef he didn't hate 'em so. No, Mis' Blakes, it ain't only thet he don't never drink ice-water. I wouldn't mind a little thing like that.

"You ricollec' ol' Mis' Meredy, she used to preside over one thet they had, an' somehow he taken a distaste to her an' to ice-pitchers along with her, an' he don't never lose a chance to express his disgust. When them new folks was in town last year projec'in' about the railroad, he says to me, 'I hope they won't stay, they'd never suit Simpkinsville on earth. They're the regular swingin' ice-pitcher sort. Git folks like that in town an' it wouldn't be no time befo' they'd start a-chargin' pew rent in our churches.' We was both glad when they give out thet they wasn't a-goin' to build the road. They say railroads is mighty corruptin', an' me, with my sick headaches, an' a' ingine whistle in town, no indeed! Besides, ef it was to come I know I'd be the first one run over. It's bad enough to have bulls in our fields without turnin' steam-ingines loose on us. Jest one look at them cow-ketchers is enough to frustrate a person till he'd stand stock still an' wait to be run over—jest like poor crazy Mary done down here to Cedar Springs.

"They say crazy Mary looked that headlight full in the face, jes' the same ez a bird looks at a snake, till the thing caught her, an' when the long freight train had passed over her she didn't have a single remain, not a one, though I always thought they might've gethered up enough to give her a funeral. When I die I intend to have a funeral, even if I'm drownded at sea. They can stand on the sho'e, an' I'll be jest ez likely to know it ez them thet lay in view lookin' so ca'm. I've done give him my orders, though they ain't much danger o' me dyin' at sea, not ef we stay in Simpkinsville.

"How much are them willer rockers, Mr. Lawson? I declare that one favors my old man ez it sets there, even without him in it. Nine dollars? That's a good deal for a pants-tearin' chair, seems to me, which them willers are, the last one of 'em, an' I'm a mighty poor hand to darn. Jest let me lay my stitches in colors, in the shape of a flower, an' I can darn ez well ez the next one, but I do despise to fill up holes jest to be a-fillin'. Yes, ez you say, them silver-mounted brier-wood pipes is mighty purty, but he smokes so much ez it is, I don't know ez I want to encourage him. Besides, it seems a waste o' money to buy a Christmas gif' thet a person has to lay aside when company comes in, an' a silver-mounted pipe ain't no politer to smoke in the presence o' ladies than a corncob is. An' ez for when we're by ourselves—shucks.

"Ef you don't mind, Mr. Lawson, I'll stroll around through the sto'e an' see what you've got while you wait on some o' them thet know their own minds. I know mine well enough. *What I want is that swingin' ice-pitcher*, an' my judgment tells me thet they ain't a more suitable present in yo' sto'e for a settled man thet has built hisself a residence an' furnished it complete the way *he* has, but of co'se 'twouldn't never do. I always think how I'd enjoy it when the minister called. I wonder what Mr. Lawson thinks o' me back here a-talkin' to myself. I always like to talk about the things I'm buyin'. That's a mighty fine saddle-blanket, indeed it is. He was talkin' about a new saddle-blanket the other day. But that's a thing a person could pick up almost any day, a saddle-blanket is. A' ice-pitcher now——

"Say, Mr. Lawson, lemme look at that tiltin'-pitcher again, please, sir. I jest want to see ef the spout is gold-lined. Yes, so it is—an' little holes down in the throat of it, too. It cert'n'y is well made, it cert'n'y is. I s'pose them holes is to strain out grasshoppers or anything thet might fall into it. That musician thet choked to death at the barbecue down at Pump Springs last summer might 'a' been livin' yet ef they'd had sech ez this to pass water in, instid o' that open pail. *He's* got a mighty keerless way o' drinkin' out open dippers, too. No tellin' what he'll scoop up some day. They'd be great safety for him in a pitcher like this—ef I could only make him see it. It would seem a sort o' awkward thing to pack out to the well every single time, an' he won't drink no water but what he draws fresh. An' I s'pose it would look sort o' silly to put it in here jest to drink it out again.

"Sir? Oh, yes, I saw them saddle-bags hangin' up back there, an' they are fine, mighty fine, ez you say, an' his are purty near wo'e out, but lordy, I don't want to buy a Christmas gif' thet's hung up in the harness room half the time. What's that you say? Won't you all never git done a-runnin' me about that side-saddle? You can't pleg me about that. I got it for his pleasure, ef it was for my use, an', come to think about it, I'd be jest reversin' the thing on the pitcher. It would be for his use an' my pleasure. I wish I could see my way to buy it for him. Both goblets go with it, you say—an' the slop bowl? It cert'n'y is handsome—it cert'n'y is. An' it's expensive—nobody could accuse me o' stintin' 'im. Wonder why they didn't put some polar bears on the goblets, too.

They'd 'a' had to be purty small bears, but they could 'a' been cubs, easy.

"I don't reely believe, Mr. Lawson, indeed I don't, thet I could find a mo' suitable present for him ef I took a month, an' I don't keer what he's a-pickin' out for me this minute, it can't be no handsomer'n this. Th' ain't no use—I'll haf to have it—for 'im. Jest charge it, please, an' now I want it marked. I'll pay cash for the markin', out of my egg money. An' I want his full name. Have it stamped on the iceberg right beside the bear. 'Ephraim N. Trimble.' No, you needn't to spell out the middle name. I should say not. Ef you knew what it was you wouldn't ask me. Why, it's Nebuchadnezzar. It'd use up the whole iceberg. Besides, I couldn't never think o' Nebuchadnezzar there an' not a spear o' grass on the whole lan'scape. You needn't to laugh. I know it's silly, but I always think o' sech ez that. No, jest write it, 'Ephraim N. Trimble, from his wife, Kitty.' Be sure to put in the Kitty, so in after years it'll show which wife give it to him. Of co'se, them thet knew us both would know which one. Mis' Mary Jane wouldn't never have approved of it in the world. Why, she used to rip up her old crocheted tidies an' things an' use 'em over in bastin' thread, so they tell me. She little dremp' who she was a-savin' for, poor thing. She was buyin' this pitcher then, but she didn't know it. But I keep a-runnin' on. Go on with the inscription, Mr. Lawson. What have you got? 'From his wife, Kitty'—what's the matter with 'affectionate wife'? You say affectionate is a purty expensive word? But 'lovin'' 'll do jest ez well, an' it comes cheaper, you say? An' plain 'wife' comes cheapest of all? An' I don't know but what it's mo' suitable, anyhow—at his age. Of co'se, you must put in the date, an' make the 'Kitty' nice an' fancy, please. Lordy, well, the deed's done—an' I reckon he'll threaten to divo'ce me when he sees it—till he reads the inscription. Better put in the 'lovin',' I reckon, an' put it in capitals—they don't cost no more, do they? Well, good-bye, Mr. Lawson, I reckon you'll be glad to see me go. I've outstayed every last one thet was here when I come. Well, good-bye! Have it marked immejiate, please, an' I'll call back in an hour. Good-bye, again!"

Part III

When old man Trimble stood before the fireplace at midnight that night, stuffing little parcels into the deep, borrowed stocking, he chuckled noiselessly, and glanced with affection towards the corner of the room where his young wife lay sleeping. He was a fat old man, and as he stood with shaking sides in his loose, home-made pajamas, he would have done credit to a more conscious impersonation of old Santa himself.

His task finally done, he glanced down at a tall bundle that stood on the floor almost immediately in front of him, moved back with his hands resting on his hips, and thoughtfully surveyed it.

"Well, ef anybody had 'a' told it on me I never would 'a' believed it," he said, under his breath. "The idee o' me, Ephe Trimble, settin' up sech a thing ez that in his house—at my time o' life." Then glancing towards the sleeper, he added, with a chuckle, "an' ef they'd 'a' prophesied it I wouldn't 'a' believed sech ez *thet*, neither—at my time o' life—bless her little curly head."

He sat down on the floor beside the bundle, clipped the twine, and cautiously pushed back the wrappings. Then, rising, he carefully set each piece of the water-set up above the stocking on the mantel. He did not stop to examine it. He was anxious to get it in place without noise.

It made a fine show, even in the dim, unsteady light of a single taper that burned in its tumbler of oil close beside the bed. Indeed, when it arose in all its splendor, he was very much impressed.

"A thing like that ought to have a chandelier to set it off right," he thought—"yas, and she'll have one, too—she'll have anything she wants—thet I can give her."

Sleep came slowly to the old man that night, and even long after his eyes were closed, the silver things seemed arrayed in line upon his mental retina. And when, after a long while, he fell into a troubled slumber, it was only to dream. And in his dream old Judge Robinson's mother-in-law seemed to come and stand before him—black dress, side curls, and all—and when he looked at her for the first time in his life unabashed—she began to bow, over and over again, and to say with each salutation, "Be seated"—"be seated"—

"be seated," getting farther and farther away with each bow until she was a mere speck in the distance—and then the speck became a spot of white, and he saw that the old lady had taken on a spout and a handle, and that she was only an ice-pitcher, tilting, and tilting, and tilting,—while from the yellow spout came a fine metallic voice saying, "Be seated"—"be seated"—again and again. Then there would be a change. Two ladies would appear approaching each other and retreating—turning into two ice-pitchers, tilting to each other, then passing from tilting pitchers to bowing ladies, until sometimes there seemed almost to be a pitcher and a lady in view at the same time. When he began to look for them both at once the dream became tantalizing. Twin ladies and twin pitchers—but never quite clearly a lady and a pitcher. Even while the vision tormented him it held him fast—perhaps because he was tired, having lost his first hours of sleep.

He was still sleeping soundly, spite of the dissolving views of the novel panorama, when above the two voices that kept inviting him to "be seated," there arose, in muffled tones at first, and then with distressing distinctness, a sound of sobbing. It made the old man turn on his pillow even while he slept, for it was the voice of a woman, and he was tender of heart. It seemed in the dream and yet not of it—this awful, suppressed sobbing that disturbed his slumber, but was not quite strong enough to break it. But presently, instead of the muffled sob, there came a cumulative outburst, like that of a too hard-pressed turkey-gobbler forced to the wall. He thought it was the old black gobbler at first, and he even said, "Shoo," as he sprang from his bed. But a repetition of the sound sent him bounding through the open door into the dining-room, dazed and trembling.

Seated beside the dining-table there, with her head buried in her arms, sat his little wife. Before her, ranged in line upon the table, stood the silver water-set—her present to him. He was beside her in a moment—leaning over her, his arms about her shoulders.

"Why, honey," he exclaimed, "what on earth——"

At this she only cried the louder. There was no further need for restraint. The old man scratched his head. He was very much distressed.

"Why, honey," he repeated, "tell its old man all about it. Didn't it like the purty pitcher thet its old husband bought for it? Was it too big—or too little—or too heavy for it to tote all the way out here from that high mantel? Why didn't it wake up its lazy ol' man and make him pack it out here for it?"

It was no use. She was crying louder than ever. He did not know what to do. He began to be cold and he saw that she was shivering. There was no fire in the dining-room. He must do something. "Tell its old man what it would 'a' ruther had," he whispered in her ear, "jest tell him, ef it don't like its pitcher——"

At this she made several efforts to speak, her voice breaking in real turkey-gobbler sobs each time, but finally she managed to wail:

"It ain't m-m-m-mi-i-i-ne!"

"Not yours! Why, honey. What can she mean? Did it think I bought it for anybody else? Ain't yours! Well, I like that. Lemme fetch that lamp over here till you read the writin' on the side of it, an' I'll show you whose it is." He brought the lamp.

"Read that, now. Why, honey! Wh-wh-wh-what in thunder an' lightnin'! They've done gone an' reversed it. The fool's put my name first—'Ephraim N. Trimble. From— his——'

"Why Jerusalem jinger!

"No wonder she thought I was a low-down dog—to buy sech a thing an' mark it in my own name—no wonder—here on Christmus, too. The idee o' Rowton not seein' to it thet it was done right——"

By this time the little woman had somewhat recovered herself. Still, she stammered fearfully.

"R-r-r-owton ain't never s-s-s-saw that pitcher. It come from L-l-l-awson's, d-d-down at Washin'ton, an' I b-brought it for y-y-y-you!"

"Why, honey-darlin'——" A sudden light came into the old man's eyes. He seized the lamp and hurried to the door of the bed-chamber, and looked in. This was enough. Perhaps it was mean—but he could not help it—he set the lamp down on the table, dropped into a chair, and fairly howled with laughter.

Christmas in Modern Story

"No wonder I dremp' ol' Mis' Meredy was twins!" he screamed. "Why, h-h-honey," he was nearly splitting his old sides—"why, honey, I ain't seen a thing but these two swingin' pitchers all night. They've been dancin' before me—them an' what seemed like a pair o' ol' Mis' Meredys, an' between 'em all I ain't slep' a wink."

"N-n-either have I. An' I dremp' about ol' Mis' M-m-m-eredy, too. I dremp' she had come to live with us—an' thet y-y-you an' me had moved into the back o' the house. That's why I got up. I couldn't sleep easy, an' I thought I might ez well git up an' see wh-wh-what you'd brought me. But I didn't no mor'n glance at it. But you can't say you didn't sleep, for you was a-s-s-snorin' when I come out here——"

"An' so was you, honey, when I 'ranged them things on the mantel. Lemme go an' git the other set an' compare 'em. That one I picked out is mighty purty."

"I'll tell you befo' you fetch 'em thet they're exactly alike"—she began to cry again—"even to the p-p-polar bear. I saw that at a glance, an' it makes it s-s-so much more ridic'——"

"Hush, honey. I'm reely ashamed of you—I reely am. Seems to me ef they're jest alike so much the better. What's the matter with havin' a pair of 'em? We might use one for butter-milk."

"Th-that would be perfectly ridiculous. A polar bear'd look like a fool on a buttermilk pitcher. N-n-no, the place for pitchers like them is in halls, on tables, where anybody comin' in can see 'em, an' stop an' git a drink. They couldn't be nothin' tackier'n pourin' buttermilk out of a' ice-pitcher."

"Of co'se, if you say so, we won't—I jest thought maybe—or, I tell you what we might do. I could easy take out a panel o' banisters out of the side po'ch, an' put in a pair o' stair-steps, so ez to make a sort o' side entrance to the house, an' we could set one of 'em in *it*. It would make the pitcher come a little high, of co'se, but it would set off that side o' the house lovely, an' ef you say so——

"Lemme go git 'em all out here together."

As he trudged in presently loaded up with the duplicate set he said, "I wonder ef you know what time it is, wife?"

She glanced over her shoulder at the clock on the wall.

Christmas in Modern Story

"Don't look at that. It's six o'clock last night by that. I forgot to wind her up. No, it's half-past three o'clock—that's all it is." By this time he had placed his water-set beside hers upon the table. "Why, honey," he exclaimed, "where on earth? I don't see a sign of a' inscription on this—an' what is this paper in the spout? Here, you read it, wife, I ain't got my specs."

"Too busy to mark to-day—send back after Christmas—sorry.

"Rowton."

"Why, it—an' here's another paper. What can this be, I wonder?"

"To my darling wife, from her affectionate husband."

The little wife colored as she read it.

"Oh, that ain't nothin' but the motter he was to print on it. But ain't it lucky thet he didn't do it? I'll change it—that's what I'll do—for anything you say. There, now. Don't that fix it?"

She was very still for a moment—very thoughtful. "An' affectionate is a mighty expensive word, too," she said, slowly, glancing over the intended inscription, in her husband's handwriting. "Yes. Your pitcher don't stand for a thing but generosity—an' mine don't mean a thing but selfishness. Yes, take it back, cert'nly, that is ef you'll get me anything I want for it. Will you?"

"Shore. They's a cow-topped butter-dish an' no end o' purty little things out there you might like. An' ef it's goin' back, it better be a-goin'. I can ride out to town an' back befo' breakfast. Come, kiss me, wife."

She threw both arms around her old husband's neck, and kissed him on one cheek and then on the other. Then she kissed his lips. And then, as she went for pen and paper, she said: "Hurry, now, an' hitch up, an' I'll be writin' down what I want in exchange—an' you can put it in yo' pocket."

In a surprisingly short time the old man was on his way—a heaped basket beside him, a tiny bit of writing in his pocket. When he had turned into the road he drew rein for a moment, lit a match, and this is what he read:

My dear Husband,—I want one silver-mounted brier-wood pipe and a smoking set—a nice lava one—and I want a set of them fine overhauls like them that Mis Pope give Mr. Pope that time I said she was too extravagant, and if they's any money left over I want some nice tobacco, the best. I want all the price of the ice-set took up even to them affectionate words they never put on.

Your affectionate and loving wife,

Kitty.

When Ephraim put the little note back in his pocket, he took out his handkerchief and wiped his eyes.

Her good neighbors and friends, even as far as Simpkinsville and Washington, had their little jokes over Mis' Trimble's giving her splendor-despising husband a swinging ice-pitcher, but they never knew of the two early trips of the twin pitcher, nor of the midnight comedy in the Trimble home.

But the old man often recalls it, and as he sits in his front hall smoking his silver-mounted pipe, and shaking its ashes into the lava bowl that stands beside the ice-pitcher at his elbow, he sometimes chuckles to himself.

Noticing his shaking shoulders as he sat thus one day his wife turned from the window, where she stood watering her geraniums, and said:

"What on earth are you a-laughin' at, honey?" (She often calls him "honey" now.)

"How did you know I was a-laughin'?" He looked over his shoulder at her as he spoke.

"Why, I seen yo' shoulders a-shakin'—that's how." And then she added, with a laugh, "An' now I see yo' reflection in the side o' the ice-pitcher, with a zig-zag grin on you a mile long—yo' smile just happened to strike a iceberg."

He chuckled again.

"Is that so? Well, the truth is, I'm just sort o' tickled over things in general, an' I'm a-settin' here gigglin', jest from pure contentment."

THE GIFT OF THE MANGER[5]
Edith Barnard Delano

Christine's frail body bent slightly forward to meet the force of the gale. She kept her face lowered, shielded by her muff; yet now and again she raised it for an instant to glance upward at Norwood, with a bright flash of the eyes and a gleam of teeth. Invariably he met the look and warmed to it as to a flame, smiled back, or shook his head. To speak in the face of such a gale was all but impossible, yet once or twice she bent close enough to call in her sweet, high tones, "I love it! I adore it!"

It was at such times that he shook his head. He was keen enough for adventure, good sport enough to meet it halfway, to make the utmost of it when it came; but this—the snow, the early fall of night, the upward climb over roads tantalizingly but half remembered—this was more than he had counted upon, and, truly, more than he wanted. He was beginning to wonder whether, even for Christine's sake, the journey were a wise one.

They had planned, weeks earlier, to take the noon train as far as River Junction, where his father, with the pair of sturdy grays, was to meet them for the eight-mile drive to the old home farm over the hills. But young doctors cannot always keep their best-laid plans, and Christine had waited in vain at the station while Norwood officiated at an entrance into the world and an exit therefrom—the individuals most concerned in both instances taking their own time. Christine, waiting beside the suit-cases, boxes, and parcels, whose number and variety of shapes unmistakably proclaimed Christmas gifts, had watched the express pull out of the station. Then, with a dull pounding at her temples and a barely controlled choking in her throat, she had gathered up the Christmas impedimenta and gone home. Norwood found her there an hour later, still dressed as for the journey, and sobbing wildly in a heap at the foot of the bed—his Christine,

---

[5] Reprinted from "Harper's Magazine" by special permission of Edith Barnard Delano. All rights reserved by the author.

Christmas in Modern Story

to whose courage during the past ten months his very soul had done homage many a time.

"I cannot bear it! I cannot bear it!" she had sobbed out at last, when the tenderness of his arms had begun to soothe her outburst of grief. "To be with your father and mother, to make Christmas for the poor old darlings, to work and keep busy all day—that was bad enough; but I could have done that——"

"I know, dear, I know," he said, holding her firmly, his professional sense alive to every pulse in the racked body.

"But to stay here, where Teddy was last year—I cannot, I cannot!"

"Christine!" he besought her.

"Oh, Ned, I have seen him watch me tie up every parcel—I have heard him on the stairs—I have caught myself wondering which toys he would wish for this Christmas—and he isn't here! I cannot bear it! I cannot stay here without him! I want my boy, my little boy—my baby! It is Christmas eve—and I want my boy!"

And this was his Christine who, during the ten months since the child had died, had faced the world and her husband with her head held high, with a smile on her lips and courage in the clasp of her hand! Not once before to-day had he heard her cry out in grief or rebellion—his Christine!

"Then we will not stay here," he said. "We will go to the farm whether we have missed the train or not! We will go to the end of the world, or beyond it, if that will help!"

"Ned! What do you mean?" she cried, drawing back from his clasp to look up into his face.

"It is only a matter of sixty miles or so, and it isn't yet two o'clock; we can make it with the big car!"

She sprang to her feet with a choking laugh, her hands on her throat, her eyes shining like stars of hope.

"Hurry!" she cried; and in scarcely half an hour they were on their way, the multitude of the Christmas bundles tumbled, helter-skelter, into the tonneau, she fur-clad and glowing beside him.

The big "sixty" stood up to its task, and the first part of the journey was as nothing. It had been one of those winters when autumn prolongs itself into December, when people begin to talk of a green Christmas, and the youngsters feel almost hopeless about sleds and skates; but to-day, Christmas eve, the children's hopes had revived; a sudden drop in temperature, a leaden sky, an unwonted briskness among the sparrows—it might not be a green Christmas, after all.

That was one of the little things that Christine talked about along the way; and when the first few flakes of snow came wavering down she held out her muff, as if trying to catch them all, and laughed.

"Oh, see, Ned! We'll snowball each other to-morrow!"

But he had replied, "Let's hope that we shall have to postpone the snow-balling until we get to the farm, anyway. By Jove! I had forgotten how steep these roads were!"

"Don't you remember them?" she asked. "Have you forgotten your way?"

He got the teasing note in her tone. "That's all right," he said, "but it has been many years since I came this way; and roadsides have a way of changing, even in Vermont; and with this storm coming along worse every minute, I am not anxious to negotiate them by dark."

"'Fraid cat," she laughed, and then cried: "Oh, see! The snow is coming! It's coming, coming, coming!"

It had come, indeed, on the wings of a quick, wild gust; its particles cut like bits of ice, and presently flew in swirling eddies beside the car and in front of it, and, for all their speed, built itself into little drifts wherever a curve or crevice or corner made a possible lodging-place. It pierced their barrier of windshield and curtains, and heaped itself on their fur wrappings, until swept away again by a new fierce breath of the storm. Then it was that Christine's cheeks flamed, but she bent forward to meet the force of the wind, and now and again turned to call up to Norwood that she loved it.

Night fell almost with the swiftness of a stage curtain, blotting out the distant hills, the pastures, the fields, and scattered houses; blotting out at last even the roadsides, its blackness emphasized by the ever-swirling, steadily descending snow. Once or twice Norwood stopped the car and got out to reconnoiter. Christine felt his uneasiness by means of that sixth sense of wifehood; yet all the while, by another of wifehood's endowments, she rested secure, serene in the feeling that all was well and must continue well with her man at the wheel; while side by side with his own feeling of uneasiness, Norwood was proud of his wife's courageous serenity, unaware in his masculine simplicity that her courage had its fount of being in himself.

Nobly the big car responded to their demand upon it, yet they had gone not more than a few miles beyond the last recognized sign-post when it began to show symptoms of reluctance, of distress. Norwood muttered under his breath, and once more Christine turned a laughing face toward him.

"It's a real adventure," she cried. "I do believe you are lost!"

Norwood's answering laugh held no merriment. "You are not so bad at guessing," he remarked, dryly. "Suppose you try to guess the way!"

Her keen eyes were peering forward through the veil of snow. "Here we come! I think I see a house ahead of us," she said. "We can ask our way of the people who live there."

"They won't know," said Norwood, with a man's pessimism. "Probably foreigners. Half the old places around here are bought up by people who can't speak English and don't know anything when they can."

"Oh, you just don't want to ask questions," said Christine. "Men always hate to! I never can see why!"

The day had held many things for him; now his nerves were beginning to jump. "All right, we'll ask," he said, shortly.

The car, in its inanimate way, seemed glad enough to stop. "I will run in and ask," said Christine, and Norwood was already busy over some of the mysterious attentions men love to bestow upon their engines.

"All right," he said, without raising his head.

But in a moment she was back. "It isn't a house, Ned! It's only a barn!"

Still bent over his engine, he replied: "House probably across the road. They often fix them that way up here."

But in another moment or two she was calling to him, above the voice of the gale: "Ned! Ned! There has been a fire! It must have been quite lately, for the snow melts as it falls on the place where the house was! How horrible to think of those poor people, burned out just before Christmas."

At that he stood up. "Burned out, is it? They may be camping in the barn. We'll see if we can't rout them out."

He went back a step or two and reached over to his horn, sending forth one honking, raucous blast after another. "That ought to fetch them," he said.

There was, indeed, an answering sound from the barn—trampling of hoofs, the suffering call of an unmilked cow. Christine went toward the denser blackness, which was the door.

"Hoo—hoo!" she cried. "Is any one here?"

She held a little pocket flash-light in her hand, and threw its light here and there through the interior darkness. Norwood, still busy with his engine, was not aware when she went within; he was busy with mind and fingers. But all at once he sprang into a fuller activity—the activity of the man who hears the one cry that would recall him from another world; his wife had called to him, had cried aloud a wordless message which held wonder and fear, bewilderment, and—a note of joy?

He ran around the car into the open doorway of the barn. The air of the vast space within was redolent with the scent of stored hay, the warm, sweet breath of beasts, the ghost of past summers, the promised satisfaction of many a mealtime. He could hear the movement of the animals in the stalls; the roof of the barn arched far above in cavelike darkness; in a quick flash of memory there came to him the story of another cave where patient beasts were stabled; and this was Christmas eve....

Far back in the gloom there shone a tiny light. He was curiously breathless. "Christine!" he called, a quick, foolish fear clutching at his heart, "Christine!"

She answered with another wordless call that was partly an exclamation of wonder, partly a crooning. Blundering forward, he could see the dim outline of a form—Christine's form—kneeling in the dimness that was sparsely lighted by the pocket-light which she had dropped on the floor beside her. It was scarcely more than the space of a breath before he was at her side, yet in that space there had arisen another cry—a cry which he, the doctor, had also heard many times before. He felt as though he were living in a dream—but a dream as old as time.

"Ned, it's a baby! Look! Here, alone, in the manger!"

It was, truly, a manger beside which she knelt; and she held gathered closely in her arms a child which was now crying lustily. Norwood spoke, she answered, and together they bent over the little form. It had been warmly wrapped in an old quilt; it was dressed in a queer little dress of brilliant pink, with strange, dark woolen underthings the like of which Christine had never seen before. Its cradle had been warm and safe, for all the gale without, and it had slept there peacefully in the manger until the honking horn and this strange woman had brought it back to a world of very cruel hunger.

Norwood laughed aloud as its little waving, seeking fists closed on one of his fingers. "Good healthy youngster," he said; "three or four months old, I should say." Then he added, "Hey, old man, where are your folks?"

At that Christine held the baby more closely to her breast. "Oh, I suppose it does belong to some one," she said. "But, oh, Ned, I found it! Here in the manger—like the Christ-child! It seemed to me that I found something I had lost, something of my own!"

Norwood felt the danger of this sort of talk, as he mentally termed it, and hastened to interrupt. "Sure you found it!" he said. "That's just what the baby is trying to tell you, among other things. He cries as if he were starved. Can't you keep him quiet? Lord! how he yells!"

But Christine had sprung to her feet with the baby still held closely to her in all its strange wrappings. She was staring into the blackness of the barn. There must have been a new sound, for Norwood also turned quickly.

"Who's there?" he called. He had taken Christine's light from the floor and now flashed it toward the sound.

"All a-right! I mak-a de light," a voice called; and with the careless noisiness of one who feels himself at home, the new-comer stumbled toward a shelf near the door and presently succeeded in lighting a dingy lantern. It revealed him to be, as Norwood had foreseen, a person distinctly un-American; and as they drew nearer his features disclosed themselves, though undoubtedly old, as of that finished adherence to type which is the result, perhaps, of the many-centuries-old Latin ideal of human perfection—the type as distinct and clear-cut as a Neapolitan cameo.

"Well," said Norwood, jocularly, "quite a fire here, I see!"

The Italian raised shoulders and palms in that gesture of his race, alike disclaiming all responsibility and at the same time imploring the blessings of a benign Providence. "Oh, de fire, de fire! He burn all up; he burn up everyt'ing!"

By gesture and broken words he made the story plain. "Dis-a morn' Maria send-a me to River—you know, River. I tak-a de horse; I go. I come back. I see-a de smoke, de smoke away up. I whip-a de horse. I come! *Dio mio!* De smoke! He flame up, up. I whip-a de horse. I come to de hill. I see Maria run out of de house wit' de babee in her arm. She tak-a de babee to de barn and she run-a back. She run-a back to Stefano. Stefano he in bed. He in bed one mont', two mont', t'ree mont'—no can move. I whip-a de horse some more. I jump down. I t'ink I go too for Stefano. *Ma! Dio mio!*" Again the gesture imploring Heaven. "De house, de floor, he go, he come down. Maria, Stefano, all—all come down, all go! *Dio!*"

He had made it graphic enough. They could see the quick tragedy of it, the wild rush of the mother taking her baby to its cradled safety in the manger, her dash back to the bedridden husband, the flames, the quickly charred timbers of the old house, the crashing fall....

Christine could feel the blood rush back to her heart; her forehead, her lips, were as cold as if an icy hand had been laid upon them; she trembled, and strained the baby to herself as if it could still the sympathetic pain at her heart. Norwood, seeing her distress, moved closer, drew her into the curve of his arm; her head bent to his shoulder, and he could feel her silently crying. Before the revelation of the pitiful tragedy they were momentarily speechless; then Norwood began to question the man.

"But the neighbors? Why did no one come to help?"

The sidewise bend of his head, the opening fingers of his gesture, spoke as plainly as the Italian's words. "No neighbor! Far away over de mount'. No can-a see! Far away!"

"He means that the nearest neighbors were too far off to see the fire," Norwood explained. "It's likely enough, in these hills!" Again he asked: "But the barn? Why didn't the barn burn, too?"

"No burn-a de barn; de wind dat-a way—" He made an expressive gesture. "De wind-a blow! De barn no burn."

"That's plain enough," said Norwood. "Well, I am mighty sorry for you, my friend. What can we do to help you? What are you going to do with the baby?"

The old man seemed to become aware for the first time of the child in Christine's arms. "Where you fin'-a heem?" he asked.

"My wife found him, back there in the manger where the poor mother laid him for safety, I suppose. What are you going to do with him?"

"Me not-a do! He not-a my babee!"

"Good Lord, man! He is some relation to you, isn't he? Your grandchild, perhaps?"

"*Ma!* No-o! Maria, Stefano, come from Ascoli! Me"—tapping his breast in a magnificent gesture—"Me *Siciliano!*"

Christine looked up and gave a little eager cry. "You are not related? He isn't your baby, then, and you don't want him?"

"Wait, dear! Make sure, first, before you set your hopes too high." Norwood understood what was passing in her mind, and he added to the old man: "You are not related? What are you doing here, then?"

Again the typical shrug. "Stefano no can work; he much-a seeck! Me come along. Maria, Stefano, dey tell-a me, 'You stay mak-a de mon. Stefano get-a well, you can-a go!' So me stay, two week, t'ree week, maybe!"

Norwood thought quickly in silence for a moment; then he asked the man, "Do you know where Squire Norwood lives?"

The man nodded vigorously: "Big-a house, white house; over dere—two, t'ree mile."

"Can you show us the way?"

"*Si!*"

"Then come on! We will give you a lift and a place to sleep in."

He led his wife and the child, now sleeping, as many centuries before another had led a woman and a sleeping babe; the beauty and wonder and mystery of it was not changed, not lessened because he led them through the snow on a modern dispeller of distance, instead of through burning wastes on a patient beast. She had taken the child from a manger on this Christmas eve; and it seemed a very gift of God.

The distance to Squire Norwood's house was only a matter of a few miles; yet it must have been an hour later when the two old people stood framed in the lamp-lighted door, hurriedly opened in response to the call of the motor's horn.

"What's this? what's this?" his father's hearty voice called out. "Thought ye were coming by train, and mother just broke down and cried when I come back without ye."

Bareheaded, the snow no whiter than his hair, he stepped out toward the dark, big shape of the car, which loomed enormous through the falling snow; then he turned to stare after the shape which moved so swiftly past him and up to the shelter of the old wife's arms. Doubtless there were hurried words, questions, answers; but the fact of the mere existence of the baby seemed to be enough for the two women—one so lately new to grief, the other so nearly beyond it for all time. They stopped, then passed within; the lighted doorway was empty.

"I swan! Where'd ye get that baby?" the old man asked of his son.

Norwood explained; his father was quick with self-reproach that such a tragedy had transpired so near, while he, the friendly "Squire" of the countryside, should have been all unaware of it.

"Summer-time I might have driven home that way; mother and me often stopped to see how Stefano was coming along. But winters we always use the state road. It's longer, but better going. Sho! Mother will feel dreadful bad. She got to be real fond of Mareea, what with the baby coming, and after. Mareea used to tell as how they hadn't any folks, poor young things!"

"Are you sure of that?" asked Norwood, sharply. "Could not Christine—could we have the baby?"

His father's eyes held a sharp question, then became quickly misty. "I *am* sure; but as selectman I can make it sure for ye beyond question."

The men's hands clasped; the squire coughed, and Norwood's doctor-sense was aroused.

"Why, father, you are standing here without your hat! You go right in, and I'll put the car in the barn. I guess we can give this man shelter over Christmas, can't we?"

It was, perhaps, some three hours later, after his mother had worn out all her persuasion in trying to coax them to eat to four times their capacity; and after they had exhausted every detail of talk about the fire and the tragedy; and after they had disposed the beribboned parcels to be opened in the morning; and after Norwood had lifted his mother fairly off the floor in his good-night "bear hug"—it was after all of this that Norwood followed Christine up to the big south room, with its white-hung four-poster, and found her kneeling over the old mahogany cradle which had been his own. The old clock in the hall below struck twelve.

Christine arose, and laid her cheek against her husband's arm. "It is Christmas," she said; and the baby, sleeping, smiled.

GOD REST YOU, MERRY CHRISTIANS[6]
George Madden Martin

It was the night before Christmas. Any Christian must have known it, apart from the calendar, by reason of a driving, haunting sense of things yet undone, and a goaded gathering together of exhausted faculties for a final sprint towards the accomplishing of all before the dawning of The Day.

Because we long have associated certain things with Christmas we have come to believe them integrant. The blended odor of orange peel, lighted tapers, and evergreens rushing upon us as the Church door opens means Christmas, even as much as the murmuring voices of the children within, each pew a variegated flower-bed of faces up-lifted to the light and tinsel of a giant tree.

Aromatic odors, other than frankincense and myrrh, mean Christmas, cedar, spices; and certain flavors, an almond kernel laid against a raisin and crushed between molars to the enravishment of the palate, seem to belong to Christmas; the translucent olive of preserved citron, exuding sugared richness, suggests Christmas, together with the crinkled layers of the myriad-seeded, luscious-hearted fig; blazing brandy means Christmas, and the velvet smoothness of egg, cream and Old Bourbon blended, seems part of Christmas too.

But because the average Christian is an unreasoning creature, and, like the ox, bending his neck to the yoke because the yoke offers, plods the way along unquestioning beneath it, the preceding mad rush means Christmas too, and the feverish dream wherein, for instance, the long strand of embroidery silk forever pulls through, unknotted. And it is expected that the bones should ache at Christmas, and the flesh cry out for weariness, and the brain be fagged to the excluding of more than a blurred impression of The Day when it is come.

In the Rumsey household the celebration of the festival began on Christmas Eve with a family gathering of children

---

[6] By permission of the author and "McClure's Magazine."

and grandchildren. There is a certain wild, last hour, preceding the moment of gracious and joyous bestowal, made up of frenzied haste and exhaustion. It was that hour now.

"Anne Rumsey calls it the tears and tissue-paper stage," was told as evidence of Anne's singular attitude towards the ways of the Christian world about her.

"And I am sure I don't know what I've done to have any one as queer as Anne for my child," Mrs. Rumsey, handsome, imposing, on her knees by the bed tying parcels, was saying to her married daughter, Florrie, come home with her babies for Christmas. "There's no one prides themselves more on the conventional than I do, and I am sure you never did an unconventional thing in your life. But I suppose every family has to have its black sheep, not"—hastily at Florrie's horrified disclaimer—"not that I mean that, of course— Florrie, how you take one up!—nor ugly duckling exactly, either, for Anne is the handsomest of you all—what did I tie in this package, do you know? I'm sure I don't—but that a child of mine should thus deliberately each year stand apart, outside the Christmas spirit, while others—it almost looks as if I had not brought my children up with a proper regard for sacred things."

Down-stairs, in the big, circular hallway, Anne Rumsey, outstretched in a long wicker chair, lay gazing into the fire. It was nice to lie there and watch the flames and listen to the crackle of the logs. Hickory logs seem to belong to Christmas. Anne's grandfather, years ago, in the country, used to bring in hickory logs for Christmas. Anne had provided these for to-night herself. She had gone to a place in the country she knew of, and walked over to a farm and negotiated for them. She had waited a week for some member of her family to find time from shopping to make the jaunt with her, and then had gone alone. It was ideal December weather; the snow crunched under foot, the sky was brilliant, a top-knotted cardinal bird and a jay on a thorn-hedge against the blue looked at her as she passed along the road. It was good to be alive.

Her mother was testy that night at dinner. Her handsome face was flushed to floridness beneath her gray pompadour. "I'm sure I haven't time to know whether the weather is perfect or not, if I half do my duty for my family at Christmas. For Heaven's sake, Anne, don't be so aggressively high-spirited; it gets on my nerves."

And to-night, Christmas Eve, Anne lay looking into the fire. It was nice to know it was snowing outside those drawn curtains, it made one love their warmth and crimson more, and snow seems part of Christmas. That morning she had put holly about, idling over the pleasure of trying it here, there. Now she reveled in the color and cheer about her. She had dressed for the evening with a sort of childlike and smiling gaiety, slowly and pleasurably, because the dress seemed part of the season and the joy, and in the scarlet gown looked some dryad of the holly-tree herself, or some Elizabethan's concept of the Twelfth Night spirit.

The outer door behind her opened to a latch-key and closed.

"Is that you, Daddy?" called Anne. "Come to the blaze and warm."

"I can't," confessed the big-headed, square little man, struggling out of his overcoat; "I'm a disheveled wreck and I've got to dress for dinner, I suppose. What time do you look for 'em all around? God bless my soul, Anne, it's good to see somebody composed and enjoying themselves. I've been looking for something for the grandchildren."

"You said you were too busy, didn't really have time——"

"Yes, yes, I did, I know I did, but——"

"—at the eleventh hour you rushed out; what did you buy, Daddy?"

"Just a trifle, a trifle around," confessed John Rumsey hastily, moving towards the stairway; "just a trifle—been putting greenery around, Anne? It looks nice—but I'm worried by a sort of after-recollection. Didn't I give Florrie's boy a silver cup before, some time or other?"

Anne laughed; a teasing, yet a provoking laugh, too, it was. "Sort of mile-stones on the road to Dover, little John's mugs will be, won't they, father? This will make the——"

John Rumsey, with a plunge up the steps, sent back a sort of frenzied snort.

"Change your shoes," called Anne after him; "it's slushy

down street, I know. I laid your clothes out; the buttons are in."

"Thank the Lord!" John Rumsey's voice came back. "I've been fighting my way through mobs, I'm exhausted."

The dear, blessed, grizzle-headed little Daddy! It was he who, after the long pull, had made hickory fires and crimson hangings and silver mugs possible. The girl's eyes softened to almost maternal tenderness. The dear, square-set, grizzled little Daddy!

Anne stretched her strong, young length in the chair and consciously luxuriated in the warmth, the richness, the beauty around her.

"It is like a hymn, the colors," she was thinking.

Again a door opened, somewhere above this time, and protesting childish voices came down the stairway, the voices of sister Florrie's babies come for Christmas. Anne's eyes deepened as she listened, laughingly, yet broodingly.

It was sister Florrie answering:

"Now go on down to Norah, John Rumsey, and take your little sister. Go on! I'll lose my mind if you say another word about Santy Claus; go on, I've got all that bed full of things to tie up yet——"

"But you said—" expostulated a small voice, the voice of little John Rumsey.

"I don't care what I said—" a door closed violently.

A wail arose on the silence, the injured cry of Mary Wingate, the baby.

"Shut up, can't you," the fraternal tones of small John were heard requesting, "and come on." Feet pattered along the hall as towards a rear stairway. "But she said afore we came to Grandpa's, she did," the voice of little John was reiterating as it grew fainter, "when she got time she'd tell me what Santy Claus looked like when she was little, afore his whiskers got white."

Anne down-stairs laughed through merry yet fierce eyes. Babies belong to Christmas. Yet they could not come down here to her because of the decorations and the preparations which Florrie would not permit them to see beforehand.

Anne waxed hot in her soul, for babies belong to Christmas, or, rather, Christmas belongs to babies, and she loved babies. They are so honest, so unconquered, they look at the adult and its inconsistencies so uncompromisingly. So do boys, and she loved boys too. Babies and boys are the honestest things in life. Had Anne but known it, there was much of baby and of boy in her own nature; she attacked nobody's convictions, only stood to her own. It gives one large liberty if one will be honest to self.

The footsteps of the babies, sent to some nether world, died away.

"Yet Christmas is meant for babies, or, rather, Christmas means A Baby."

The girl rose. There were rooms opening around the hallway. It was at times such as this, with married sisters and brothers arriving with their families and laughter and jollity, that one loved it so, the space, and the beauty, and the means. At times such as Christmas one paused and thought about it all. The dear Daddy who had given it to them!

Anne crossed to one of the arched spaces and, pulling a curtain aside, went in. She left the hangings apart. The tree, glittering with scarlet and gold, and hung with delightful woolly lambs and Noah's Arks and such like toys, would show joyously through the opening. And why not? Since it was her tree, for the tree had come to be her part and she had pottered around the whole happy, uninterrupted morning adorning it, since it was her tree it should stand unconcealed from first to last for its purpose—beauty, revel, festivity.

On salvers upon a table near the tree were bowls of glass and silver heaped with dates, figs, tamarinds, sweet pastes, nougats—luscious things that seemed to bring close, far-away Orient climes.

There seemed, too, in the colors and the appointments of the room, an Oriental sumptuousness pervading. Anne loved it, and laving in it, lent herself to it and stood with half-closed lids and parted lips, hands straight at sides, letting fancy be ravished, until she seemed to see——

Against an indigo sky wherein a star burned clear, three swift-footed, shadowy creatures swinging across sandy wastes, each uncouth back bearing in silhouette against the blue, a turbaned rider, eyes shielded by hand, gazing ahead—
—

Her eyes opened. It was lavish, the richness about her. There came a distaste. It was a simple and pastoral life those Orient Jewish people led. She had been there, she and Daddy, one delightful runaway journey together. Afterward her father had marked passages in a book and brought it to her, wherein it was put as neither he nor she could put it.

Now she walked to a bookcase, and taking out a slim volume, hunted passages, and finding them, read blissfully:

A total indifference to ... the vain appanage of the comfortable which our drearier countries make necessary to us, was the consequence of the sweet and simple life lived in Galilee.... The countries which awaken few desires are the countries of idealism and poesy. The accessories of life are there insignificant compared with the pleasure of living.... The embellishment of the house is superfluous, for it is frequented as little as possible.... This contempt, when it is not caused by idleness, contributes greatly to the elevation of the soul.

Anne, hunting passages, drew a long breath. She could love it too, the simple life of certain poverties.

We see the streets where Jesus played when a child in the stony paths or little crossways which separate the dwellings. The house of Joseph doubtless much resembled those poor shops lighted by the door, serving at once for shop, kitchen, and bedroom, having for furniture a mat, some cushions on the ground, one or two clay pots, and a painted chest.

Where the little Jesus played! The eyes of Anne, lifting from the page, sought a niche where, in a golden frame, hung a picture, royal in indigo, purple and scarlet. It was a copy, but it was an honest one. The Baby's head seemed verily to rest, to press, into the curve of Mary's arm. The little head! And the brooding, jealous ecstasy in Mary's face, and the little hand Mary was playfully uplifting! Was she dreaming great, beautiful dreams for the little son's life to come? Does every woman dream mighty deeds for her man-child's doing? And this Baby's hand, uplifted there by Mary's finger, the hand of the little Galilean peasant whose carpenter-father's house boasted a few mats, one or two clay pots, and a painted chest: this little hand was to lift the human ideal out of materialism and set it above earthly things, and behold!

Christmas in Modern Story

nineteen hundred years are gone, and still that ideal shines high, clear, a star against the dome of Time, and wise men, following its leading, still are journeying, eyes shielded by hand, as they gaze ahead——

Mary's little son, the peasant baby!

There was an opened piano in the room. Anne crossed to it. On her lips was a smile, an exultant, a jealous smile. She could feel the little head pressing into the curve of Mary's arm.

Her fingers sought the keys. The notes were rich and deep and full; they filled the room and poured out into the hallway and rose——

Above stairs, from his own doorway, John Rumsey, struggling with the last details of a toilet, stood looking into his wife's room. He was a big-headed, even a belligerent little man, but he stood as though hesitating once, twice, before speaking what was on his mind to say.

"Mary," he had begun.

Mrs. Rumsey scarcely turned from the mêlée of jeweler's boxes, ribbons, packages, surrounding her. "I can't listen now; I've forgotten whom I could have meant this for——"

"But, Mary——"

"Heavens, John, don't distract me; I have to dress yet———"

"Call Anne to help you."

"Not at all," with some asperity; "if Anne can so separate herself from the Christmas spirit as to abjure the preparing of any gifts herself, she'll not be called on——"

"Mamma"—it was Florrie speaking from her room across the hall—"did you ever order the flowers for the dinner table?" appearing as she ended.

Mrs. Rumsey arose the picture of imposing and tragic despair. A small figure turned from between the curtains, where he was drawing figures on the moisture gathering on the pane. It was little John Rumsey.

"Aunt Anne went out and got them," he said. "They are roses, they're red."

Now there were certain things destined to swell the portion of little John, as yet unwrapped.

"How did that child get in here?" demanded John's grandmamma testily, even sharply; "now go on out. Didn't your mother send you to Norah?"

"She put us out the kitchen, she's helping 'em down there. She said we weren't to see till everything was done."

"Florrie," besought Mrs. Rumsey, "please take him out. Gracious, child!" as the light fell upon the slender person of Florrie, "how ghastly tired you look! I told you that you were overdoing. There, there, don't go to crying. Pour her some aromatic ammonia, Papa, it won't hurt her; I've taken two doses myself since I got home. Sometimes I think it is a mistake to have them all here for Christmas Eve. Next year we'll send the presents around and get the business over with and Christmas Day have them here in peace and quiet."

"Mary," the voice of Mr. Rumsey was insistent, "Donald Page is in town; got in this afternoon. I asked him to dinner to-night."

There was silence. Some silences are ominous. Then from Florrie, looking from father to mother, timidly, perhaps, for Florrie loved peace:

"Does Anne know?"

"She wrote him. She brought her answer to me for sanction."

"And you?" it was his wife asking.

"I sent it. She has waited a long time on you, Mary."

Mrs. Rumsey had risen again, her lapful of ribbons and papers strewing the floor. "You sent it, and you asked him to dinner, Donald Page, absolutely come up out of the ranks——"

"I am out of the ranks," said her husband.

"——and self-made, that is, if he ever is made at all."

"I am self-made," said John Rumsey.

Mary Rumsey, imposing in her maturity, handsome, surveyed him. She was a Wingate and they are an arrogant blood.

"I am self-made," repeated John Rumsey, looking at her steadily.

"I have never forgotten it," said Mary, his wife, her eyes measuring him.

The little boy at the window was gazing at these older

people. His eyes were big.

"Oh," Florrie was saying, "Mamma."

They were looking at each other, the man and the woman, long married. Her eyes were hard, and his were sorrowful.

A few chords from the piano reached them. It was Anne; they knew her touch, and it was Anne's voice now arising, sweet, strong, trembling with the passion of it.

For it was Christmas Eve. Else why this room strewn with holly and gifts and scarlet ribbons, else why this spiciness of cedar pervading the house, else why Anne's noël arising?

The words came up to them, words that had belonged to Christmas at the small, old-fashioned church where the Rumseys once had been wont to go.

The little boy slipped out into the hall. They heard him pattering down to Anne.

Mary Rumsey, with a gesture of contrition like any girl's, went to her husband, and the next moment was crying on the little man's shoulder and his hand was patting her soothingly, gently.

For it was Christmas Eve, eve of the night when Christ was born, and Anne was singing of it:

"For yonder breaks a new and glorious morn,
Fall on your knees! O hear the angel voices!
O night divine, O night when Christ was born,
O night, O night divine!"

And down-stairs Anne, turning from the piano to the little nephew standing there, drew him to her with a kind of rapture, for children belong to Christmas, children and simple joys and memories and loves.

And then, a servant opening the door, Donald Page came in out of the night, big, steadfast-looking Donald, with something somewhere of the grimness of the fight in his eyes, and Anne went from the room out to the hall to meet him.

It was very big and simple, the gesture of her hands, as with one who gives all.

And then little John Rumsey gasped, for his Aunty Anne was lifting her face even as baby sister might, to a tall and strange man to be kissed.

Gifts had been given and the evening was almost over. Anne Rumsey's sister-in-law was speaking, under cover of voices and merriment and confusion, to Anne's sister:

"It saves Anne trouble, of course, but to put one's self outside it all, and give nothing at Christmas, I don't see how Anne can."

TO SPRINGVALE FOR CHRISTMAS[7]
Her children rise up and call her blessed.

Zona Gale

When President Arthur Tilton of Briarcliff College, who usually used a two-cent stamp, said "Get me Chicago, please," his secretary was impressed, looked for vast educational problems to be in the making, and heard instead:

"Ed? Well, Ed, you and Rick and Grace and I are going out to Springvale for Christmas.... Yes, well, I've got a family too, you recall. But mother was seventy last Fall and—Do you realize that it's eleven years since we've all spent Christmas with her? Grace has been every year. She's going this year. And so are we! And take her the best Christmas she ever had, too. Ed, mother was *seventy* last Fall——"

At dinner, he asked his wife what would be a suitable gift, a very special gift, for a woman of seventy. And she said: "Oh, your mother. Well, dear, I should think the material for a good wool dress would be right. I'll select it for you, if you like—" He said that he would see, and he did not reopen the subject.

In town on December twenty-fourth he timed his arrival to allow him an hour in a shop. There he bought a silver-gray silk of a fineness and a lightness which pleased him and at a price which made him comfortably guilty. And at the shop, Ed, who was Edward McKillop Tilton, head of a law firm, picked him up.

"Where's your present?" Arthur demanded.

Edward drew a case from his pocket and showed him a tiny gold wrist-watch of decent manufacture and explained: "I expect you'll think I'm a fool, but you know that mother has told time for fifty years by the kitchen clock, or else the shield of the black-marble parlor angel who never goes—you get the idea?—and so I bought her this."

At the station was Grace, and the boy who bore her bag bore also a parcel of great dimensions.

---

[7] By permission of the author and the "Delineator."

Christmas in Modern Story

"Mother already has a feather bed," Arthur reminded her.

"They won't let you take an automobile into the coach," Edward warned her.

"It's a rug for the parlor," Grace told them. "You know it *is* a parlor—one of the few left in the Mississippi valley. And mother has had that ingrain down since before we left home——"

Grace's eyes were misted. Why would women always do that? This was no occasion for sentiment. This was a merry Christmas.

"Very nice. And Ricky'd better look sharp," said Edward dryly.

Ricky never did look sharp. About trains he was conspicuously ignorant. He had no occupation. Some said that he "wrote," but no one had ever seen anything that he had written. He lived in town—no one knew how—never accepted a cent from his brothers and was beloved of every one, most of all of his mother.

"Ricky won't bring anything, of course," they said.

But when the train had pulled out without him, observably, a porter came staggering through the cars carrying two great suitcases and following a perturbed man of forty-something who said, "Oh, here you are!" as if it were they who were missing, and squeezed himself and his suitcases among brothers and sister and rug. "I had only a minute to spare," he said regretfully. "If I'd had two, I could have snatched some flowers. I flung 'em my card and told 'em to send 'em."

"Why are you taking so many lugs?" they wanted to know.

Ricky focused on the suitcases. "Just necessities," he said. "Just the presents. I didn't have room to get in anything else."

"Presents! What?"

"Well," said Ricky, "I'm taking books. I know mother doesn't care much for books, but the bookstore's the only place I can get trusted."

They turned over his books: Fiction, travel, biography, a new illustrated edition of the Bible—they were willing to admire his selection. And Grace said confusedly but appreciatively: "You know, the parlor bookcase has never had a thing in it excepting a green curtain *over* it!"

And they were all borne forward, well pleased.

Springvale has eight hundred inhabitants. As they drove through the principal street at six o'clock on that evening of December twenty-fourth, all that they expected to see abroad was the pop-corn wagon and a cat or two. Instead they counted seven automobiles and estimated thirty souls, and no one paid the slightest attention to them as strangers. Springvale was becoming metropolitan. There was a new church on one corner and a store-building bore the sign "Public Library." Even the little hotel had a rubber-plant in the window and a strip of cretonne overhead.

The three men believed themselves to be a surprise. But, mindful of the panic to be occasioned by four appetites precipitated into a Springvale ménage, Grace had told. Therefore the parlor was lighted and heated, there was in the air of the passage an odor of brown gravy which, no butler's pantry ever having inhibited, seemed a permanent savory. By the happiest chance, Mrs. Tilton had not heard their arrival nor—the parlor angel being in her customary eclipse and the kitchen grandfather's clock wrong—had she begun to look for them. They slipped in, they followed Grace down the hall, they entered upon her in her gray gingham apron worn over her best blue serge, and they saw her first in profile, frosting a lemon pie. With some assistance from her, they all took her in their arms at once.

"Aren't you surprised?" cried Edward in amazement.

"I haven't got over being surprised," she said placidly, "since I first heard you were coming!"

She gazed at them tenderly, with flour on her chin, and then she said: "There's something you won't like. We're going to have the Christmas dinner to-night."

Their clamor that they would entirely like that did not change her look.

"Our church couldn't pay the minister this Winter," she said, "on account of the new church-building. So the minister and his wife are boarding around with the congregation. To-morrow's their day to come here for a week. It's a hard life and I didn't have the heart to change 'em."

Her family covered their regret as best they could and entered upon her little feast. At the head of her table, with her four "children" about her, and father's armchair left vacant, they perceived that she was not quite the figure they had been thinking her. In this interval they had grown to think of her as a pathetic figure. Not because their father had died, not because she insisted on Springvale as a residence, not because of her eyes. Just pathetic. Mothers of grown children, they might have given themselves the suggestion, were always pathetic. But here was mother, a definite person with poise and with ideas, who might be proud of her offspring, but who, in her heart, never forgot that they *were* her offspring and that she was the parent stock.

"I wouldn't eat two pieces of that pie," she said to President Tilton; "it's pretty rich." And he answered humbly: "Very well, mother." And she took with composure Ricky's light chant:

"Now, you must remember, wherever you are,

That you are the jam, but your mother's the jar."

"Certainly, my children," she said. "And I'm about to tell you when you may have your Christmas presents. Not tonight. Christmas Eve is no proper time for presents. It's stealing a day outright. And you miss the fun of looking forward all night long. The only proper time for the presents is after breakfast on Christmas morning, *after* the dishes are washed. The minister and his wife may get here any time from nine on. That means we've got to get to bed early!"

President Arthur Tilton lay in his bed looking at the muslin curtain on which the street-lamp threw the shadow of a bare elm which he remembered. He thought:

"She's a pioneer spirit. She's the kind who used to go ahead anyway, even if they had missed the emigrant party, and who used to cross the plains alone. She's the backbone of the world. I wish I could megaphone that to the students at Briarcliff who think their mothers 'try to boss' them!"

"Don't leave your windows open too far," he heard from the hall. "The wind's changed."

In the light of a snowy morning the home parlor showed the cluttered commonplace of a room whose furniture and ornaments were not believed to be beautiful and most of them known not to be useful. Yet when—after the dishes were washed—these five came to the leather chair which bore the gifts, the moment was intensely satisfactory. This in spite of the sense of haste with which the parcels were attacked—lest the minister and his wife arrive in their midst.

"That's one reason," Mrs. Tilton said, "why I want to leave part of my Christmas for you until I take you to the train to-night. Do you care?"

"I'll leave a present I know about until then too," said Ricky. "May I?"

"Come on now, though," said President Arthur Tilton. "I want to see mother get her dolls."

It was well that they were not of an age to look for exclamations of delight from mother. To every gift her reaction was one of startled rebuke.

"Grace! How could you? All that money! Oh, it's beautiful! But the old one would have done me all my life.... Why, Edward! You extravagant boy! I never had a watch in my life. You ought not to have gone to all that expense. Arthur Tilton! A silk dress! What a firm piece of goods! I don't know what to say to you—you're all too good to me!"

At Ricky's books she stared and said: "My dear boy, you've been very reckless. Here are more books than I can ever read—now. Why, that's almost more than they've got to start the new library with. And you spent all that money on me!"

It dampened their complacence, but they understood her concealed delight and they forgave her an honest regret at their modest prodigality. For, when they opened her gifts for them, they felt the same reluctance to take the hours and hours of patient knitting for which these stood.

"Hush, and hurry," was her comment, "or the minister'll get us!"

The minister and his wife, however, were late. The second side of the turkey was ready and the mince pie hot when, toward noon, they came to the door—a faint little woman and a thin man with beautiful, exhausted eyes. They were both in some light glow of excitement and disregarded Mrs. Tilton's efforts to take their coats.

"No," said the minister's wife. "No. We do beg your

pardon. But we find we have to go into the country this morning."

"It is absolutely necessary to us that we go into the country," said the minister earnestly. "This morning," he added impressively.

"Into the country! You're going to be here for dinner."

They were firm. They had to go into the country. They shook hands almost tenderly with these four guests. "We just heard about you in the post-office," they said. "Merry Christmas—oh, Merry Christmas! We'll be back about dark."

They left their two shabby suitcases on the hall floor and went away.

"All the clothes they've got between them would hardly fill these up," said Mrs. Tilton mournfully. "Why on earth do you suppose they'd turn their back on a dinner that smells so good and go off into the country at noon on Christmas Day? They wouldn't do that for another invitation. Likely somebody's sick," she ended, her puzzled look denying her tone of finality.

"Well, thank the Lord for the call to the country," said Ricky shamelessly. "It saved our day."

They had their Christmas dinner, they had their afternoon—safe and happy and uninterrupted. Five commonplace-looking folk in a commonplace-looking house, but the eye of love knew that this was not all. In the wide sea of their routine they had found and taken for their own this island day, unforgettable.

"I thought it was going to be a gay day," said Ricky at its close, "but it hasn't. It's been heavenly! Mother, shall we give them the rest of their presents now, you and I?"

"Not yet," she told them. "Ricky, I want to whisper to you."

She looked so guilty that they all laughed at her. Ricky was laughing when he came back from that brief privacy. He was still laughing mysteriously when his mother turned from a telephone call.

"What do you think!" she cried. "That was the woman that brought me my turkey. She knew the minister and his wife were to be with me to-day. She wants to know why they've been eating a lunch in a cutter out that way. Do you suppose——"

They all looked at one another doubtfully, then in abrupt conviction. "They went because they wanted us to have the day to ourselves!"

"Arthur," said Mrs. Tilton with immense determination, "let me whisper to you, too." And from that moment's privacy he also returned smiling, but a bit ruefully.

"Mother ought to be the president of a university," he said.

"Mother ought to be the head of a law firm," said Edward.

"Mother ought to write a book about herself," said Ricky.

"Mother's mother," said Grace, "and that's enough. But you're all so mysterious, except me."

"Grace," said Mrs. Tilton, "you remind me that I want to whisper to you."

Their train left in the late afternoon. Through the white streets they walked to the station, the somber little woman, the buoyant, capable daughter, the three big sons. She drew them to seclusion down by the baggage-room and gave them four envelopes.

"Here's the rest of my Christmas for you," she said. "I'd rather you'd open it on the train. Now, Ricky, what's yours?"

She was firm to their protests. The train was whistling when Ricky owned up that the rest of his Christmas present for mother was a brand-new daughter, to be acquired as soon as his new book was off the press. "We're going to marry on the advance royalty," he said importantly, "and live on—" The rest was lost in the roar of the express.

"Edward!" shouted Mrs. Tilton. "Come here. I want to whisper——"

She was obliged to shout it, whatever it was. But Edward heard, and nodded, and kissed her. There was time for her to slip something in Ricky's pocket and for the other good-bys, and then the train drew out. From the platform they saw her brave, calm face against the background of the little town. A mother of "grown children" pathetic? She seemed to them at that moment the one supremely triumphant figure in life.

They opened their envelopes soberly and sat soberly over the contents. The note, scribbled to Grace, explained:

Mother wanted to divide up now what she had had for them in her will. She would keep one house and live on the rent from the other one, and "here's all the rest." They laughed at her postscript:

"Don't argue. I ought to give the most—I'm the mother."

"And look at her," said Edward solemnly. "As soon as she heard about Ricky, there at the station, she whispered to me that she wanted to send Ricky's sweetheart the watch I'd just given her. Took it off her wrist then and there."

"That must be what she slipped in my pocket," said Ricky.

It was.

"She asked me," he said, "if I minded if she gave those books to the new Springvale public library."

"She asked me," said Grace, "if I cared if she gave the new rug to the new church that can't pay its minister."

President Arthur Tilton shouted with laughter.

"When we heard where the minister and his wife ate their Christmas dinner," he said, "she whispered to ask me whether she might give the silk dress to her when they get back tonight."

All this they knew by the time the train reached the crossing where they could look back on Springvale. On the slope of the hill lay the little cemetery, and Ricky said:

"And she told me that if my flowers got there before dark, she'd take them up to the cemetery for Christmas for father. By night she won't have even a flower left to tell her we've been there."

"Not even the second side of the turkey," said Grace, "and yet I think——"

"So do I," her brothers said.

EMMY JANE'S CHRISTMAS[8]
Julia B. Tenney

Mawnin', Miss Johnson. Is yer out doin' yer Chris'mas shoppin'? You sure is de forehandestest pusson I eber did see. Here 'tis five whole days 'fore Chris'mas, an' you 'most frough gettin' ready.

What 's we goin' ter do? Why, jes as usu'l, an' dat 's good 'nough fer we. You see, we spends Chris'mas day sorter foragin' roun' 'mongst de white folks, an' c'llectin' things tergether, an' ketchin' 'em Chris'mas gif'; den de nex' day we all has *our* Chris'mas.

What? We ain't got it on de right date? What's dat got to do wid de 'joyment ob it, I'd like to know? An', anyhow, no one doan' know fer sure what is de right date nohow, 'ca'se dere ain't no one erlivin' now what was erlive when Chris'mas started in on us, an' if dere was, I wouldn' b'lieve him nohow, 'ca'se he'd be too ole ter trus' his mem'ry. So one day's as good as anudder, an' maybe better. Dis here way suits *me*, an' it saves er lot ob trouble an' hard wuk, not ter speak ob de money.

Dis is de way we wuks it, an' 'scusin' de walkin' roun' an' totin' de load home, it ain't no trouble 't all.

We 'vides de city up into pahts. I teks de av'nues, 'Lindy teks de lengthways streets, li'le Polly Ann an' John Andrew de cross streets, an' Jeemes William—my ole man—de gen'lemen's clubs. We all has our own way ob doin' it, but we all gits de things.

Jeemes William he jes' stan's near de do' ob de club-houses wid his hat in his han', an' as de gen'men goes in, he says ter all ob de sassy-lookin' ones, "Chris'mas gif', Gen'al," an' p'ints ter de army-button what he foun' in de White Lot, an' what he puts in his buttonhole on dese 'casions. Den as de South'rn gen'men goes in, he hol's dat li'le 'Federate flag ober de button an' says, "Chris'mas gif', Massa." An' I've knowed him ter come home wid as much as twelve dollars in his pocket jes f'om his good manners; dey

---

[8] By permission of The Century Co.

is so skase nowerdays, wid all dis passle ob young niggers growin' up roun' here, dat de white folks is willin' ter pay high fer 'em when dey do come 'cross 'em.

'Lindy she puts on dat black alpacky frock of hern an' er white collar an' a starched white ap'on, an' she takes de rich-lookin' houses an' rings de bells an' asks kin she hope out wid de extra wuk jes fur er tas'e ob de Chris'mas-time, an' dat fetches someone 'fore she's made more 'n five or six tries, an' den she jes lays herse'f out ter please de white folks, an' ebery endurin' one ob dem gibs her sumpen 'nudder what they doan' want an' what somebody else done gib *dem*, an' as 'Lindy mos' in gen'al picks out de big famblies, dere ain't no mean showin' f'om her.

Polly Ann an' John Andrew dey sings "I 's er-rovin' li'le darky all de way f'om Alabam'" an' some yudder sech chunes un'er de winders, an' folks t'rows dem pennies an' nickels, an' lots ob 'em gibs 'em cakes an' or'nges an' candy an' de like er dat.

Me? How do I git my share? Now yer 'll laugh! Jeemes William say', "No one would n't thunk er sech er thing 'cep'in' you, Emmy Jane," but I ain't nuss nine li'le white chillun, 'sides thirteen ob my own piccaninnies, countin' de halves an' de dade ones, an' not learn nothin' ter hope me 'long in dis world.

I jes puts on er clean purple caliker frock an' er stiff white ap'on wid er white handkuchief roun' my neck, an' I ties er colored handkuchief ober my h'ad ter make our kind er white folks 'member de days when we all uster be jes like one family, an' laugh an' cry togeder, an' dat 's how come it dat I done foun' out so many ob de quality.

What I do 'sides dress up like ole times? Well, all de endurin' year I saves up all de putty fedders f'om de tu'keys an' chickens an' geese an' sech, an' I gets me er ball ob red cord fer five cents, an' I ties de fedders up in li'le bunches an' puts 'em in er basket.

Chris'mas I teks dat basket on my arm, an' I s'lec's de houses where dey is babies, an' dere is plenty ob 'em on de av'nues, too, 'spite ob Mr. Roosterfelt er-sayin' rich chillun is fallin' off in comin' ter our big cities. He oughter hab my job one year an' see fer hisse'f.

Christmas in Modern Story

Well, I rings de bell an' asks kin I gib de baby er Chris'mas gif', an' 'most ebery fambly say "Yes," an' brings de baby out, an' acts pleased-like. Den I hol's out my arms to de li'le chile an' says, "Come ter Mammy, Honey!" an' most in gen'al dey jumps right to me, an' dat settles de mas an' pas.

Den I s'lec's er bunch ob fedders an' gibs dem to de baby. All chillun, white or black, loves to play wid fedders. Reckon it's 'ca'se dey ain't so long lef' dem off in de wing-country what dey come f'om, an' I tell you dat basket is er heap sight heavier on de home trip dan on de goin' out.

Next day we all brings out our pickin's an' we builds er fire in de bes' room, an' *den's* our Chris'mas.

Doan' we *give* no presen's? Co's we does. We s'lec's all de things what we doan' want, same as de white folks does, an' we makes er pile ob 'em, den we makes a lis' ob de names ob de people what we wants ter gib to,—'Lindy she does dat paht, 'ca'se she's had schoolin' an' kin write grand,—den we blin'fol's li'le John Andrew, an' 'Lindy she calls out er name, an' John Andrew grabs er gif'. Dat's how come you ter git er pair of gallusses, an' Daddy Bundy er long gingham ap'on las' year.

I hopes de givin' dis year will turn ter tu'key an' cranberry, jes fer de sake ob ole times down home. I sure does get lonesome fer de ole place roun' 'bout Chris'mas.

DAVID'S STAR OF BETHLEHEM[9]
Christine Whiting Parmenter

Scott Carson reached home in a bad humor. Nancy, slipping a telltale bit of red ribbon into her workbasket, realized this as soon as he came in.

It was the twenty-first of December, and a white Christmas was promised. Snow had been falling for hours, and in most of the houses wreaths were already in the windows. It was what one calls "a Christmasy-feeling day," yet, save for that red ribbon in Nancy's basket, there was no sign in the Carson home of the approaching festival.

Scott said, kissing her absent-mindedly and slumping into a big chair, "This snow is the very limit. If the wind starts blowing there'll be a fierce time with the traffic. My train was twenty minutes late as it is, and—There's the bell. Who can it be at this hour? I want my dinner."

"I'll go to the door," said Nancy hurriedly, as he started up. "Selma's putting dinner on the table now."

Relaxing into his chair Scott heard her open the front door, say something about the storm and, after a moment, wish someone a Merry Christmas.

A Merry Christmas! He wondered that she could say it so calmly. Three years ago on Christmas morning, they had lost their boy—swiftly—terribly—without warning. Meningitis, the doctor said. Only a few hours before the child had seemed a healthy, happy youngster, helping them trim the tree; hoping, with a twinkle in the brown eyes so like his mother's, that Santa Claus would remember the fact that he wanted skis! He had gone happily to bed after Nancy had read them "The Night Before Christmas," a custom of early childhood's days that the eleven-year-old lad still clung to. Later his mother remembered, with a pang, that when she kissed him good night he had said his head felt kind of funny. But she had left him light-heartedly enough and gone down to help Scott fill the stockings. Santa had not forgotten the

---

[9] Reprinted from the "American Magazine" by permission of the author.

skis; but Jimmy never saw them.

Three years—and the memory still hurt so much that the very thought of Christmas was agony to Scott Carson. Jimmy had slipped away just as the carolers stopped innocently beneath his window, their voices rising clear and penetrating on the dawn-sweet air:

"Silent night—holy night...."

Scott arose suddenly. He *must* not live over that time again. "Who was it?" he asked gruffly as Nancy joined him, and understanding the gruffness she answered tactfully, "Only the expressman."

"What'd he bring?"

"Just a—a package."

"One naturally supposes that," replied her husband, with a touch of sarcasm. Then, suspicion gripping him, he burst out, "Look here! If you've been getting a Christmas gift for me, I—I won't have it. I told you I wanted to forget Christmas. I——"

"I know, dear," she broke in hastily. "The package was only from Aunt Mary."

"Didn't you tell her we weren't keeping Christmas?" he demanded irritably.

"Yes, Scott; but—but you know Aunt Mary! Come now, dinner's on and I think it's a good one. You'll feel better after you eat."

But Scott found it unaccountably hard to eat; and later, when Nancy was reading aloud in an effort to soothe him, he could not follow. She had chosen something humorous and diverting; but in the midst of a paragraph he spoke, and she knew that he had not been listening.

"Nancy," he said, "is there any place—any place on God's earth where we can get away from Christmas?"

She looked up, answering with sweet gentleness, "It would be a hard place to find, Scott."

He faced her suddenly: "I feel as if I couldn't stand it—the trees—the carols—the merrymaking, you know. Oh, if I could only sleep this week away! But ... I've been thinking.... Would—would you consider for one moment going up to camp with me for a day or two? I'd gone alone, but——"

"Alone!" she echoed. "Up there in the wilderness at

Christmas time? Do you think I'd let you?"

"But it would be hard for you, dear, cold and uncomfortable. I'm a brute to ask it, and yet——"

Nancy was thinking rapidly. They could not escape Christmas, of course. No change of locality could make them forget the anniversary of the day that Jimmy went away. But she was worried about Scott, and the change of scene might help him over the difficult hours ahead. The camp, situated on the mountain a mile from any neighbors, would at least be isolated. There was plenty of bedding, and a big fireplace. It was worth trying.

She said, cheerfully, "I'll go with you, dear. Perhaps the change will make things easier for both of us."

This was Tuesday, and on Thursday afternoon they stepped off the north-bound train and stood on the platform watching it vanish into the mountains. The day was crisp and cold. "Two above," the station master told them as they went into the box of a station and moved instinctively toward the red-hot "air-tight" which gave forth grateful warmth.

"I sent a telegram yesterday to Clem Hawkins, over on the mountain road," said Scott. "I know you don't deliver a message so far off; but I took a chance. Do you know if he got it?"

"Yep. Clem don't have a 'phone, but the boy come down for some groceries and I sent it up. If I was you, though, I'd stay to the Central House. Seems as if it would be more cheerful—Christmas time."

"I guess we'll be comfortable enough if Hawkins airs out, and lights a fire," replied Scott, his face hardening at this innocent mention of the holiday. "Is there anyone around here who'll take us up? I'll pay well for it, of course."

"Iry Morse'll go; but you'll have to walk from Hawkinses. The road ain't dug out beyond.... There's Iry now. You wait, an' I'll holler to him. Hey, Iry!" he called, going to the door, "Will you carry these folks up to Hawkinses? They'll pay for it."

"Iry," a ruddy-faced young farmer, obligingly appeared, his gray work horse hitched to a one-seated sleigh of ancient and uncomfortable design.

"Have to sit three on a seat," he explained cheerfully;

"but we'll be all the warmer for it. Tuck the buffalo robe 'round the lady's feet, mister, and you and me'll use the horse blanket. Want to stop to the store for provisions?"

"Yes, I brought some canned stuff, but we'll need other things," said Nancy. "I've made a list."

"Well, you got good courage," grinned the station master. "I hope you don't get froze to death up in the woods. Merry Christmas to yer, anyhow!"

"The same to you!" responded Nancy, smiling; and noted with a stab of pain that her husband's sensitive lips were trembling.

Under Ira's cheerful conversation, however, Scott relaxed. They talked of crops, the neighbors, and local politics—safe subjects all; but as they passed the district school, where a half-dozen sleighs or flivvers were parked, the man explained: "Folks decoratin' the school for the doin's to-morrow afternoon. Christmas tree for the kids, and pieces spoke, and singin'. We got a real live school-ma'am this year, believe *me*!"

They had reached the road that wound up the mountain toward the Hawkins farm, and as they plodded on, a sudden wind arose that cut their faces. Snow creaked under the runners, and as the sun sank behind the mountain Nancy shivered, not so much with cold as with a sense of loneliness and isolation. It was Scott's voice that roused her:

"Should we have brought snowshoes? I didn't realize that we couldn't be carried all the way."

"Guess you'll get there all right," said Ira. "Snow's packed hard as a drum-head, and it ain't likely to thaw yet a while. Here you are," as he drew up before the weatherbeaten, unpainted farm house. "You better step inside a minute and warm up."

A shrewish-looking woman was already at the door, opening it but a crack, in order to keep out fresh air and cold.

"I think," said Nancy, with a glance at the deepening shadows, "that we'd better keep right on. I wonder if there's anybody here who'd help carry our bags and provisions."

"There ain't," answered the woman, stepping outside and pulling a faded gray sweater around her shoulders. "Clem's gone to East Conroy with the eggs, and Dave's up to the camp keepin' yer fire goin'. You can take the sled and carry yer stuff on that. There 'tis, by the gate. Dave'll bring it back when he comes. An' tell him to hurry. Like as not, Clem won't get back in time fer milkin'."

"I thought Dave was goin' to help Teacher decorate the school this afternoon," ventured Ira. He was unloading their things as he spoke and roping them to the sled.

"So'd he," responded the woman; "but there wa'n't no one else to light that fire, was they? Guess it won't hurt him none to work for his livin' like other folks. That new school-ma'am, she thinks o' nothin' but——"

"Oh, look here!" said the young man, straightening up, a belligerent light in his blue eyes, "it's Christmas! Can Dave go back with me if I stop and milk for him? They'll be workin' all evenin'—lots o' fun for a kid like him, and——"

"No, he can't!" snapped the woman. "His head's enough turned now with speakin' pieces and singin' silly songs. You better be gettin' on, folks. I can't stand here talkin' till mornin'."

She slammed the door, while Ira glared after her retreating figure, kicked the gate post to relieve his feelings, and then grinned sheepishly.

"Some grouch! Why, she didn't even ask you in to get warm! Well, I wouldn't loiter if I was you. And send that kid right back, or he'll get worse'n a tongue-lashin'. Well, good-by to you, folks. Hope you have a Merry Christmas."

The tramp up the mountain passed almost entirely in silence, for it took their united energy to drag the sled up that steep grade against the wind. Scott drew a breath of relief when they beheld the camp, a spiral of smoke rising from its big stone chimney like a welcome promise of warmth.

"Looks grand, doesn't it? But it'll be dark before that boy gets home. I wonder how old——"

They stopped simultaneously as a clear, sweet voice sounded from within the cabin:

"Silent night ... holy night...."

"My God!"

Scott's face went suddenly dead white. He threw out a hand as if to brush something away, but Nancy caught it in hers pulling it close against her wildly beating heart.

Christmas in Modern Story

"All is calm ... all is bright."

The childish treble came weirdly from within, while Nancy cried, "Scott—dearest, don't let go! It's only the little boy singing the carols he's learned in school. Don't you see? Come! Pull yourself together. We must go in."

Even as she spoke the door swung open, and through blurred vision they beheld the figure of a boy standing on the threshold. He was a slim little boy with an old, oddly wistful face, and big brown eyes under a thatch of yellow hair.

"You the city folks that was comin' up? Here, I'll help carry in yer things."

Before either could protest he was down on his knees in the snow, untying Ira's knots with skillful fingers. He would have lifted the heavy suit case himself, had not Scott, jerked back to the present by the boy's action, interfered.

"I'll carry that in." His voice sounded queer and shaky. "You take the basket. We're late, I'm afraid. You'd better hurry home before it gets too dark. Your mother said——"

"I don't mind the dark," said the boy quietly, as they went within. "I'll coast most o' the way down, anyhow. Guess you heard me singin' when you come along." He smiled, a shy, embarrassed smile as he explained: "It was a good chance to practice the Christmas carols. They won't let me, 'round home. We're goin' to have a show at the school to-morrow. I'm one o' the three kings—you know—'We three kings of Orient are.' I sing the first verse all by myself," he added with childish pride.

There followed a moment's silence. Nancy was fighting a desire to put her arms about the slim boyish figure, while Scott had turned away, unbuckling the straps of his suit case with fumbling hands. Then Nancy said, "I'm afraid we've kept you from helping at the school this afternoon. I'm so sorry."

The boy drew a resigned breath that struck her as strangely unchildlike.

"You needn't to mind, ma'am. Maybe they wouldn't have let me go anyway; and I've got to-morrow to think about. I—I been reading one o' your books. I like to read."

"What book was it? Would you like to take it home with you for a—" She glanced at Scott, still on his knees by the

Christmas in Modern Story

suit case, and finished hurriedly—"a Christmas gift?"

"Gee! Wouldn't I!" His wistful eyes brightened, then clouded. "Is there a place maybe where I could hide it 'round here? They don't like me to read much to home. They" (a hard look crept into his young eyes), "they burned up the book Teacher gave me a while back. It was 'David Copperfield,' and I hadn't got it finished."

There came a crash as Scott, rising suddenly, upset a chair. The child jumped, and then laughed at himself for being startled.

"Look here, sonny," said Scott huskily, "you must be getting home. Can you bring us some milk to-morrow? I'll find a place to hide your book and tell you about it then. Haven't you got a warmer coat than this?"

He lifted a shabby jacket from the settle and held it out while the boy slipped into it.

"Thanks, mister," he said. "It's hard gettin' it on because it's tore inside. They's only one button," he added, as Scott groped for them. "She don't get much time to sew 'em on. I'll bring up the milk to-morrow mornin'. I got to hurry now or I'll get fits! Thanks for the book, ma'am. I'd like it better'n anything. Good night."

Standing at the window Nancy watched him start out in the fast descending dusk. It hurt her to think of that lonely walk; but she thrust the thought aside and turned to Scott, who had lighted a fire on the hearth and seemed absorbed in the dancing flames.

"That's good!" she said cheerfully. "I'll get things started for supper, and then make the bed. I'm weary enough to turn in early. You might bring me the canned stuff in your suit case, Scott. A hot soup ought to taste good to-night."

She took an apron from her bag and moved toward the tiny kitchen. Dave evidently knew how to build a fire. The stove lids were almost red, and the kettle was singing. Nancy went about her preparations deftly, tired though she was from the unaccustomed tramp, while Scott opened a can of soup, toasted some bread, and carried their meal on a tray to the settles before the hearthfire. It was all very cozy and "Christmasy," thought Nancy, with the wind blustering outside and the flames leaping up the chimney. But she was strangely quiet. The thought of that lonely little figure trudging off in the gray dusk persisted, despite her efforts to forget. It was Scott who spoke, saying out of a silence, "I wonder how old he is."

"The—the little boy?"

He nodded, and she answered gently, "He seemed no older than—I mean, he seemed very young to be milking cows and doing chores."

Again Scott nodded, and a moment passed before he said, "The work wouldn't hurt him though, if he were strong enough; but—did you notice, Nancy, he didn't look half fed? He is an intelligent little chap, though, and his voice—Good lord!" he broke off suddenly, "how can a shrew like that bring such a child into the world? To burn his book! Nancy, I can't understand how things are ordered. Here's that poor boy struggling for development in an unhappy atmosphere—and our Jimmy, who had love, and understanding, and—Tell me, why is it?"

She stretched out a tender hand; but the question remained unanswered, and the meal was finished in silence.

Dave did not come with the milk next morning. They waited till nearly noon, and then tramped off in the snow-clad, pine-scented woods. It was a glorious day, with diamonds sparkling on every fir tree, and they came back refreshed, and ravenous for their delayed meal. Scott wiped the dishes, whistling as he worked. It struck his wife that he hadn't whistled like that for months. Later, the last kitchen rites accomplished, she went to the window, where he stood gazing down the trail.

"He won't come now, Scott."

"The kid? It's not three yet, Nancy."

"But the party begins at four. I suppose everyone for miles around will be there. I wish—" She was about to add that she wished they could have gone too, but something in Scott's face stopped the words. She said instead, "Do you think we'd better go for the milk ourselves?"

"What's the use? They'll all be at the shindig, even that sour-faced woman, I suppose. But somehow—I feel worried about the boy. If he isn't here bright and early in the morning I'll go down and see what's happened. Looks as if it were clouding up again, doesn't it? Perhaps we'll get snowed in!"

Big, lazy-looking snowflakes were already beginning to drift down. Scott piled more wood on the fire, and stretched out on the settle for a nap. But Nancy was restless. She found herself standing repeatedly at the window looking at the snow. She was there when at last Scott stirred and wakened. He sat up blinking, and asked, noting the twilight, "How long have I been asleep?"

Nancy laughed, relieved to hear his voice after the long stillness.

"It's after five."

"Good thunder!" He arose, putting an arm across her shoulders. "Poor girl! I haven't been much company on this trip! But I didn't sleep well last night, couldn't get that boy out of my mind. Why, look!" Scott was staring out of the window into the growing dusk. "Here he is now! I thought you said——"

He was already at the door, flinging it wide in welcome as he went out to lift the box of milk jars from the sled. It seemed to Nancy, as the child stepped inside, that he looked subtly different—discouraged, she would have said of an older person; and when he raised his eyes she saw the unmistakable signs of recent tears.

"Oh, David!" she exclaimed, "why aren't you at the party?"

"I didn't go."

The boy seemed curiously to have withdrawn into himself. His answer was like a gentle "none of your business"; but Nancy was not without a knowledge of boy nature. She thought, "He's hurt—dreadfully. He's afraid to talk for fear he'll cry; but he'll feel better to get it off his mind." She said, drawing him toward the cheerful hearthfire, "But why not, Dave?"

He swallowed, pulling himself together with an heroic effort.

"I had ter milk. The folks have gone to Conroy to Gramma Hawkins's! I *like* Gramma Hawkins. She told 'em to be sure an' bring me; but there wasn't no one else ter milk, so ... so...."

It was Scott who came to the rescue as David's voice

Christmas in Modern Story

failed suddenly.

"Are you telling us that your people have gone away, for *Christmas*, leaving you home alone?"

The boy nodded, winking back tears as he managed a pathetic smile.

"Oh, I wouldn't ha' minded so much if—if it hadn't been for the doin's at the school. Miss Mary was countin' on me ter sing, and speak a piece. I don't know who they could ha' got to be that wise man." His face hardened in a way not good to see in a little boy, and he burst out angrily, "Oh, I'd have gone—after they got off! *Darn 'em!* But they hung 'round till almost four, and—and when I went for my good suit they—they'd *hid* it—or carried it away!... And there was a Christmas tree...."

His voice faltered again, while Nancy found herself speechless before what she recognized as a devastating disappointment. She glanced at Scott, and was frightened at the consuming anger in his face; but he came forward calmly, laying a steady hand on the boy's shoulder. He said, and, knowing what the words cost him, Nancy's heart went out to her husband in adoring gratitude, "Buck up, old scout! We'll have a Christmas tree! And we'll have a party too, you and Mother and I—darned if we don't! You can speak your piece and sing your carols for us. And Mother will read us 'The'"—for an appreciable moment Scott's voice faltered, but he went on gamely—"'The Night Before Christmas.' Did you ever hear it? And I know some stunts that'll make your eyes shine. We'll have our party to-morrow, Christmas Day, sonny; but now" (he was stooping for his overshoes as he spoke), "now we'll go after that tree before it gets too dark! Come on, Mother. We want you, too!"

Mother! Scott hadn't called her that since Jimmy left them! Through tear-blinded eyes Nancy groped for her coat in the diminutive closet. Darkness was coming swiftly as they went into the snowy forest, but they found their tree, and stopped to cut fragrant green branches for decoration. Not till the tree stood proudly in its corner did they remember the lack of tinsel trimmings; but Scott brushed this aside as a mere nothing.

"We've got pop corn, and nothing's prettier. Give us a bit

of supper, Nancy, and then I'm going to the village."

"The village! At this hour?"

"You take my sled, mister," cried David, and they saw that his eyes were happy once more, and childlike. "You can coast 'most all the way, like lightning! I'll pop the corn. I'd love to! Gee! it's lucky I milked before I come away!"

The hours that followed passed like magic to Nancy Carson. Veritable wonders were wrought in that small cabin; and oh, it was good to be planning and playing again with a little boy! Not till the child, who had been up since dawn, had dropped asleep on the settle from sheer weariness, did she add the finishing touches to the scene.

"It's like a picture of Christmas," she murmured happily. "The tree, so green and slender with its snowy trimmings—the cone-laden pine at the windows—the bulging stocking at the fireplace, and—and the sleeping boy. I wonder——"

She turned, startled by a step on the creaking snow outside, but it was Scott, of course. He came in quietly, not laden with bundles as she expected, but empty-handed. There was, she thought, a strange excitement in his manner as he glanced 'round the fire-lit room, his eyes resting for a moment on David's peaceful face. Then he saw the well-filled stocking at the mantel, and his eyes came back unswervingly to hers.

"Nancy! Is—is it——?"

She drew nearer, and put her arms about him.

"Yes, dear, it's—Jimmy's—just as we filled it on Christmas Eve three years ago. You see, I couldn't quite bear to leave it behind us when we came away, lying there in his drawer so lonely—at Christmas time. Tell me you don't mind, Scott—won't you? We have our memories, but David—he has so little. That dreadful mother, and——"

Scott cleared his throat; swallowed, and said gently, "He has, I think the loveliest mother in the world!"

"What do you mean?"

He drew her down onto the settle that faced the sleeping boy, and answered, "Listen, Nancy. I went to the school-house. I thought perhaps they'd give me something to trim the tree. The party was over, but the teacher was there with Ira Morse, clearing things away. I told them about David—

why he hadn't shown up; and asked some questions. Nancy—what do you think? That Hawkins woman isn't the child's mother! I *knew* it!

"Nobody around here ever saw her. She died when David was a baby, and his father, half crazed, the natives thought, with grief, brought the child here, and lived like a hermit on the mountain. He died when Dave was about six, and as no one claimed the youngster, and there was no orphan asylum within miles, he was sent to the poor farm, and stayed there until last year, when Clem Hawkins wanted a boy to help do chores, and Dave was the cheapest thing in sight. Guess you wonder where I've been all this time? Well, I've been interviewing the overseer of the poor—destroying red tape by the yard—resorting to bribery and corruption! But—Hello, old man, did I wake you up?"

David, roused suddenly, rubbed his eyes. Then, spying the stocking, he wakened thoroughly, and asked, "Say! Is—is it Christmas?"

Scott laughed, and glanced at his watch.

"It will be, in twelve minutes. Come here, sonny."

He drew the boy onto his knee, and went on quietly: "The stores were closed, David, when I reached the village. I couldn't buy you a Christmas gift, you see. But I thought if we gave you a *real mother*, and—and a father——"

"Oh, Scott!"

It was a cry of rapture from Nancy. She had, of course, suspected the ending to his story, but not until that moment had she let herself really believe it. Then, seeing the child's bewilderment, she explained, "He means, dear, that you're our boy now—for always."

David looked up, his brown eyes big with wonder.

"And I needn't go back to Hawkins's? Not *ever*?"

"Not ever," Scott promised, while his throat tightened at the relief in the boy's voice.

"And I'll have folks, same as the other kids?"

"You've guessed right." The new father spoke lightly in an effort to conceal his feeling. "That is, if you think we'll do!" he added, smiling.

"Oh, you'll——"

Suddenly inarticulate, David turned, throwing his thin

arms around Scott's neck in a strangling, boylike hug. Then, a bit ashamed because such things were new to him, he slipped away, standing with his back to them at the window, trying, they saw with understanding hearts, to visualize this unbelievable thing that had come, a miracle, into his starved life. When after a silence they joined him, the candle on the table flared up for a protesting moment, and then went out. Only starlight and firelight lit the cabin now; and Nancy, peering into the night, said gently, "How beautifully it has cleared! I think I never saw the stars so bright."

"Christmas stars," Scott reminded her and, knowing the memory that brought the roughness to his voice, she caught and clasped his hand.

It was David who spoke next. He was leaning close to the window, his elbows resting on the sill, his face cupped in his two hands. He seemed to have forgotten them as he said dreamily, "It's Christmas.... Silent night ... holy night ... like the song. I wonder—" He looked up trustfully into the faces above him—"I wonder if—if maybe one of them stars isn't the Star of Bethlehem!"

A GOD IN ISRAEL[10]
Norman Duncan

James Falcontent, of Groot & McCarthy, was in the most singular fashion to be imagined struck with ominous amazement. And big James Falcontent had got well past the years of simplicity; he was not easily startled. The Fifth Avenue bus had stopped; Falcontent had glanced up from his musing—a purely commercial calculation, being nothing more romantic than some trick of the trade having to do with the sale of boots and shoes. But what Falcontent had then observed—he was gently yawning at the time—nevertheless astounded him beyond recent experience. Moreover, it led him eventually to far-away places and engrossed him in preposterous emotions. Here, indeed, was the first flutter of the wings of Fate. No; it was not a woman. A splendid, high-stepping, modish creature, of impeccable propriety, of gracious, aristocratic demeanor, might mildly have interested James Falcontent in passing. But since the last departure of Matilda—well, since the death of Falcontent's wife, Falcontent had persuaded himself that women were not at all pertinent to his life in the world. No; it was not a woman. Nothing of the sort! A church had dumfounded Falcontent.

Nobody was going in or out; the bronze doors were closed and doubtless locked fast against untimely intrusion.

"Shut down for the week, by George!" Falcontent commented, in astonishment.

It was a gigantic building occupying a great block of what Falcontent called in his business lingo high-class real estate. And it was truly a magnificent edifice. It occurred all at once to Falcontent that a plant of this spaciousness and exquisite exterior, running full time, as it were, only on Sundays, with occasional week-day operations, situated in a neighborhood in which real-estate values were of such an appalling character that few men could look upon them and live thereafter without horrified envy, must have an enormous patronage to support it. That is to say, a good many people of

---

[10] By permission of Dr. E. H. Duncan and Harper & Brothers.

consequence must still be going to church. And it astonished Falcontent to the very deeps of his knowledge of the world to confront this visible evidence of what he had for a good many years conceived to have become an old-fashioned and generally abandoned habit of piety. Moreover, Falcontent could recall other churches. There were hundreds of them. There were thousands. Good Lord, there must be millions— the country over! And most of them, Falcontent was shocked to remember, were of an extravagant magnitude and elegance, each according to its community.

What the deuce did people still go to church for, anyhow? Nobody that Falcontent was intimate with ever went to church. But there must still be something in it!

Falcontent began to ponder this odd disclosure when the bus got under way. Thus: Well, anyhow, the young women, God bless 'em! went to church to display their dainty little attractions and to assert each her peculiar interpretation of the fashions of the day. Of course! That was plain enough. It always had been that way. It was tenderly feminine, too—a most engaging weakness of the sex. And the young men— amorous young sparks of the town—followed the young women. A very natural and proper thing! It always had been that way. And Falcontent had done it himself—long ago. The delectable business of mating, then, accounted for a good deal. But not for very much. Still, there were the aged. They went to church, of course, for the traditional consolations of religion. Falcontent wondered, flushed with melancholy, whether or not they got what they went for. Probably not. Falcontent did not know. He had heard rumors to the contrary; and these rumors now mightily incensed him. Hang it all, anyhow! There was nothing specific or downright any more. Doubtless the old-fashioned religion, such as Falcontent had known as a boy, was in these days altogether a thing of the past.

"The devil!" Falcontent thought, out of temper with the times; "they might at least have preserved that institution for a while—for one more generation—if for nothing more than mere sentiment's sake."

Deuce take it all!

"Of course the thing had to go to the scrap-heap; but

still—for a few more years——"

Other folk went to church, as Falcontent very well knew; men of largest riches, for example, whose hobby was pious behavior in private life, and who voiced with amusing precision in the Sunday-schools the antique platitudes of piety. Falcontent grinned grimly when this crossed his mind with significance. Groot, of Groot & McCarthy, was a man cut from that cloth. But never mind Groot! The upkeep of these expensive establishments was not by any means to be accounted for by the piety of Falcontent's unctuous boss. What the deuce *did* keep the churches on their feet? Well, there was just one adequate answer; there must still be a vast body of—of—well, of consumers of religion, so to speak—of paying patrons of religious exercises—whom Falcontent had forgotten, and of whose needs and ancient practices he had continued in surprising ignorance. It was these substantial folk who kept the churches in what was obviously a thriving state of health. Churches in the city, churches in the towns—churches the whole country over. Steeples everywhere, by George! Good Lord, there must be a big bunch of people in the country—like that!

They were the real people, too. They were always the real people. No matter what sort of big industry their patronage kept on its feet—*they were the real people*! And every business man knew it.

"These people are not giving something for nothing," Falcontent reflected, somewhat disturbed by this novelty of truth. "They're getting *something* out of it."

That was a business proposition.

"I wonder," Falcontent puzzled, "what the deuce they *do* get out of it—in these days."

Falcontent was himself a robust fellow. He was highly efficient: he was a hustler—of the most up-to-date and scientifically efficient sort. And he conformed: he was sane according to every notion of the times. In shirts, shoes, hose, cravats, hair-cut, occupation, waist-line, language, habits, interest, antipathies, finger-nails, clean-shaven condition, oaths, charities—in everything a man might be disposed to call in question—Falcontent was of the day and proper beyond quibble. He gave no sign even of the subtle beginnings of peculiarity. He was precisely like everybody else in the world: it would have horrified him—grieved and shamed him—to discover any symptom of significant difference. In brief, Falcontent was in vigorous health. Not an alienist of virtuous reputation could have discovered in him the least divergence from the straight line of normality.

Nor could a surgeon with due regard for the ethics of his profession have found in Falcontent any honest occupation for his knife; nor could a devoted practitioner of internal medicine have supplied a need of Falcontent's hearty body.

Falcontent's soul? Falcontent had no soul. Or rather, to be precise, he had a soul, of course. Everybody has a soul. Nobody doubts that any more; it is not in good taste even to discuss the thing. But Falcontent was not abnormally conscious of having a soul. Nobody in Falcontent's world acknowledged the possession of a soul. Falcontent's soul took care of itself; it did not trouble him. And had such a phantom of his childhood lingered to distress him—to cry out for the bread and water of attention,—Falcontent would with caution have concealed its aggravating habits from the normal fellows with whom he was accustomed to mingle upon terms of the most normally jovial good-fellowship. Falcontent—*with a troublesome soul*? You should have heard Falcontent laugh! A big, ruddy, big-hearted chap—that was James Falcontent; a clean, kindly, hopeful, energetic, merry fellow, given to no meanness, to no greed, to no unworthy pride, to no dishonor whatsoever.

Big James Falcontent surely stood in no peril of the machinations of mysticism.

But——

"I don't know," Falcontent brooded, as the bus sped on up Fifth Avenue, "but that little Jimmie had better start in going to Sunday-school."

All very well! But little Jimmie might contract a morbid piety. He might become—an angelic child! Oh, Lord!... Doubtless revival-meetings were still in the fashion. And some vivid gentleman with a bright brass cornet or a tinkling banjo might catch the poor little devil.... Well, how about it? That was all right, wasn't it? Jimmie had to rough it, hadn't he?—as his father had done. Jimmie was going to the public school; he was taking his chances there like a little man—and surviving, too. That kid sure had the stuff in him.... But if Jimmie should turn out a parson?... Falcontent gulped. Parsons, poets, and pianists: they were the same sort of thing in Falcontent's primitive category of the professions.... Well, anyhow, how about *that*? That was *Jimmie's* business, wasn't it? What right had Falcontent to butt in? If Jimmie really wanted to be a parson—or a poet—or even a pianist.... No: Falcontent could not with any degree of pride listen to suave sermons from Jimmie. Nor could he endure to hear Jimmie read poetry of his own composition; nor could he with fond equanimity observe Jimmie's manipulation of the piano—no matter how astonishingly skilful.

Come to think of it, it was little Jimmie's future—and the good prospect of a business partnership with little Jimmie—that kept James Falcontent the decent, kindly, upright fellow that he was. And not an uncommon sort of thing, either! Falcontent looked forward. Hope was his; also faith.

"Anyhow," he determined, "little Jimmie has got to take his chance. I took mine."

Having so determined, Falcontent's muse merged into a grinning reminiscence of New England days—long-ago times of top-boots and mufflers and chapped hands and drowsy sermons. Had Falcontent's next neighbor on the right peered over his spectacles and all at once demanded, "What is the chief end of man?" Falcontent would promptly have replied, "To glorify God and enjoy Him forever!" and would have chuckled the most hearty enjoyment of his own cleverness. And had the dainty old lady opposite inquired, "What is sanctification?" Falcontent would have been impelled to make an awkward attempt to answer the appalling old question—stumbling, of course, over the very words upon which he had always stubbed the toes of his memory. And had the prim and pretty young person to the left smilingly requested a complete statement of the Fifth Commandment, Falcontent would surely have gained her approval by reciting the Fifth Commandment with twinkling precision. Well, well, those days were long past! And since then Falcontent's attention had not been unduly aggravated in the direction of God. Falcontent had been busy making good. Queer, though, how the old doctrines would persist in a man's memory!

Falcontent had made good. He was city salesman for Groot & McCarthy—Boston, New York, and Philadelphia—earning with conspicuous merit and spending with conspicuous generosity ten thousand a year.

"It's Sunday-school for little Jimmie!" he concluded, with a smile, as he jumped off the bus and stepped jauntily to the pavement. "*I* went."

Subsequently Falcontent's attention was frequently aggravated—and with persistent assiduity—in the direction of those religious mysteries whose very existence he had forgotten in the business of getting on in the world. And Falcontent was delighted to discover that he could enlighten Jimmie—with the same enlightenment that he himself had long ago enjoyed. Almighty queer how those old doctrines just *would* continue in a man's memory!...

Some six months after his amazing experience on Fifth Avenue, Falcontent sat, a broken man, in the street arbor of an obscure French hotel in Cairo. He was alone: he was lonely. Jimmie was dead. Good God, how lonely it was without him—without the faith in his future!... And Cairo was an outlandish place. It was the real thing, too: here was no Coney Island plaster and paint. By George, how much like Coney Island the East was! But a man could not here catch the B. R. T. for New York and get there before bedtime. Falcontent was astonished and deeply disgruntled to find himself in a corner of the world so detestably foreign and far away and absurd. It was horribly outlandish. Everything was outlandish: the shuffle of the street, soft, suspicious; and the mutter of the street, not honest, hearty, but guttural, villainously low-pitched, incomprehensible; and the laughter of the street, gurgling with ridicule; and the veiled women in the carriages, and the painted, plumed women who drove with outriders, and the skirted natives, twirling flirtatious little canes or daintily fingering strings of glass beads, and the beggars, and the dark faces, the uniforms of the military, the incredible arrogance of the niggers, the ear-rings, camels, cocked red fezzes.... And the Continental women, going in and out—swishing, chattering, smeared little creatures! And the Continental men; hairy, smirking, gabbing, posturing, stage-clad caricatures—oh, ow! what waists! what mustaches! what hats! Surely one might fairly expect some comfort from the mere caravansary contact with Europeans! But—these!... It was hot weather, too. Whew! Falcontent was in a summer's-day sweat in the open—and here it was night and coming on late in November!... There were none of the shipmates of Falcontent's crossing about. They had begun to avoid Falcontent long before the landing at Alexandria; and Falcontent had taken care to avoid them since the landing. Glimpses of the familiar in the Cairo confusion only annoyed Falcontent the more by creating in his wretched spirit a mirage of that which was altogether familiar—Home.... And Falcontent determined that he must have another beastly brandy-and-soda....

Big Jim Falcontent was a broken man. Dragged from a decent seclusion, stated in clear, straightaway, brief, bald terms, which anybody can understand, Falcontent's trouble was this: he was now fully aware that he had no God. And that was all that was normally the matter with Falcontent. Queer enough, perhaps, but true. No material happening of Falcontent's life could excuse or account for the ghastly collapse of his spirit. Falcontent was an infidel: Falcontent was an atheist. He had so declared himself. It was his best boast. Falcontent had said in his heart, "There is no God." But there are no longer any infidels: the infidels of other times now denounce the social system. Nobody denounces faith. A decent man, being extraordinarily troubled, says to himself: "Oh, well, that's all right! I don't know anything about it, anyhow. I'll just have to take my chances with the rest of the boys." The talkative Falcontent found himself without listeners: he was distasteful to his company. Bartenders would not humor his argument; baseball patrons fled his neighborhood—and his approach instantly dispersed every circle of his club-mates.

"What the devil's the matter with Falcontent?"

"Why can't the fellow keep it to himself?"

"Sorry? Why, sure! But in this little old world a man

must help *himself*. It don't do Jim Falcontent any good to listen——"

"What the devil does he want to blatherskite his damned blasphemy around here for?"

Falcontent's business? Falcontent used to be "some" salesman: he was "some" salesman no longer. And everybody knew it. Groot knew it—and waited with pious patience for the imminent end. Galesworth knew it—remarked it with melancholy: though Galesworth and his wife were waiting with what patience they could command for Falcontent's more remunerative job of selling Groot & McCarthy's shoes in Boston, Philadelphia, and New York. And no wonder sales had fallen off! A buyer of shoes cannot with profitable precision look over a line of samples and at the same time indulge an argument rabidly directed against the existence of God. Nor will he attempt the perilous acrobatics involved. What has the existence of God to do with a line of shoes? Presently Falcontent himself came eye to eye with the catastrophe of his uselessness. "I'm just three months off from a Bowery lodging-house," he reflected, "and but a few weeks longer from the bread-line and the gutter. That's a devilish queer thing—to happen to me!" But he knew why; it was because he had with resentful conviction said in his own heart, "There is no God." And he would go on saying it—that selfsame thing, over and over again.

Being an honest fellow, Falcontent went straightway to Groot for a friendly discussion of a distressful situation.

"Mr. Groot," he began, "I guess I'm all in."

"I guess so," Groot admitted.

Falcontent started. "You think, then, that——"

"I said," Groot drawled, "that I thought so, too. Isn't that clear?"

Mr. Groot was the partner of privately pious inclinations in the shoe-manufacturing firm of Groot & McCarthy.

"If that's so," said Falcontent, "I guess I'm not much use to the firm anymore."

"No," Groot agreed, "Not much."

"I guess I'd better resign?"

"Huh!" Groot grunted.

"All right," sighed Falcontent, despairing. "It might as

well take effect at once."

A dreary silence fell.

"Oh, I don't know," said Groot, looking up from his office-desk. "Maybe it isn't as bad as all that. Hadn't you better try a six-months' vacation with pay?"

Falcontent was listlessly grateful. "Thanks," said he. "You're kind. It wouldn't do me any good, though. I'm all in."

"Can't sell shoes any longer?"

"Devil a shoe! I can't do *anything*. I'm in wrong—everywhere."

Groot gave gloomy assent. "I guess that's just about right," said he.

"You see, Mr. Groot," Falcontent began to explain, a blithering loquacity obviously impending, "the trouble with me is——"

"Don't tell me!" Groot ejaculated, alarmed. "I know what's the trouble with you."

"But you *can't* know, Mr. Groot!" Falcontent's voice was rising in morbid agitation. "I haven't spoken with you—about this."

"No salesman of mine can run himself to hell in this town," Groot declared, thin-lipped, his gray eyes flashing resentfully, "without my knowing pretty much what's the matter with him."

Falcontent flushed. "Well?" he inquired.

"You run over to the Holy Land for a while," said Groot, smiling a little, rubbing his lean hands like a Sunday-school Superintendent. "That'll fix you up. It fixed me." He sighed; his eyes sparkled wistfully. "I wish I could go along with you," he added. "I'd—almighty like to."

Falcontent laughed softly. "Holy Land!" he scoffed.

"You want action, don't you?" Groot demanded, grimly. "Well, a little visit to the Holy Land will make you or break you. Now—you *go*!"

And here, at last, in an obscure French hotel in Cairo, was Falcontent, bound for the Holy Land, to be made or broken, at the expense of Groot & McCarthy. It was amusing; but Falcontent was not amused. It was not possible for

Falcontent in the pass of spiritual exhaustion to which he had come to sustain even a flash of amusement. Falcontent was in a wretched condition; he was thin, weak, untidy, downcast. He was a little the worse of brandy-and-soda, too, of course—nothing to speak of; and he was so very much the worse of Life that his long, vacant face, his lusterless eyes, his listless attitude, all the evidences of spiritual fatigue, communicated melancholy even to those surroundings which had determined to be gay in spite of whatever might happen. Falcontent attracted glances—which were averted, repelled. But presently a spare, brown, alert little man—a muscular little fellow, washed by wind and sun, now clad in the fashion of a Continental dandy, with an inverted mustache, to which he was in the habit of giving a quick, defiant twist, at the same time indulging a swash-buckling scowl—sidled close to Falcontent, as though casually, and sat down beside him, again casually.

Presently the brown little man flashed a keen eye over Falcontent. He glanced off at once; but his clean, brown eyes presently returned, now smiling ingenuously, and he made bold to address the traveler.

"Good evenin', Mr. Falcontent," he ventured, politely.

"Who the devil are you?" Falcontent growled.

"Ver' proper in-qui-ry," the little man warmly agreed. His smile broadened trustfully. "I was born in Jerusalem. Mr. Amos Awad. It is I." The announcement was made with a flourish.

"Well, George," Falcontent drawled—the little man was dark of skin—"will you please tell me how you happened to know my name?"

"You wonder, eh?"

"A con game, George?"

"It is matter business; that is all."

"Business? What business? You don't mean to tell me that you've got an Oriental gold brick up in your room?"

"Gold brick!" the little man laughed. "Oh, dear me, no! Oh, my *dear* sir! Here—it is not America. I have the honor to explain," he continued, seriously. "Privilege granted? Ah! Jus' so! I am dragoman. I am jus' brought my party from Palestine. Ver' fine people. I am paid off an' mos' generously dismiss' with mos' elegant references. Egypt? It is not my ver' bes' tour. I am not ver' well acquaint' with Egyptian antiquities. But I am fully acquaint' with Holy Land an' all things pertainin' thereof. Holy Land! By Jove! What ver' good Holy Land dragoman am I! By any chance you go there, Mr. Falcontent? I hope so. I *do* hope so. I hope so in the ver' bottom of my heart. Ah!"

"Look here, George," Falcontent reproved, "you haven't told me yet how you knew my name."

"Pst!"—scornfully. "It is nothing. The hotel clerk"—contemptuously—"have his little commission for little favor like that."

"Oh, sure. I might have thought of that."

"Ver' simple thing."

"Why didn't you lie about it?"

Dignity galvanized the little man. "It do not compat' with my general behavior truth an' probity," he said, distinctly, "to tell the lie.... An' not one single thing is to be gain'—in the end."

"Oh!" Falcontent blankly ejaculated.

Falcontent's surprise was sufficiently apologetic. "You see the world, Mr. Falcontent?" the dragoman resumed, again mildly. "I do hope so. Oh my dear sir! A tour 'round the world—includin' the Holy Land? No doubt?"

"Well," Falcontent admitted, "I'm resting."

"Ah! Jus' so! I understan'. Overwork—doubtless? A Wall Street panic? Hum! Doubtless so."

"No," Falcontent sighed; "nothing like that."

Wisdom and experience enlightened the little man. He precisely comprehended.

"Oh, my dear sir!" he exclaimed.

"My little boy died," said Falcontent. "It knocked me out.... Have a drink?"

The dragoman lifted a delicate, brown hand. "I am mere child in such matters, as it were," said he. He was much like a boy jocularly invited to partake in something preposterously beyond his years.

"You won't mind," Falcontent began, "if I——"

Again a lift of the brown hand and a polite little bow. "I shall have the ver' great honor," said the dragoman, renewing the politeness of the bow, "to observe consumption of brandy-an'-soda with keen sympathy an' relish."

Falcontent almost laughed. "Where did you learn your English, old man?" he asked interested.

"In New York, sir."

"Oh, shucks!"

"An' the Moody Institute—for some small time."

"You didn't learn that kind of talk anywhere *near* New York!"

"Ah! I understan'. Oh, my, no!" the dragoman protested, quickly. "The polish," he explained, "is acquire' by myself from readin' great works of literature an' mos' modern theology."

Falcontent warmed to the little man. Awad was in health; he had the color and sure power and the limpid peace of the open places. He was companionable—possibly in a mercenary way; but what matter? He would listen. In those days Falcontent found his most engaging form of entertainment in elucidating a seditious philosophy of the universe. And into the waiting ear of the dragoman he now poured the tale of little Jimmie's death. The boy was dead and buried; there had been typhoid fever—and a long fight, through which, it seemed, Falcontent had entreated the Almighty to spare the lad. But the lad was dead; as, according to the unrelenting mysteries, many another man's young son had died before him. Falcontent was alone; he was stricken—ruined. But the death of children? They vanish in multitudes and leave all places vacant and desolate. It is nothing out of the way. Falcontent's was a commonplace sorrow: the world renews the like of it every day. But the brown little man listened, with many a pitying "Tsc, tsc, tsc!" and many a muttered "How ver' sad!" to encourage a complete disclosure. He was alive to more than the tale: he was like a physician—alert, intent, analytical, discovering from Falcontent's mawkish, and hardly coherent recital the deeper springs of Falcontent's pitiable state.

Falcontent was in rebellion. Ha! That was the trouble. But why rebel? A laughable thing—thus to rebel! A preposterous and hurtful perversity! Why not yield—presently? Why not say, "Thy will be done!"—and cultivate some form of faith? It seemed to the brown little dragoman to be a brave and sensible sort of behavior.

"Ver' sad!" he sighed, at the end.

"Sad?" Falcontent snarled.

"The Lord gives," the dragoman quoted, apparently with sincere conviction, "an' the Lord takes away."

Falcontent leaned forward in disreputable anger. "You mean to tell me," he flared, his voice risen, "that the Lord *took* him—deliberately? That the Lord put that poor little fellow through weeks of useless agony—and then killed him?"

"Hush!"

Falcontent would not be quieted. His eyes were flushed with rage; his nostrils flared; his teeth were bared. "You call that Design?" he cried. "Design—hell! That was *Chance*. There *is* no God!"

Ha! Was it so? Awad needed nothing more. It was an old problem. He gripped Falcontent's forearm to restrain him. "Sh-h!" he commanded. "It is too loud for be polite. You have shame yourself. An' me—your dragoman!" Falcontent's resentment failed. He had not the strength to sustain rage: he was able only to continue in sulky rebellion. He was listless now once more; he stared vacantly upon the scornful comment his outburst—though in English—had aroused. "Listen!" the dragoman went on, his voice low, his words clear-cut, his way authoritative. "You go the Holy Land by present intention. I know that much. It is for the cure. Some friend say, 'Go an' be heal'.' I understan'. Many peoples—many, oh many, many peoples—come the Holy Land to be cure of sorrow. Ver' commonplace to happen. But mos' dangerous practice. I have see' cure; I have also see' ruin. Now I am deep student of ver' mos' new an' modern theology. Ver' good. I prescribe. Privilege granted? Listen! We go to Jerusalem. True; but by way of Mount Sinai. By way of Suez, the Monastery of St. Catherine, Akaba, Ell Ma'an, Petra, I make no bones, sir. It is a long desert journey:—ver' harsh journey includin' dangers proceedin' from robbers' habitations. But mos' excellent health is thereby to be gain'. Ver' good. Quite satisfy? I prepare, then, my outfit of men an' animals at once.... Mm-m?"

It was an appealing suggestion. Falcontent was moved to carry his sorrow to an exceeding desolation. And he was sensible, too, of the physical advantage. There was surely bodily cure—the cure of physical folly—to be found on the caravan route.

"That listens all right, George," said he. "But what do you get out of this?"

"Surely," the dragoman replied, with a shrug, "I have honor to arrange contract with reasonable profit devolving upon me ... Expense, as it were, Mr. Falcontent—no object? Mm-m? Doubtless not?"

"Oh, anything reasonable, George," said Falcontent. "But I don't want to be stung."

"Ver' reasonable, Mr. Falcontent. No sting in contract of Mr. Amos Awad. I do so assure you upon honor."

Falcontent came to a quick decision. "All right, George," said he, with spirit. "I'll go. And we'll get to work and arrange the terms of that little contract right now."

Falcontent rode into Jerusalem near the close of day—the day before Christmas. Awad had proved a faithful, companionable fellow; he had been solicitous concerning Falcontent's first pains of travel—he had been grim, business-like, vastly determined in respect to the way and the hours of riding. There had been no discussion of Falcontent's perplexities. There had been entertainment: Awad had told many engaging stories to relieve the monotony of the sand—such Eastern tales as are told, in various forms, names varying, incidents differing somewhat from the Occidental traditions, but the moral unchanged, to while away time and weariness in all the deserts of the East. And Falcontent had indeed matched his sorrow against an exceeding desolation; a land, however, unable to wrench any complaint against Fate from its lean dwellers. Falcontent was himself now lean and brown with weeks of desert travel. His eyes were clean and quick and sure. It had been a short ride that day; he tingled with muscular exaltation. He was toned; it was a physically rehabilitated Falcontent. He was in appetite; he could sleep.... Sell shoes? Well, rather! By Jove—Falcontent would sure show old man Groot that he had "come back!" And he had not yet even seen the Holy Places! It would sure be a laugh on Groot!

Falcontent could laugh—now. But his mirth was hard, a mere reflex, without feeling. It was mirth without sure foundation. There was no spiritual health in it. At the first touch of adversity the laughter might turn to jeering cachinnation. Life was a grim experience: a man was born, lived, died. "To-morrow we die!" Falcontent stood no longer in confusion between Design and Chance. He had settled that question for good and all. And what a fool he had been to trouble about it at all! How shall a man surely know? Falcontent laughed to think of the hurtful folly of his brooding ... God? There was no God. There were many gods: gods of all peoples—a vast variety. There were many superstitions, there was much bowing down.... A flash of agitated uncertainty passed over Falcontent when he reflected that his was the only generation of all the generations of men (as he fancied) by whom the worship of God had been generally abandoned.... But why not? "The old order changeth." The times were new.... "God of our fathers!" How the old teachings persisted in a man's imagination! Falcontent could recall the psalm—and the nasal singing. It aggravated him to remember. He concerned his thoughts with the road.... It was crisp weather; it was much like a harvest evening—at home. Light lingered upon the city. It was a city lying soft and half revealed in a mist of twilight.

"Jerusalem!" Falcontent thought. "Well—I'm damned! Jim Falcontent, of Groot & McCarthy—in Jerusalem!"

Falcontent was subconsciously disappointed to find no glory of heavenly light upon the flat roofs, and no glow of peace and beneficence upon the countenances of the sinister-appearing inhabitants. He had, like a child—it was a legacy of childhood—looked for some continued manifestation of the story of the Divine residence.

"Nice town, Awad?" he inquired.

"Ver' modern city accordin' Eastern standards," the dragoman replied, with a flirt of his dainty mustache. "Ver' human peoples live here. Disappoint', eh?" he ran on. "Jus' so. Ver' much like all tourist' excep' ver' old people. You think to see pearly gates an' golden streets, eh? Ha, ha! Oh, dear me, no! Ver' human city of present day. Ver' up-to-date town. Always was, I take it. Possibly so in time of King Solomon. An' in days of King David—doubtless so? Why not? Mm-m?"

It occurred to Falcontent for the first time with significant conviction that Jerusalem was a reality; that the city had been real from generation to generation—here situated—near by—and that the happenings recorded were realities like the events of profane history—of the American Revolution.

But——

"Garden of Gethsemane still around here?" he yawned.

"Oh, yes. Ver' close by the city. Carriage an' all fees suppli' by terms of my contract."

"Got a fence around it?" Falcontent joked.

"Oh, yes."

"What!" Falcontent exclaimed.

"Not what you call precisely picket fence," the dragoman replied. "Much more substantial. A ver' solid wall."

"Sure they got the right spot fenced in?"

"My habit truth an' probity compel me say I personally ver' much doubt. Right place? What matter? Pst!"

What *did* it matter?

"Haven't moved the Mount of Olives, have they?"

"Oh, my *dear* sir!" Awad laughed. "Impossible job for to perform. An' Palestine antiquities, my dear sir, not for sale for decorate landscape of the American millionaire."

"Calvary?"

"Same ol' place, sir," the dragoman replied, gravely, "but naturally ver' much change'. Ver' well authenticate', too, accordin' by latest authorities. Which thing I am ver' happy to state—with perfect truth, at last."

Falcontent rode on in silence. It was dark in the city. There were no details: there was the mystery of dim-lit habitations—of narrow streets—of shuffling forms.... And this was Jerusalem! There was actually such a place! Falcontent all at once realized the existence of the city as a physical fact. It had a place in history—not wholly in legend. It was of old time. It was real.... The American Revolution and the Civil War were legendary conflicts in Falcontent's

111

consciousness until he had with amazed understanding set foot on the battle-fields and stared about.... And Gethsemane was near by! Precise location? Pst! What matter? There had been a Garden of Gethsemane! The Mount of Olives, too: it was a remarkable hill—now within reach, like Grant's Tomb at home. And Calvary! There had been a place called Calvary!... Falcontent was profoundly moved by his proximity to these places which now at last were real. Falcontent was shocked; his unbelief in the tradition—was it tradition?—of the Divine Presence upon earth was disturbed. A presence in Jerusalem—roundabout: here and beyond.... Falcontent began to whistle a snatch from "The Queen of the Great White Way." It was incongruous; he could not bear to continue.... There had been a Teacher: that was true—it was as true as Grant and Lincoln and Washington—and the teaching was not yet forgotten in the world. Falcontent knew it all well enough—the life and philosophy which somewhere near by these very places had had their origin.... To relieve the agitation of these disclosures Falcontent tried once more the topical song from "The Queen of the Great White Way." It was impossible.

"Cold?" Awad inquired.

"No," Falcontent answered. "I'm not cold. I'm shivering, though. That's funny, isn't it?"

"Well, no," said Awad. "Ver' commonplace thing to happen. I should not have be surprise' if, on the other hand, you have swear ver' harshly."

Falcontent had experienced—and had thereby been horrified—a curious impulse to blaspheme.

"That's queer," he drawled now.

"Ver' commonplace thing," the dragoman repeated. He shrugged. "I recommend, if I be permit," he went on, impassively, "a hot bath, food, an' perusal of Holy Scriptures for historical data. I am great believer in original sources. Let us say, Gospel accordin' St. Luke—chapter two, especially. It is Christmas Eve. To-night—accordin' by itinerary—we visit Bethlehem. Carriage an' all fees my pleasure to provide accordin' by terms of my contract."

When, late that Christmas Eve, the little dragoman

knocked on the door of Falcontent's room in a hotel by the Jaffa Gate, Falcontent had gathered a deal of historical data from the original sources.... *And there were in the same country shepherds abiding in the field, keeping watch on their flocks by night. And, lo, the angel of the Lord came upon them, and the glory of the Lord shone round about them, and they were sore afraid. And the angel said unto them, Fear not, for, behold, I bring you tidings of great joy, which shall be to all people: for unto you is born this day, in the city of David, a Saviour, which is Christ the Lord. And this shall be a sign unto you: Ye shall find the babe wrapped in swaddling clothes, lying in a manger. And suddenly there was with the angel a multitude of the heavenly host, praising God, and saying, Glory to God in the highest, and on earth peace and good-will toward men. And it came to pass that as the angels were going away from them into heaven the shepherds said one to another, Let us now go even unto Bethlehem, and see the thing which has come to pass, which the Lord has made known to us....* And Falcontent had perused the tragedy from that beginning to its heroic end. It was all familiar, to be sure—had continued in Falcontent's memory since those old New England days; but was now new with reality and meaning.

"I'm tired," Falcontent protested to the dragoman. "I guess we'd better put the Bethlehem trip off."

"Ha!" the dragoman ejaculated. "We go," he announced, calmly. "It is my greates' ambition to serve my gentlemen. I fail—never! We go. I am flat in it."

Falcontent was presently rattling over the road to Bethlehem. It was a clear night. There were stars—brilliantly shining. A moon was imminent. A shadowy country—waste like a wilderness in the night—was on either side. The road lay white and dusty. It was an old road—an old, old way of going and coming. It had felt the imprint of dusty feet these many long, forgotten years.... The world was surely very old: that which persisted from generation to generation was of value—new things doubtful.... Falcontent was cold. But the night was warm. Yet Falcontent shivered; his hands trembled—teeth clicked together. He was hardly able to command this nervous spasm.... There came, by and by, dark, winding streets, rough, narrow. The horses stumbled.... There was the Church of the Nativity: it was like a fortification. There was a narrow door—there were wide, cathedral spaces—there was the light of candles—there were ecclesiastical robes—there was incense—there were many voices distantly chanting—there was the wonder of some mystical ceremony by which Falcontent was shaken from his hold on the commonplaces of life.... And Falcontent stared and listened, transported so far from Broadway by the vision and music of these mysteries that Broadway was no longer with his recollection, save as a blurred, contrasting horror.

Thereafter Falcontent stood for a long time midway of a narrow stone stair—gazing awed now into the Grotto of the Nativity. It was a small space. The yellow light of many candles illuminated it.... Many people knelt below in adoration: these were Russian pilgrims—folk of a race cruelly oppressed; yet their countenances gave no sign of oppression, but were clean of guile and fear and suspicion and all manner of trouble. Peace was upon all them that adored: such peace—Falcontent reflected in the terms of other times—as the world can neither give nor take away.... And so it had been: a faith continuing from generation to generation, comforting, inspiring, peace-bringing, giving hope and courage—the integrity of its essentials preserved, after all, against the cocksure philosophies of all these new days.

"Ver' much regret," the dragoman whispered in Falcontent's ear. "Accordin' my Bethlehem itinerary, it is time for visit Field of Shepherds."

Falcontent started.

"Oh, we'll cut that out!" he whispered, hastily. "I guess I better get back to the hotel."

But Falcontent followed a rocky pathway, leading down, leading on, inclining toward the stars, to a hill, near by some ancient ruins, below which a field lay in a mist of moonlight.... Falcontent was cold; but yet it was a warm night. It was not the cold. He was afraid; he trembled—and was afraid.... Awad withdrew. Falcontent stood alone.... It is related of Saul of Tarsus, as Falcontent then singularly recalled, that, being on the road to Damascus, *there shined round about him a light from heaven, and he fell to the earth, and heard a voice, saying unto him, Saul, why persecutest thou me?* And the narrative continues: *And he said, Who art thou, Lord? And the Lord said, I am Jesus, whom thou persecutest. It is hard for thee to kick against the pricks. And he trembling and astonished, said, Lord, what wilt thou have me to do?...* No light from heaven shined round about James Falcontent, of Groot and McCarthy; but yet he trembled and was astonished—in a great illumination of the spirit. It was a simple thing: it concerned only the realities of Falcontent's experience.... *And the angel said unto them, Fear not, for behold, I bring you tidings of great joy, which shall be to all people: for unto you is born this day, in the city of David, a Saviour....* And it was true! Salvation had proceeded from that Birth: all liberty in the world, as Falcontent knew the world and the ages of its spinning—every simple kindness—all pure aspiration—every good deed—all true forms of love and virtue and high courage and justice.... And the God of Falcontent's fathers was the only God Falcontent knew anything about.

There was a peal of bells; the ringing came liquid-sweet through the moonlight from the Church of the Nativity on the hills of Bethlehem.

"Amos!" Falcontent called.

"Sir? I am here."

"What they ringing the bells for?"

"It is Christmas mornin', Sir."

Falcontent stood staring into the mist of moonlight below. "I guess you better leave me alone for a little while, Amos," he said, presently, without turning. "I—want to be alone." After that Falcontent lifted his face to the sky and prayed. It should astonish no one. Many a good man has done the like of it since the world began....

Well, what miracle? What amazing transformation? Falcontent looked fit: that was true. The same old Falcontent! the Falcontent of his heartiest days. Back in New York now, still a bit lean and brown with desert travel. To the eye—to the ear—to the heart of his intimates—he was the same man he had been at his best. He was selling shoes for Groot &

McCarthy, too, in vast quantities, in Boston, Philadelphia, and New York. There were some little omissions of behavior, to be sure, as he went about. They were not obtrusive: they earned—they deserved—no comment. A big, ruddy, big-hearted man—that was James Falcontent: a clean, kindly, hopeful, energetic, merry fellow, given to no meanness, to no greed, to no unworthy pride, to no dishonor whatsoever. And he was sane according to every goodly notion of the times. It would have alarmed him—shamed and grieved him—to discover any symptom of peculiarity. Not an alienist of virtuous reputation could have discovered in Falcontent the least divergence from the straight line of normality. Nor could a surgeon with due regard for the ethics of his profession have found in Falcontent any honest employment for his knife; nor could a devoted practitioner of internal medicine have supplied a need of Falcontent's hearty body. Falcontent was a robust fellow. Falcontent was in vigorous health. What need had Falcontent of a physician or a surgeon?

Falcontent's soul? Oh, yes, Falcontent had a soul—and had in some way established peace with it!

VAN VALKENBERG'S CHRISTMAS GIFT[11]
Elizabeth G. Jordan

The "Chicago Limited" was pulling out of the Grand Central Station in New York as Dr. Henry Van Valkenberg submitted his ticket to the gateman. He dashed through, pushing the indignant official to one side, and made a leap for the railing of the last car of the train. It was wet and slippery and maddeningly elusive, but he caught it, and clung to it valiantly, his legs actively seeking a resting-place on the snow-covered steps of the platform. Even as he hung there, offering to his fellow-travelers this inspiring illustration of athletic prowess and the strenuous life, he was painfully conscious that the position was not a dignified one for a stout gentleman of sixty with an exalted position in the scientific world. He pictured to himself the happy smiles of those who were looking on, and he realized that his conception of their hearty enjoyment had not been exaggerated when he glanced back at them after a friendly brakeman had dragged him "on board." Dr. Van Valkenberg smiled a little ruefully as he thanked the man and rubbed the aching surface of his hand, which not even his thick kid gloves had protected. Then he pulled himself together, picked up the books and newspapers he had dropped and which the bystanders had enthusiastically hurled after him, and sought his haven in the sleeping-car. When he reached his section he stood for a moment, with his back to the passengers, to put some of his belongings in the rack above his head. As he was trying to arrange them properly he heard a voice behind him.

"O-oh! Were you hurt?" it said. "I was so 'fraid you were going to fall."

Dr. Van Valkenberg, who was a tall man, turned and looked down from his great height. At his feet stood a baby; at least she seemed a baby to him, although she was very dignified and wholly self-possessed and fully four years old. She was looking up at him with dark brown eyes, which wore an absurdly anxious expression. In that instant of quick

---

[11] By special permission of the author.

observation he noticed that her wraps had been removed and that she wore a white dress and had yellow curls, among which, on one side of her head, a small black bow lay sombrely.

She was so delicious in her almost maternal solicitude that he smiled irrepressibly, though he answered with the ceremoniousness she seemed to expect.

"Why, no, thank you," he said. "I am not hurt. Didn't you see the kind man help me onto the car?"

There was a subdivided titter from the other passengers over this touching admission of helplessness, but the human atom below drew a long, audible sigh of relief.

"I'm very glad," she said, with dignity. "I was 'fraid he hurt you." She turned as she spoke, and toddled into the section opposite his, where a plain but kindly faced elderly woman was sitting. She lifted her charge to the seat beside her, and the child rose to her knees, pressed her pink face against the window-pane, and looked out at the snow that was falling heavily.

Dr. Van Valkenberg settled back in his seat and tried to read his newspaper, but for some reason the slight incident in which he and the little girl had figured moved him strangely. It had been a long time since anyone had looked at him like that! He was not a person who aroused sympathy. He conscientiously endeavored to follow the President's latest oracular utterances on the Trust problem, but his eyes turned often to the curly head at the window opposite. They were well-trained, observant eyes, and they read the woman as not the mother, but a paid attendant—a trained nurse, probably, with fifteen years of admirable, cold, scientific service behind her. Why was she with the child, he wondered.

It was Christmas eve—not the time for a baby girl to be travelling. Then his glance fell again on the black bow among the yellow curls and on the white dress with its black shoulder-knots, and the explanation came to him. An orphan, of course, on her way West to a new home, in charge of the matter-of-fact nurse who was dozing comfortably in the corner of her seat. To whom was she going? Perhaps to grandparents, where she would be spoiled and wholly happy; or quite possibly to more distant relatives where she might find a grudging welcome. Dear little embryo woman, with her sympathetic heart already attuned to the world's gamut of pain. She should have been dancing under a Christmas tree, or hanging up her tiny stocking in the warm chimney-corner of some cozy nursery. The heart of the man swelled at the thought, and he recognized the sensation with a feeling of surprised annoyance. What was all this to him—to an old bachelor who knew nothing of children except their infantile ailments, and who had supposed that he cared for them as little as he understood them? Still, it was Christmas. His mind swung back to that. He himself had rebelled at the unwelcome prospect of Christmas eve and Christmas day in a sleeping-car—he, without even nephews and nieces to lighten the gloom of his lonely house. The warm human sympathy of the man and the sweet traditions of his youth rose in protest against this spectacle of a lonely child, travelling through the night toward some distant home which she had never seen, and where coldness, even neglect, might await her. Then he reminded himself that this was all imagination, and that he might be wholly wrong in his theory of the journey, and he called himself a fool for his pains. Still, the teasing interest and an elusive but equally teasing memory held his thoughts.

Darkness was falling, but the porter had not begun to light the lamps, and heavy shadows were rising from the corners of the car. Dr. Van Valkenberg's little neighbor turned from the gloom without to the gloom within, and made an impulsive movement toward the drowsy woman opposite her. The nurse did not stir, and the little girl sat silent, her brown eyes shining in the half-light and her dimpled hands folded in her lap. The physician leaned across the aisle.

"Won't you come over and visit me?" he asked. "I am very lonely, and I have no one to take care of me."

She slid off the seat at once, with great alacrity.

"I'd like to," she said, "but I must ask Nana. I must always ask Nana now," she added, with dutiful emphasis, "'fore I do anyfing."

She laid her hand on the gloved fingers of the nurse as she spoke, and the woman opened her eyes, shot a quick glance at the man, and nodded. She had not been asleep. Dr.

Christmas in Modern Story

Van Valkenberg rose and lifted his visitor to the seat beside him, where her short legs stuck out in uncompromising rigidity, and her tiny hands returned demurely to their former position in her lap. She took up the conversation where it had been interrupted.

"I can take care of you," she said, brightly. "I taked care of mamma a great deal, and I gave her her med'cin'."

He replied by placing a cushion behind her back and forming a resting-place for her feet by building an imposing pyramid, of which his dressing-case was the base. Then he turned to her with the smile women loved.

"Very well," he said. "If you really are going to take care of me I must know your name. You see," he explained, "I might need you in the night to get me a glass of water or something. Just think how disappointing it would be if I should call you by the wrong name and some other little girl came!"

She laughed.

"You say funny things," she said, contentedly. "But there isn't any other little girl in the car. I looked, soon as I came on, 'cos I wanted one to play with. I like little girls. I like little boys, too," she added, with innocent expansiveness.

"Then we'll play I'm a little boy. You'd never believe it, but I used to be. You haven't told me your name," he reminded her.

"Hope," she said, promptly. "Do you think it is a nice name?" She made the inquiry with an anxious interest which seemed to promise immediate change if the name displeased him. He reassured her.

"I think Hope is the nicest name a little girl could have, except one," he said. "The nicest little girl I ever knew was named Katharine. She grew to be a nice big girl, too,—and has little girls of her own now, no doubt," he added, half to himself.

"Were you a little boy when she was a little girl?" asked his visitor, with flattering interest.

"Oh, no; I was a big man, just as I am now. Her father was my friend, and she lived in a white house with an old garden where there were all kinds of flowers. She used to play there when she was a tiny baby, just big enough to crawl along the paths. Later she learned to walk there, and then the gardener had to follow her to see that she didn't pick *all* the flowers. I used to carry her around and hold her high up so she could pull the apples and pears off the trees. When she grew larger I gave her a horse and taught her to ride. She seemed like my very own little girl. But by-and-by she grew up and became a young lady, and—well, she went away from me, and I never had another little girl."

He had begun the story to interest the child. He found, as he went on, that it still interested him.

"Did she go to heaven?" asked the little girl, softly.

"Oh, dear, no," answered the doctor, with brisk cheerfulness.

"Then why didn't she keep on being your little girl always?" was the next leading question.

The doctor hesitated a moment. He was making the discovery that after many years old wounds can reopen and throb. No one had ever been brave enough to broach to him the subject of this single love-affair, which he was now discussing, he told himself, like a garrulous old woman. He was anxious to direct the conversation into other channels, but there was a certain compelling demand in the brown eyes upturned to his.

"Well, you see," he explained, "other boys liked her, too. And when she became a young lady other men liked her. So finally—one of them took her away from me."

He uttered the last words wearily, and the sensitive atom at his side seemed to understand why. Her little hand slipped into his.

"Why didn't you ask her to please stay with you?" she persisted, pityingly.

"I did," he told her. "But, you see, she liked the other man better."

"Oh-h-h." The word came out long-drawn and breathless. "I don't see how she possedly could!"

There was such sorrow for the victim and scorn for the offender in the tone, that, combined with the none too subtle compliment, it was too much for Dr. Van Valkenberg's self-control. He threw back his gray head, and burst into an almost boyish shout of laughter, which effectually cleaned the

Christmas in Modern Story

atmosphere of sentimental memories. He suddenly realized, too, that he had not been giving the child the cheerful holiday evening he had intended.

"Where are you going to hang up your stockings tonight?" he asked. A shade fell over her sensitive face.

"I can't hang them up," she answered, soberly. "Santa Claus doesn't travel on trains, Nana says. But p'r'aps he'll have something waiting for me when I get to Cousin Gertie's," she added, with sweet hopefulness.

"Nana is always right," said the doctor, oracularly, "and of course you must do exactly as she says. But I heard that Santa Claus was going to get on the train to-night at Buffalo, and I believe," he added, slowly and impressively, "that if he found a pair of small black stockings hanging from that section he'd fill them!"

Her eyes sparkled.

"Then I'll ask Nana," she said. "An' if she says I may hang them, I will. But one," she added, conscientiously, "has a teeny, weeny hole in the toe. Do you think he would mind that?"

He reassured her on this point, and turned to the nurse, who was now wide awake and absorbed in a novel. The car was brilliantly lighted, and the passengers were beginning to respond to the first dinner call.

"I beg your pardon," he said. "I've taken a great fancy to your little charge, and I want your help to carry out a plan of mine. I have suggested to Hope that she hang up her stockings tonight. I have every reason to believe that Santa Claus will get on this train at Buffalo. In fact," he added, smiling, "I mean to telegraph him."

The nurse hesitated a moment. He drew his card-case from his pocket and handed her one of the bits of pasteboard it contained.

"I have no evil designs," he added, cheerfully. "If you are a New-Yorker you may possibly know who I am."

The woman's face lit up as she read the name. She turned toward him impulsively, with a very pleasant smile.

"Indeed I do, doctor," she said. "Who does not? Dr. Abbey sent for you last week," she added, "for a consultation over the last case I had—this child's mother. But you were out of town. We were all so disappointed. It seems strange that we should meet now."

"Patient died?" asked the physician, with professional brevity.

"Yes, doctor."

He rose from his seat.

"Now that you have my credentials," he added, cordially, "I want you and Hope to dine with me. You will, won't you?"

The upholstered cheerfulness of the dining-car found favor in the sight of Hope. She conducted herself, however, with her usual dignity, broken only occasionally by an ecstatic wriggle as the prospective visit of Santa Claus crossed her mind. Her dinner, superintended by an eminent physician and a trained nurse, was naturally a simple and severely hygienic one, but here, too, her admirable training was evident. She ate cheerfully her bowl of bread and milk, and wasted no longing glances on the plum-pudding.

Later, in the feverish excitement of hanging up her stockings, going to bed, and peeping through the curtains to catch Santa Claus, a little of her extraordinary repose of manner deserted her; but she fell asleep at last, with great reluctance.

When the curtains round her berth had ceased trembling, a most unusual procession wended its silent way toward Dr. Van Valkenberg's section. In some occult manner the news had gone from one end to the other of the "Special" that a little girl in section nine, car *Floradora*, had hung up her stockings for Santa Claus. The hearts of fathers, mothers, and doting uncles responded at once. Dressing-cases were unlocked, great valises were opened, mysterious bundles were unwrapped, and from all these sources came gifts of surprising fitness. Small daughters and nieces, sleeping in Western cities, might well have turned restlessly in their beds had they seen the presents designed for them drop into a pair of tiny stockings and pile up on the floor below these.

A succession of long-drawn, ecstatic breaths and happy gurgles awoke the passengers on car *Floradora* at an unseemly hour Christmas morning, and a small white figure, clad informally in a single garment, danced up and down the aisle, dragging carts and woolly lambs behind it.

Occasionally there was the squeak of a talking doll, and always there was the patter of small feet and the soft cooing of a child's voice, punctuated by the exquisite music of a child's laughter. Dawn was just approaching, and the lamps, still burning, flared pale in the gray light. But in the length of that car there was no soul so base as to long for silence and the pillow. Crabbed old faces looked out between the curtains and smiled; eyes long unused to tears felt a sudden, strange moisture. Dr. Van Valkenberg had risen almost as early as Hope, and possibly the immaculate freshness of his attire, contrasted with the scantiness of her own, induced that young lady to retire from observation for a short time and emerge clothed for general society. Even during this brief retreat in the dressing-room the passengers heard her breathless voice, high-pitched in her excitement, chattering incessantly to the responsive Nana.

Throughout the day the snow still fell, and the outside world seemed far away and dreamlike to Dr. Van Valkenberg. The real things were this train, cutting its way through the snow, and this little child, growing deeper into his heart with each moment that passed. The situation was unique, but easy enough to understand, he told himself. He had merely gone back twenty-five years to that other child, whom he had petted in infancy and loved and lost in womanhood. He had been very lonely—how lonely he had only recently begun to realize, and he was becoming an old man whose life lay behind him. He crossed the aisle suddenly and sat down beside the nurse, leaving Hope singing her doll to sleep in his section. There was something almost diffident in his manner as he spoke.

"Will you tell me all you know about the child?" he asked. "She interests me greatly and appeals to me very strongly, probably because she's so much like someone I used to know."

The nurse closed her book and looked at him curiously. She had heard much of him, but nothing that would explain this interest in a strange child. He himself could not have explained it. He knew only that he felt it, powerfully and compellingly.

"Her name is Hope Armitage," she said, quietly. "Her

mother, who has just died, was a widow—Mrs. Katharine Armitage. They were poor, and Mrs. Armitage seemed to have no relations. She had saved a little, enough to pay most of her expenses at the hospital, and—" She hesitated a moment, and then went on: "I am telling you everything very frankly, because you are you, but it was done quietly enough. We all loved the woman. She was very unusual, and patient, and charming. All the nurses who had had anything to do with her cried when she died. We felt that she might have been saved if she had come in time, but she was worked out. She had earned her living by sewing, after her husband's death, three years ago, and she kept at it day and night. She hadn't much constitution to begin with, and none when she came to us. She was so sweet, so brave, yet so desperately miserable over leaving her little girl alone in the world——"

Dr. Van Valkenberg sat silent. It was true, then. This was Katharine's child. Had he not known it? Could he have failed to know it, whenever or wherever they had met? He had not known of the death of Armitage nor of the subsequent poverty of his widow, but he had known Katharine's baby, he now told himself, the moment he saw her.

"Well," the nurse resumed, "after she died we raised a small fund to buy some clothes for Hope, and take her to Chicago to her new home. Mrs. Armitage has a cousin there, who has agreed to take her in. None of the relatives came to the funeral; there are not many of them, and the Chicago people haven't much money, I fancy. They offered to send Hope's fare, or even to come for her if it was absolutely necessary; but they seemed very much relieved when we wrote that I would bring her out."

Dr. Van Valkenberg did not speak at once. He was hardly surprised. Life was full of extraordinary situations, and his profession had brought him face to face with many of them. Nevertheless, a deep solemnity filled him and a strange peace settled over him. He turned to the nurse with something of this in his face and voice.

"I want her," he said, briefly. "Her mother and father were old friends of mine, and this thing looks like fate. Will they give her to me—these Chicago people—do you think?"

Tears filled the woman's eyes.

"Indeed they will," she said, "and gladly. There was"—she hesitated—"there was even some talk of sending her to an institution before they finally decided to take her. Dear little Hope—how happy she will be with you!"

He left her, and went back to the seat where Hope sat, crooning to the doll. Sitting down, he gathered them both up in his arms, and a thrill shot through him as he looked at the yellow curls resting against his breast. Her child—her little helpless baby—now his child, to love and care for. He was not a religious man; nevertheless a prayer rose spontaneously in his heart. But there was a plea to be made—a second plea, like the one he had made the mother; this time he felt that he knew the answer.

"Hope," he said, gently, "once, long ago, I asked a little girl to come and live with me, and she would not come. Now I want to ask you to come, and stay with me always, and be my own little girl, and let me take care of you and make you happy. Will you come?"

The radiance of June sunshine broke out upon her face and shone in the brown eyes upturned to his. How well he knew that look! Hope did not turn toward Nana, and that significant omission touched him deeply. She seemed to feel that here was a question she alone must decide. She drew a long breath as she looked up at him.

"Really, truly?" she asked. Then, as he nodded without speaking, she saw something in his face that was new to her. It was nothing to frighten a little girl, for it was very sweet and tender; but for one second she thought her new friend was going to cry! She put both arms around his neck, and replied softly, with the exquisite maternal cadences her voice had taken on in her first words to him when he entered the car:

"I'll be your own little girl, and I'll take care of you, too. You know, you said I could."

Dr. Van Valkenberg turned to the nurse.

"I shall go with you to her cousin's, from the train," he announced. "I'm ready to give them all the proofs they need that I'm a suitable guardian for the child, but," he added, with a touch of the boyishness that had never left him, "I want this matter settled now."

The long train pounded its way into the station at Chicago, and the nurse hurriedly put on Hope's coat and gloves and fastened the ribbons of her hood under her chin. Dr. Van Valkenberg summoned a porter.

"Take care of all these things," he said, indicating both sets of possessions with a sweep of the arm. "I shall have my hands full with my little daughter."

He gathered her into his arms as he spoke, and she nestled against his broad chest with a child's unconscious satisfaction in the strength and firmness of his clasp. The lights of the great station were twinkling in the early dusk as he stepped off the train, and the place was noisy with the greetings exchanged between the passengers and their waiting friends.

"Merry Christmas," "Merry Christmas," sounded on every side. Everybody was absorbed and excited, yet there were few who did not find time to turn a last look on a singularly attractive little child, held above the crowd in the arms of a tall man. She was laughing triumphantly as he bore her through the throng, and his heart was in his eyes as he smiled back at her.

A BEGGAR'S CHRISTMAS[12]
A FABLE

Edith Wyatt

Once upon a time there was a beggar-maid named Anitra, who lived in a cellar in the largest city of a wealthy and fabulous nation.

In spite of the fact that the country was passing through an era of great commercial prosperity, it contained such large numbers of beggars, and the competition among them was so keen, that on Christmas Eve at midnight, Anitra found herself without a single cent.

She turned away from the street-corner, where she had been standing with her little stack of fortune-cards, and hurried through the alleys to the shelter of her cellar. These fortune-cards of hers were printed in all languages; and, had the public but known, it could not go wrong among them, for every single card promised good-luck to the chooser. But, in spite of all this tact on Anitra's part, and her complete dependence upon universal chivalry, qualities which are woman's surest methods of success in the real world, in the wealthy and fabulous kingdom she now found herself not only hungry, ragged, and penniless, but also without a roof over her head. For when she reached her cellar-door it was nailed shut: and, as she had not paid her rent for a long time, she knew she could not persuade her fabulous landlord to open it for her.

She walked away, holding her little torn shawl fast around her, and shaking her loose black hair around her cheeks to try to keep them warm. But the cold and the damp struck to her very bones. Her little feet in their ragged shoes and stockings were as numb as clubs; and she limped along, scarcely able to direct them, to know where she was going, or to know anything in fact, except that she would freeze to death if she stood still.

Soon she reached a large dark building with a broad

---

[12] By permission of the author and the "Atlantic Monthly."

flight of steps and a pillared entrance. Nobody seemed to be guarding it, and she managed to creep up the steps and in between the pillars out of the snow.

Behind the pillars rose enormous closed doors. Under the doors shone a chink of light. Anitra stooped down and put her hand against the crack. There was a little warmth in the air sifting through. She laid her whole body close against the opening. That pushed the doors inward slightly, and she slipped inside the entrance.

She was in a tremendous gilded, carven, and pillared hall of great tiers of empty seats and far dark galleries, all dimly lighted and all garlanded with wreaths of mistletoe and holly. For a long time she sat on the floor with her head thrown back against the door, staring quietly about her, without moving a hair for fear of being driven away. But no one came. The whole place was silent.

After about an hour, she rose softly, and stepped without a sound along the dark velvet carpet of the centre aisle and up a flight of steps at the end, to a great gold throne with cushions of purple velvet and ermine. She rested her wrists on the gold ledge of the seat, and with a little vault she jumped up on the cushions. They were warm and soft. She curled up among them, and pulled her little shawl over her, meaning to jump down the instant she heard the least noise. And while she was listening she fell fast asleep.

She was awakened by the cool gray light of the December daybreak falling through the long windows, over all the gold-carven pillars and high beams and arches, all the empty seats and dark velvet cushions and high garlands of holly.

She held her breath. Three men, who had plainly not seen her, had entered at a side-door. She recognized them all from their pictures in the papers. They were the aged Minister, the middle-aged Chancellor, and the young King of the kingdom. The King carried a roll of parchment in his hand and seemed very nervous, and the Chancellor was speaking to him about "throwing the voice," as they all came up the centre aisle, and then straight up the steps, toward the throne.

Dumb with fright, Anitra raised her head from the cushions. The three men suddenly saw her. The young King started and dropped the parchment, the Chancellor stumbled and nearly fell, and the aged Minister darted toward her.

"What are you doing here?" he cried angrily.

"Nothing," said Anitra, sitting up, with her shawl held tightly around her, and her little ragged shoes dangling from the throne.

"Who are you?" said the Chancellor suspiciously, staring at her. He was very short-sighted.

"Nobody," said Anitra.

"She is just a stray who has got in here somehow," said the Minister rather kindly. "Run away, my child," he added, giving her a coin. "Can't you see the King wants to practice his speech here, now?"

But the Chancellor seemed to be considering. "Do you know," he said softly to the Minister, as the King, who had picked up the parchment, stood absorbed, whispering his speech over to himself, "an idea has struck me. I don't know but that we might let her stay there till the reporters come to photograph the new hall. It would look rather well, you know, if something like this should get into the papers, 'Mighty Monarch Finding Stray Asleep on Throne, on Christmas Morn, Refuses to Break Slumbers.'"

The old Minister looked a little doubtful. "You can't tell what she might say afterwards," he said.

"We can easily arrange that," replied the Chancellor; and he turned towards Anitra and said sternly, "If we let you stay here will you promise not to say one word to anyone about the matter or about anything you see or hear in this hall, without our permission?"

"Yes," said Anitra readily.

"Consider what you are saying, my child," said the Minister mildly. "Do you know this means that if you say one word the administration dislikes you will be hung?"

"No, indeed," said Anitra in misery. "How could I know that?"

"You should not have promised so rashly," said the Chancellor. "But now that it is done, we will trust that everything will fall out so that it will not be necessary to hang you."

"What do you want me to do?" said Anitra.

"Simply remain here now, just as you were when we came in, except with your eyes shut," said the Chancellor, "and then when we tell you to do so, go down and sit on the throne-steps until the audience-hall is filled with all the populace who are coming to see the new audience-chamber, and to listen to the judgments of the King, on Christmas Day. If anybody asks you how you came to be here, you might mention the fact that you had strayed in from the cold, and tell about the royal clemency shown in permitting you to remain. Then, at the end of the day, if you have done as you should, you can go out with the rest of the people."

"Go to sleep again, now," said the aged Minister, "just as you were when we came in."

Anitra put her head down on the cushion again, but she could not sleep, for the King began to read his proclamation at the top of his lungs, so that it could be heard in the furthest galleries, where the Chancellor stood and kept calling, "Louder! Louder!" The speech was all about the wealth and prosperity and happiness and good fortune of the kingdom, and how no one needed to be hungry or cold or poor in any way, because there was such plenty.

When the King had finished, he said rather crossly to the Chancellor, "Well, are you suited?"

The Chancellor expressed his content, and they talked over the prisoners who were to be judged, which ones were to be hanged, and which ones were to be pardoned, till the Chancellor had to hurry away to attend to some other matters. The King left moodily soon afterwards. The Chancellor's opinions and methods were often obnoxious to him; but he disliked greatly to wound or oppose him in any way. He had been an old and intimate friend of the King's father, and besides he was very powerful in the country.

All this time Anitra had kept her eyes closed; and she now lay still, while strange footsteps sounded on the marble floors and she heard the reporters coming to photograph the new audience-hall, heard them asking the aged Minister why she was there, and heard him telling them about the early visit of the King to inspect the new audience-chamber, and his wish that the slumber of the beggar-girl should not be disturbed till the arrival of the audience made it absolutely necessary. Then she heard them tiptoeing away to a little distance, heard their fountain-pens scratching and their cameras clicking through the empty galleries, and at last she heard them going away.

"Now you can jump down, and run around for a little while," said the Minister, waiting a minute before following them. "Some of the Democratic papers will have extras out, by three o'clock this afternoon, with photographs of you asleep on the throne, and there will be editorials in the Republican papers about the King's tact and grace in the matter."

Although Anitra wished to answer that she was too faint from hunger to jump down and run around, she made no reply for fear of being hung. But she slipped down from the throne, and sat on the throne-step, on the tread nearest the floor, in the hope of not being seen and questioned by the entering audience, for some time at least.

For it was ten o'clock now. The great doors had swung wide open and a tremendous crowd of people surged into the hall,—men, women, and children, laughing, talking, exclaiming over the beauty of the new audience-chamber, and wondering what would happen to the three murderers the King would judge that day. It was a prosperous, well-dressed city crowd, and it poured in till it had filled the hall, the galleries, the aisles, and the staircases, and till the latest comers had even climbed upon the shoulders of the others, to the window-sills and the ledges of the wainscoting. With the rest came two old, wrinkled, clumsy shepherds from the country, with staffs in their hands and sheepskins on their backs, and sharp, aged eyes looking out from under their shaggy eyebrows, as though they could watch well for wolves. Although they came among the last, they somehow made their way up to the very front of the hall. Except for these old shepherds and Anitra, all the people wore their very best clothes. The sun sparkled over everything. Outside, the Christmas bells rang, and Anitra looked at it all, and listened to it all, and hoped she would not faint with hunger, and wondered whether she could go through the day without saying something the Chancellor would dislike and being hung for it.

The people in the first row stared hard at her, and one usher wished to put her out because she was sitting inside the red velvet cordon intended to separate the royal platform from the populace. But another usher came hurrying up to say that he had received official orders to the effect that she was to be permitted to remain just where she was.

Before anyone in the first row had time to ask her how she came to be there inside the red velvet cordon, the heralds blew on the trumpets, and everybody turned to see the entrance of the prisoners.

They were a man, a woman, and a boy. The woman was a cotton-spinner, Elizabeth, a poor neighbor of Anitra's, who had left a fatherless child of hers upon a doorstep where it died. The boy was a Moorish merchant's son, Joseph, who had stabbed another boy in a street-brawl. The man was a noble, Bernardino, who had killed his adversary in a duel. The turnkeys marched on either side of the prisoners and marshaled them into their seats on the platform.

No one in the court knew about Elizabeth or the Moorish boy Joseph, or paid any attention to them, except that Joseph's father stood with haggard eyes close to the cordon, and he looked at his son and his son looked back at him with a deep glance of devotion when the prisoners marched by to judgment. Six or seven rows back in the audience sat Elizabeth's little sister, and when the prisoners were standing at the bar, she leaned far forward and threw a little sprig of holly down at Elizabeth's feet, and Elizabeth stooped and picked it up.

But there was a great buzz in the crowd when Bernardino, the nobleman, marched by. He was well known at court. His best friends sat together, and they cheered, and there was constant applause as he passed, and he bowed grandly to everybody.

Then there was another flourish of trumpets, and the pages and ladies-and-lords-in-waiting and knights and chamberlains came in, and the Minister and the Chancellor, and last of all the young King. The whole room rang with applause and cheers. All the heralds blew on the bugles. The bells rang and the young King took his seat on the throne between the Minister and the Chancellor, and waited till the audience-chamber was still.

The herald came forward and cried, "Oyez! Oyez! Oyez! Bernardino, Duke of Urba, Lord of Rustica, come into the Court!" Bernardino, with his fur cape swinging from his broad shoulders and his plume tossing, stepped forward from the bar, and his trial began. The King heard evidence upon one side and heard evidence upon the other for a long, long time: and at last he pardoned Bernardino. The bells rang, and the trumpets sounded again, and Bernardino's friends went nearly wild with joy. And Bernardino kissed the King's hand and walked down the throne-steps a free man.

Only, the two aged clumsy shepherds turned and looked at each other, as if they felt some contempt for what was happening. And while Anitra watched them, as she thought how hungry she was, it seemed to her that they were far younger than she had noticed at first. They appeared to be about fifty years old.

Bernardino's trial had occupied a great length of time; and just after it was over, and the applause and tumult after the decision had died down, and the herald had called, "Oyez! Oyez! Oyez! Joseph, son of the merchant Joseph, come into the Court!" then Anitra noticed that everyone was looking at her, and whispering. She saw papers passed from hand to hand, and knew that the extras the King had spoken of must have come out.

Everybody was so entertained and preoccupied with comparing the newspaper pictures of Anitra with Anitra herself, and with reading, "Mighty Monarch Finding Stray on Throne on Christmas Morn Refuses to Break Slumbers," that Joseph's trial seemed to slip by almost without public notice.

Only, Joseph's father hung on every word. The King heard evidence upon one side and heard evidence upon the other for a long, long time, and every few minutes, on account of the buzz about Anitra's being permitted to sleep on the throne, the herald would be obliged to ask for silence in the audience-chamber. For no one knew Joseph, and no one cared about his fate except in so far as there was a general feeling that a murder committed by a Moor was more dangerous than a murder committed by anybody else. So that toward the end, when the evidence seemed to show more and more that

Joseph had fought only to defend himself, the court was more silent, and there was a certain tenseness in the air. The King turned white. He condemned Joseph to death; but he did not look at him, he looked away. Joseph stood proudly before him, without moving an eyelash, without moving a muscle. Joseph's father looked as proud as his son. But his face had changed to the face of an old man, and in his eyes burned the painful glance of a soul enduring an injustice.

Everyone else seemed to be satisfied, however. Only, the two aged, clumsy shepherds turned and looked at each other as though they felt a certain contempt for what was happening. And while Anitra watched, as she thought how hungry she was, it seemed to her that they were not aged at all. They appeared to be about forty years old.

Then the herald called, "Oyez! Oyez! Oyez! Elizabeth, spinner of cotton, come into the Court!" And everything turned so black before Anitra that she could hardly see Elizabeth come out and stand before the King. For she loved Elizabeth and Elizabeth's sister, and she knew that Elizabeth had deserted her baby when she was beside herself with sickness and disgrace and poverty, and she knew that the father who had deserted her and deserted the baby was one of those trumpeters of the King, who had just been blowing the blasts of triumph for him, to the admiration of the whole court.

Then the King heard evidence upon one side, and heard evidence upon the other. But almost everything was against Elizabeth; though the King in his mercy changed her sentence from death to imprisonment and disgrace for her whole life. Everyone applauded his clemency. But the little sister sobbed and cried like a crazy thing, though Elizabeth raised her chin and smiled bravely at her, to comfort her.

The shepherds turned and looked at each other with a glance of contempt for what was happening. And now they were not aged or clumsy at all. They were strong, straight young men, more beautiful than anything else Anitra had seen in her whole life; and they looked at her beautifully as though they were her brothers.

Then the heralds all came out and blew upon the trumpets to announce the King's proclamation; and the King read about all the wealth and prosperity and peace and good fortune and happiness and plenty of the nation; and every minute Anitra grew more and more faint with hunger.

When the proclamation was done the people screamed and shouted. The Christmas bells rang. The fifes and bugles sounded. Everybody cheered the King, and the King rose and responded. Then everybody cheered the Chancellor, and he bowed and responded. Then there were cries of "Long Live Bernardino!" and the bugles were sounded for him; and he bowed and responded. And then some one called "Long Live Anitra, the Beggar-girl!" And there was an uproar of cheers and bugles and applause and excitement.

Anitra rose and stood upon the throne-steps. But she looked only at the shepherds, who were more beautiful than anything else she had ever seen in her whole life, and who looked at her beautifully as though they were her brothers. She thought, "I must have died some day at any rate. So I will die to-day and speak the truth."

When the audience-chamber was still she said, "I am Anitra the Beggar-girl. But I do not praise the King for his kindness, for though he let me stay on his throne he is letting me die of hunger. And I do not praise the King for his justice, for in his court the man who deserts his child and his child's mother walks free, and the woman who deserts her child must die in prison. And in his court the King pardons one man and condemns another for exactly the same fault."

Then the two shepherds walked up the steps of the throne. Everything was still. Not a bell rang. Not a trumpet blew. But as the shepherds walked, the audience-chamber seemed to vanish away; and all around, beyond the pillared arches, and beyond the prosperous people, stood all the poor people, all the hungry people, all the unjustly-paid and overworked and sick and struggling people in the nation. And in the judges and judged, and the prosperous people and the poor people, there rose like the first quiver of dawn a sense simply of what was really true for each one and for everyone.

The younger shepherd said, "In this Court to-day stand those who are more strong than all the triumphs of the world. We are the Truth and Death."

And as he spoke, all thought of judgment and of

condemnation and pardon and patronage vanished away; and in everybody's soul the thought simply of what was really true for each one and for every one opened like the clear flower of daybreak.

Not a bell rang. Not a trumpet blew. "We are the Truth and Death," repeated the older shepherd.

And the thought simply of what was really true for each one and for everyone, and the thought that all were common fellow mortals thrilled through everybody's soul more keenly and more fully than the light of morning and the tones of all the trumpets of the world.

After that, the shepherds did not again turn and glance at each other as though they felt a contempt for what was happening. For from that time on, everything was done in the Court only with the thought of what was really true for each one and for everyone, and the thought that all were fellow mortals; and before the next Christmas, there were no beggars at all in the fabulous nation. And the Truth and Death, there, always looked at everybody beautifully, as though they were their brothers.

A CHRISTMAS MYSTERY[13]
THE STORY OF THREE WISE MEN
William J. Locke

I cannot tell how the truth may be;
I say the tale as 'twas said to me.

Three men who had gained great fame and honor throughout the world met unexpectedly in front of the bookstall at Paddington Station. Like most of the great ones of the earth they were personally acquainted, and they exchanged surprised greetings.

Sir Angus McCurdie, the eminent physicist, scowled at the two others beneath his heavy black eyebrows.

"I'm going to a God-forsaken place in Cornwall called Trehenna," said he.

"That's odd; so am I," croaked Professor Biggleswade. He was a little, untidy man with round spectacles, a fringe of grayish beard and a weak, rasping voice, and he knew more of Assyriology than any man, living or dead. A flippant pupil once remarked that the Professor's face was furnished with a Babylonic cuneiform in lieu of features.

"People called Deverill, at Foullis Castle?" asked Sir Angus.

"Yes," replied Professor Biggleswade.

"How curious! I am going to the Deverills, too," said the third man.

This man was the Right Honorable Viscount Boyne, the renowned Empire Builder and Administrator, around whose solitary and remote life popular imagination had woven many legends. He looked at the world through tired gray eyes, and the heavy drooping blonde mustache seemed tired, too, and had dragged down the tired face into deep furrows. He was smoking a long black cigar.

"I suppose we may as well travel down together," said Sir Angus, not very cordially.

Lord Boyne said courteously: "I have a reserved

---

[13] Reprinted by permission of W. J. Locke.

carriage. The railway company is always good enough to place one at my disposal. It would give me great pleasure if you would share it."

The invitation was accepted, and the three men crossed the busy, crowded platform to take their seats in the great express train. A porter laden with an incredible load of paraphernalia, trying to make his way through the press, happened to jostle Sir Angus McCurdie. He rubbed his shoulder fretfully.

"Why the whole land should be turned into a bear garden on account of this exploded superstition of Christmas is one of the anomalies of modern civilization. Look at this insensate welter of fools traveling in wild herds to disgusting places merely because it's Christmas!"

"You seem to be traveling yourself, McCurdie," said Lord Boyne.

"Yes—and why the devil I'm doing it, I've not the faintest notion," replied Sir Angus.

"It's going to be a beast of a journey," he remarked some moments later, as the train carried them slowly out of the station. "The whole country is under snow—and as far as I can understand we have to change twice and wind up with a twenty-mile motor drive."

He was an iron-faced, beetle-browed, stern man, and this morning he did not seem to be in the best of tempers. Finding his companions inclined to be sympathetic, he continued his lamentation.

"And merely because it's Christmas I've had to shut up my laboratory and give my young fools a holiday—just when I was in the midst of a most important series of experiments."

Professor Biggleswade, who had heard vaguely of and rather looked down upon such new-fangled toys as radium and thorium and helium and argon—for the latest astonishing developments in the theory of radio-activity had brought Sir Angus McCurdie his worldwide fame—said somewhat ironically:

"If the experiments were so important, why didn't you lock yourself up with your test tubes and electric batteries and finish them alone?"

"Man!" said McCurdie, bending across the carriage, and

speaking with a curious intensity of voice, "d'ye know I'd give a hundred pounds to be able to answer that question."

"What do you mean?" asked the Professor, startled.

"I should like to know why I'm sitting in this damned train and going to visit a couple of addle-headed society people whom I'm scarcely acquainted with, when I might be at home in my own good company furthering the progress of science."

"I myself," said the Professor, "am not acquainted with them at all."

It was Sir Angus McCurdie's turn to look surprised.

"Then why are you spending Christmas with them?"

"I reviewed a ridiculous blank-verse tragedy written by Deverill on the Death of Sennacherib. Historically it was puerile. I said so in no measured terms. He wrote a letter claiming to be a poet and not an archæologist. I replied that the day had passed when poets could with impunity commit the abominable crime of distorting history. He retorted with some futile argument, and we went on exchanging letters, until his invitation and my acceptance concluded the correspondence."

McCurdie, still bending his black brows on him, asked him why he had not declined. The Professor screwed up his face till it looked more like a cuneiform than ever. He, too, found the question difficult to answer; but he showed a bold front.

"I felt it my duty," said he, "to teach that preposterous ignoramus something worth knowing about Sennacherib. Besides I am a bachelor and would sooner spend Christmas, as to whose irritating and meaningless annoyance I cordially agree with you, among strangers than among my married sisters' numerous and nerve-racking families."

Sir Angus McCurdie, the hard, metallic apostle of radio-activity, glanced for a moment out of the window at the gray, frost-bitten fields. Then he said:

"I'm a widower. My wife died many years ago and, thank God, we had no children. I generally spend Christmas alone."

He looked out of the window again. Professor Biggleswade suddenly remembered the popular story of the great scientist's antecedents, and reflected that as McCurdie had once run, a barefoot urchin, through the Glasgow mud, he was likely to have little kith or kin. He himself envied McCurdie. He was always praying to be delivered from his sisters and nephews and nieces, whose embarrassing demands no calculated coldness could repress.

"Children are the root of all evil," said he. "Happy the man who has his quiver empty."

Sir Angus McCurdie did not reply at once; when he spoke again it was with reference to their prospective host.

"I met Deverill," said he, "at the Royal Society's Soirée this year. One of my assistants was demonstrating a peculiar property of thorium and Deverill seemed interested. I asked him to come to my laboratory the next day, and found he didn't know a damned thing about anything. That's all the acquaintance I have with him."

Lord Boyne, the great administrator, who had been wearily turning over the pages of an illustrated weekly chiefly filled with flamboyant photographs of obscure actresses, took his gold glasses from his nose and the black cigar from his lips, and addressed his companions.

"I've been considerably interested in your conversation," said he, "and as you've been frank, I'll be frank too. I knew Mrs. Deverill's mother, Lady Carstairs, very well years ago, and of course Mrs. Deverill when she was a child. Deverill I came across once in Egypt—he had been sent on a diplomatic mission to Teheran. As for our being invited on such slight acquaintance, little Mrs. Deverill has the reputation of being the only really successful celebrity hunter in England. She inherited the faculty from her mother, who entertained the whole world. We're sure to find archbishops, and eminent actors, and illustrious divorcées asked to meet us. That's one thing. But why I, who loathe country house parties and children and Christmas as much as Biggleswade, am going down there to-day, I can no more explain than you can. It's a devilish odd coincidence."

The three men looked at one another. Suddenly McCurdie shivered and drew his fur coat around him.

"I'll thank you," said he, "to shut that window."

"It's shut," said Boyne.

"It's just uncanny," said McCurdie, looking from one to the other.

"What?" asked Boyne.

"Nothing if you didn't feel it."

"There did seem to be a sudden draught," said Professor Biggleswade. "But as both window and door are shut, it could only be imaginary."

"It wasn't imaginary," muttered McCurdie.

Then he laughed harshly. "My father and mother came from Cromarty," he said with apparent irrelevance.

"That's the Highlands," said the Professor.

"Ay," said McCurdie.

Lord Boyne said nothing, but tugged at his mustache and looked out of the window as the frozen meadows and bits of river and willows raced past. A dead silence fell on them. McCurdie broke it with another laugh and took a whisky flask from his handbag.

"Have a nip?"

"Thanks, no," said the Professor. "I have to keep to a strict dietary, and I only drink hot milk and water—and of that sparingly. I have some in a thermos bottle."

Lord Boyne also declining the whisky, McCurdie swallowed a dram and declared himself to be better. The professor took from his bag a foreign review in which a German sciolist had dared to question his interpretation of a Hittite inscription. Over the man's ineptitude he fell asleep and snored loudly.

To escape from his immediate neighborhood McCurdie went to the other end of the seat and faced Lord Boyne, who had resumed his gold glasses and his listless contemplation of obscure actresses. McCurdie lit a pipe, Boyne another black cigar. The train thundered on.

Presently they all lunched together in the restaurant car. The windows steamed, but here and there through a wiped patch of pane a white world was revealed. The snow was falling. As they passed through Westbury, McCurdie looked mechanically for the famous white horse carved into the chalk of the down; but it was not visible beneath the thick covering of snow.

"It'll be just like this all the way to Gehenna—Trehenna,

I mean," said McCurdie.

Boyne nodded. He had done his life's work amid all extreme fiercenesses of heat and cold, in burning draughts, in simoons and in icy wildernesses, and a ray or two more of the pale sun or a flake or two more of the gentle snow of England mattered to him but little. But Biggleswade rubbed the pane with his table-napkin and gazed apprehensively at the prospect.

"If only this wretched train would stop," said he, "I would go back again."

And he thought how comfortable it would be to sneak home again to his books and thus elude not only the Deverills, but the Christmas jollities of his sisters' families, who would think him miles away. But the train was timed not to stop till Plymouth, two hundred and thirty-five miles from London, and thither was he being relentlessly carried. Then he quarreled with his food, which brought a certain consolation.

The train did stop, however, before Plymouth—indeed, before Exeter. An accident on the line had dislocated the traffic. The express was held up for an hour, and when it was permitted to proceed, instead of thundering on, it went cautiously, subject to continual stoppings. It arrived at Plymouth two hours late. The travelers learned that they had missed the connection on which they had counted and that they could not reach Trehenna till nearly ten o'clock. After weary waiting at Plymouth they took their seats in the little, cold local train that was to carry them another stage on their journey. Hot-water cans put in at Plymouth mitigated to some extent the iciness of the compartment. But that only lasted a comparatively short time, for soon they were set down at a desolate, shelterless wayside junction, dumped in the midst of a hilly snow-covered waste, where they went through another weary wait for another dismal local train that was to carry them to Trehenna. And in this train there were no hot-water cans, so that the compartment was as cold as death. McCurdie fretted and shook his fist in the direction of Trehenna.

"And when we get there we have still a twenty miles' motor-drive to Foullis Castle. It's a fool name and we're fools to be going there."

"I shall die of bronchitis," wailed Professor Biggleswade.

"A man dies when it is appointed for him to die," said Lord Boyne, in his tired way; and he went on smoking long black cigars.

"It's not the dying that worries me," said McCurdie. "That's a mere mechanical process which every organic being from a king to a cauliflower has to pass through. It's the being forced against my will and my reason to come on this accursed journey, which something tells me will become more and more accursed as we go on, that is driving me to distraction."

"What will be, will be," said Boyne.

"I can't see where the comfort of that reflection comes in," said Biggleswade.

"And yet you've traveled in the East," said Boyne. "I suppose you know the Valley of the Tigris as well as any man living."

"Yes," said the Professor, "I can say I dug my way from Tekrit to Bagdad and left not a stone unexamined."

"Perhaps, after all," Boyne remarked, "that's not quite the way to know the East."

"I never wanted to know the modern East," returned the Professor. "What is there in it of interest compared with the mighty civilizations that have gone before?"

McCurdie took a pull from his flask.

"I'm glad I thought of having a refill at Plymouth," said he.

At last, after many stops at little lonely stations they arrived at Trehenna. The guard opened the door and they stepped out on to the snow-covered platform. An oil lamp hung from the tiny pent-house roof that, structurally, was Trehenna Station. They looked around at the silent gloom of white undulating moorland, and it seemed a place where no man lived and only ghosts could have a bleak and unsheltered being. A porter came up and helped the guard with the luggage. Then they realized that the station was built on a small embankment, for, looking over the railing, they saw below the two great lamps of a motor car. A fur-clad chauffeur met them at the bottom of the stairs. He clapped his hands together and informed them cheerily that he had been waiting for four hours. It was the bitterest winter in these parts within the memory of man, said he, and he himself had not seen snow there for five years. Then he settled the three travelers in the great roomy touring car covered with a Cape cart hood, wrapped them up in many rugs and started.

After a few moments, the huddling together of their bodies—for, the Professor being a spare man, there was room for them all on the back seat—the pile of rugs, the serviceable and all but air-tight hood, induced a pleasant warmth and a pleasant drowsiness. Where they were being driven they knew not. The perfectly upholstered seat eased their limbs, the easy swinging motion of the car soothed their spirits. They felt that already they had reached the luxuriously appointed home which, after all, they knew awaited them. McCurdie no longer railed, Professor Biggleswade forgot the dangers of bronchitis, and Lord Boyne twisted the stump of a black cigar between his lips without any desire to relight it. A tiny electric lamp inside the hood made the darkness of the world to right and left and in front of the talc windows still darker. McCurdie and Biggleswade fell into a doze. Lord Boyne chewed the end of his cigar. The car sped on through an unseen wilderness.

Suddenly there was a horrid jolt and a lurch and a leap and a rebound and then the car stood still, quivering like a ship that has been struck by a heavy sea. The three men were pitched and tossed and thrown sprawling over one another onto the bottom of the car. Biggleswade screamed. McCurdie cursed. Boyne scrambled from the confusion of rugs and limbs and, tearing open the side of the Cape cart hood, jumped out. The chauffeur had also just leaped from his seat. It was pitch dark save for the great shaft of light down the snowy road cast by the acetylene lamps. The snow had ceased falling.

"What's gone wrong?"

"It sounds like the axle," said the chauffeur ruefully.

He unshipped a lamp and examined the car, which had wedged itself against a great drift of snow on the off side. Meanwhile McCurdie and Biggleswade had alighted.

"Yes, it's the axle," said the chauffeur.

"Then we're done," remarked Boyne.

"I'm afraid so, my lord."

"What's the matter? Can't we get on?" asked Biggleswade in his querulous voice.

McCurdie laughed. "How can we get on with a broken axle? The thing's as useless as a man with a broken back. Gad, I was right. I said it was going to be an infernal journey."

The little Professor wrung his hands. "But what's to be done?" he cried.

"Tramp it," said Lord Boyne, lighting a fresh cigar.

"It's ten miles," said the chauffeur.

"It would be the death of me," the Professor wailed.

"I utterly refuse to walk ten miles through a Polar waste with a gouty foot," McCurdie declared wrathfully.

The chauffeur offered a solution of the difficulty. He would set out alone for Foullis Castle—five miles further on was an inn where he could obtain a horse and trap—and would return for the three gentlemen with another car. In the meanwhile they could take shelter in a little house which they had just passed, some half mile up the road. This was agreed to. The chauffeur went on cheerily enough with a lamp, and the three travelers with another lamp started off in the opposite direction. As far as they could see they were in a long, desolate valley, a sort of No Man's Land, deathly silent. The eastern sky had cleared somewhat, and they faced a loose rack through which one pale star was dimly visible.

"I'm a man of science," said McCurdie as they trudged through the snow, "and I dismiss the supernatural as contrary to reason; but I have Highland blood in my veins that plays me exasperating tricks. My reason tells me that this place is only a commonplace moor, yet it seems like a Valley of Bones haunted by malignant spirits who have lured us here to our destruction. There's something guiding us now. It's just uncanny."

"Why on earth did we ever come?" croaked Biggleswade.

Lord Boyne answered: "The Koran says, 'Nothing can befall us but what God hath destined for us.' So why worry?"

"Because I'm not a Mohammedan," retorted Biggleswade.

"You might be worse," said Boyne.

Presently the dim outline of the little house grew perceptible. A faint light shone from the window. It stood unfenced by any kind of hedge or railing a few feet away from the road in a little hollow beneath some rising ground. As far as they could discern in the darkness when they drew near, the house was a mean, dilapidated hovel. A guttering candle stood on the inner sill of the small window and afforded a vague view into a mean interior. Boyne held up the lamp so that its rays fell full on the door. As he did so, an exclamation broke from his lips and he hurried forward, followed by the others. A man's body lay huddled together on the snow by the threshold. He was dressed like a peasant, in old corduroy trousers and rough coat, and a handkerchief was knotted round his neck. In his hand he grasped the neck of a broken bottle. Boyne set the lamp on the ground and the three bent down together over the man. Close by the neck lay the rest of the broken bottle, whose contents had evidently run out into the snow.

"Drunk?" asked Biggleswade.

Boyne felt the man and laid his hand on his heart.

"No," said he, "dead."

McCurdie leaped to his full height. "I told you the place was uncanny!" he cried. "It's fey." Then he hammered wildly at the door.

There was no response. He hammered again till it rattled. This time a faint prolonged sound like the wailing of a strange sea-creature was heard from within the house. McCurdie turned round, his teeth chattering.

"Did ye hear that, Boyne?"

"Perhaps it's a dog," said the Professor.

Lord Boyne, the man of action, pushed them aside and tried the door-handle. It yielded, the door stood open, and the gust of cold wind entering the house extinguished the candle within. They entered and found themselves in a miserable stone-paved kitchen, furnished with poverty-stricken meagerness—a wooden chair or two, a dirty table, some broken crockery, old cooking utensils, a flyblown missionary society almanac, and a fireless grate. Boyne set the lamp on the table.

"We must bring him in," said he.

They returned to the threshold, and as they were bending over to grip the dead man the same sound filled the air, but this time louder, more intense, a cry of great agony. The sweat dripped from McCurdie's forehead. They lifted the dead man and brought him into the room, and after laying him on a dirty strip of carpet they did their best to straighten the stiff limbs. Biggleswade put on the table a bundle which he had picked up outside. It contained some poor provisions—a loaf, a piece of fat bacon, and a paper of tea. As far as they could guess (and as they learned later they guessed rightly) the man was the master of the house, who, coming home blind drunk from some distant inn, had fallen at his own threshold and got frozen to death. As they could not unclasp his fingers from the broken bottle neck they had to let him clutch it as a dead warrior clutches the hilt of his broken sword.

Then suddenly the whole place was rent with another and yet another long, soul-piercing moan of anguish.

"There's a second room," said Boyne, pointing to a door. "The sound comes from there."

He opened the door, peeped in, and then, returning for the lamp, disappeared, leaving McCurdie and Biggleswade in the pitch darkness, with the dead man on the floor.

"For heaven's sake, give me a drop of whisky," said the Professor, "or I shall faint."

Presently the door opened and Lord Boyne appeared in the shaft of light. He beckoned to his companions.

"It is a woman in childbirth," he said in his even, tired voice. "We must aid her. She appears unconscious. Does either of you know anything about such things?"

They shook their heads, and the three looked at each other in dismay. Masters of knowledge that had won them world-wide fame and honor, they stood helpless, abashed before this, the commonest phenomenon of nature.

"My wife had no child," said McCurdie.

"I've avoided women all my life," said Biggleswade.

"And I've been too busy to think of them. God forgive me," said Boyne.

The history of the next two hours was one that none of the three men ever cared to touch upon. They did things blindly, instinctively, as men do when they come face to face with the elemental. A fire was made, they knew not how, water drawn they knew not whence, and a kettle boiled. Boyne, accustomed to command, directed. The others obeyed. At his suggestion they hastened to the wreck of the car and came staggering back beneath rugs and traveling bags which could supply clean linen and needful things, for amid the poverty of the house they could find nothing fit for human touch or use. Early they saw that the woman's strength was failing, and that she could not live. And there, in that nameless hovel, with death on the pitiful bed, the three great men went through the pain and the horror and squalor of birth, and they knew that they had never yet stood before so great a mystery.

With the first wail of the newly born infant a last convulsive shudder passed through the frame of the unconscious mother. Then three or four short gasps for breath, and the spirit passed away. She was dead. Professor Biggleswade threw a corner of the sheet over her face, for he could not bear to see it.

They washed and dried the child as any crone of a midwife would have done, and dipped a small sponge which had always remained unused in a cut-glass bottle in Boyne's dressing-bag in the hot milk and water of Biggleswade's thermos bottle, and put it to his lips; and then they wrapped him up warm in some of their own woolen undergarments, and took him into the kitchen and placed him on a bed made of their fur coats in front of the fire. As the last piece of fuel was exhausted they took one of the wooden chairs and broke it up and cast it into the blaze. And then they raised the dead man from the strip of carpet and carried him into the bedroom and laid him reverently by the side of his dead wife, after which they left the dead in darkness and returned to the living. And the three grave men stood over the wisp of flesh that had been born a male into the world. Then, their task being accomplished, reaction came, and even Boyne, who had seen death in many lands, turned faint. But the others, losing control of their nerves, shook like men stricken with palsy.

Suddenly McCurdie cried in a high-pitched voice, "My

God! Don't you feel it?" and clutched Boyne by the arm. An expression of terror came on his iron features. "There! It's here with us."

Little Professor Biggleswade sat on a corner of the table and wiped his forehead.

"I heard it. I feel it. It was like the beating of wings."

"It's the fourth time," said McCurdie. "The first time was just before I accepted the Deverills' invitation. The second in the railway carriage this afternoon. The third on the way here. This is the fourth."

Biggleswade plucked nervously at the fringe of whisker under his jaws and said faintly, "It's the fourth time up to now. I thought it was fancy."

"I have felt it, too," said Boyne. "It is the Angel of Death." And he pointed to the room where the dead man and woman lay.

"For God's sake let us get away from this," cried Biggleswade.

"And leave the child to die, like the others?" said Boyne.

"We must see it through," said McCurdie.

A silence fell upon them as they sat round by the blaze with the new-born babe wrapped in its odd swaddling clothes asleep on the pile of fur coats, and it lasted until Sir Angus McCurdie looked at his watch.

"Good Lord," said he, "it's twelve o'clock."

"Christmas morning," said Biggleswade.

"A strange Christmas," mused Boyne.

McCurdie put up his hand. "There it is again! The beating of wings." And they listened like men spellbound. McCurdie kept his hand uplifted, and gazed over their heads at the wall, and his gaze was that of a man in a trance, and he spoke:

"Unto us a child is born, unto us a son is given——"

Boyne sprang from his chair, which fell behind him with a crash.

"Man—what the devil are you saying?"

Then McCurdie rose and met Biggleswade's eyes staring at him through the great round spectacles, and met the eyes of Boyne. A pulsation like the beating of wings stirred the air.

The three wise men shivered with a queer exaltation.

Something strange, mystical, dynamic had happened. It was as if scales had fallen from their eyes and they saw with a new vision. They stood together humbly, divested of all their greatness, touching one another like children, as if seeking mutual protection, and they looked, with one accord, irresistibly compelled, at the child.

At last McCurdie unbent his black brows and said hoarsely:

"It was not the Angel of Death, Boyne, but another Messenger that drew us here."

The tiredness seemed to pass away from the great administrator's face, and he nodded his head with the calm of a man who has come to the quiet heart of a perplexing mystery.

"It's true," he murmured. "Unto us a child is born, unto us a son is given. Unto the three of us."

Biggleswade took off his great round spectacles and wiped them.

"Gaspar, Melchior, Balthazar. But where are the gold, frankincense and myrrh?"

"In our hearts, man," said McCurdie.

The babe cried and stretched its tiny limbs.

Instinctively they all knelt down together to discover if possible and administer ignorantly to its wants. The scene had the appearance of an adoration.

Then these three wise, lonely, childless men who, in furtherance of their own greatness, had cut themselves adrift from the sweet and simple things of life and from the kindly ways of their brethren, and had grown old in unhappy and profitless wisdom, knew that an inscrutable Providence had led them as it had led three Wise Men of old, on a Christmas morning long ago, to a nativity which should give them a new wisdom, a new link with humanity, a new spiritual outlook, a new hope.

And when their watch was ended they wrapped up the babe with precious care, and carried him with them, an inalienable joy and possession, into the great world.

A CHRISTMAS CONFESSION[14]
Agnes McClelland Daulton

Philamaclique lay wrapped softly in snow. The trees arching the wide streets swayed in the stinging winter wind and silently dropped their white plumes upon the head of the occasional pedestrian. Over the old town peace brooded. The snow deadened the passing footstep; the runners of the rude sleds, the hoofs of the farm horses, made no sound; sleepy quiet prevailed but for the rare jingle of sleigh-bells or the gay calling of children's voices.

The rollicking morning sun, having set the town a-glitter without adding a hint of warmth, smiled broadly as he peeped into the snowy-curtained window of a little red brick house on the north side of High Street. Here in the quaint, low sitting-room he found good cheer a-plenty. The red geraniums on the window-sill, the worn but comfortable furniture, the crackling wood fire upon the hearth, the dozing cat upon the hearth-rug, even the creaking of the rocking-chairs, whispered of warmth and rest and homeliness.

"So I just run over to tell you, seein' the snow was too deep for you to get out to prayer-meetin'," wheezed Mrs. Keel, blinking at the sun and creaking heavily back and forth in the old rush-bottomed rocker. "Says I to Joel at breakfast, 'Granny Simmers will be pleased as Punch, for she always did love a frolic, so I'll just run over and tell her while Mellie is washin' the dishes and I'm waitin' for the bread to raise'."

"It was real kind of you, Sister Keel, with your asthmy an' rheumatiz," quavered Granny, folding her checked breakfast shawl more closely about her slender shoulders, as she sat excitedly poised like a little gray bird on the edge of her chair. "Jest to think of us Methodists havin' a Christmas-tree after all these years. My! how I wish it had come in John's time! I remember once, when we was livin' out on the farm, says he to me, 'Polly, if the preacher says we'll have a tree this year, you and me'll hitch up Dolly an' go to town an' buy a gif' fer every man, woman, an' child.' Dolly was our

---

[14] By permission of the author and the "Outlook."

bay buggy-beast, an' the best mare in the neighborhood, so John was as choice of her as he was of me 'most, an' that was a deal for him to offer."

"Law, Granny, how well I remember him and you ridin' so happy in that little green wicker sleigh!" exclaimed Mrs. Keel, as she ponderously drew herself from the deeps of her chair. "I must be goin' now. It was awful nice of Brother Sutton to decide for the Christmas tree when he found the infant class was achin' for it. His face was beamin' last night like a seryphim. The children are about wild; Emmie says she wants a pony; guess we'd have some trouble hangin' that on the tree! Mart wants a gold watch and chain, and Billy says marbles and a gun is good enough for him; but I reckon they'll all take what they can get. Joel said this mornin' he's afraid there'll be lots of achin' hearts. There is them little Cotties—who's a-goin' to give to them, and the Jacksons, and old Miss Nellie, and Widow Theat. I don't see how the Millers can do much for Tessie; and poor old Sister Biddle, says she to me last night as we was comin' out, says she, 'It'll be awful sweet to hear Brother Knisley readin' out, Mis' Sallie Biddle; seems 'most as if I couldn't stand it, it'll be so sweet. I ain't had a Christmas gif' since Biddle was courtin' me sixty years ago.' The poor old body was just chucklin' over it; but who's goin' to give her anything, I'd like to know?"

"Oh, my me!" sighed Granny, clasping her little wrinkled hands wistfully as she stood at the open door. "I ain't thought of the gif's. It was the lights, and the candles a-twinklin', an' the music, an' the children most bustin' with gladness and wishes. Land! when I was a little girl, how I used to wish we was Moravians; they was always havin' trees, or candle feasts, or children's feasts, or Easterin's, an' us Methodists didn't have no excitement 'cept revivals. Law me, what am I sayin'!" she broke off with a chuckle. "As if I didn't thank the Lord every night for makin' me a Methodist bred, a Methodist born, a Methodist till I die. It's the children I'm thinkin' about."

Mrs. Keel laughed and held up a fat reproving finger as she called from the gate:

"I guess you ain't growed up yourself, Granny, for all

your eighty years. I've said to Joel often, says I, 'There ain't a child in this town that is younger at heart than Granny Simmers,' and says he, 'Ner a child that's sweeter ner prettier!'"

"My me!" whispered Granny as she closed the door, her soft wrinkled cheeks delicately flushed at the unexpected compliment. "John said I'd never git over bein' a girl, an' here I be blushin' like a fool 'cause old Joel Keel says I ain't bad-lookin'."

There was much bustling going on in the trim little "brick" that morning. Martha Morris, Granny's "help," had never known her mistress to be so concerned about the crispness of the pepper-cakes, the spiciness of the pig and horse ginger cookies, the brownness of the twisted doughnuts, or the flakiness of the mince pies that were resting by noon in savory richness on the pantry shelf. Then, when dinner was over and the dishes washed, Granny demanded that she herself be taken in hand.

"Law, Granny, you ain't goin' up town in such a snow as this!" protested Martha, as she lovingly tucked the thin white hair under the velvet cap and folded the kerchief about her neck.

"Indeed I am, Marthy," replied Granny with prompt decision. "The sun is shinin' grand, an' Billy Sharp went along with the snow shovel while you was washin' the dishes. Just wrap me up warm an' I'll get along first rate."

"Better let me go, too," argued Martha, as she pinned Granny's "Bay State" firmly under her chin with the big glass brooch with its precious lock of gray hair safely inclosed, and tied her nubia over her cap. "You might slip and fall. I won't feel safe one minute till you are back home."

"Land, Marthy! every born soul knows me. Ain't I Granny to the hull town, for all I ain't got a chick ner a child? My me! it's sixty years since John an' me laid 'Rastus away; fifty since little Mary, her father's darlin', slipped off to heaven. Seems like my old heart goes out in love to everybody 'count of them three, John and my two babies, waitin' for me in one of the Father's mansions. Hope there's a chimbly corner—John always loved it so on a winter's night; an' I hope there's roses growin' by the doorstep, so it will seem like home to 'em all; an', Marthy, if I fall there ain't a soul but would be ready to pick me up, an' a smile for me, bless 'em! I jest wonder sometimes how it comes everybody is so kind an' good. It's a lovely world, that's what it is."

"Now," said Granny to herself, as she teetered along on the icy walk toward the busy stores, "John said a gif' for every man, woman, an' child. Guess I can remember the hull lot, as there's only six men an' I've got the women writ down; an' for the children, well, I'll buy till my money gives out, an' I reckon I'll get enough. Kind of pitiful about Sister Biddle. My! what a dashin', lovely girl she was when I first see her at the Beals' apple-parin'! She was Sallie Neely then, pretty as a picture, hair and eyes like jet, an' cheeks pink as roses, an' so tall an' slender. I recollect how she picked me up an' whirled me round; she was as light as a feather on her feet, an' said, 'Polly Whitehead, was there ever such a morsel of a girl as you are? If I was a man, I'd marry you 'fore night.' An' John said he said to himself she'd have had a hard time of it, for he made up his mind then an' there to have me himself. Yes, I'll get Sallie Neely a red plush album an' put John's picture in it; she'd admire to get that!"

Granny hesitated.

"Well, did you ever!" she gasped. "I ain't never thought of it before; who'll give anything to me, Polly Simmers? John would, dear John, but he's gone, an' I ain't got a blood akin in the town, an' they've all got such a lot to give to. Mebby I wouldn't mind much, but it—would—be kind of mortifyin' to be the only one forgot, for I'm bound they sha'n't be another soul left out. I wonder if I dare!"

Long shafts of light from the bare, uncurtained windows of the old church lay across the snow, as the cracked bell jangled through the crisp air its Christmas greeting. The jingle of sleigh-bells, the creaking of the runners, merry voices, bits of song, gay laughter, united in a Christmas carol redolent with Christmas spirit—Peace on earth, good will to men.

Granny, leaning on Martha's strong arm, fairly shivered with excitement and delight. She knew that not a soul called by the clamor of that bell had been forgotten. There had been no need of stinting, for Granny's acres were broad and fruitful and her wants few. Gift after gift had her withered hands tied into pretty parcels. The pen had creaked and sputtered across the paper as she marked them, for she had refused all help from curious but loving Martha, only asking that there be a good fire made in the air-tight stove in the spare chamber. There she worked alone, but happy, Martha well knew, as she stood with her ear pressed to the crack of the door, having found the keyhole stopped with cotton.

"While shepherds watched their flocks by night,
All seated on the ground,
The angels of the Lord came down,
And glory shone around,"

quavered the old voice. And Martha never knew it was not Granny Simmers who sang so joyfully within, but pretty Polly Whitehead in the choir of the old meeting-house, looking on the same hymn-book with handsome young John Simmers, the catch of the valley.

"Just fairly takes my breath away," wheezed Mrs. Keel, meeting Granny at the door of the church. "Don't seem like the same place. Now ain't it pretty?"

Granny caught her breath.

Could this be the little church she knew so well? Before that altar, she, a bride, had stood with John; there they had carried Baby Rastus and Mary for baptism; there the casket had rested that awful day when she had found herself alone.

A crude little sanctuary, always bare and cheerless to the beauty-loving eye, yet rich with tenderest memories to Granny; to-night, ablaze with lights, roped with greenery, gay with flags, joyful with the hum of merry voices, it seemed some new and unexplored fairyland. And there upon the rostrum in all its glory, tall, straight, and beautiful, twinkling with candles, festooned with strings of popcorn and cranberries, glittering with tinsel stars and silver crowns, adorned with bobinet stockings cubby and knubby with candy and nuts, hung with packages big and little, stood the tree, the tree!

"Let me set down till I get my breath, Marthy," cackled Granny, excitedly. "Jest get my specks out of my pocket, will you, child? My, my! if only John an' 'Rastus an' little Mary was here now!"

Sitting straight in the corner of her pew, her spectacles on the extreme end of her nose, her bonnet tipped rakishly to one side in her joy, her black-woolen-mittened hands crossed demurely in her lap, she, the happiest child of them all, listened to the exercise. Carolers and speech-makers found naught but sympathy in her sweet face.

When the last speaker had tiptoed to his seat and the infant class was growing unruly in the amen corner—the sight of the bobinet stockings and mysterious packages being too much for the patience of their baby souls—Brother Knisley carefully mounted the step-ladder and the distribution of the gifts began.

"Billy Keel, Tessie Miller—Dora Jackson, Mrs. Sallie Biddle," haltingly read the Brother. The sight of Sallie's wild delight over the red plush album almost moved Granny to tears. "Mrs. Polly Simmers, Martha Morris—Mrs. Polly Simmers, Mrs. Joel Keel—Mrs. Polly Simmers," then again and again until the pew in which Granny sat was filled and overflowed into her lap. Wide-eyed, at first happy, then more and more distressed grew the small face under its rakish bonnet.

"Mrs. Polly Simmers, Miss Nelly Sanford—Mrs. Polly Simmers—" Oh, would they never cease? Martha, chuckling with joy, gathered them in one by one.

"There, Granny, guess it ain't hard to see who is the favorite in this town," she whispered vehemently. "Law's sakes, if here ain't another; that makes twenty-one! Wonder what it is? It feels for all the world like a milk-strainer, but I never heard of such a thing hung on a tree."

Granny's face flushed, puckered, and flamed into crimson.

"Don't talk so loud, Marthy. Ain't you got no manners! Oh, whatever, ever shall I do?"

"Do?" wheezed Mrs. Keel, leaning over the back of her pew. "Do? Why, take every one of 'em and enjoy 'em. Ain't one but what's filled with love, even if it is a milk-strainer, though I can't see why anybody come to think of that."

"Goodness knows, we needed it bad enough," returned Martha, shrilly, over Mrs. Keel's shoulder. "I've been jawsmithin' about it fer the last month, but she wus always forgittin' it."

"Looks to me as if that was a coal-hod," remarked Billy Keel, prodding a bulky bundle on Granny's lap with a fat forefinger.

"You hush up, Billy Keel," exclaimed Granny, resentfully. "I ain't makin' any remark about your gif's, be I?"

Billy, as much astonished as if one of his pet doves had pecked him, hung his head in shame.

"Mrs. Polly Simmers," announced the Brother, pompously, as he slowly clambered to the floor; "that is the last gif'."

"Ahem!" began Brother Sutton, his mild old eyes beaming with joy as he looked over his congregation. He drew his tall length to its uttermost, set the tips of his fingers together, and teetered slowly back and forth from toe to heel. "Ahem! It has been gratifying indeed to see so much generosity. But most of all it has pleased us to see that the receiver of the lion's share has been our aged sister, Mrs. Polly Simmers. It is delightful that her unselfish life, her high sense of honor, her sweet sympathy, has been appreciated."

Granny, her face deathly pale, every hint of the Christmas joy of the early evening gone from her eyes, now dulled with agony, arose trembling in her pew.

But Brother Sutton's eyes brightened as he saw her.

"Our aged sister wishes to speak to us, I see," he said, kindly, "and I know all the little folks will be very quiet."

"I jest want to say," gasped Granny, clutching nervously at the pew in front of her, "I jest want to say that I'm a wicked old sinner, that I'm a liar and a cheat and a disgrace to my church."

The audience, as if electrified, turned toward her in amazement; even the children dropped their gifts to stare at Granny, as she stood pale, wild-eyed, and self-accusing.

"My heart's 'most bustin' with your goodness," went on the quavering old voice, "and I've got to tell or I'll die 'fore mornin', an' I can't go to John an' 'Rastus an' little Mary with a lie on my soul, even if the good Lord would forgive me for their sakes an' let me in. That day I set out to buy a gif' fer every man, woman, an' child in the church the devil kept tellin' me they wouldn't be nothin' fer old Granny Simmers, an' the more I thought the more I got a hankerin' to hear my name read with the rest; an' the bad man he said to me, says he, 'Granny Simmers, why don't you buy some things for yourself an' put them on the tree; nobody'd be the wiser. Needn't buy anything extravagant,' says he, 'jest plain needcessities that Marthy's been urgin'. Since you are buyin' for everybody in the church, there's no harm—John said every man, woman, an' child.'

"I didn't have an idee that anybody would think of old me, so I says to the bad man at last, says I, 'Jest a few things, devil, jest a few—a milk-strainer that Marthy has been jawin' about, a coal-hod, a tack-hammer, an' a new calico I had been needin' for some time; then I got a couple of new pie tins an' a soapstone 'cause Marthy cracked the old one. An' I never once thought of it bein' a sin, an' I tied 'em up with ribbons an' tissue-paper, an' sung as I did it—I was just as happy as a child. But when I saw how you'd all remembered me, an' heard Brother Knisley readin' gif' after gif', an' I seed how I'd doubted your friendship an' knowed you never dreamed I was actin' a lie, I just felt so pusly mean I couldn't stand that you should believe all them gif's come from love. I guess I ain't fit for anything but churchin'."

Shaking with sobs, the little woman dropped back in her seat to be received into Martha's loving arms.

"Brother Sutton"—it was Mrs. Keel's asthmatic wheeze that broke the silence—"Brother Sutton, I've got a few words to say, and as I look about at the streamin' eyes of this congregation I know you'll all agree with me. If there is a dear saint on earth, who has stood by us in our sorrows an' our joys, who's hovered over our death-beds and welcomed our babies, it's Granny Simmers. If there's a soul of honor, a childlike conscience, and one of the Lord's own, it is this blessed little woman. I don't know how the rest of you feel, but my heart's 'most broke for the poor little soul. Ain't no more sin in her gentle little heart than there is in a baby's."

"Amen!" came from every side.

But Brother Sutton, his face beaming with tenderness, had come swiftly down the aisle and was bending over

Granny.

"Sister," he said, taking her little wrinkled hands in his, "believe me, God forgave you this before you asked it; and as for us, look about you, and what do you see in the faces of your friends? Come one and all and give her your tenderest greetings."

Kneeling by the bed that night in her little white gown and cap, as she pressed her face in the pillow where John's head had rested for so many years, Granny poured out a humble and a contrite heart. "An', Lord," she added, "please tell John an' the children that I give every one of them things to Mis' Cottie, an' I'm startin' out again with falterin' steps toward the heavenly home."

THE DAY OF DAYS[15]
Elsie Singmaster

Upon three hundred and sixty-five days in the year Miss Mary Britton gave; upon one day Miss Mary received. That day was the day before Christmas.

Miss Mary did not receive, however, from the same persons to whom she gave. Miss Mary gave to all the village, a lift here in sickness, a little present of money there in case of need. To Sally Young went a new bonnet, to old Carrie Burrage a warm shawl, to the preacher and his large family unnumbered articles. Miss Mary took old Carrie Burrage, tiresome, ungrateful, self-centered, into her house for a month; she took the Arundel baby for three.

None of these persons remembered Miss Mary at Christmas. The village was poor; it considered Miss Mary rich; it expected her to be generous. Miss Mary's present came from far away New York; it was the most treasured gift received in the state of Ohio. Years ago, when the Britton fortune was large, when kinsfolk were numerous, when the broad doors of this Britton house stood open to relatives removed to the fourth degree, a young cousin had spent a happy summer under its roof. He had been ill; here, in the country, ministered to with unfailing kindness, he had fully recovered.

Since then, he had never failed to remember his hosts at Christmas time. He had never come again; he grew to be a famous man with whom it was an honor to be connected, but he was never too busy to remember the tastes of his cousins. Miss Mary's father had had his magazine, her mother a bit of lace, Miss Mary's brother a riding whip, Miss Mary herself a book. After the father died, two gifts came to Miss Mary's mother; when all had gone but the lonely daughter, her gift was quadrupled. Of late years, the gift had increased—instead of four books, Miss Mary received twenty.

"You have now more time for reading," wrote the cousin.

---

[15] By permission of the author and the "Youth's Companion." This story was printed in the "Youth's Companion," December 23, 1926.

"If my taste in books does not please you, you must tell me. It will be just as easy to send you what you like as what I like."

Miss Mary had no quarrel with her cousin's taste. If he had sent her a Greek dictionary, she would have treasured it. But he sent her the books she loved, novels, essays, poetry. With them came always a letter with reminders of that happy summer, and expressions of affection.

The box came usually on the last train on Christmas Eve. It was sometimes earlier, but it had never yet been late. Miss Mary always opened the box herself, with many failures of hammer and screwdriver to do proper execution, with excited examination of bindings, to see that no harm had come to them on their long journey, with pauses and exclamations while titles and frontispieces were examined. Miss Mary had this year a new bookcase for which she had been a long time saving the extra pennies that remained after baker's and butcher's bills were paid and the repairs made on the homestead and the outfit for the Arundel baby purchased. The bookcase was already half filled with the overflow from Miss Mary's other bookcases.

Miss Mary woke on the morning of the day before Christmas with flushed cheeks and an accelerated pulse. This condition was no warning of approaching illness, it indicated only Miss Mary's usual condition of excitement on this day. For three months past, the Arundel baby in the next room had wakened her drowsy hostess at the crack of dawn, but this morning Miss Mary was dressed before the Arundel baby had opened her brown eyes. Miss Mary's excitement, however, was not entirely that of joyful anticipation; it was partly alarm. Each year, she prepared herself for disappointment, for the coming of the evening train without any precious freight for her. The cousin was old, ten years older than Miss Mary; he could not live to send her gifts on every Christmas, and when he died, when his box failed to come, she would be alone in the world, without kin, without interests beyond the sleepy village, with nothing to look forward to all her life long.

"I must be prepared for it," Miss Mary often said to herself.

But she never succeeded in preparing herself. When she woke, she sprang from bed as she used to spring in her childhood.

"I am like the children who call out 'Christmas gift' and pound at the door," said Miss Mary, amused at herself.

It was about nine o'clock when the Arundel baby's aunt came for her. She was to have come at eight; she was, indeed, to have come yesterday and last week, and, indeed, last month. But the Arundel baby belonged to a weak and shiftless family.

She was much inconvenienced by the delay of the baby's aunt. To the day before Christmas Miss Mary postponed various duties, her intention being to keep the hours as full as possible so that the time might not drag until the evening train.

The house was yet to be put in order, the wreaths must be hung in the windows, sundry baskets must be packed for distribution in the morning and sundry presents be wrapped for the butcher's boy and the baker's man and for James Vanderslice, the expressman. To the baker's man Miss Mary gave a tie, to the butcher's boy a pair of suspenders, alternating the gifts with the years, but to James Vanderslice, eagerly watched for at twilight, she gave both, and a little present of money besides.

The Arundel baby's aunt not only came an hour late, but she stayed for an hour talking about nothing.

The aunt began presently to gossip, and Miss Mary moved uneasily in her chair. She did not like gossip or persons who repeated it. Fortunately, the baker's horn interrupted with its loud demand, and Miss Mary asked to be excused. When she returned, she brought with her the baby's hat and coat. Miss Mary was able to dismiss unpleasant persons without their being aware of it. She wrapped the baby up herself and tucked her into the carriage she had bought and kissed her goodbye.

"She has been a good girl," she said. "You must bring her to see me every week. When she is a little older, I will begin to teach her to read and afterwards to sew patchwork. That is the way I was brought up."

Miss Mary remained standing, and the baby's aunt had

perforce to remain standing too.

"A child is a great care," said she, as she raised the corner of her apron to her pale eyes.

"Not if she's managed with system," answered Miss Mary in her curt way. "This baby's been very little care to me; she need be very little to you if you're systematic."

"I'm sure I'll try," said the baby's aunt, as she wiped away more tears.

Then the baby carriage was trundled down the street. Miss Mary suffered a slight pang as she saw how cheerfully the baby went, how willing she was to associate with unattractive incompetence, and a sharper pang as she beheld the bump with which the coach took the first crossing; then she went indoors. This was her day, the happiest day of all the year; she could think no more of the Arundel baby.

Miss Mary went first of all to put the baby's room in order. She took down the white crib and carried the pieces, one by one, into the attic. Except the bed, nothing belonging to the baby remained, since all had been sent earlier in the day to the house of the aunt. Then, with capable strokes of her strong arms, she swept the room. She had not been brought up to work of this kind, but when change of fortune made it necessary she was quick to teach herself. This morning the swift moving back and forth of the broom gave her pleasure.

When the baby's room was finished, Miss Mary went to look at the clock. She was surprised to see that it was only half past ten. She was conscious of a jumping feeling in her heart, and she looked out the window as if to ease it. She saw nothing but the familiar houses with their familiar dooryards. It was Miss Mary's custom to look often out the window on the day before Christmas.

Now, sternly, as usual she began to prepare herself for disappointment.

"Nothing is more probable than that it will not come," said Miss Mary.

At eleven o'clock, having wrapped her packages and packed her baskets, she looked at the clock again, expecting the hand to stand at twelve. Thereupon she determined that she would look no more. Her simple lunch was usually eaten at one; she decided to have it earlier, in order to have a long afternoon for what she wished to do. In her heart of hearts she knew that the chief of her occupations would be waiting.

Miss Mary washed her dishes slowly, then she brushed up the kitchen, which needed no brushing. She wished now that she was only beginning her lunch instead of finishing it.

Again Miss Mary went to the window and looked out. The street was still empty, and at sight of it Miss Mary shivered.

"I must not expect anything," she said sternly.

By half past one she had tied up those of her Christmas packages which remained and had hung the holly wreaths in the front windows. Then she cried out "O dear!" and went to the door. She had not been mistaken: drops of water were falling, the sky was thickly overclouded, the wind was east. Already it sighed mournfully round the corner of the house.

"A rainy Christmas Eve!" cried Miss Mary tragically. "A rainy Christmas Day!"

At two o'clock, she began to give her sitting-room an unnecessary dusting; at half past, she sat down at the window with some sewing; at three, she went to the door again, as if pulled by a rope. When she saw the expressman coming down the street, she clutched the side of the door. But the expressman stopped at the corner house and then turned the head of his old white horse back toward the station.

At half past three, Miss Mary took up some crocheting. The Arundel baby would need new petticoats in the spring, and Miss Mary realized that new petticoats, and the lace for them, if any were had, would have to come from her. But the thread clung to her fingers, the needle slipped from her hand.

"It's the rheumatism," she said to herself, grimly. "Old age is here."

At four o'clock Miss Mary took a book, and in three minutes laid it down. It was one of Cousin John's books.

"I am a goose," she announced aloud to her quiet house. "I could even buy a few books for myself and make shift to subscribe to a few magazines if the box does not come. But,"—here Miss Mary covered her face with her hands—"it will mean that I am alone in the world!"

At half past four Miss Mary began to prepare supper,

though she usually ate at six. She no longer made excuses to herself; she did not pretend that she was having supper early so as to make the evening long; she sought only to fill the next minute and the next; she was reckless about the later hours.

The evening train came in at six. It was only a country way train with a short run, and it was on time, even on Christmas Eve. With a great jump of her heart, Miss Mary heard its familiar whistle. Allowing for all James Vanderslice's slowness, he should reach her house in fifteen minutes. It was probable that hers would be the only package he would have to deliver.

Moving with a slow step, she descended to the cellar and put coal on the furnace fire. Temptingly, mockingly, the hammer and screwdriver seemed to thrust themselves to the top of the toolbox on the table which she had to pass. Miss Mary did not touch them. She played the part of expecting nothing.

When Miss Mary came up from the cellar, the hands of the clock pointed to twenty minutes after six. She grew red, then pale. Then she opened the door and stood with the rain beating against her. The street was dark and quiet.

"He *must* come," whispered Miss Mary.

But the expressman did not come. When Miss Mary went indoors, it was half past six. Until seven she walked up and down her sitting-room. Then her lips tightened.

"I am going to bed," she said aloud.

Miss Mary fixed her fires for the night; she set out the milk pail on the shelf on the back porch; she wound the clock and took her lamp and climbed the stairway and undressed and lay down in her bed. Then, metaphorically and actually, she turned her face to the wall.

But at eight o'clock she was still awake. At half past eight she sprang from bed, thinking she heard a rap at the door; at nine she lighted her lamp and looked at the clock. All within and without the house was as silent as midnight. Then poor Miss Mary yielded herself to despair.

"I do not know what is the matter with me. This had to happen sometime! But I am utterly desolate and forlorn. Christmas is a dreadful time when you grow old. But I have been trying to prepare myself for years! I do not know what is the matter with me."

The ticking of the clock seemed to fill the quiet house. Miss Mary grew more and more nervous. Again she sprang from bed.

"If I have some exercise, perhaps I shall sleep!"

But exercise did not bring sleep. Miss Mary went into her father's room and her brother's room, and into her mother's room, which had lately been the Arundel baby's, and tears ran down her cheeks. It was not a journey from which she need have expected much repose of spirit.

"If they could only come back!" she cried. "If things could only be as they used to be on Christmas! If I were only not alone in the world!"

Then Miss Mary did an extraordinary thing. She was standing in her mother's room, where the Arundel baby's bed had stood. In this room her childish difficulties had been adjusted, her childish troubles soothed. She lifted her head as if she heard a voice speaking to her, and then she laughed almost hysterically.

"I *will* have a merry Christmas," she cried suddenly.

At once, hurrying back to her bedroom, she began to dress feverishly, hastily, with fingers that trembled over hooks and buttons. Still she talked to herself. She seemed to be saying over and over that she would get herself a Christmas gift. When she was dressed, she hurried down the steps at perilous speed and went into the cellar and put the draught on the furnace. Apparently grief had crazed her.

Still Miss Mary's strange course was not at an end. She put on her shawl and bonnet and opened the door and went out, forgetting to turn the key, and hurried down the street in the rain without an umbrella. Following straight the course that the Arundel baby's aunt had taken, she knocked at a mean little door. Within was a light and the sound of voices. In answer to a loud "Come in!" Miss Mary opened the door and entered.

The Arundel baby's aunt, however lugubrious and tearful she might be in the presence of Miss Mary, had other moments when she allowed herself to be merry and comfortable. She was now surrounded by her friends,—Miss

Mary recognized each one of the doubtful guests,—refreshments were being passed, hilarity was at its height. The Arundel baby—Miss Mary saw her at the same instant that she beheld the hands of the clock pointing to midnight—lay asleep in her carriage in the corner. She had not been undressed; her cheeks were flushed as if a slight fever might have added a stain of red to cheeks already red from crying.

Miss Mary said not a word in reproof; she lifted the baby from the carriage and took her under her shawl and bade the baby's aunt come to see her on the morrow and stalked out. Neither the baby's aunt nor her guests made reply. They all had been at some time Miss Mary's pensioners; it was more than probable that they would need her help again.

Miss Mary walked with rapid steps back to her house. The clouds had parted, the dashes of rain were fitful, the wind had veered to the north; but she was not aware of the change. In the dark corner of her porch stood a wooden box, and pinned to it was a scrap of paper on which James Vanderslice explained that he would tell her tomorrow why he had been so late in delivering her parcel. Miss Mary saw neither box nor paper; she would not see them until morning.

In the kitchen the fire was glowing, and Miss Mary sat down before it, bonneted and shawled, with the Arundel baby in her arms. She was trembling, her breath came in gasps. Presently she opened the shawl and looked down. The Arundel baby was still sleeping, with her mouth pursed up in her funny fashion, and her damp hair curled tightly over her head. Miss Mary regarded her solemnly, even with awe, as if she beheld some unaccountable object. Then she heaved a long and happy sigh, and her tears began to fall. She remembered that Christmas Day had come; she thought with tender heart of that other Baby, whom she had for a little while forgotten; she prayed that He would help her make the Arundel baby a good girl.

"I shall have something to think of! I shall have someone that is mine! This," said good Miss Mary with trembling lips, "this was what was the matter with me!"

HOLLY AT THE DOOR[16]
Agnes Sligh Turnbull

On the outside—that is, in the smart little suburban town of Branchbrook—Christmas week had begun most auspiciously. A light fall of snow made the whole place look like an old-fashioned holiday greeting card; the neat English stuccos and Colonial clapboards set back in wide lawns, seemed to gather their flocks of clipped little pine and spruce shrubbery closer to them and suggest through their fresh curtained windows the thought of bright wood fires and mistletoe and shining Christmas cheer soon to come.

In the parish room of St. Andrew's small gray stone church the children were practicing carols while pigeons cooed on the roof. And down in the village center great boxes of holly wreaths stood in the street before all the grocery store windows, and bevies of slender little virgin pine trees, ready and waiting for the great moment to which they had been born, leaned against all the shop door-ways.

The postman smiled beneath his staggering load, thinking of later benefactions; and the windows of Beverly's Fine Food Stuffs, the town's most exclusive market, were caparisoned with every delicacy which even a Christmas epicure might desire.

Strangers spoke to each other, children laughed gleefully, shop men made jokes with their customers, everybody was busy, friendly, somehow relaxed from the ordinary conventional aloofness, because Christmas was only five days away. Everything was just as it should be, on the outside.

But on the inside—that is to say, in the big Colonial home of the Bartons which had been built just long enough before prices went up to make it seem now more of an abode of wealth than it really was—here the week had begun in the worst way possible. Monday morning had started with a quarrel.

---

[16] By permission of the author and "McCall's Magazine." Copyright 1926 by "McCall's Magazine."

Alice Barton had not rested well the night before. She had fully planned to spend all Sunday afternoon and evening addressing Christmas cards. That would have seen them all safely in the postman's hands this morning.

But the plan had been frustrated by the Levitts' dropping in for a call, staying to tea and spending the evening. And it had been Tom's fault entirely. He was the one that simply kept them. Of course she had to be decently polite. They sat listening to the radio until eleven. After that she had been too tired to start the cards. And here they were all to do now, this morning, more than a hundred of them, on top of all the regular day's work and the committee meeting at eleven. And she must get a few more hours shopping in! That would be hectic now but there was no help for it. And all her packages were yet to be tied up, and Mrs. Dunlop's bridge-luncheon on Wednesday and Catherine's friend coming Thursday! She *must* not forget about the guest room curtains! Why had she let Catherine have anyone come at Christmas time!

The dull headache she had when she rose became a splitting pain. She scarcely spoke to Tom as she dressed except for one brief and fitting retort to his: "Now don't spend all day in the bathroom. I have to shave!"

She went downstairs, mechanically checking off the things she must tell Delia, the maid.

Tom was down before the children. He opened the front door for the newspaper which Delia always forgot to bring in and came toward the table with his brows drawn. It was not a propitious moment, but the thing had to be done.

"Tom."

"Darned if they haven't given that murderer another reprieve! How do they ever expect to have...."

"Listen, Tom! There's something I want to ask you."

"A pretty kind of justice! Wrap all the little murderers up in pink wool blankets for fear they get cold in the neck, and forget the poor cuss that's been killed! You know, Alice, what ought to be done is this...."

"Yes, but Tom, listen. I'll simply have to have a little more money." (It was dreadful to have to ask him now when he was all stirred up over this thing in the paper!) "I'll just have to do some more shopping, just a few little things I forgot, and I'd rather be free to go about instead of sticking to the charge accounts. If you could give me...."

Tom was suddenly all attention. His dark eyes were looking at her keenly. He broke in.

"Why I gave you an extra twenty-five last Friday."

"I know, Tom, but it took every cent of it for the cards. And even then I had to spend most of the day trying to find respectable ones within my price." Tom's face looked thunderous.

"Do you mean to tell me that it takes *twenty-five dollars* now to send out Christmas cards? *Twenty-five dollars!* Why, Good Heavens, that would buy two tons of coal. That's the sheerest piece of criminal waste I ever heard of!"

Alice's face darkened too. "Well, what are you going to do about it? You know the kind everybody sends us. We can't look like pikers. It would have cost fifty dollars to get the engraved kind I wanted. I won't send out cheap stereotyped ones, so all that's left for me is to try to pick out something artistic and individual, at least for the people we care most about. It's no easy job, and this is the thanks I get!"

"You bet you'll get none from me. Do you know how I feel? I hate Christmas! Nothing but money, money beforehand, and nothing but bills, bills, bills afterward. It's enough to drive a man crazy. And what's the sense of it? You send a lot of cards to people that barely look at 'em and throw 'em in the fire! You women exchange a bunch of junk that you never use. And as a family, we spend money like drunken sailors on a lot of extravagant things we've no business having. And old Dad, poor boob, gets a good dinner out of it and then he pays and pays and pays for the next six months! That's the way I've got it doped out!"

Alice's face was frozen in sharp lines. "If that's the way you feel about it I suppose I needn't hope for my coat."

"Coat! What coat?"

"Tom, as if you didn't know perfectly well what I wanted this year more than anything. The short fur coat! Why I've talked about it all fall. I think every woman in town has one but me. I can't wear my big seal one shopping and marketing! And my cloth one is simply gone! Why, I thought all the time you knew, and that you'd surely...." There were almost tears in her voice.

"So it's come to that, has it! A woman has to have a special kind of fur coat to do her marketing in! Too bad! Well, I'm sorry to disappoint you but you can't bank on one this year—unless you'd like to mortgage the house!"

He got up abruptly from the table. Young Tom and Catherine had just come into the dining room in time for the last speech. They looked at their parents with cool, amused eyes. It was not the first quarrel they had witnessed in the last years since they had left childhood behind. Catherine, a day pupil at Miss Bossart's finishing school, and young Tom, a Senior in High School, were startlingly mature. They were calmer, more cynical, more unemotional than their parents. They touched life with knowing fingers that never trembled. Alice marveled at them.

She rose now too and followed Tom into the library. He sat down a moment at the desk and then flicked her a slip of paper.

"There's fifty. And that's all, remember, until next month's allowance!"

Alice's voice was like cold steel. "Thanks. I'm sure I'll enjoy spending it since it's so very generously given."

Tom did not answer. He got into his overcoat, called a general goodbye and left the house.

Alice came back to the children. Young Tom looked up quizzically. "Well, Mums, that ought to hold him for a while, eh, what?" he remarked as he helped himself hugely to the omelette.

Catherine's brows were slightly puckered. "Say, Mother, am I going to get my watch? Dad was in such a vile humor, I'm scared. Really I'll feel like a pauper down there at Miss Bossart's unless I get something a little bit flossy. And this old watch, I've had since I was twelve. There isn't another round gold one in school. Everything's platinum now! Heavens, it's not much to ask for compared to what most of the girls are getting. Jean and Hilda know they're getting cars of their own! And flocks of them are getting marvelous fur coats."

"Well, you have your new coat," Alice reminded her.

"Oh, yes," Catherine agreed with a faint, deprecating sigh, "such as it is."

Alice opened her lips for a quick remonstrance and closed them again. Oh, what was the use! The children were always ungrateful. They had no real appreciation these days of what their parents gave them. With them it was take, take, take, and never a thought of value received.

Young Tom looked up from his toast and marmalade with his most winning smile.

"Say, Mums, can you let me have a fiver out of your new pile? I'm in the very dickens of a hole."

Alice fastened quick eyes upon him. "Where has your allowance gone?" she asked sharply.

"Well, gee, it's so small to begin with I can hardly see it and then just now round Christmas time there's always such a darned lot of extras!"

Catherine cut in sweetly: "Such as bouquets of orchids for Miss Doris Kane!"

"Orchids!" Alice almost screamed the word. "Tom, you don't mean for a minute to tell me you're sending orchids to a girl! High School children sending orchids! I never in my life heard of anything so wickedly absurd!"

"Well, gosh, Mums, what are you going to do? That's what all the girls want now for the dances, and a fellow can't look like a piker! I've got to order some for to-night. Lend me five, won't you, just to run me over? What we ought to have is a charge account at the florist's. That's what all the other fellows' folks have."

"No doubt," Alice said sarcastically. "It's barely possible that some of your friends' fathers may have more money to pay their bills than your father has. But I suppose you never thought of that! Well, I'll give you five this time, but I don't want you ever to ask me again for such a purpose."

"And now if he's through," Catherine broke in, "what about me? Is there any reason why I should be broke while my handsome young brother sends orchids to Doris Kane? You should see what the girls are giving each other for Christmas. It makes me sick to hand out the things I have. They look like a rummage sale compared with the rest! I did want one decent thing for Jean, but I'm terribly short."

She looked at her mother challengingly.

Alice made a desperate gesture with her hands. "All right," she said, "you can have it. Of course it doesn't matter whether I'm short or not! I'm at the place where I don't care much what happens!"

Her head throbbed miserably as she borrowed the two five-dollar bills from her housekeeping purse and gave them to the children. She had a vivid perception that each thought they should have been tens. Their thanks were scant and careless. They had only received their just due, and scarcely that!

Alice felt sick as she climbed the stairs to the den where she kept her desk. Now for the cards. Christmas was a hard, trying time. She would be glad when it was over.

She began in frantic haste, selecting, addressing, searching her notebook and the telephone directory for streets and numbers. Five, ten, fifteen finished, stamped, ready.

Suddenly she picked up an alien from the carefully chosen mass that lay about her, a cheap little card that she knew she had never bought. Either she or the salesgirl must have caught it up by mistake with some of the others. It was a commonplace little card of the folder variety that carries a sentimental verse inside. Alice opened it mechanically before tossing it into the waste basket. And there beneath her eyes were these words:

Oh what, my dear, of Christmas cheer could anyone wish more,

Than candle-light and you within, and holly at the door!

She stared at the words unbelievingly. Not for thirty years had she thought of that old song. And now suddenly she heard it in her father's voice, just as he used to sing it Christmas after Christmas as he went through the house with his hammer in one hand and a dangling bough of green in the other.

And holly at the door, and holly at the door!

With candle-light and you within, and holly at the door!

She hummed the old melody under her breath, and then she found herself bending over the desk, face in hands, weeping, while over her swept great waves of homesickness, poignant pangs of yearning for a place and a time that had drifted out of her consciousness.

At last she raised her head and leaned it against the high back of the chair. It seemed almost as though invisible fingers had pressed it there, had closed her eyes, had made the pen drop from her passive hand. All at once she was back in the little town of her childhood where she had not been, and where not even her mind had traveled vividly, these long years.

Christmas time in Martinsville! Christmas in the small frame house that had been home. Mother singing blithely as she stuffed the turkey in the kitchen. Father standing proudly by, watching her every movement. For the turkey was an event. One turkey a year, to be ordered after due consideration from one of the farmers near town, to be received with a small flurry of excitement when it arrived and to be picked and prepared for the oven by Mother's own skilful fingers.

"I suppose we should ask Miss Amanda for dinner tomorrow. The Smiths usually have her but they're away this year," Mother was saying.

Father agreed. "Maybe we'd better. It's not nice to think of anybody sitting down all by themselves to a cold bite on Christmas!"

"When we have so much," Mother went on. "You'd better stop and ask her when you go for the mail to-night."

Footsteps on the porch. Father and Mother break into smiles. "There's Alice," they exclaim in unison.

Quick stamping of snow on the scraper, quick opening of the door, a quick rush of cold wind and a quick, joyous child's voice.

"Mother, the holly's come; Father, look at this! Isn't it lovely? Mr. Harris just got in now with the wagon from Wanesburg. And he brought a big box of it. He has wreaths, too, but they're a quarter apiece. I think the bunch is prettier and it was only a dime. Look at the berries!"

The child's cheeks are as scarlet as her red toboggan and sweater, that Mother herself had knitted. Her blue eyes are shining and eager, her light hair tossed by the wind.

"Put it up quick, Father, and I'll get the red ribbon for it."

She flies up stairs, stumbling in her haste.

Suddenly, laughter below, expostulation, hurrying feet in the front hall. "Alice, Alice, don't open the under drawer of my bureau! You *didn't*, did you? Mercy, we had such a scare! The ribbon's in the top drawer, left hand side. Now mind, no looking any where else!"

"And holly at the door...."

Father's big voice booming out happily.

Alice skips down the stairs. "I never peeped! Honestly. But what can it be you have for me? It's something to wear! Oh, I can't wait."

"And holly at the door...."

Father's hammer tapping smartly, then the gay swinging green branch with its brave little bow of red. They all have to go out to admire it.

"And, Father, you should see the church! It's wonderful this year. George Davis and Mr. Parmley climbed up on two ladders and tied the greens to the big cross rafter and fastened a silver star right at the top. It's never been so pretty. And the tree! Mother, it reaches the ceiling! And Mrs. Davis was putting little white lambs under it and shepherds. We saw it when we were there practicing for to-night. Oh, I *hope* I don't forget my speech."

Immediately, concentrated, proud interest. Father and Mother sit down to listen once again. Alice stands in front of the table, her hands primly by her sides, her face upraised in gentle seriousness.

"The milk-white sheep looked up one night,
And there stood an angel all in white,
And though he spoke no words to them,
He was there on the hills of Bethlehem,
That very first Christmas morning!
"The lowing cattle meekly stood
Near to a manger rough and rude...."
On and on goes the sweet childish voice to the end.
"And the time will come, so the wise men say,
When the wolf and the lamb together shall play,
And a little child shall lead the way,
The child of that first Christmas morning."

"Pshaw!" says Father, poking the fire to hide the tender

mist in his eyes. "You couldn't forget that if you tried!"

"Of course you couldn't," Mother reassures. "Only remember to speak loud enough that they can hear you in the back of the church."

"And all the girls have new dresses," Alice exclaims, coming excitedly down to earth again. "And I said I had one too. That wasn't a fib, was it, Mother? It really is new, for me, even if it is Aunt Jennie's old one dyed."

"Of course," Mother stoutly agrees. "And all the trimmings are new. That light cashmere certainly took the dye well."

"I don't see how you got it such a beautiful shade of red. It's just like the holly!"

"You must remember, my dear," Father puts in with loving pride, "that your mother is a very wonderful person."

The soft early dusk of Christmas Eve falls upon Martinsville. Father starts down to the post-office for the mail. Mother prepares a light supper to be eaten in the kitchen because of the general haste. For the big Sunday School entertainment and "treat" is at seven-thirty. Alice sets out with her small pail to go to a neighbor's for the daily supply of milk.

It is so still in the village street. All white and hushed. Just a little stirring like wings in the church yard pines. The child stops, breathless, clasping her hands to her breast, the small pail dangling unheeded, her whole tender young soul caught up suddenly in a white mystery. Christmas Eve! The baby in the manger. The gold stars looking down just as they were to-night, and the angels sweeping through the sky on soft shining wings, singing *singing*.

It seemed almost as though they would appear any moment there where the stars were brightest, right back of the church steeple.

Why, it was real. It was true! Christmas Eve was happening again, within her, down deep, deep in her heart somewhere, as she stood there all quiet and alone in the snow. The wonderful aching beauty of it! It was as though she and the big wide star-swept night had a secret together. Or perhaps it was she *and God*.

Down the street comes a quick, clear jingle-jangle-jingle. A sleigh has just turned the corner. Alice starts and runs the rest of the way to the neighbors!

"And two quarts, please, Mother says, if you can spare it, because to-morrow's Christmas!"

She is dressed for the entertainment in the new dyed dress, her long curls showing golden above its rich red. Father and Mother suddenly begin to consult together in low voices in the kitchen. They come out at last impressively.

"Would she rather have one of her presents, not the big one but the other one, now, so she could wear it to-night? Would she?"

Alice stands considering delightedly, blue eyes like stars, "The big present would still be left for to-morrow?" she queries eagerly.

"You bet!" Father assures her.

"Then—I—believe—I'll—take the other—*now*!"

Mother brings it out. A hair ribbon! Just the color of the dress. Bigger and broader than any she has ever had. It is finally perched like a scarlet tanager above the golden curls!

There is the sound of talking, laughing voices passing outside. Scrunch, scrunch, scrunch, of many feet in the snow. People going to the entertainment. The little church up the street is all alight. It is time to go! They start out in the fresh, frosty air. Father follows her and Mother along the narrow snowy path, humming the Holly Song softly to himself.

All at once there was a shrill persistent ringing. It was not of a church bell or passing sleighs. It kept on ringing. The woman in the chair before the desk littered with Christmas cards came slowly back to her surroundings. She grasped the telephone dazedly. "This is Mrs. Barton. What meeting?... Oh, yes.... No, I can't come.... I'm—I'm not well."

She hung up the receiver abruptly. The Committee meeting at eleven! It seemed suddenly far away. Her one longing was to get back again to the past where she had just now been living; to those fresh, sweet realities of long ago. She closed her eyes, terrified lest the illusion was lost completely. But slowly, softly, surely, the little snowy village of Martinsville closed in again around her. She was once more the child, Alice.

She was falling asleep on Christmas Eve. The

entertainment had been wonderful. She hadn't forgotten her speech, not a word, and the girls all thought her dress was lovely and her hair ribbon had felt so big and pretty and floppy on her head, and the Ladies Quartette had sung "O Holy Night" for a surprise. Nobody knew they had been practicing, and it was so beautiful it had hurt her inside. And the treat candy had ever so many more chocolates in it than last year, and it was snowing again and she could hear the faint jingle-jangle-jingle of the sleighs still going up and down Main Street, and she was so happy! And to-morrow would really be Christmas.

Then all at once it was morning. Father and Mother were talking in low, happy voices in their room. She could hear Father creaking softly down the back stairs to start the fire before she got awake. The stockings would be all filled. Goodness, it was hard to wait.

Then at last a great noise in the front hall. Father shouting "Merry Christmas! My Christmas gift! Merry Christmas up there!"

It is time now. She flings her chill little body into her red wrapper and slippers and scurries down the stairs. A big fire in the grate! The three big bulging stockings! Father and Mother stand by until she empties hers first. She feels it with delicious caution. Oranges, apples and nuts in the toe. A funny little bumpy thing above. That would be one of Father's jokes. But at the top a mysterious soft, squashy package! She withdraws it slowly. She opens one tiny corner, gasps, opens a little more. Then gives a shrill cry. "*Mother!* It *couldn't* be a—a *muff!*"

She pulls it out, amazed ecstasy on her face. "It *is* a muff! Oh, Father, to think of your getting me a muff." She clasps the small scrap of cheap fur to her breast. "Oh, Mother, I never was so happy."

A subdued sound drew louder, became a sharp rap at the door. Martinsville receded. The woman in the chair opened her eyes with a dull realization of the present. Delia stood in the door-way, black and ominous. "What about them bedroom curtains?" she demanded.

Alice Barton rose slowly. With a great effort she brought her mind back to the problems of the day. She led the way to

Christmas in Modern Story

the guest room with Delia after her, grumbling inaudibly. Perhaps her eyes were still misted over with sweet memories, for somehow the curtains did not look so bad. "We'll let them go as they are, Delia. You have enough extras to do."

Delia departed in pleased surprise, and Alice sat down in the quiet room before a mirror, and peered into it. Almost she expected to see the child she had once been, the tender, smiling young mouth, the soft, eager eyes, the tumbled curls.

Instead she saw a middle aged face with all the spontaneous light gone out of it. There were hard lines in it which no amount of expensive "facials" had been able to smooth away. There was a bitter, unlovely droop to the lips.

Alice regarded herself steadily. Where along the way had she lost the spirit of that child who had this day come back to her?

The outward changes of her life passed in review. It was soon after that last happy Christmas in Martinsville that the little town had been swept by disease. The old village doctor had neither knowledge nor equipment to restrain it. When it was over, many homes had been desolated, and Alice, a bewildered little orphan, had gone to Aunt Jennie's in the city.

The changed way of living had been at first startling and then strangely commonplace. She had been fluidly adaptable. She had gone to a fashionable finishing school, had made a smart début, had met Tom, fallen deeply in love and then married him with all the circumstance Aunt Jennie had ordained.

Then had come life in Branchbrook and the beginning for herself of the curious nameless game Aunt Jennie had taught her, of belonging, of keeping up with most; of being ahead of many. A game with no noticeable beginning and no possible end. And of course one had to keep on playing it, for if one stopped it meant being dropped. Life would be insupportable after that.

And yet, would it? The game wasn't making any of them happy as it was. Back of her own restless home she saw again Father and Mother and the little girl named Alice. They had all been so joyously content with each other, had found life with its few small pleasures so wholesome and sweet to the taste.

The woman rose trembling to her feet. Suppose she stopped playing the game! Suppose she didn't care whether she belonged or not. What if she tried walking in the simple ways of her mother?

She stood there thinking in new terms, startled out of all her old standards, crying out to the past to guide her. And then suddenly she raised her arms above her head in a gesture of emancipation.

She examined her extra shopping list for which she had asked the money that morning. All the items were expensive courtesies that need not be rendered if considered apart from the game. She crossed them out one by one.

All that day as she went about her duties, she was conscious of an invisible companion: a child with eager, happy eyes walked beside her, watched her as she helped Delia with the big fruit cake, as she fastened a bough of holly to the door with her own hands.

The child was still close to her in the shadows when she lighted the tall candelabra at dusk and drew the tea-table to the fireside. Just the fire-light and candle shine to greet Tom when he came. She sat very still on the big divan, waiting. Would he feel the new quiet that possessed her? Would he forgive her for having made all the other Christmases times of confusion and worry? She wondered.

The children were not home yet when Tom came. He hung his coat in the hall closet and entered the living room heavily. He looked tired. His glance swept over the tall lighted candles, and the shining tea table. "What's coming off here? A tea-fight?" he said.

Alice stretched her hands toward him.

"You are the only guest, Tom. You and the children."

The man came nearer in surprise, caught her hands, peered into her face. Then his own softened. "What is it?" he asked.

They sank down together on the divan, hands still clasped tightly, something old and yet new, flooding back and forth between them.

"What is it?" Tom asked again. "There is something ... tell me."

And then suddenly the woman knew that into her own

hard faded eyes there had come again the gladness of youth.

"I had a visit to-day," she said slowly, "from a little girl of thirty years ago. A little girl I had forgotten. She brought me something precious."

Tom looked at her wonderingly. "Will she come *again*? *Often?*" he begged.

Alice shook her head and smiled. "There is no need," she answered softly. "For she and her gift have come *to stay!*"

TEACHER JENSEN[17]
Karin Michaelis

If the school-children had cared to look about them while they were playing hide-and-seek during recess, they would have seen the sharp tower of a mighty building piercing the air beyond a distant clump of trees. Unless you knew better, you would have believed that it was a castle where knights and beautiful ladies ate game off golden plates and on Sundays regaled themselves with macaroons. But the school-children did know better. They knew, forgot, and remembered again, that it was a prison standing near them, where prisoners lived, each in his own cell, never seeing each other except at church, where black masks disguised their faces. They knew and forgot and remembered again.

Lauritz Thomsen belonged there. Not that he had done anything to be ashamed of—God forbid! But his father was the cook for the prison, and Lauritz knew what the prisoners got to eat—and what they did not get. He lived, so to speak, in prison, but apart from these men with the black masks. He was so accustomed to taking the short cut across the fields to the high red wall and walking through the entrance portal, which was immediately closed and bolted after him, that it all seemed like nothing extraordinary. He could see it in no other light. But if his schoolmates began to ask him questions he would hold his peace and blush to the roots of his hair.

His mother worried and grieved about the prison, and sought as best she could to forget what was going on. Filling her windows with flowers, she tried to silence her unpleasant thoughts about the poor creatures breathing the deathly cellar air behind those iron bars. She laid by penny upon penny in the hope of saving enough to buy a little country inn, or any kind of establishment far away from the Living Cemetery, as the prison was called. During her dreams she cried aloud, waking her children, for she always saw people with black masks on their faces swarming behind walls and windows and threatening to kill her. Evil dreams arise from evil

---

[17] Reprinted from the "Living Age" by permission.

thoughts, it is said, but Frau Thomsen could have no evil thoughts. She had only once in her life gone through the prison. It still froze her with terror to think of it, and she could not understand how her husband could sing and enjoy himself at the end of his day's work. Nor could she comprehend how he could speak of the prisoners as if they were friends or comrades. When he began to carry on in this way she would leave the room and not come back until he had promised to talk about something else.

Children are children. They can accustom themselves to wading in a river where crocodiles sleep, or to playing in a jungle where snakes hang from the trees. Children become accustomed to living near a prison just as they get used to a father who drinks or a mother who scolds. They think of it, forget it, and remember it again. Thoughts glide across their minds like shadows; for a moment everything seems dark, and suddenly the sun shines once more.

Whenever a prisoner escaped, the school-children were thrown into a great commotion. They followed the pursuit from afar, listening to the shots, the alarm signals, the whistles. They leaned out of windows and saw the prison wardens rushing in all directions, on foot, and on horseback. Nothing was so exciting as a man hunt, either over winter snow or over green summer fields. When the fugitive was taken, peace descended upon all their souls. Now the only question was what punishment would be meted out to the victim, and all eyes were turned toward Lauritz. But Lauritz said nothing. He was ashamed without quite knowing why.

Prison and the prisoners would be forgotten save when a boy or girl at play would suddenly gape at the high towers to the east, jutting up there above the forest.

The children had a new teacher. He was called Teacher Jensen—nothing more. If he had a Christian name, he was never called by it. Just Teacher Jensen. And Teacher Jensen was little and frail, and Teacher Jensen's voice was as little and frail as he. But there was a wonderful quality in his voice, like a violin that makes a much louder noise than anyone would believe possible. The children did not sleep in his classes. They were not even drowsy. In his classes they forgot to write notes to each other or secretly to eat bread and butter behind their desks. They only listened and asked questions. Teacher Jensen had an answer for everything. They could ask Teacher Jensen all kinds of questions. But sometimes he would shake his head and say: "I seem to have forgotten it. Let me think a minute." Or worse yet: "I don't know. I never knew it. But I will look it up. It is to be found in some book, or a friend will tell me the answer." The children found that there was something splendid about having a teacher of whom you could ask all kinds of questions and who sometimes did not know the answer offhand.

Teacher Jensen talked about new things and old, and his speech was not like pepper shaken from a pepper pot. Even while the children were playing in the fields, they would remember what he had said. Yes, it remained fast in their minds.

One day Teacher Jensen said that murder was by no means the worst thing a man could do, and that it was much worse to think or say or do evil to another human being, or to make a defenseless animal suffer. And the children were full of wonder. It seemed that a new door had been opened to them, and each passed through it, one after another. Yes, it was true, what he said. They understood his meaning clearly, but they cast their eyes down, for all of them knew they had often done what was much worse than murder. Perhaps they would do it again, but not willingly, never willingly. Yet there was another thing worse than murder, and that was to act without using your will.

One day Teacher Jensen brought with him a sick, whining little cat which he had found on his way to school. He had put it under his cloak to keep it warm, and he stroked its back and its sharp little head. It was an ugly, gray, dirty cat. Teacher Jensen did not tell the children what he was going to do with it, but simply sat with the cat in his lap and rubbed his cheek against its head. To the children this poor little sick gray cat was the whole world. They took a silent vow that they would cure it. Through Teacher Jensen's little gray cat they had peered deep into the soul of an animal, and what they saw was more beautiful and more pure than a human soul.

Teacher Jensen often went on Sunday excursions with

the children. Whoever wanted to could come, and all of them wanted to. It so happened that one Sunday morning in the autumn they were walking among falling leaves, and the earth clung to their shoes in little lumps. It had been raining, and was likely to rain again. Traversing a bit of open country, they soon entered the big forest in the distance. Ahead of them was the "castle" that was a prison. Lauritz ran in to get a scarf. Teacher Jensen saw him and drew his hand over his eyes, and as he cast down his eyes it was clear that he had been crying; but no one asked anything, no one spoke. They arrived at a vast grove of fir trees standing in long rows, with their evergreen branches above and their yellow trunks below. Teacher Jensen explained that such a forest could grow from a mere handful of tiny grains. The children knew this perfectly well; yet it sounded quite new. They suddenly understood that trees lived, breathed, and thought, that they strove for the light as poor people strive for bread.

"Now let's begin the game," said Teacher Jensen. "Let's imagine that this forest of fir trees is a prison, and that we are all prisoners, each in his own cell. Let us do this for one hour. I am holding a watch in my hand. During that hour let no one speak, for we are prisoners, and speech is forbidden."

This was a new game, a peculiar game. The rain had stopped some time ago, but drops were still falling from the high trees. The children stood, each under his own tree, and felt the water dripping and dripping on cheeks and hands. The children stood with the water dripping off them, laughing and shouting to each other side by side cell by cell. Slowly the laughter died and their faces became serious. All eyes were directed toward Teacher Jensen, who stood with the watch in his hand. He seemed to see nobody, and did not announce when the hour should begin.

The children felt as if they ought to hold their breath, for surely something important and serious was afoot. It was not like the times when they had gone out with other teachers, when hatred and pride cropped up as soon as the school door was closed. This was serious, and each breath was like a bucketful of water from a deep, deep well. Was time standing still? Had not many hours already passed? Were they really prisoners after all? They did not crawl away, though there was nothing to stop them. Teacher Jensen did not look around him at all, yet as soon as any of the children thought of creeping away they could not help remembering what happened when a prisoner escaped and they heard the shots ring out, the alarm bells clang, the whistles blow, and saw the wardens riding off in all directions hunting the fugitive. Their feet would not obey them—they were bound fast by Teacher Jensen's word; the outstretched hand with the watch held them in their places. Yes, they were prisoners, each in his own cell, and darkness settled and a gentle mist descended, veil upon veil.

Was this what it was like being a prisoner?

The hour was up.

Every one sighed with relief, yet they all stood quiet for a moment, as if they could not really believe that they had regained their freedom. Then they sprang up and clustered around Teacher Jensen, asking him questions. It was growing dark, and he put his watch in his pocket, saying: "It is just as hard to be a prison watchman as to be a prisoner."

The children had never thought of this before, and after a long pause Teacher Jensen added: "The lot of the prison warden is the hardest of all, for he can do nothing for the prisoners; and in his heart he wants to help them all he can, yet they are not able to read his thoughts."

And after another pause he said: "I knew a man who spent seventeen years in prison and then died there."

When Lauritz reached home his mother was sitting at the piano playing and singing. The smell of freshly baked cake filled the room. On the table stood a glass bowl of apples. Lauritz's father sat on a chair smoking his pipe. Without knowing just what he said or why he said it, Lauritz went up to the piano and whispered in his mother's ear: "When I am a big man I shall be a prison warden."

"What did you say?" she cried. "A prison warden, Lauritz? In there with those people? Never!"

Lauritz repeated: "When I am a big man I shall be a prison warden."

And then something happened that was never explained. Who had the idea first no one knew. Perhaps it entered all those little heads at the same time, in that hour when they were standing, each a prisoner under his own tree, each in his own cell—just in a single hour.

When Teacher Jensen was told about the plan, he only nodded as if he had known about it long ago. But when they begged him to talk to the prison inspector, since their scheme was contrary to all regulations, he shook his head, saying: "It is your idea. You must carry it out. It is up to you, if you believe in yourselves, to stand fast by your beliefs."

That was two months before Christmas, and all the school-children, big and little, boys and girls, were there. Money was the first necessity, and it had to be collected in modest amounts and earned in an honorable way. Teacher Jensen said that if the gift was not honest no good came of it. The children all saved the money that they would ordinarily have spent on sweets and on stamps for their albums. They went on little errands, chopped wood, carried water, and scrubbed milk cans, wooden buckets, and copper tubs. The money was put into a big earthenware pig that Teacher Jensen had put in the wardrobe at school. No one knew who gave the most or who gave the least.

Lauritz announced that, including the seventeen sick people, there were three hundred and ten prisoners in the jail.

In the middle of December the pig was broken and the money was counted over and over, but it did not amount to much. Then a little fellow came with his little private savings bank, and a girl with a little earthen receptacle in which she kept her spare pennies. That started them off. Many little hoardings destined for Christmas presents were emptied into the great common fund at school. See how it grew! Shiny paper was now brought, and flags and walnuts. Every day the whole school stayed until supper time cutting out and pasting. The little girls made white and red roses. They wove baskets, gilded walnuts, pasted flags on little sticks, and cut out cardboard stars, painting them gold and silver. The little ones made, out of clay, birds' nests with eggs in them, and little horses and cows that they covered with bright colors so they looked like real live animals. The boys cut out photographs and made little boxes. With jig saws they fashioned napkin rings and paper weights.

Christmas trees were bought—three hundred and ten real

fir trees, for which the gardener charged only twenty-five pfennigs apiece.

Teacher Jensen emptied his purse on the desk. It had once been black, but it had long since turned brown, and was full of cracks. "That belonged to the man who spent seventeen years in prison," he announced. "He had it there with him. He kept it there for seventeen long years."

No one asked who the man was, but the money had to be counted over many times, for the children's eyes were moist and they had to keep wiping the tears away.

On the Sunday before Christmas the children went with Teacher Jensen to the local store and bought a lot of tobacco and chocolate, almonds and raisins, playing cards and brightly colored handkerchiefs, and writing paper. And they got a lot of old Christmas books too, which were given to them free because they were at the bottom of the pile and were out of date.

The parents of the children had to contribute whether they wanted to or not, and bags full of cookies and nuts, playing cards and books, came out of each house.

Lauritz's father had spoken in all secrecy to the prison chaplain, who went as a representative to the inspector. But the inspector hemmed and hawed saying: "That goes against all regulations. It's impossible. It can't be allowed on any ground whatever." The chaplain was to have told this to Lauritz's father, and Lauritz was to have brought the news to the children that the plan had to be abandoned. But the chaplain said nothing to Lauritz's father, and the children did not know that it was impossible and could never be allowed.

All the parents, no matter how much they had to do, made a point of going into the schoolhouse the day before Christmas and seeing the three hundred little sparkling Christmas trees, each laden with joy, each with its star on the top, each with its white and red roses, white and red flags, and white and red candles, each decorated with tinsel and hung with gifts. To every tree a little letter was fastened, written by a boy or a girl. What was in this letter only the writer and perhaps Teacher Jensen knew—for Teacher Jensen had to help the little ones who only knew how to print numbers and capital letters.

The church bells rang over the town and called the faithful to God's worship. The prison bells rang out over the prison and called the prisoners to the prison church. Before the school was drawn up a row of wagons which had been laden with the little Christmas trees. Each child then took his tree under his arm and set out, following the wagons, singing as he went. It was a Christmas party without snow, but a Christmas party just the same.

Stopping before the prison, they rang the bell, and asked to speak to the inspector. He came out, and the moment he appeared Teacher Jensen and all the children began to sing: "*O du fröhliche, o, du selige, gnaden-bringende Weihnachtszeit....*"

The inspector shook his head sadly and raised his hands in the air. It was impossible, absolutely impossible—he had said so. But the children kept right on singing, and seemed not to hear him. As the inspector afterward said, when the director of all the prisons in that district demanded an explanation: "A man is only human, and had you been in my place, Mr. Director, you would have done as I did, even if it had cost you your position."

Thus it came to pass that this one time Christmas was celebrated in each cell of the big prison—a good, happy, cheerful Christmas. When the prisoners came back from the worship of God with their black masks on their faces they found a Christmas tree in every cell, and the cell doors stood open until the candles had burned out, and the prisoners received permission to go freely from cell to cell all through the corridor to look at each other's Christmas trees and gifts—to look at them and to compare them. But each prisoner thought that his little tree and his present were the most beautiful and the best of all.

When the last light had burned out, the doors were closed, and far into the night the prisoners sang the Christmas carols of their childhood, free from distress, grief, and all spitefulness.

And as the last light flickered out behind the high walls the thin figure of a man with his coat collar up over his ears and his hat pulled over his face crept along the prison wall. Through the night air he heard the voices singing, "*Stille*

Nacht, heilige Nacht."

Clasping his hands tightly together and raising them aloft into the darkness, he cried: "I thank thee, father. Thy guilt has been atoned for ten times over."

HONORABLE TOMMY[18]
Mary E. Wilkins Freeman

It was the day before Christmas, long ago, when Christmas was seldom observed in New England. There were two houses in the village separated by a wide yard in which the grass, of a dirty dun color, lay like a frost-woven mat underfoot, crunching when the children sped over it.

It was difficult to understand what the boy and girl found amusing in that dismal wintry yard, flanked on one side by the Dunbar farmhouse, with its enormous barns and outbuildings, on the other by the more modern house where the Roseberrys lived. There was probably nothing except the indomitable spirit of youth. The boy, Tommy Dunbar, and the girl, Cora Roseberry, raced back and forth between the leafless, creaking old cherry trees. They made leaps over a ledge of rock. The girl gave little squeals of merriment from time to time. The boy, although radiant, was silent. They were pretty children, but the fashions of their day detracted from their beauty.

The girl, charmingly graceful, pink and white, with long blond curls, wore a hoop skirt and a frock of royal Stuart plaid. She wore white stockings and ugly half-low shoes, a red knitted hood, and a shawl over her mother's sontag. As she ran, the fringed corners of the blue and green plaid shawl flew out.

"You will catch cold," said the boy thoughtfully. "Stop, Cora; you must let me tie the ends of your shawl."

"It is cold," agreed the girl: "but I have on Mother's sontag under the shawl." She glanced down admiringly and guiltily at the brilliant circle of her royal Stuart skirt. "Mother didn't know I was going to wear this dress," said she.

"What made you?" asked the boy soberly. He was smaller than the girl, although of the same age. He was also paler. His attire was as absurd: trousers which seemed a queer evolution from skirts, an uncouth jacket, and wool cap and

---

[18] By permission of the author and the "Woman's Home Companion."

muffler. His features were good, but their expression of extreme seriousness baffled. His blue eyes under a high forehead were almost aggressively thoughtful for a mere child.

"Will your mother scold you?"

"My mother scold me!" The girl burst into a roulade of laughter. "Mother never scolds me, neither does Father. Everybody loves me, you know," she said prettily.

Tommy Dunbar gazed reflectively at Cora. He was considering what would have happened to him had he clad himself, without permission from his aunts Nancy and Sarah and his Uncle Reuben, in the bright blue broadcloth suit with a white frill round the neck which he wore Sundays.

Cora looked at him curiously. "Do your folks treat you bad if you do things you want to?" she inquired. Tommy was silent.

"Why don't you answer?"

"My folks do the way they think is right, I guess," said Tommy, with a stolid air.

Cora gave her long curls a toss. She dismissed the subject.

"You can't catch me, running around every one of the cherry trees three times," declared she, and was off.

Cora ran round the trees, with Tommy following at a fixed distance, according to his code of honor, then stopped, squealing with glee. "Couldn't! Told you so," said she. Cora was charming. She conquered her ugly clothes. In a way, Tommy Dunbar conquered his. There was a very noble, manly expression on his young face above the uncouth jacket and muffler.

Cora sniffed. "What are they cooking over at your folks'?" said she.

"They're doing pig work," replied Tommy. "That's lard trying out you smell."

"Seems to me funny work to be doing the day before Christmas," said Cora.

Tommy stared.

Cora stared back. "You look as if you'd never heard of Christmas," said she. "Are you going to have a tree, or hang up your stocking?"

193

Tommy hesitated; then he said feebly: "I guess I'll hang up my stocking."

"That's what I'm going to do this Christmas." Cora lowered her voice. "That's really what Mother went to Boston for," she whispered. "You see, I know perfectly well that Father and Mother and Aunt Emmy and Grandpa and Cousin Ellen give the things that go in my stocking. But I like to make believe it's Santa Claus, and it pleases the others, so I do."

To Tommy the remark was enigmatical, but he made no comment.

"I shall hang my stocking by the fireplace in the sitting-room," said Cora. "Where will you hang yours?"

"Guess I'll hang mine by the fireplace in the sitting-room, too," muttered Tommy; but he had an anxious, bewildered expression.

It did not dawn upon Cora that Tommy Dunbar had never in his life hung up his stocking, but so it was.

Cora saw her mother getting out of the stage-coach, and summarily ran home. Tommy also went home, sniffing the smell of lard and roast meat.

He enjoyed his supper of crisp roast spare-ribs, turnips, baked potatoes and pumpkin pie. At the table were his Uncle Reuben and his aunts Sarah and Nancy. His grandmother was confined to her room with a cold, otherwise things would have been different. Tommy's grandmother could not have connived in the after-happenings of that day. Before going up-stairs to bed Tommy stopped to say good night to her. She sat propped up in her great bed, with a white shawl over her shoulders, and she was knitting. She smiled serenely at Tommy.

If anything, serenity was a fault in Grandmother Dunbar. No minor trials of life disturbed her, and she often assumed erroneously that they did not disturb other people. However, she was the mother of children, and when a child was in question the surface of her sweet calm could be ruffled. If only she had known—but she did not know. She smiled at Tommy, and her large pink-and-white face, framed in white ruffles, represented to the child personified love. His mother had died when he was a baby, his father two years ago, and

Tommy had speeded to this grandmotherly shelter.

Tommy kissed her good night with effusion. It was a pity that he did not confide in her; but he was very shy and shamed before the unwonted idea in his mind. His grandmother gave him a peppermint, and told him not to forget his prayers, and he climbed up-stairs to his own bedroom. It was an icy room, and almost reproachfully neat.

Tommy said his prayers, and went to bed, but not to sleep. His room was over the sitting-room. He could hear the hum of conversation below. He knew each voice, although he could not distinguish one word. Aunt Nancy's was very shrill, punctuated by frequent bursts of laughter. Aunt Sarah's was of lower pitch. Uncle Reuben had a deep bass growl. Tommy listened. Presently they would all go out in the back kitchen to grind sausage meat.

Soon silence settled down upon the floor below. They were all out in the back kitchen. Tommy crept very softly out of bed. He took one of his knitted blue yarn stockings, and he went down-stairs, padding on his bare feet. Tommy wore a red flannel nightgown. When he opened the sitting-room door and the fire-light on the hearth illumined him, he looked like a little Fra Angelico angel. His fair hair, crested smoothly over his forehead, caught the light. His pale cheeks were rosy with reflection.

He tiptoed across the floor and hung the blue yarn stocking in the fire-place. Then he beat a retreat; but he had been discovered. His aunt Nancy, whose hearing was almost preternatural, had heard the stairs creak under his little feet and had pulled the others along with her. They were all peeking around the kitchen door. However, they were out of range of the fireplace. They only saw Tommy approach, then steal away in that flickering red light. Reuben held them back until the sitting-room door was closed, and the pit-pat of Tommy's bare feet had ceased upon the stairs. Then the three hearty, healthy, kindly, but obtuse, young people entered the sitting-room.

"He certainly was fussing about something in the fireplace," said Nancy. Suddenly she made a pounce. She pointed. She shook and bent with stifled laughter. The others looked. They saw poor Tommy's blue stocking, symbolic of childish faith, hanging in the fireplace. Nancy laughed, and Sarah laughed, but cautiously. Reuben stared.

"What's the stockin' doin' there?" he inquired, with no lowering of his deep voice.

Tommy up-stairs heard him, and trembled. Then he heard no more, for his aunts hushed his uncle peremptorily. They pulled him out into the kitchen.

"What in creation—?" began Reuben.

"Reuben, do hush up. He'll hear you," gasped Nancy. "It's—it's——"

"It's what? What did he come down like that for, and hang his stockin' there? Is he crazy?"

"It's Christmas to-morrow," replied Nancy, choking with laughter.

"And he was out in the yard with Cora this afternoon, and she must have told him she was going to hang her stocking, and put him up to it," said Sarah between giggles.

"Grace went to Boston this morning," said Nancy. "I know she went to buy presents for Cora. They're just spoiling that child."

Reuben scowled. "If," said he, "Grace wants to fill her child's head with such nonsense, I do wish she would tell her not to talk to Tommy. Hangin' his stockin' in the chimney!"

However, Reuben, who was not an ill-natured man, grinned as he spoke. Into his small brown eyes leapt a spark of malicious mischief.

"I'll fix up his stockin'; I vum I will," declared Reuben. He began to laugh. They all laughed.

"What are you going to do, Reuben?" inquired Nancy.

Reuben whispered. The heads of the three conspirators were close together. When Reuben finished, they all laughed until the tears ran down their cheeks. Reuben's plan seemed to them such a joke.

The three, stifling their laughter, filled the blue yarn stocking. When it hung bulging, they fairly clung together and reeled, they were so overcome by the fun of the thing.

"He will come down by dawn to find it," giggled Nancy. She and Sarah slept on the ground floor, Reuben above.

"I will sleep with one ear open," said he. "I shall hear him come downstairs."

"Mind you don't let him hear you," cautioned Sarah. "Nancy and I will be on the lookout."

Soon the house was still. The street was still, hushed by an evening of fast-falling snow. Everybody slept except Tommy. He lay awake in a sort of ecstasy. He did not know what he expected. Afterward he was never able to define the nature of his joyful expectancy, but he lay awake in one of the transports of awaited happiness which do not come often in a lifetime. All the beautiful symbolism of Christmas was astir in him, like a strain of wonderful music. Little New England boy, who had never known a Yuletide, it may be that ancestral memory had been awakened in him, that the joy of his ancestors over the merry holy time of the year thrilled him.

The storm clouds had passed. He could see a great star from his window. He gazed at it so steadily that its rays became multiplied. Finally the star, to his concentrated vision, seemed surrounded by a halo of rainbows. He lay there waiting for the dawn, in such bliss as he might never again in his whole life attain, since that bliss was to be dashed back into the very face of his soul with a shock as of spiritual ice.

That Christmas morning the dawn was beautiful, and Tommy's window faced the east. He saw first a pallor of light along the horizon; then beams of cowslip-gold, rose and violet shot upward like an aurora. Tommy crept out of bed. He padded down-stairs. The cold was bitter, but he did not feel it. The poor little man in his red flannel nightgown entered the sitting-room. There was a faint glow on the hearth. He stole near. Yes, his stocking was full, bulging with unknown treasures.

He did not hear his uncle Reuben coming down-stairs behind him, then hiding observant in a dark corner of the front entry. He did not see his aunts' faces peering around a crack of their bedroom door. He clutched the stocking. He was trembling with delight. He had intended to run up-stairs and discover his wealth in his own room, but he could not wait. He sat down on the hearth and began to explore.

When it was over, just one little sharp sound broke the silence. Nancy said afterward it sounded as if some boy had stepped on a very little dog and killed him. After that, silence came again. Somehow the watchers did not feel like laughing. Tommy stood up. The dawn light fell full upon his white, stern little face. He crammed the miserable travesties of Christmas treasures back into the stocking. He went straight to the outer door. He shot the bolt. He went out.

"Mercy on us!" gasped Nancy.

"He will catch his death of cold going out in his nightgown," said Sarah. She was very pale.

Reuben came into the room. He looked frightened. "Where has he gone?" he demanded.

Sarah and Nancy hushed him and drew him into their own room. They peered out, and saw the boy, with the stern white face of a man, march in. He held his blue yarn stocking dangling limply. He went up-stairs. They heard his door close. The three went together into the sitting-room. Nancy was almost weeping, Reuben scowled, Sarah's pale face wore a puzzled expression.

"I did not think he would take it like that," half sobbed Nancy. Sarah looked accusingly at her brother.

"I don't see why you did it," she said.

"You thought it was as good a joke as I did," retorted Reuben. He shook himself, took his cap from a peg, and went out.

Nancy and Sarah, left alone, stood and stared at each other in dismay. They did not give speech to it, but at that moment both realized that childhood was a land left far behind them. Nancy's lover had died two years before. Queerly enough, she thought of him now. Sometime he had been a little boy like poor Tommy.

"I s'pose we ought to have known better," Sarah thought. All she said was, "I guess Grace Roseberry will think we're heathen."

"Perhaps he—won't—tell," said Nancy hesitatingly.

"Children always tell," returned Sarah. "Let him tell. It is all Grace's fault, spoiling Cora and having her put such ideas into Tommy's head. Come, it's time to get breakfast. You go in and see how Mother is; if she had a good night."

"Mother wouldn't like it," murmured Nancy.

"She'll give him some pep'mints and coddle him up

when he tells her," said Sarah.

"Perhaps he won't tell," returned Nancy.

"Of course he'll tell; children always tell. Let him. I've done nothing that I'm ashamed of. It was only a joke. It will cure him of being so silly, too. I'll start the breakfast while you look after Mother."

Then Tommy was heard on the stairs. He entered the room, clad in his uncouth suit, and went soberly through on his way to the wood-shed. It was his morning task to chop up the kindling wood. Tommy's face was still white and unchildlike, and the sisters regarded each other with something like fear when he had disappeared.

"All I've got to say is, a child as silly as that ought to be taught sense, and I guess it's just as well it happened," said Sarah.

"He's had time enough to tell Mother; but I don't believe he has."

"Well, if he has told, Mother has coddled him; but he looked just the same."

"Maybe we are making too much fuss over nothing," said Nancy. Sarah went into the kitchen, stepping heavily and quickly, and Nancy entered her mother's room. The old woman was awake, and she smiled serenely at her daughter.

"He hasn't told," thought Nancy with relief. When she joined her sister in the kitchen she said, "Sarah, he hasn't told Mother. He's a good boy."

"He will tell," returned Sarah grimly, "and he can, for all me."

But Tommy did not tell, although as time went on he was subjected to a severe ordeal. It began that very morning out in the yard under the cherry trees. The light fall of snow was not enough to admit of sleighing, but enough to make as good an excuse for using a Christmas sled as a child could wish. Out there, on the thin glistening rime of snow was Cora Roseberry, dragging a superfine sled, gaudily painted and named "Snow Bird." Cora wore a set of furs, although the muff was dreadfully in her way. It was a Christmas present. She also wore a bright red cloak lined with plaid, another Christmas present, and on one hand a kid glove. The other hand was bare, because it was decorated with a gold ring with

Christmas in Modern Story

a garnet stone.

When she saw Tommy she hailed him. "Come here, quick, quick!" she called in her thin sweet voice.

"Oh, Tommy Dunbar, you are *so* slow!" she cried as he came up. "I want you to just look at my Christmas presents! See my sled, see my furs, see my red cape, see my kid gloves, real kid, the first I've had. And oh, Tommy, see my ring! See how it shines!"

Tommy nodded soberly. He was not jealous, but he could not bring himself to show hilarity after his own experience.

"And these ain't near all," boasted Cora. "I've got two books, a red one and a blue one, with pictures, and a photograph album, and oranges, and candy, and a game, and lots of other things. Say, can't you come in our house and see them?"

"I guess I can't just now," replied Tommy gravely.

"I've got a new doll with real hair and a pink spangled dress, and a stereoscope with lots of pictures. Say, Tommy, don't you want to look at the pictures through my stereoscope?"

Tommy shook his head. He would have liked to own a stereoscope.

"They're real pretty. They couldn't all go into my stocking. They were all round it on the floor. Say, Tommy, did you hang your stocking?"

Tommy hesitated just one moment. Then—he had the blood of honest soldiers in his veins—he nodded.

"Oh, Tommy, what did you have in your stockings?"

"Useful things," replied Tommy gruffly.

"What kind of useful things? Mittens?"

"I said useful things," replied Tommy with masculine dignity and finality. He walked away with the proud carriage of a victor leaving a hardly won battlefield, while Cora screamed after him. "Tommy Dunbar, I think you are real mean, so there!"

Nancy and Sarah had seen Tommy out in the yard talking to Cora.

"I wonder if Tommy's telling Cora," said Nancy uneasily.

"Let him, if he wants to; I'm sure I don't care. This

hanging stockings Christmas and talking about Santa Claus, is silly and heathenish, anyway."

Nancy still looked uneasy. When Tommy entered she did not hesitate. "What did Cora mean by speaking to you like that? What had you done?" she said.

"I hadn't done anything."

"What did she mean?" persisted Aunt Nancy. Aunt Sarah was looking at him; so was his uncle.

The little boy looked at them. In his small face was an expression of scorn so high that it was entirely above all petty, childish resentment. "She said that because I wouldn't tell her what was in my stocking," he replied.

"Why wouldn't you tell her?" inquired his aunt Sarah sharply.

"Because I am ashamed," said Tommy. "I shall never tell anybody, because I am ashamed."

"Ashamed of what?" demanded Sarah. Her face was flushed.

"Ashamed of you all," replied Tommy simply.

Then Tommy walked out. Another morning task of his was replenishing the hearth fire and cleaning the hearth in the sitting-room. They heard him about it. The three looked at one another. A dim conception of the nobility of the trust of childhood and the enormity of its betrayal was over them. Nancy whimpered a little.

"We never ought to have done such a thing," she said unsteadily.

Reuben echoed her. "No, we shouldn't."

"Well, what's done can't be undone," said Sarah, but she also looked disturbed.

"Suppose Reuben hitches up, and we go down to the store and get some things for him," suggested Nancy timidly.

Reuben denied the motion peremptorily. "If you think you can salve over matters that way, with a boy like that, you are mistaken," said he. "I could tell you that, both of you."

There was the sharp tinkle of a bell, and Nancy started. "That's Mother's bell," said she.

"I'll go see what she wants," said Sarah.

Sarah entered her mother's room, and the old woman looked up at her from her feather-bed nest. "What did you ring your bell for, Mother?" Sarah asked.

"Is that door shut tight?" asked her Mother.

"Yes, it is."

"I don't want Tommy to hear. Sarah, what ails Tommy?"

Sarah was a truthful woman, but she hedged. "What do you mean, Mother?"

"I called him in here a minute ago to give him a pep'mint, and that child don't look a mite well. Has he been complaining?"

"No, he ain't."

"You don't think he's et too much sassage?"

"I know he didn't." Sarah's voice gained emphasis. She was relieved at being able to tell the truth without evasion.

"Well, all I've got to say is that child don't look right this morning," said her mother. "If I was up and about I'd put him to bed and dose him. I'm afraid he's in for a sick spell. What's that?"

There had been a sound of a sudden fall in the sitting-room. The grandmother sat up. "I knew it!" said she. "I'm going to get up."

"You keep still, Mother," said Sarah, who had turned white.

"Then you run and see, and you leave my door wide open, or I'll get up."

Sarah obeyed. On the floor in the sitting-room lay Tommy in a little sprawl of unconsciousness. Over him knelt Nancy and Reuben.

"Stop asking him what the matter is when he's fainted dead away, and fetch me the bottle of cordial from the top butt'ry shelf, Reuben; and you, Nancy, get the camphor bottle, quick," commanded Sarah.

After a while Tommy was revived, but he was a sick little boy. He was put to bed in the little room out of his grandmother's, and the doctor was called. At that date the medical fraternity was not very anxious concerning shocks to the nerves. Tommy swallowed valerian and was afterward comforted with peppermints. He had a hot brick at his feet, and nobody spoke out loud anywhere near him.

"He is a very delicate child," said the doctor out in the sitting-room with the door tightly closed. "Don't give him much to eat to-day."

"A little jelly?" sobbed Nancy, who was quite overcome.

"Oh, yes, jelly and toast and weak tea when he wakes up," said the doctor.

Tommy slept for hours. He was a delicate child, and his night of rapt wakefulness, his terrible disillusionment, his lack of food, for he had eaten no breakfast, had all been too much for him.

It was after the noon dinner when he awaked and had his tea and toast and jelly. He had just finished it when there was a sound of wheels and horse hoofs in the yard. The snow had all melted and the ground was quite bare. Nancy and Reuben ran to the windows.

"It's Tom Loring," exclaimed Nancy. Tom Loring was Tommy's mother's brother, his uncle Tom.

Sarah came running out from Tommy's bedside. "He's better," said she joyfully. "He has eaten every mite."

"Tom Loring has come," announced Nancy.

"I suppose now there will be a to-do. I suppose that child will tell the whole thing, and we can't ever make Tom Loring understand," said Sarah.

"Tommy won't tell," said Reuben grimly. He had not eaten much dinner himself, and he looked downcast. He was really fond of Tommy.

Sarah ushered Uncle Tom Loring into the sitting-room. He was a youngish man, stout and rosy. "Where's Tommy?" he demanded.

"Tommy had a little sick spell just before dinner," said Sarah entering, wiping her hands on her apron. "How do you do, Tom?"

"Sick spell!" repeated Uncle Tom Loring.

Reuben followed after Sarah. He greeted Tom, who turned to him hopefully. "What do they mean by a sick spell?"

"Fainted dead away," replied Reuben shortly.

Uncle Tom made an exclamation of dismay. "Why, I came out thinking I would take him back to Boston with me," he said. "Sister Annie has come to live with me now her husband's dead and her children are all married; and I thought little Tommy could come and make us a visit, maybe live with us most of the time, if he likes it. And now he's sick! Annie will be dreadfully disappointed. She's got a tree all rigged up for him, and a big dinner, and everything."

"He can go," Reuben stated firmly.

"Oh, Reuben, do you think he's well enough?" gasped Nancy.

"Of course he is. What's a little fainting spell? He can go. The air will do him good. His grandmother will miss him, and we shall, too, but it will do him good to have a change."

Just then Tommy, who heard his uncle's voice and got into his clothes, came weakly out. Tom grabbed him and looked at him.

"Say, young man, you do look peaked," he said.

Grandmother's voice was heard from her bedroom.

"Tom Loring, you take that child home with you. When I'm up again you can bring him back. He's all run down."

"All right, Grandma," called back Uncle Tom. He shook the boy lovingly. "Well, little Tommy, I'm going to take you back to Boston with me. Your aunt Annie is there, and there's a great Christmas tree all trimmed with candles. I suppose you didn't have a tree?"

"No, sir," said little Tommy.

"Hung up your stocking, eh?"

"Yes, sir."

Sarah and Nancy were pale, Reuben looked dogged. Then came the question direct.

"Well, what was in the stocking?"

"Useful things," replied little Tommy.

Sarah was a courageous woman. She was really ashamed of the miserable joke they had tried on the child, but she was quite prepared to face the consequences.

"You tell your uncle what was in your stocking, Tommy," said she.

Reuben echoed her. "No use beating about the bush," said he, while Tom looked puzzled. "Go ahead and tell him, Tommy."

"Useful things," repeated stanch little Tommy.

Uncle Tom gave a shrewd glance at him. "Well, useful things are very good things to have," said he; "but I think your aunt Annie has a lot of the other kind for you."

"You get that child ready right away, Nancy and Sarah," ordered Grandmother from the bedroom, "and mind you wrap him up warm. It's a cold ride to Boston."

"I have a lot of fur robes," said Uncle Tom. "And we are going to stop in at The Sign of the Lion on our way home, and get some hot milk for him, and anything else he wants."

In a very short time little Tommy was riding beside his uncle Tom. He was enveloped in furs. He had a hot brick at his feet. He was happy again, but his rapt ecstasy of the night before, which even without the after-shock of disillusionment had been a strain, had settled down into a deep peace of realization.

Nancy and Sarah were in their mother's room. They had told her. Nancy was sobbing and Sarah looked sober. Reuben stood in the doorway, looking soberer still.

"I wish he would tell," sobbed Nancy.

"He never will, and we can't any of us have the comfort of thinking he is anywhere near as mean as the rest of us," said Reuben gloomily.

"Don't you make too much of it, Reuben," said Grandmother. "You didn't any of you mean any harm. You couldn't know that what seemed funny to you—and it was sort of funny—would be taken in dead earnest by a child like that. I could have told you."

After that Christmas, Tommy lived much of the time in Boston with his uncle Tom and his aunt Annie. He spent the summers with his aunts and uncle on the farm. He seemed as fond of them as ever. Nobody mentioned the stocking.

When Tommy and Cora were grown up they fell in love and were married, and lived in Boston. On Christmas Day Cora asked Tommy a question. "Tommy dear, what was in that stocking you were so mysterious about when you were a little boy?" said she. "Tell me now, please."

Tommy laughed, but he shook his head. "Just something useful, dear," said he. The man was faithful to his code of honor of childhood.

Cora, however, remained curious. The next summer when she and Tommy were staying at the farm, she asked Sarah to tell her what had been in the stocking.

"Aunt Sarah," said pretty Cora, "do please tell me what

was in Tommy's stocking that Christmas when he was a little boy. He won't tell me, and I want to know."

"You ought to know," said Sarah. "We have always been ashamed of it, although we meant it to be only a joke, and never realized what we were doing. We did not understand how a child like Tommy might take it. We were doing pig work that Christmas, and"—Sarah laughed a little and colored—"we put in some pigs' ears nicely wrapped up, and a pig's tail, and a potato, and a turnip, and two beets."

"Goodness!" said Cora.

"We were all ashamed of it," said Aunt Sarah.

Cora went over and kissed her. "Don't you worry one bit," said she. "Maybe Tommy's having such awful things in his stocking, poor little boy, made him better all his life. Perhaps his keeping still and not telling made him so honorable and honest. Aunt Sarah, it can't have done Tommy much harm, for he is certainly about the best man who ever lived now."

"He certainly is," said Sarah, "but if I had to live over again, I wouldn't try such a way of making him so, for my own sake."

THE SAD SHEPHERD[19]
Henry Van Dyke

I
Darkness

Out of the Valley of Gardens, where a film of new-fallen snow lay smooth as feathers on the breast of a dove, the ancient Pools of Solomon looked up into the night sky with dark, tranquil eyes, wide-open and passive, reflecting the crisp stars and the small, round moon. The full springs, overflowing on the hill-side, melted their way through the field of white in winding channels, and along their course the grass was green even in the dead of winter.

But the sad shepherd walked far above the friendly valley, in a region where ridges of gray rock welted and scarred the back of the earth, like wounds of half-forgotten strife and battles long ago. The solitude was forbidding and disquieting; the keen air that searched the wanderer had no pity in it; and the myriad glances of the night were curiously cold.

His flock straggled after him. The sheep, weather beaten and dejected, followed the path with low heads nodding from side to side, as if they had travelled far and found little pasture. The black, lop-eared goats leaped upon the rocks, restless and ravenous, tearing down the tender branches and leaves of the dwarf oaks and wild olives. They reared up against the twisted trunks and crawled and scrambled among the boughs. It was like a company of gray downcast friends and a troop of merry little black devils following the sad shepherd afar off.

He walked looking on the ground, paying small heed to them. Now and again, when the sound of pattering feet and panting breath and the rustling and rending among the copses fell too far behind, he drew out his shepherd's pipe and blew a strain of music, shrill and plaintive, quavering and

---

[19] From "The Unknown Quantity"; copyright, 1916, by Charles Scribner's Sons. By permission of the publishers.

lamenting through the hollow night. He waited while the troops of gray and black scuffled and bounded and trotted near to him. Then he dropped the pipe into its place and strode forward, looking on the ground.

The fitful, shivery wind that rasped the hill-top fluttered the rags of his long mantle of Tyrian blue, torn by thorns and stained by travel. The rich tunic of striped silk beneath it was worn thin, and the girdle about his loins had lost all its ornaments of silver and jewels. His curling hair hung down dishevelled under a turban of fine linen, in which the gilt threads were frayed and tarnished; and his shoes of soft leather were broken by the road. On his brown fingers the places of the vanished rings were still marked in white skin. He carried not the long staff nor the heavy nail-studded rod of the shepherd, but a slender stick of carved cedar battered and scratched by hard usage, and the handle, which must once have been of precious metal, was missing.

He was a strange figure for that lonely place and that humble occupation—a branch of faded beauty from some royal garden tossed by rude winds into the wilderness—a pleasure craft adrift, buffeted and broken, on rough seas.

But he seemed to have passed beyond caring. His young face was as frayed and threadbare as his garments. The splendour of the moonlight flooding the wild world meant as little to him as the hardness of the rugged track which he followed. He wrapped his tattered mantle closer around him, and strode ahead, looking on the ground.

As the path dropped from the summit of the ridge toward the Valley of Mills and passed among huge broken rocks, three men sprang at him from the shadows. He lifted his stick, but let it fall again, and a strange ghost of a smile twisted his face as they gripped him and threw him down.

"You are rough beggars," he said. "Say what you want, you are welcome to it."

"Your money, dog of a courtier," they muttered fiercely; "give us your golden collar, Herod's hound, quick, or you die!"

"The quicker the better," he answered, closing his eyes.

The bewildered flock of sheep and goats, gathered in a silent ring, stood at gaze while the robbers fumbled over their master.

"This is a stray dog," said one, "he has lost his collar, there is not even the price of a mouthful of wine on him. Shall we kill him and leave him for the vultures?"

"What have the vultures done for us," said another, "that we should feed them? Let us take his cloak and drive off his flock, and leave him to die in his own time."

With a kick and a curse they left him. He opened his eyes and lay quiet for a moment, with his twisted smile, watching the stars.

"You creep like snails," he said. "I thought you had marked my time to-night. But not even that is given to me for nothing. I must pay for all, it seems."

Far away, slowly scattering and receding, he heard the rustling and bleating of his frightened flock as the robbers, running and shouting, tried to drive them over the hills. Then he stood up and took the shepherd's pipe from the breast of his tunic. He blew again that plaintive, piercing air, sounding it out over the ridges and distant thickets. It seemed to have neither beginning nor end; a melancholy, pleading tune that searched forever after something lost.

While he played, the sheep and the goats, slipping away from their captors by roundabout ways, hiding behind the laurel bushes, following the dark gullies, leaping down the broken cliffs, came circling back to him, one after another; and as they came, he interrupted his playing, now and then, to call them by name.

When they were nearly all assembled, he went down swiftly toward the lower valley, and they followed him, panting. At the last crook of the path on the steep hillside a straggler came after him along the cliff. He looked up and saw it outlined against the sky. Then he saw it leap, and slip, and fall beyond the path into a deep cleft.

"Little fool," he said, "fortune is kind to you! You have escaped from the big trap of life. What? You are crying for help? You are still in the trap? Then I must go down to you, little fool, for I am a fool too. But why I must do it, I know no more than you know."

He lowered himself quickly and perilously into the cleft, and found the creature with its leg broken and bleeding. It was not a sheep but a young goat. He had no cloak to wrap it in, but he took off his turban and unrolled it, and bound it around the trembling animal. Then he climbed back to the path and strode on at the head of his flock, carrying the little black kid in his arms.

There were houses in the Valley of the Mills; and in some of them lights were burning; and the drone of the mill-stones, where the women were still grinding, came out into the night like the humming of drowsy bees. As the women heard the pattering and bleating of the flock, they wondered who was passing so late. One of them, in a house where there was no mill but many lights, came to the door and looked out laughing, her face and bosom bare.

But the sad shepherd did not stay. His long shadow and the confused mass of lesser shadows behind him drifted down the white moonlight, past the yellow bars of lamplight that gleamed from the doorways. It seemed as if he were bound to go somewhere and would not delay.

Yet with all his haste to be gone, it was plain that he thought little of where he was going. For when he came to the foot of the valley, where the paths divided, he stood between them staring vacantly, without a desire to turn him this way or that. The imperative of choice halted him like a barrier. The balance of his mind hung even because both scales were empty. He could act, he could go, for his strength was untouched; but he could not choose, for his will was broken within him.

The path to the left went up toward the little town of Bethlehem, with huddled roofs and walls in silhouette along the double-crested hill. It was dark and forbidding as a closed fortress. The sad shepherd looked at it with indifferent eyes; there was nothing there to draw him.

The path to the right wound through rock-strewn valleys toward the Dead Sea. But rising out of that crumpled wilderness, a mile or two away, the smooth white ribbon of a chariot-road lay upon the flank of a cone-shaped mountain and curled in loops toward its peak. There the great cone was cut squarely off, and the levelled summit was capped by a palace of marble, with round towers at the corners and flaring beacons along the walls; and the glow of an immense fire, hidden in the central court-yard, painted a false dawn in the eastern sky. All down the clean-cut mountain slopes, on terraces and blind arcades, the lights flashed from lesser pavilions and pleasure-houses.

It was the secret orchard of Herod and his friends, their trysting-place with the spirits of mirth and madness. They called it the Mountain of the Little Paradise. Rich gardens were there; and the cool water from the Pools of Solomon plashed in the fountains; and trees of the knowledge of good and evil fruited blood-red and ivory-white above them; and smooth, curving, glistening shapes, whispering softly of pleasure, lay among the flowers and glided behind the trees. All this was now hidden in the dark. Only the strange bulk of the mountain, a sharp black pyramid girdled and crowned with fire, loomed across the night—a mountain once seen never to be forgotten.

The sad shepherd remembered it well. He looked at it with the eyes of a child who has been in hell. It burned him from afar. Turning neither to the right nor to the left, he walked without a path straight out upon the plain of Bethlehem, still whitened in the hollows and on the sheltered side of its rounded hillocks by the veil of snow.

He faced a wide and empty world. To the west in sleeping Bethlehem, to the east in flaring Herodium, the life of man was infinitely far away from him. Even the stars seemed to withdraw themselves against the blue-black of the sky. They diminished and receded till they were like pinholes in the vault above him. The moon in mid-heaven shrank into a bit of burnished silver, hard and glittering, immeasurably remote. The ragged, inhospitable ridges of Tekoa lay stretched in mortal slumber along the horizon, and between them he caught a glimpse of the sunken Lake of Death, darkly gleaming in its deep bed. There was no movement, no sound, on the plain where he walked, except the soft-padding feet of his dumb, obsequious flock.

He felt an endless isolation strike cold to his heart, against which he held the limp body of the wounded kid, wondering the while, with a half-contempt for his own foolishness, why he took such trouble to save a tiny scrap of the worthless tissue which is called life.

Even when a man does not know or care where he is going, if he steps onward he will get there. In an hour or more of walking over the plain the sad shepherd came to a sheepfold of grey stones with a rude tower beside it. The fold was full of sheep, and at the foot of the tower a little fire of thorns was burning, around which four shepherds were crouching, wrapped in their thick woollen cloaks.

As the stranger approached they looked up, and one of them rose quickly to his feet, grasping his knotted club. But when they saw the flock that followed the sad shepherd, they stared at each other and said: "It is one of us, a keeper of sheep. But how comes he here in this raiment? It is what men wear in king's houses."

"No," said the one who was standing, "it is what they wear when they have been thrown out of them. Look at the rags. He may be a thief and a robber with his stolen flock."

"Salute him when he comes near," said the oldest shepherd. "Are we not four to one? We have nothing to fear from a ragged traveller. Speak him fair. It is the will of God—and it costs nothing."

"Peace be with you, brother," cried the youngest shepherd; "may your mother and father be blessed."

"May your heart be enlarged," the stranger answered, "and may all your families be more blessed than mine, for I have none."

"A homeless man," said the old shepherd, "has either been robbed by his fellows, or punished by God."

"I do not know which it was," answered the stranger; "the end is the same, as you see."

"By your speech you come from Galilee. Where are you going? What are you seeking here?"

"I was going nowhere, my masters; but it was cold on the way there, and my feet turned to your fire."

"Come then, if you are a peaceable man, and warm your feet with us. Heat is a good gift; divide it and it is not less. But you shall have bread and salt too, if you will."

"May your hospitality enrich you. I am your unworthy guest. But my flock?"

"Let your flock shelter by the south wall of the fold: there is good picking there and no wind. Come you and sit with us."

So they all sat down by the fire; and the sad shepherd ate of their bread, but sparingly, like a man to whom hunger brings a need but no joy in the satisfying of it; and the others were silent for a proper time, out of courtesy. Then the oldest shepherd spoke:

"My name is Zadok the son of Eliezer, of Bethlehem. I am the chief shepherd of the flocks of the Temple, which are before you in the fold. These are my sister's sons, Jotham, and Shama, and Nathan: their father Elkanah is dead; and but for these I am a childless man."

"My name," replied the stranger, "is Ammiel the son of Jochanan, of the city of Bethsaida, by the Sea of Galilee, and I am a fatherless man."

"It is better to be childless than fatherless," said Zadok, "yet it is the will of God that children should bury their fathers. When did the blessed Jochanan die?"

"I know not whether he be dead or alive. It is three years since I looked upon his face or had word of him."

"You are an exile, then? he has cast you off?"

"It was the other way," said Ammiel, looking on the ground.

At this the shepherd Shama, who had listened with doubt in his face, started up in anger. "Pig of a Galilean," he cried, "despiser of parents! breaker of the law! When I saw you coming I knew you for something vile. Why do you darken the night for us with your presence? You have reviled him who begot you. Away, or we stone you!"

Ammiel did not answer or move. The twisted smile passed over his face again as he waited to know the shepherds' will with him, even as he had waited for the robbers. But Zadok lifted his hand.

"Not so hasty, Shama-ben-Elkanah. You also break the law by judging a man unheard. The rabbis have told us that there is a tradition of the elders—a rule as holy as the law itself—that a man may deny his father in a certain way without sin. It is a strange rule, and it must be very holy or it would not be so strange. But this is the teaching of the elders: a son may say of anything for which his father asks him—a sheep, or a measure of corn, or a field, or a purse of silver—

'it is Corban, a gift that I have vowed unto the Lord'; and so his father shall have no more claim upon him. Have you said 'Corban' to your father, Ammiel-ben-Jochanan? Have you made a vow unto the Lord?"

"I have said 'Corban,'" answered Ammiel, lifting his face, still shadowed by that strange smile, "but it was not the Lord who heard my vow."

"Tell us what you have done," said the old man sternly, "for we will neither judge you, nor shelter you, unless we hear your story."

"There is nothing in it," replied Ammiel indifferently. "It is an old story. But if you are curious you shall hear it. Afterward you shall deal with me as you will."

So the shepherds, wrapped in their warm cloaks, sat listening with grave faces and watchful, unsearchable eyes, while Ammiel in his tattered silk sat by the sinking fire of thorns and told his tale with a voice that had no room for hope or fear—a cool, dead voice that spoke only of things ended.

II
Nightfire

"In my father's house I was the second son. My brother was honoured and trusted in all things. He was a prudent man and profitable to the household. All that he counselled was done, all that he wished he had. My place was a narrow one. There was neither honour nor joy in it, for it was filled with daily tasks and rebukes. No one cared for me. My mother sometimes wept when I was rebuked. Perhaps she was disappointed in me. But she had no power to make things better. I felt that I was a beast of burden, fed only in order that I might be useful; and the dull life irked me like an ill-fitting harness. There was nothing in it.

"I went to my father and claimed my share of the inheritance. He was rich. He gave it to me. It did not impoverish him and it made me free. I said to him 'Corban,' and shook the dust of Bethsaida from my feet.

"I went out to look for mirth and love and joy and all that is pleasant to the eyes and sweet to the taste. If a god made me, thought I, he made me to live, and the pride of life was strong in my heart and in my flesh. My vow was offered to that well-known god. I served him in Jerusalem, in Alexandria, in Rome, for his altars are everywhere and men worship him openly or in secret.

"My money and youth made me welcome to his followers, and I spent them both freely as if they could never come to an end. I clothed myself in purple and fine linen and fared sumptuously every day. The wine of Cyprus and the dishes of Egypt and Syria were on my table. My dwelling was crowded with merry guests. They came for what I gave them. Their faces were hungry and their soft touch was like the clinging of leeches. To them I was nothing but money and youth; no longer a beast of burden—a beast of pleasure. There was nothing in it.

"From the richest fare my heart went away empty, and after the wildest banquet my soul fell drunk and solitary into sleep.

"Then I thought, Power is better than pleasure. If a man will feast and revel let him do it with the great. They will favour him and raise him up for the service that he renders them. He will obtain place and authority in the world and gain many friends. So I joined myself to Herod."

When the sad shepherd spoke this name his listeners drew back from him as if it were a defilement to hear it. They spat upon the ground and cursed the Idumean who called himself their king.

"A slave!" Jotham cried, "a bloody tyrant and a slave from Edom! A fox, a vile beast who devours his own children! God burn him in Gehenna."

The old Zadok picked up a stone and threw it into the darkness, saying slowly, "I cast this stone on the grave of the Idumean, the blasphemer, the defiler of the Temple! God send us soon the Deliverer, the Promised One, the true King of Israel!" Ammiel made no sign, but went on with his story.

"Herod used me well—for his own purpose. He welcomed me to his palace and his table, and gave me a place among his favourites. He was so much my friend that he borrowed my money. There were many of the nobles of Jerusalem with him, Sadducees, and proselytes from Rome and Asia, and women from everywhere. The law of Israel was observed in the open court, when the people were watching. But in the secret feasts there was no law but the will of Herod, and many deities were served but no god was worshipped. There the captains and the princes of Rome consorted with the high-priest and his sons by night; and there was much coming and going by hidden ways. Everybody was a borrower or a lender, a buyer or a seller of favours. It was a house of diligent madness. There was nothing in it.

"In the midst of this whirling life a great need of love came upon me and I wished to hold some one in my inmost heart.

"At a certain place in the city, within closed doors, I saw a young slave-girl dancing. She was about fifteen years old, thin and supple; she danced like a reed in the wind; but her eyes were weary as death, and her white body was marked with bruises. She stumbled, and the men laughed at her. She fell, and her mistress beat her, crying out that she would fain be rid of such a heavy-footed slave. I paid the price and took her to my dwelling.

"Her name was Tamar. She was a daughter of Lebanon. I robed her in silk and broidered linen. I nourished her with tender care so that beauty came upon her like the blossoming of an almond tree; she was a garden enclosed, breathing spices. Her eyes were like doves behind her veil, her lips were a thread of scarlet, her neck was a tower of ivory, and her breasts were as two fawns which feed among the lilies. She was whiter than milk, and more rosy than the flower of the peach, and her dancing was like the flight of a bird among the branches. So I loved her.

"She lay in my bosom as a clear stone that one has bought and polished and set in fine gold at the end of a golden chain. Never was she glad at my coming, or sorry at my going. Never did she give me anything except what I took from her. There was nothing in it.

"Now whether Herod knew of the jewel that I kept in my dwelling I cannot tell. It was sure that he had his spies in all the city, and himself walked the streets by night in a disguise. On a certain day he sent for me, and had me into his secret chamber, professing great love toward me and more confidence than in any man that lived. So I must go to Rome for him, bearing a sealed letter and a private message to Cæsar. All my goods would be left safely in the hands of the king, my friend, who would reward me double. There was a certain place of high authority at Jerusalem which Cæsar would gladly bestow on a Jew who had done him a service. This mission would commend me to him. It was a great occasion, suited to my powers. Thus Herod fed me with fair promises, and I ran his errand. There was nothing in it.

"I stood before Cæsar and gave him the letter. He read it and laughed, saying that a prince with an incurable hunger is a servant of value to an emperor. Then he asked me if there was nothing sent with the letter. I answered that there was no gift, but a message for his private ear. He drew me aside and I told him that Herod begged earnestly that his dear son, Antipater, might be sent back in haste from Rome to Palestine, for the king had great need of him.

"At this Cæsar laughed again. 'To bury him, I suppose,' said he, 'with his brothers, Alexander and Aristobulus! Truly, it is better to be Herod's swine than his son! Tell the old fox he may catch his own prey.' With this he turned from me and I withdrew unrewarded, to make my way back, as best I could with an empty purse, to Palestine. I had seen the Lord of the World. There was nothing in it.

"Selling my rings and bracelets I got passage in a trading ship for Joppa. There I heard that the king was not in Jerusalem, at his Palace of the Upper City, but had gone with his friends to make merry for a month on the Mountain of the Little Paradise. On that hill-top over against us, where the lights are flaring to-night, in the banquet-hall where couches are spread for a hundred guests, I found Herod."

The listening shepherds spat upon the ground again, and Jotham muttered, "May the worms that devour his flesh never die!" But Zadok whispered, "We wait for the Lord's salvation to come out of Zion." And the sad shepherd, looking with fixed eyes at the firelit mountain far away, continued his story:

"The king lay on his ivory couch, and the sweat of his disease was heavy upon him, for he was old, and his flesh was corrupted. But his hair and his beard were dyed and perfumed and there was a wreath of roses on his head. The hall was full of nobles and great men, the sons of the high-priest were there, and the servants poured their wine in cups of gold. There was a sound of soft music; and all the men were watching a girl who danced in the middle of the hall; and the eyes of Herod were fiery, like the eyes of a fox.

"The dancer was Tamar. She glistened like the snow on Lebanon, and the redness of her was ruddier than a pomegranate, and her dancing was like the coiling of white serpents. When the dance was ended her attendants threw a veil of gauze over her and she lay among her cushions, half covered with flowers, at the feet of the king.

"Through the sound of clapping hands and shouting, two slaves led me behind the couch of Herod. His eyes narrowed as they fell upon me. I told him the message of Cæsar, making it soft, as if it were a word that suffered him to catch his prey. He stroked his beard and his look fell on Tamar. 'I have caught it,' he murmured; 'by all the gods, I have always caught it. And my dear son, Antipater, is coming home of his own will. I have lured him, he is mine.'

"Then a look of madness crossed his face and he sprang up, with frothing lips, and struck at me. 'What is this,' he cried, 'a spy, a servant of my false son, a traitor in my banquet-hall! Who are you?' I knelt before him, protesting that he must know me; that I was his friend, his messenger; that I had left all my goods in his hands; that the girl who had danced for him was mine. At this his face changed again and he fell back on his couch, shaken with horrible laughter. 'Yours!' he cried, 'when was she yours? What is yours? I know you now, poor madman. You are Ammiel, a crazy shepherd from Galilee, who troubled us some time since. Take him away, slaves. He has twenty sheep and twenty goats among my flocks at the foot of the mountain. See to it that he gets them, and drive him away.'

"I fought against the slaves with my bare hands, but they held me. I called to Tamar, begging her to have pity on me, to speak for me, to come with me. She looked up with her eyes like doves behind her veil, but there was no knowledge of me in them. She laughed lazily, as if it were a poor comedy, and flung a broken rose-branch in my face. Then the silver cord was loosened within me, and my heart went out, and I struggled no more. There was nothing in it.

"Afterward I found myself on the road with this flock. I led them past Hebron into the south country, and so by the Vale of Eshcol, and over many hills beyond the Pools of Solomon, until my feet brought me to your fire. Here I rest on the way to nowhere."

He sat silent, and the four shepherds looked at him with amazement.

"It is a bitter tale," said Shama, "and you are a great sinner."

"I should be a fool not to know that," answered the sad shepherd, "but the knowledge does me no good."

"You must repent," said Nathan, the youngest shepherd, in a friendly voice.

"How can a man repent," answered the sad shepherd, "unless he has hope? But I am sorry for everything, and most of all for living."

"Would you not live to kill the fox Herod?" cried Jotham fiercely.

"Why should I let him out of the trap," answered the sad shepherd. "Is he not dying more slowly than I could kill him?"

"You must have faith in God," said Zadok earnestly and gravely.

"He is too far away."

"Then you must have love for your neighbour."

"He is too near. My confidence in man was like a pool by the wayside. It was shallow, but there was water in it, and sometimes a star shone there. Now the feet of many beasts have trampled through it, and the jackals have drunken of it, and there is no more water. It is dry and the mire is caked at the bottom."

"Is there nothing good in the world?"

"There is pleasure, but I am sick of it. There is power, but I hate it. There is wisdom, but I mistrust it. Life is a game and every player is for his own hand. Mine is played. I have nothing to win or lose."

"You are young, you have many years to live."

"I am old, yet the days before me are too many."

"But you travel the road, you go forward. Do you hope

for nothing?"

"I hope for nothing," said the sad shepherd. "Yet if one thing should come to me it might be the beginning of hope. If I saw in man or woman a deed of kindness without a selfish reason, and a proof of love gladly given for its own sake only, then might I turn my face toward that light. Till that comes, how can I have faith in God whom I have never seen? I have seen the world which he has made, and it brings me no faith. There is nothing in it."

"Ammiel-ben-Jochanan," said the old man sternly, "you are a son of Israel, and we have had compassion on you, according to the law. But you are an apostate, an unbeliever, and we can have no more fellowship with you, lest a curse come upon us. The company of the desperate brings misfortune. Go your way and depart from us, for our way is not yours."

So the sad shepherd thanked them for their entertainment, and took the little kid again in his arms, and went into the night, calling his flock. But the youngest shepherd Nathan followed him a few steps and said:

"There is a broken fold at the foot of the hill. It is old and small, but you may find a shelter there for your flock where the wind will not shake you. Go your way with God, brother, and see better days."

Then Ammiel went a little way down the hill and sheltered his flock in a corner of the crumbling walls. He lay among the sheep and the goats with his face upon his folded arms, and whether the time passed slowly or swiftly he did not know, for he slept.

He waked as Nathan came running and stumbling among the scattered stones.

"We have seen a vision," he cried, "a wonderful vision of angels. Did you not hear them? They sang loudly of the Hope of Israel. We are going to Bethlehem to see this thing which is come to pass. Come you and keep watch over our sheep while we are gone."

"Of angels I have seen and heard nothing," said Ammiel, "but I will guard your flocks with mine, since I am in debt to you for bread and fire."

So he brought the kid in his arms, and the weary flock

straggling after him, to the south wall of the great fold again, and sat there by the embers at the foot of the tower, while the others were away.

The moon rested like a ball on the edge of the western hills and rolled behind them. The stars faded in the east and the fires went out on the Mountain of the Little Paradise. Over the hills of Moab a grey flood of dawn rose slowly, and arrows of red shot far up before the sunrise.

The shepherds returned full of joy and told what they had seen.

"It was even as the angels said unto us," said Shama, "and it must be true. The King of Israel has come. The faithful shall be blessed."

"Herod shall fall," cried Jotham, lifting his clenched fist toward the dark peaked mountain. "Burn, black Idumean, in the bottomless pit, where the fire is not quenched."

Zadok spoke more quietly. "We found the new-born child of whom the angels told us wrapped in swaddling clothes and lying in a manger. The ways of God are wonderful. His salvation comes out of darkness. But you, Ammiel-ben-Jochanan, except you believe, you shall not see it. Yet since you have kept our flocks faithfully, and because of the joy that has come to us, I give you this piece of silver to help you on your way."

But Nathan came close to the sad shepherd and touched him on the shoulder with a friendly hand. "Go you also to Bethlehem," he said in a low voice, "for it is good to see what we have seen, and we will keep your flock until you return."

"I will go," said Ammiel, looking into his face, "for I think you wish me well. But whether I shall see what you have seen, or whether I shall ever return, I know not. Farewell."

III
Dawn

The narrow streets of Bethlehem were waking to the first stir of life as the sad shepherd came into the town with the morning, and passed through them like one walking in his sleep.

Christmas in Modern Story

The court-yard of the great khan and the open rooms around it were crowded with travellers, rousing from their night's rest and making ready for the day's journey. In front of the stables half hollowed in the rock beside the inn, men were saddling their horses and their beasts of burden, and there was much noise and confusion.

But beyond these, at the end of the line, there was a deeper grotto in the rock, which was used only when the nearer stalls were full. Beside the entrance of this cave an ass was tethered, and a man of middle age stood in the doorway.

The sad shepherd saluted him and told his name.

"I am Joseph the carpenter of Nazareth," replied the man. "Have you also seen the angels of whom your brother shepherds came to tell us?"

"I have seen no angels," answered Ammiel, "nor have I any brothers among the shepherds. But I would fain see what they have seen."

"It is our first-born son," said Joseph, "and the Most High has sent him to us. He is a marvelous child: great things are foretold of him. You may go in, but quietly, for the child and his mother Mary are asleep."

So the sad shepherd went in quietly. His long shadow entered before him, for the sunrise was flowing into the door of the grotto. It was made clean and put in order, and a bed of straw was laid in the corner on the ground.

The child was asleep, but the young mother was waking, for she had taken him from the manger into her lap, where her maiden veil of white was spread to receive him. And she was singing very softly as she bent over him in wonder and content.

Ammiel saluted her and kneeled down to look at the child. He was nothing different from other young children. The mother waited for him to speak of angels, as the other shepherds had done. The sad shepherd did not speak, but only looked. And as he looked his face changed.

"You have suffered pain and danger and sorrow for his sake," he said gently.

"They are past," she answered, "and for his sake I have suffered them gladly."

"He is very little and helpless; you must bear many

troubles for his sake."

"To care for him is my joy, and to bear him lightens my burden."

"He does not know you, he can do nothing for you."

"But I know him. I have carried him under my heart, he is my son and my king."

"Why do you love him?"

The mother looked up at the sad shepherd with a great reproach in her soft eyes. Then her look grew pitiful as it rested on his face.

"You are a sorrowful man," she said.

"I am a wicked man," he answered.

She shook her head gently.

"I know nothing of that," she said, "but you must be very sorrowful, since you are born of a woman and yet you ask a mother why she loves her child. I love him for love's sake, because God has given him to me."

So the mother Mary leaned over her little son again and began to croon a song as if she were alone with him.

But Ammiel was still there, watching and thinking and beginning to remember. It came back to him that there was a woman in Galilee who had wept when he was rebuked; whose eyes had followed him when he was unhappy, as if she longed to do something for him; whose voice had broken and dropped silent while she covered her tear-stained face when he went away.

His thoughts flowed swiftly and silently toward her and after her like rapid waves of light. There was a thought of her bending over a little child in her lap, singing softly for pure joy,—and the child was himself. There was a thought of her lifting a little child to the breast that had borne him as a burden and a pain, to nourish him there as a comfort and a treasure,—and the child was himself. There was a thought of her watching and tending and guiding a little child from day to day, from year to year, putting tender arms around him, bending over his first wavering steps, rejoicing in his joys, wiping away the tears from his eyes, as he had never tried to wipe her tears away,—and the child was himself. She had done everything for the child's sake, but what had the child done for her sake? And the child was himself: that was what he had come to,—after the night fire had burned out, after the darkness had grown thin and melted in the thoughts that pulsed through it like rapid waves of light,—that was what he had come to in the early morning,—*himself*, a child in his mother's arms.

Then he arose and went out of the grotto softly, making the three-fold sign of reverence; and the eyes of Mary followed him with kind looks.

Joseph of Nazareth was still waiting outside the door.

"How was it that you did not see the angels?" he asked. "Were you not with the other shepherds?"

"No," answered Ammiel, "I was asleep. But I have seen the mother and the child. Blessed be the house that holds them."

"You are strangely clad for a shepherd," said Joseph. "Where do you come from?"

"From a far country," replied Ammiel; "from a country that you have never visited."

"Where are you going now?" asked Joseph.

"I am going home," answered Ammiel, "to my mother's and my father's house in Galilee."

"Go in peace, friend," said Joseph.

And the sad shepherd took up his battered staff, and went on his way rejoicing.

CHRISTMAS BREAD[20]
Kathleen Norris

"But what time will your operation be over, mother?"

A silence. The surgeon opened three letters, looked at them, tore them in two, cast them aside, glanced at her newspaper, glanced at her coffee cup, and took a casual sip of the smoking liquid. But she did not answer.

"If you were thr-r-rough at 'leven o'clock—" Merle began again hopefully. She paid some attention to consonants, because until recently she had called through "froo," and she was anxious to seem grown-up. "I could go to the hospital with Miss Frothingham," she suggested, "and wait for you?"

"I thought Miss Frothingham was going to take you to Mrs. Winchester's?" Doctor Madison countered in surprise, at last giving a partial attention to her little daughter. "Don't you want to spend Christmas Day with little Betty?" she went on, easily, half-absently. "It seems to me that is a very nice plan—straighten your shoulders, dear. It seems to me that it was extremely nice of Mrs. Winchester to want you to come. Most people want only their own families on Christmas Day!"

She was paying small heed to her own words. "That band really did straighten her teeth," she was thinking. "I must remind Miss Frothingham to order some more of the little smocks; she doesn't look half so well in the blue-jacket blouses. How like George she is growing!... What did you say, Merle?" she added, realizing that the child's plaintive voice was lingering still in the air.

"I said that *I* would like my own family, too, on Christmas," the child repeated, half-daring, half-uncertain.

"Ring the bell, dear," her mother said from the newspaper.

"I wish I didn't know what you were going to give me for Christmas, mother!"

"You what?"

---

[20] By permission of the author and "Good Housekeeping."

"I wish I didn't know what you were going to give me!" Silence.

"For Christmas, you know?" Merle prompted. "I love your present. I love to have a little desk all my own. It's just like Betty's, too, only prettier. But I would drather have it a surprise, and run down Christmas morning to see what it was!"

"Don't say 'drather,' dear."

"Rather." With a gold spoon, Merle made a river through her cream of wheat in the monogrammed gold bowl and watched the cream rivers flood together. "What interests you in the paper, mother?" she asked politely.

"Why, they are going to have the convention in California next summer," her mother said.

"And shall you go, mother?"

"Oh, I think so! Perhaps you and Miss Frothingham will go with me."

"To hotels?"

"I suppose so."

Merle sighed. She did not like large strange hotels. "Mother, doesn't it seem funny to you that a patient would have his operation on Christmas Day? Couldn't he have it to-morrow, or wait till Wednesday?"

The doctor's fine mouth twitched at the corners. "Poor fellow, they only get him here to-morrow, Merle, Christmas morning. And they tell me there is no time to lose."

Tears came into the little girl's eyes. "It doesn't seem—much—like Christmas," she murmured under her breath. "To have you in the surgery all morning, and me with the Winchesters, that aren't my relations at all——"

"Tell me exactly what you had planned to do, Merle," her mother suggested reasonably. "Perhaps we can manage it for some other day. What did you especially want to do?"

The kindly, logical tone was that of the surgeon used to matters no less vital than life and death. Merle raised her round, childish eyes to her mother's pleasant, keen ones. Then with a great sigh she returned to the golden bowl and spoon. Nothing more was said until Lizzie came in for the orders.

"Dear me, I miss Miss Frothingham!" said

Doctor Madison then. "Tell Ada to use her own judgment, Lizzie. Tell her—you might have chicken again. That doesn't spoil, in case I'm late."

"You wouldn't have a turkey, Doctor? To-morrow's Christmas, you know."

"Well—if Ada thinks so. I don't particularly care for turkey—yes, we may as well have a turkey. But no pudding, and above all, no mince pie, Lizzie. Have something simple—prune whip, applesauce, I don't care! Merle will be with the Winchesters all day, and she'll need only a light supper. If there are any telephones, I'm at the hospital. Miss Frothingham will be back this afternoon."

Then she was gone, and there was a long lonely day ahead of her small daughter. But Merle was accustomed to them. She went into the kitchen and watched Ada and Ada's friend, Mrs. Catawba Hercules, until Miss Watson came. Then she had a music lesson, and a French lesson, and after lunch she posted herself at a front window to watch the streets and wait for pretty Miss Frothingham, who filled the double post of secretary and governess, and who had gone home yesterday to her sister's house for a Christmas visit.

Outside was Christmas weather. All morning the streets had been bare and dark, and swept with menacing winds that hurried and buffeted the marketing and shopping women. But at noon the leaden sky had turned darker and darker, and crept lower and lower, and as Merle watched, the first timid snowflakes began to flutter whitely against the general grayness.

Then there was scurrying and laughter in the streets, bundles dampened, boys shouting and running, merry faces rouged by the pure, soft cold. The shabby leather-sheathed doors of St. Martin's, opposite Merle's window, creaked and swung under the touch of wet, gloved hands. Merle could see the Christmas trees and the boxed oranges outside the State Street groceries coated with eider-down; naked gardens and fences and bare trees everywhere grew muffled and feathered and lovely. In the early twilight the whole happy town echoed with bells and horns and the clanking of snow-shovels.

By this time Miss Frothingham was back again, and was helping Merle into the picturesque black velvet with the deep lace collar. Merle, sputtering through the blue embroidered cloth while her face was being washed, asked how Miss Frothingham's little niece had liked her doll.

"Oh, my dear, she doesn't get it until she comes downstairs to-morrow morning, of course!"

"Will she be excited?" Merle asked, excited herself.

"She'll be perfectly frantic! I see that your mother's present came."

"My desk. It came last night. I moved all my things into it to-day," Merle said. "It doesn't feel much like Christmas when a person gets their presents two days before," she observed.

"His presents. Her presents," corrected the governess.

"Her presents. Will your sister's little girls have a tree?"

"Oh, my, yes! It's a gorgeous tree!"

"And did you see my cousins while you were there?"

Miss Frothingham nodded. Her married sister lived next to Doctor Madison's brother, a struggling young engineer with a small family, in a certain not-too-fashionable suburb. There had been a difference of opinion regarding a legacy, between the physician and her brother some years earlier, and a long silence had ensued, but Merle took a lively interest in the little cousins of whom she had only a hazy and wistful memory, and her mother had no objection to an occasional mention of them.

"I saw Rawley—that's the second little boy—playing with my niece," Miss Frothingham said. "And I saw Tommy—he's older than you—taking care of the baby. I think he was going to the grocery for his mother; he was wheeling the baby very carefully. But I think those children are going to have a pretty sad Christmas because their Daddy is very sick, you know, and they all had whooping-cough, and I think their mother is too tired to know whether it's Christmas or Fourth of July!"

"Maybe their father's going to die like my father," Merle suggested stoically. "I guess they won't hang up their stockings," she added suddenly.

For it had been reported that this was their custom, and Merle liked to lie awake in her little bed, warm and cosy on a winter night, and think thrillingly of what it would be to explore a bulging and lumpy stocking of her own.

Miss Frothingham looked doubtful. "I don't suppose they will!" she opined.

Merle was shocked. "Will they cry?"

"I don't suppose so. My sister says they're extremely good children and will do anything to help their mother."

"Maybe they'll hang them up anyway, and they'll be empty?" Merle said, wide-eyed.

But the governess had lost interest in the subject, as grown-ups so often and so maddeningly did, and was manicuring her pretty nails, and humming, so Merle had to abandon it for the moment.

However, she thought about it continually, and after dinner she said suddenly and daringly to her mother:

"The Rutledge children's father is sick, and they aren't going to hang up their stockings! Miss Frothingham said so!"

When this was said, she and Miss Frothingham and her mother were all in the attic. Merle had not been there for weeks, nor her mother for months, and it was enchanting to the child to find herself bustling about, so unexpectedly in this exciting atmosphere, which, if it was not typically Christmassy, was at least unusual. It had come about suddenly, as did much that affected her mother's movements.

The doctor had arrived home at half-past four, and Miss Frothingham had lost no time in reminding her that the promised bundle for the New Year's rummage sale for some charity was to have been ready this evening. Doctor Madison had said—did she remember?—that she had any amount of old clothing to dispose of.

"Oh, that attic is full of it!" Merle's mother had said, wearily. "You know this was my grandmother's house, and goodness only knows the rubbish that is up there! I've meant to get at it all sometime—I couldn't do it in her lifetime. What time is it? Suppose we go up there and get a start?"

There was twilight in the attic, and outside the dormer windows the snow was falling—falling. Merle performed a little pirouette of sheer ecstasy when they mounted the stairs. Her mother lighted the lights in a business-like fashion.

"Here, take this—take this—take this!" she began to say carelessly, picking one garment after another from the low row of ghostly forms dangling against the eaves. "Mr. Madison's army coats——"

"But, Mrs. Madison, this is beautiful beaver on this suit—yards of it!"

"Take it—take it!" Merle's equable mother said feverishly, almost irritably. "Here, I shall never wear this fur coat again, and all these hats—I suppose those plumes are worth something!"

She was an energetic, restless creature. The hard work strangely calmed her, and just before dinner she was settling down to it almost with enjoyment. The summons to the meal annoyed her.

"Suppose we come back to it and make a thorough job?" she suggested.

Merle's heart leaped for joy.

"But you ought to be in bed, Kiddie," her mother said, not urgently, when dinner was over.

"Oh, mother, please! It's Christmas Eve!" Merle begged, with all the force of her agonized eight years.

So here they all were again, and the snow was still falling outside, and the electric lights on their swinging cords were sending an eerie light over the miscellaneous shapes and contours of the attic, now making the shadow of an old what-not rush across the floor with startling vitality, now plunging the gloomy eaves behind Merle into alarming darkness.

Pyramids of books were on the floor, magazines tied in sixes with pink cord, curtains, rugs, beds, heaped mattresses, trunks, boxes, the usual wheel-chair and the usual crutch—all the significant, gathered driftwood of sixty years of living was strewn and packed and heaped and hung about.

"Here, here's a wonderful patent preserving kettle, do you suppose they could use that? And what about these four terrible patent rockers?"

"Oh, Mrs. Madison, I imagine they would be only too delighted! Their idea is to open a regular store, you know, and make the sale permanent. But ought you——"

"I ought to have done it years before! But Doctor Madison—" His widow's breast rose on a sharp sigh; she lost the words for a second. "Doctor Madison and I never lived here, you know," she resumed. "And I stayed abroad for years after his death, when Merle was a baby. And for a long time I was like a person dazed—" She stopped.

"I had my work," she resumed, after a pause. "It saved my reason, I think. Perhaps—perhaps I went into it too hard. But I had to have—to do—something! My grandparents died and left me this place and the Beachaways' place, but I've had no time for housekeeping!"

"I should think not, indeed!" Miss Frothingham said, timidly respectful.

These fingers, that could cleave so neatly into the very stronghold of life, that could touch so boldly hearts that still pulsated and lungs that still were fanned by breath, were they to count silver spoons and quilt comforters?

The governess felt a little impressed; even a little touched. She did not often see her employer in this mood. Kind, just, reasonable, interested, capable, good, Doctor Madison always was. But this was something more.

"I had no intention of becoming rich, of being—successful!" the older woman added presently, in a dreamy tone. She was sitting with the great spread of a brocaded robe across her knee. Her eyes were absent.

"All the more fun!" Miss Frothingham said youthfully.

"I was alone—" Mary Madison said drearily and quietly, in a low tone, as if to herself. And in the three words the younger caught a glimpse of all the tragedy and loneliness of widowhood. "Doctor Madison was so wise," she began again. "I've always thought that if he had lived my life would have been different."

"You lost your parents, I know, and were you an only child?" Miss Frothingham ventured, after a respectful silence. But immediately the scarlet, apologetic color flooded her face, and she added hastily: "I beg your pardon! Of course I knew that you have a brother—I know Mr. Rutledge and his wife!"

"Yes, I have a brother," the doctor answered, rousing, and beginning briskly to assort and segregate again. The tone chilled her companion, and there was a pause.

"Your brother is Tommy's and Rawley's and the baby's father," Merle broke it by announcing flatly.

Her mother looked at her with an indulgent half-smile.

She usually regarded Merle much as an amused stranger might have done; the odd little black-eyed, black-maned child who was always curling herself into corners about the house. Merle was going to be pretty, her mother thought tonight, in satisfaction. Her little face was blazing, her eyes shone, and she had pulled over her disheveled curls a fantastic tissue-paper cap of autumn leaves left from some long-ago Hallowe'en frolic her mother could only half-remember.

"What do you know about them?" she asked good-naturedly. "You never saw them!"

"You told me once about them, when I was a teeny little girl," Merle reminded her. "When we were in the cemetery you did. And Miss Frothingham told me."

"So there's a third child?" Doctor Madison asked, musing. Miss Frothingham nodded.

"A gorgeous boy. The handsomest baby I ever saw!... John," she said.

"John was my father's name. Sad, isn't it?" Doctor Madison asked after a silence during which she had folded the brocade and added it to the heap.

"A costumier would buy lots of this just as it stands," Miss Frothingham murmured by way of answer.

"I mean when families quarrel," persisted the doctor.

"Oh, I think it is very sad!" the secretary said fervently.

"We were inseparable, as children," Mary Madison said suddenly. "Tim is just a year younger than I."

"You're not going to give away all these beautiful Indian things, Doctor?"

The doctor, who had been staring absently into the shadows of the attic, roused herself. "Oh, why not? Merle here isn't the sort that will want to hoard them! I loathe them all. It was just this sort of rubbish——"

She had risen, to fling open the top of one more trunk. Now she moved restlessly across the attic, and Merle, who did not know her mother in this mood, hopped after her.

"It was just this sort of rubbish, little girl," Mary Madison said gently, one of her thin, clever hands laid against the child's cheek, "that made trouble between—your Uncle Timothy and me. Just pictures and rugs—and Aunt Lizzie's will.... Well, let's get through here, and away from these ghosts!"

"I wish *we* had three children," Merle said longingly. "You had your brother. But I haven't any one! Did you hang up your stockings?"

"Dear me, yes! At the dining-room mantel."

"Then I would hang mine there, if I—hanged—it," Merle decided.

"But we have the big open fireplace in the sitting-room now, dear. We didn't have that when we were little, Timmy and I."

"But I'd drather in the dining-room, mother, if that's what you did!"

"Here are perfectly good new flannels—" Miss Frothingham interposed.

"Take them. But Merle," the doctor said, a little troubled, "I would have filled a stocking for you if I had known you really wanted me to, dear. Will you remind me, next Christmas, and I'll see to it?"

"Yes, mother," Merle promised, suddenly lifeless and subdued. "But next Christmas is so—so far," she faltered, with watering eyes and a trembling lip.

"But all the shops are closed now, dear," her mother reminded her sensibly. "You know my brother and I never had a quarrel before," she added, after a space, to the younger woman. "And this was never an open breach."

"Was?" Miss Frothingham echoed, anxious and eager.

"Wasn't. No," said her employer thoughtfully. "It was just a misunderstanding—the wrong word said here, and the wrong construction put upon it there, and then resentment—and silence—our lives separated——"

She fell silent herself, but it was Merle, attentively watching her, who said now,

"Their father's sick, and they aren't going to hang up their stockings!"

"Oh, they've had a great deal of trouble," Miss Frothingham added with a grave expression, as the older woman turned inquiring eyes upon her. "Mr. Rutledge has been ill for weeks, and the baby is quite small—six or seven months old, I suppose."

"Why, he's a successful man!" his sister said impatiently as the other paused.

"Oh, yes, they have a good Swedish girl, I know, and a little car, and all that! But I imagine this has been a terribly hard winter for them. They're lovely people, Doctor Madison," added little Miss Frothingham bravely and earnestly. "So wonderful with their children, and they have a little vegetable garden, and fruit trees, and all that! But all the children in that neighborhood had whooping cough last fall, and I know Mrs. Rutledge was pretty tired, and then he got double pneumonia before Thanksgiving, and he hasn't been out of the house since."

"He's a wonderful boy!" Doctor Madison said in a silence. "We were orphans, and he was a wonderful little brother to me. My grandparents were the stern, old-fashioned sort, but Timmy could put fun and life into punishment, even. Many an hour I've spent up here in this very attic with him—in disgrace."

She got up, walked a few paces across the bare floor, picked an old fur buggy-robe from a chair, looked at it absently, and put it down again.

"What insanity brought me up to this attic on a snowy Christmas Eve!" she demanded abruptly, laughing, but with the tears Miss Frothingham had never seen there before in her eyes. "It all comes over me so—what life was when Timmy and George—Merle's father—were in it! Poor little girl," she added, sitting down on a trunk and drawing Merle toward her; "you were to have seven brothers and sisters, and a big Daddy to adore you and spoil you! And he had been two months in his grave when she was born," she added to the other woman.

"But then couldn't you afford to have all my brothers and sisters?" Merle demanded anxiously.

"It couldn't be managed, dear. Life gets unmanageable, sometimes," her mother answered, smiling a little sadly. "But a brother is a wonderful thing for a small girl to have. Everything has robbed this child," she added, "the silence between her uncle and me—her father's death—my profession. If I had been merely a general practitioner, as I was for three years," she went on, "there would have been a score of what we call 'G. P.'s' to fill her poor little stocking!

But half my grateful patients hardly know me by sight, much less that I have a greedy little girl who has a stocking to be filled!"

"Mother, I love you," Merle said, for the first time in her life stirred by the unusual hour and mood, and by the tender, half-sorrowful, and all-loving voice she had never heard before.

"And I love you, little girl, even if I am too busy to show it!" her mother answered seriously. "But here! Do let's get done with this before we break our hearts!" she added briskly, in a sudden change of mood. And she sank upon her knees before a trunk and began vigorously to deal with its contents. "And I'll tell you what I'll do, Merle," her mother went on, briskly lifting out and inspecting garments of all sorts. "I'll go to see Mr. Waldteufel on Wednesday——"

"Not Waldteufel of the Bazaar, mother?"

"The very same. You know your daddy and I were boarding with his mother in Potsdam when the war broke out, and two years ago your mother saved his wife and his tiny baby—after two dear little babies had died. So he thinks a great deal of the Madisons, my dear, and he'll give me the very nicest things in that big shop for my little girl's stocking. And suppose you hang it up New Year's Eve this year, and next year—well, we won't say anything about next year now, but just you *wait!*"

"Oh, mother—mother!" Merle sang, her slippered feet dancing. And there was no question at this minute that she would some day be beautiful.

"Don't strangle me. There, I remember that dress—look at the puffed sleeves, Merle," said her mother, still exploring the trunk. "I suppose the velvet is worth something—and the lace collar. That was my best dress."

"Mother, mayn't I keep it? And wear it some day?"

"Why, I suppose you may. I wish," said the doctor in an undertone, whimsically to the other woman, "I wish I had more of that sort of sentiment—of tenderness—in me! I did have, once."

"Perhaps it was the sorrow—and then your taking your profession so hard?" Miss Frothingham suggested timidly.

"Perhaps—Here, this was my brother Timmy's sweater,"

said the doctor, taking a bulky little garment of gray wool from the trunk. "How proud he was of it! It was his first—'my roll-top sweater,' he used to call it. I remember these two pockets——"

She ran her fingers—the beautifully-tempered fingers of the surgeon—into one of the pockets as she spoke, and Merle and the secretary saw an odd expression come into her face. But when she withdrew her hand and exposed to them the palm, it was filled with nothing more comprehensible than eight or ten curled and crisped old crusts of bread.

"Mother, what is it?" Merle questioned, peering.

"Bait?" Miss Frothingham asked, smiling.

"Crusts," the older woman said in an odd voice.

"Crusts?" echoed the other two, utterly at a loss.

There was that in the doctor's look that made the moment significant.

"Yes," said Merle's mother. And for a full minute there was silence in the attic, Miss Frothingham covertly and somewhat bewilderedly studying her employer's face, Merle looking from one to the other with round eyes like those of a brunette doll, and the older woman staring into space, as if entirely unconscious of their presence.

The lights stirred, and shadows leaped and moved in answer. Snow made a delicate, tinkling sound outside, in the dark, on the roof beyond the dormers. The bell of Saint Paul's rang nine o'clock on Christmas Eve.

"I was always a stubborn child, and I hated the crusts of my bread, but they insisted that I eat them," said Mary Madison suddenly, in an odd, rather low voice. "I used to cry and fight about it, and—and Timmy used to eat them for me."

"Did he like them, mother?" Merle demanded, highly interested.

"Did he—? No, I don't know that he did. But he was a very good little brother to me, Merle. And grandmother and Aunt Lizzie used to be stern with me, always trapping me into trouble, getting me into scenes where I screamed at them and they at me."

Her voice stopped, and for a second she was silent.

"Crusts were a great source of trouble," she resumed after a while.

"I like them!" Merle said encouragingly, to feed the conversation.

"Yours is a very different world, baby. People used to excite and bewilder children thirty years ago. I've spent whole mornings sobbing and defiant. 'You will say it!' 'I won't say it'—hour after hour after hour."

Merle was actually pale at the thought.

"Timmy was the favorite, and how generous he was to me!" his sister said, musing. And suddenly she raised the little dried crusts in both hands to her face, and laid her cheek against them. "Oh, Timmy—Timmy—Timmy!" she said, between a laugh and a sob. "To think of the grimy little hand that put these here just because Molly was so naughty and so stubborn!"

"Miss Frothingham," said Doctor Madison quietly, looking up with one of those amazing changes of mood that were the eternal bewilderment of those who dealt with her, "I wonder if you could finish this up? Get Lizzie to help you if you like; we're all but done anyway! Use your own judgment, but when in doubt—destroy! I believe—it's only nine o'clock! I believe I'll go and see my brother! Come, Merle, get your coat with the squirrel collar—it's cold!"

So then it was all Christmas magic, and just what Christmas Eve should be. Saunders brought the little closed car to the door, to be sure, but there he vanished from the scene, and it was only mother and Merle.

The streets were snowy, and snow frosted the windshield, and lights and people and the bright windows of shops were all mixed up together, in a pink and blue and gold dazzle of color.

But all this was past before they came to the "almost country," as Merle called it, and there were gardens and trees about the little houses, where lights streamed out with an infinitely heartening and pleasant effect.

They stopped. "Put your arms tight about my neck, Baby. I can't have you walking in this!" said her mother then.

And Merle tightened her little furry arms about her mother's furry collar, and they somehow struggled and stumbled up to Uncle Tim's porch. There was light in one of the windows, but no light in the hall. But after a while footsteps came——

"Molly!" said the pale, tall, gentle woman who opened the door, "and your dear baby!"

"Cassie—may we come in?" Merle had never heard her mother speak in quite this tone before.

They went in to a sort of red-tinted dimness. But in the dining-room there was sudden light, and they all blinked at each other. And Merle instantly saw that over the mantel two short stockings and tiny socks were suspended.

The women were talking in short sentences.

"Molly!"

"Cassie——"

"But in all this snow——"

"We didn't mind it."

"I'm so glad."

"Cassie—how thin you are, child! And you look so tired!"

"Timmy's been so ill!"

"But he's better?"

"Oh, yes—but so weak still!"

"You've had a nurse?"

"Not these last two weeks. We couldn't—we didn't—really need her. I have my wonderful Sigma in the kitchen, you know."

"But, my dear, with a tiny baby!"

The worn face brightened. "Ah, he's such a dear! I don't know what we would have done without him!"

A silence. Then Mrs. Rutledge said: "The worst is over, we hope. And the boys have been such a comfort!"

"They hung up their stockings," Merle commented in her deep, serious little voice.

"Yes, dear," their mother said eagerly, as if she were glad to have the little pause bridged. "But I'm afraid Santa Claus is going to be too busy to remember them this year! I've just been telling them that perhaps he wouldn't have time to put anything but some candy and some fruit in, this year!"

"*They* believe in Santa Claus," Merle remarked, faintly reproachful, to her mother. "But I'm younger than Tommy, and I don't!"

"But you may if you want to, dear!" Doctor Madison

said, shaken, yet laughing, and kneeling down to put her arms about the little girl. "Cassie, what can I do for Tim?" she pleaded. "We're neither of us children. I don't have to say that I'm sorry—that it's all been a bad dream of coldness and stupidity."

"Oh, Molly—Molly!" the other woman faltered. And tears came into the eyes that had not known them for hard and weary weeks. "He was to blame more than you—I always said so. He knew it! And he did try to write you! He's grieved over it so. But when he met you in the street that day——"

"I know it! I know it! He was wrong—I was wrong—you were the only sensible one, the peacemaker, between us!" the doctor said eagerly and quickly. "It's over. It's for us now to see that the children are wiser in their day and generation!"

"Ah, Molly, but you were always so wonderful!" faltered Cassie Rutledge. And suddenly the two women were in each other's arms. "Molly, we've missed—just *you*—so!" she sobbed.

Two small shabby boys in pajamas had come solemnly in from the direction of the kitchen, whence also proceeded the fretting of a baby. Merle was introduced to Tommy and Rawley and was shy. But she immediately took full charge of the baby.

"Santa Claus may not give us anything but apples and stuff," Rawley, who was six, confided. "Because Dad was sick, and there are lots of poor children this year!"

"And we aren't going to have any turkey because Dad and John couldn't have any, anyway!" Tommy added philosophically.

John was the baby, who now looked dewily and sleepily at the company from above the teething biscuit with which he was smearing his entire countenance.

"He's getting a great, big, hard back tooth, Molly, at eight months," said his mother, casting aside the biscuit and wiping the exquisite, little velvet face. "Isn't that early?"

"It seems so to me. I forget! Any fever?"

"Oh, no, but his blessed little mouth is so hot! Timmy's asleep," said Cassie anxiously. "But Molly, if you could stay to see him just a minute when he wakes! Could Merle—we have an extra bed in the little room right off the boys' room, where the nurse slept. She couldn't spend Christmas with the boys? That would be better than any present to us!"

She spoke as one hardly hoping, and Merle felt no hope whatever. But to the amazement of both, the handsome, resolute face softened, and the doctor merely said:

"Trot along to bed then, Merle, with your cousins. But mind you don't make any noise. Remember Uncle Timmy is ill!"

Merle strangled her with a kiss. There was a murmur of children's happy voices on the stairs; a messenger came back to ask if Tom's nine-year-old pajamas or Rawley's seven-year-old size would best suit the guest. Another messenger came discreetly down and hung a fourth stocking at the dining-room mantel, with the air of one both invisible and inaudible.

"He's terrified," said Cassie in an aside, with her good motherly smile; "he knows he has no business downstairs at this hour!"

Then Cassie's baby fretted himself off in her arms, and the two women sat in the dim light, and talked and talked and talked.

"Cassie, we've an enormous turkey—I'll send it over the first thing in the morning."

"But, Molly, when Tim knows you've been here, he'll not care about any turkey!"

"Their stockings—" mused the doctor, unhearing.

With a suddenly lighting face, after deep thought, she went to the telephone in the dining-room, and three minutes later a good husband and father, a mile away across the city, left his own child and the tree he was trimming and went to answer her summons.

"Mr. Waldteufel? This is Doctor Madison."

"Oh, Doctor!" came rushing the rich European voice. "Merry Christmas to you! I wish could you but zee your bapey—so fat we don't weigh him Sundays no more! His lecks is like——"

The surgeon's voice interrupted. There was excited interchange of words. Then the toy-king said:

"I meet you at my store in ten minutes! It is one more

kindness that you ask me to do it! My employees go home at five—the boss he works late, isn't it? I should to work hard for this boy of mine—an egg he eats to-day, the big roughneck feller!"

"Oh, Molly, you can't!" Cassie protested. But there was color in her face.

"Oh, Cassie, I can! Have we a tree?"

"I couldn't. It wasn't the money, Molly—don't think that. But it was just being so tired ... the trimmings are all there from last year ... oh, Molly, into this darkness and cold again! You shouldn't!"

She was gone. But the hour that Cassie waited, dreaming, with the baby in her lap, was a restful hour, and when it was ended, and Molly was back again, the baby had to be carried upstairs, up to his crib, for there was heavy work to do below stairs.

Molly had a coaster and an enormous rocking-horse. She had the car loaded and strapped and covered with packages. She had a tree, which she said she had stolen from the grocer; he would be duly enlightened and paid to-morrow.

She flung off her heavy coat, pinned back her heavy hair, tied on an apron. She snapped strings, scribbled cards. And she personally stuffed the three larger stockings.

Cassie assisted. Neither woman heard the clock strike ten, strike eleven.

"You'll be a wreck to-morrow, my dear!"

"Oh, Molly, no! This is just doing me a world of good. I had been feeling so depressed and so worried. But I believe—I do believe—that the worst of it is over now!"

"Which one gets this modeling clay? It's frightfully smelly stuff, but they all adore it! My dear, does Timmy usually sleep this way? I've looked in at him twice, he seems troubled—restless——"

"Yes—the scissors are there, right under your foot. Yes, he is like that, Molly, no real rest, and he doesn't seem to have any particular life in him. He seems so languid. Nothing tastes exactly right to him and of course the children are noisy, and the house is small. I want him——"

Mrs. Rutledge, working away busily in the litter, and fastening a large tinsel ball to a fragrant bough with thin, work-worn hands, stepped back, squinted critically, and turned to the next task. The homely little room was fire-warmed. Mary Madison remembered some of the books, and the big lamp, and the arm-chair that had belonged to her father. Cassie had a sort of gift for home-making, even in a perfectly commonplace eight-room suburban house, she mused.

"I want him," Cassie resumed presently, "to take us all down south somewhere—or to go by himself, for that matter!—and get a good rest. But he feels it isn't fair to Jim Prescott—his partner, you know. Only—" reasoned the wife, threading glassy little colored balls with wire, "only Tim is the real brains of the business, and Jim Prescott knows it. Timmy does all the designing, and this year they've seemed to get their first real start—more orders than they can fill, really. And it worries Timmy to fall down just now! He wants to get back. But I feel that if he had a real rest——"

"I don't know," the physician answered, setting John's big brown bear in an attitude of attack above the absurd little sock. "It's a very common attitude, and nine times out of ten a man is happier in his work than idling. I'd let him go back, if I were you, I think."

"Oh, would you, Molly?" Cassie demanded in relief and surprise.

"I think so. And then perhaps you could all get away early to Beachaways——"

"Molly!"

"Don't use that tone, my dear. The place wasn't even opened last year. I went to Canada for some hospital work, and took Merle with me and left her at the Lakes with my secretary. I wanted then to suggest that you and Timmy use Beachaways. It's in a bad condition, I know——"

"Bad condition! Right there on the beach, and all to ourselves! And he can get away every Friday night!"

"Perhaps you'll have my monkey down with her cousins, now and then. She doesn't seem to have made strangers of them, exactly."

"Not exactly," agreed Cassie with her quiet smile. "They were all crowded into the boys' big bed when I went up. I carried Rawley into the next room. Tom and Merle had their hands clasped, even in their sleep. Molly," she added suddenly, in an odd tone, "what—I have to ask you!—what made you come?"

"Christmas, perhaps," the doctor answered gravely, after a moment. "I've always wanted to. But, I'm queer. I couldn't."

"Tim's always wanted to," his wife said. "He's always said: 'There's no real reason for it! But life has just separated us, and we'll have to wait until it all comes straight naturally again.'"

"I don't think those things ever come straight, naturally," said Mary Madison thoughtfully. "One thinks, 'Well, what's the difference? People aren't necessarily closer, or more congenial, just because they happen to be related!' But at Christmas time you find it's all true; that families do belong together; that blood is thicker than water!"

"Or when you're in trouble, Molly, or in joy," the other woman said, musing. "Over and over again I've thought that I must go to you—must try to clear up the whole silly business! But you are away so much, and so busy—and so famous now—that somehow I always hesitated! And just lately, when it seemed—" her voice thickened, "when it seemed as if Timmy really might die," she went on with a little difficulty, "I've felt so much to blame! He's always loved you so, admired you—his big sister! He is always quoting you, what Molly says and does. And just to have the stupid years go on and on, and this silence between us, seemed so—so wasted!"

"Die!" Molly echoed scornfully. "Why should he? With these lovely boys and you to live for!"

"Yes, I know. But don't you remember saying years ago, when you were just beginning to study medicine to have an intelligent interest in George's work—don't you remember saying then that dying is a point of view? That you had seen a sudden sort of meekness come over persons who really weren't very sick, just as if they thought to themselves: 'What now? Oh, yes, I'm to die?' I remember our all shouting when you said it, but many a time since I've thought it was true. And somehow it's been almost that way with Timmy, lately. Just—dying, because he was through—living!"

"Cassie, what utter foolishness to talk that way, and get yourself crying when you are tired out, anyway!"

"Ah, well, I believe just the sight of you when he wakes up is going to cure him, Molly!" his wife smiled through her tears.

But only a little later, the invalid fell, as it chanced, into the most restful sleep he had known for weeks, and Mary, creeping away to her car, under the cold, high moon, and hearing the Christmas bells ring midnight as she went over the muffling snow toward her own room and her own bed, could only promise that when she had had a bath, and some sleep, she would come back and perhaps be beside him when he awakened.

And so it happened that in the late dawn, when three little wrapped forms were stirring in the Rutledge nursery, and when thrilled whispers were sounding in the halls, Merle Madison was amazed to see her mother coming quietly up from the kitchen and could give her an ecstatic Christmas kiss.

"We know it's only oranges and candy," breathed Merle, "but we're going down to get our stockings now!"

"Is the tree lighted?" Mary Madison, who was carrying a steaming bowl, asked in French.

"It is simply a vision!" the other mother, whose pale face was radiant, answered, with her lips close to the curly head of the excited baby she was carrying. "Timmy's waking," she added, with a nod toward the bedroom door.

"I'll go in."

The other woman carried her burden across the threshold—in the quiet orderly sick room her eyes and her brother's eyes met for the first time in years.

He was very white and thin, unshorn, and somehow he reminded her of the unkempt little motherless boy of years ago.

"Molly!" he whispered, his lips trembling.

And her own mouth shook as she put the bowl on the bedside table, and sat down beside him, and clasped her fine, strong, warm hand over his thin one.

"Hello, Timmy," she said gently, blinking, and with a little thickness of speech.

"Molly," he whispered again in infinite content. And she felt his fingers tighten, and saw two tears slip through the closed eyelids as his head was laid back against the pillow.

"Weak—" he murmured, without stirring.

"You've been so sick, dear."

A silence. Then he said, "Molly, were you here in the night?"

"Just to peep at you, Timmy!"

"I thought you were. It was so delicious even to dream it. I didn't dare ask Cassie, for fear it was only a dream. Cassie's been an angel, Molly!"

"She always was, Tim. You and I were the demon liars."

"'Demon liars!' Oh, do you remember the whipping we got for yelling that at each other?"

"Do you remember that we agreed that 'yellow cats' would mean all the very worst and naughtiest things that ever were, and the grown-ups would never know what it meant?"

He submitted childishly to her ministrations. She washed his face, brushed his hair, settled herself beside him with the steaming bowl.

"Come now, Timmy, Christmas breakfast!"

"Do you remember crying for mother, that first Christmas in this house?"

"Ah, my dear! Fancy what she must have felt, to leave us!"

"I've thought of that so often, since the boys have grown big enough to love us, and want to be with us!"

"My girl is with them downstairs—I'll have to tell you what a Christmas we've made for them! The place looks like a toy-shop! Timmy, I hope they'll always like her, be to her like the own brothers that she never had!" So much Mary said aloud. But to herself she was saying: "He doesn't seem to know it, but that's fully two ounces—three ounces—of good hot bread and milk he's taken. Well, was it a riot?" she added to Cassie, who came quietly in to sit on the foot of the bed and study the invalid with loving and anxious smiling eyes.

"Mary, you should have seen it! It was too wonderful," said Cassie, who had been crying. "I never saw anything like the expression on their little faces when I opened the door. Merle was absolutely white—Tom gave one yell! It was a sight—the candles all lighted, the floor heaped, the mantel loaded—I suppose there never was such a Christmas!"

"Cassie, you wouldn't taste this? It is the most delicious milk-toast I ever tasted in my life!" Tim said.

"If it tastes good to you, dearest!"

"I don't know how Molly makes it. Molly, do you suppose you would show Sigma how you do it?"

"I think so, Tim." The women exchanged level quick glances of perfect comprehension, and there was heaven in their eyes.

"There isn't any more downstairs?"

"I don't know that I would now, Timmy," dictatorial and imperious Doctor Madison said mildly. "You can have more when I get back from the hospital, say at about one. Now you have to sleep—lots, all the time, for days! I'm going to take all the children to my house for dinner and overnight. You're not to hear a sound. Look at the bowl, Cassie!"

She triumphantly inverted it. It was clean.

"Do you remember," Mary Madison asked, holding her brother's hands again, "do you remember years ago, when you used to eat my crusts for me, Timmy?"

"And is this bread upon the water, Molly?" he asked, infinitely satisfied to lie smiling at the two women who loved him. "I ate your crusts, and now you come and turn other crusts into milk-toast for me!"

"But don't you remember?"

He faintly shook his head. It was long ago forgotten, the little-boy kindness and loyalty, in the days of warts and freckles, cinnamon sticks and skate-keys, tears that were smeared into dirty faces, long incomprehensibly boring days in chalk and ink-scented schoolrooms, long blissful vacation forenoons dreaming under bridges, idling in the sweet dimness of old barns. There had been a little passionate Molly, alternately satisfactory and naughty, tearing aprons and planning Indian encampments, generous with cookies and taffies, exacting and jealous, marvelous, maddening, and always to be protected and admired. But she was a dim, hazy long-ago memory, merged now into the handsome, brilliant woman whose fine hand held his.

"He used to fill his little pockets with them, Cassie. I can remember passing them to him, under the table."

"Our Tom is like that," Cassie nodded.

"Think of your remembering—" Tim murmured contentedly.

He did not, but then it did not matter. It was Christmas morning, the restless dark night was over. Sun was shining outdoors on the new snow. His adored boys were happy, and the baby was asleep, and Cassie, instead of showing the long strain and anxiety, looked absolutely blooming as she smiled at him. Best of all, here was Molly, back in his life again, and talking of teaching the boys swimming, down at beloved old Beachaways. He had always thought, when he was a little boy, that no felicity in heaven or earth equaled a supper on the shore at Beachaways. The grown-ups of those days must have been hard, indeed, thought Tim mildly, drifting off to sleep, for he could remember begging for the joy of taking sandwiches down there, and being coldly and, unreasonably—he could see now—refused. Well, it would be different with his kids. They could be pirates, smugglers, beachcombers, whale fishers, anything they pleased. They could build driftwood fires and cook potatoes and toast bread——

"Crusts, hey?" he said drowsily. "Bread upon the waters."

"Bread is oddly symbolical anyway, isn't it, Molly?" Cassie said, in her quiet, restful voice. "Bread upon the waters, and the breaking of bread, and giving the children stones when they ask for bread! Even the solemnest words of all—'Do this in commemoration'—are of bread."

"Perhaps there is something we don't understand about it," Molly answered very softly. "The real sacrament of love—the essence of all religion and all sacraments."

She thought of the little crusts still in the pocket of the roll-top sweater, she looked at the empty bowl, and she held Tim's thin hand warmly, steadily.

"Christmas bread," she said, as if to herself.

Milton Keynes UK
Ingram Content Group UK Ltd.
UKHW031443291124
451807UK00005B/391